Love

AND

Ghost

Letters

Love

AND

Ghost

Letters

CHANTEL ACEVEDO

ST. MARTIN'S PRESS   ♔   NEW YORK

CR

www.stmartins.com

Library of Congress Cataloging-in-Publication Data

Acevedo, Chantel.
    Love and ghost letters : a novel / Chantel Acevedo.— 1st ed.
        p. cm.
    ISBN 0-312-34046-X
    EAN 978-0-312-34046-9
    1. Police—Family relationships—Fiction.   2. Parent and adult child—Fiction.   3. Fathers and daughters—Fiction.   4. Married women—Fiction.   5. Poor women—Fiction.   6. Exiles—Fiction.   7. Cuba—Fiction.   I. Title.

PS3601.C47L68 2005
813'.6—dc22

                                                        2005046316

First Edition: September 2005

10 9 8 7 6 5 4 3 2 1

For Orlando, with love

You do me wrong to take me out o' the grave.
—Shakespeare, *King Lear,* act 4, scene 7

BOOK I

1933-1945

1

When Josefina Navarro was an infant, her fortune was told. The maid, Regla, knew nothing of coffee grinds, she did not throw shells, nor did she have visions. She did what the country people always do—she looked at the tiny fingernails of the baby, at the white flecks embedded underneath, and proclaimed to Josefina's father that the child was to be unhappy and tormented all her life. Perhaps the reason she saw such a future was the time itself, the past century still a part of the island's memory, a place where the poor were fearsomely poor and the rich awesomely rich, with Regla trapped by both conditions. Her employer and Josefina's father, Antonio Navarro, a sergeant of Havana's police who never lost his Spaniard's lisp, was wary of the divinations of his black servant and began the habit of pressing his lips together with his fingers whenever the superstitious maid spoke of prophecy. When Josefina was old enough to understand, Regla would whisper stories of the saints and the sacrifices made to them, she'd fill Josefina's bath with daisy petals and rub honey in her hair when she was ill, and she'd string chains of colored beads and slip them around the girl's neck at night. These were the rituals she knew, and she did all of them to protect the child and to make sure that the long-ago vision would not come true.

Years later, Josefina would spend her nights pulling together scraps of detail from Regla's stories, dreaming of damp little houses with dirt floors muddied with chicken blood and Regla somewhere inside, stamping her feet and praying to the listening saints. In these dreams she always saw a beautiful woman on her knees in the corner of the room, praying through the noise of the sacrificial killing. She liked to imagine the lovely figure was her mother, though Josefina had only seen her in the portrait her father kept hidden in his closet.

In the mornings, Josefina would wonder at the presence of her mother in the dreams, since Josefina thought little of her in the daylight. Her mother had died in childbirth, and Josefina often scolded herself for not loving her mamá more, for not lighting a candle for her on the day of her death, the day of Josefina's own birth. When Josefina was eight, she had come to her father in a guilty, crying fit brought on by a nun, who had said it was a mortal sin to forget your mother, even if you had never known her. The sergeant wagged a heavy finger at her and said that he found nuns to be extraordinarily stupid.

Josefina found herself somewhere between her father's heretic views and Regla's undying faith. She loved the romance of Regla's beads and her African gods, and these were the ones she found herself praying to every year on the anniversary of her mamá's death. At the same time she loved the arrogance and pomp of her father's world, with its music lessons and society dances.

It was at one of those society dances, held by La Sociedad Juvenil de la Habana during the month of May, in 1933, that Josefina first met Lorenzo and finally chose somewhere between her father's world and Regla's. She was seventeen—old enough for the monotony of marriage, young enough that the air around her was still redolent with passion and romantic notions. The dance was held in the courtyard of the society's hall, with hibiscus blooming yellow around the dancing youth and clinging to the iron gates that encircled the building. The society mothers lit the courtyard with torches and made paper roses in the red, white, and blue colors of the flag, tying them to the trunks of the courtyard palms.

Silver buffet trays, also adorned with the colorful paper roses, held lobster tails and fresh fruit, diced into perfect cubes. On that evening, Josefina was dancing a long *danzón* with a boy who was the governor's nephew, when she saw a pale face looking out from a pair of golden blooms outside the fence.

Lorenzo Concepción, whose visage was made whiter by the harvest of black hair on his head that was framed between twisted iron rails, tracked her while she danced. Josefina matched the steps of her dance partner, every shuffle and rotation. While he spoke to her of next month's dance and the space on her dance card that was surely just for him, she watched the white face behind the iron gate as he watched her, too.

Near the end of the evening, she feigned a headache, stumbling away from the governor's nephew. She promised him another *danzón* and pulled a chair near the white face behind the gate. She slipped the gloves off her hands and folded them, twirled a painted Spanish fan around her wrist, and remembered to press at her temple, frowning, when someone looked in her direction. Often, she'd turn to look at the dancers and would be able to see the white face out of the corner of her eye, and once, she looked at him directly by mistake, then pretended to admire the flowers on the gate, going so far as to purse her lips and pull together her eyebrows as if she were studying the blooms. Though he had moved considerably closer, still the white-faced boy would not speak. She could see his toes, pushing through the green branches of the hibiscus, covered in wet grass. A beetle crawled over his foot. When she gasped at the sight, the foot, as well as the face, disappeared into the night.

I have seen thousands of beetles in my lifetime, she chided herself for gasping, noting how quickly he had gone at her small pant. She picked a fork from a table nearby, sat down once more, and began raking the dirt where the beetle had been, pulling up skinny roots, cigarette butts, and several gnats that flew into the air. And then, as if by magic, the white-faced boy appeared again. And this time, he spoke.

"Why are you getting your hands dirty?" he asked.

She drew the fan open and covered her mouth, keeping one hand over her temple.

"I was looking for the beetle that you frightened away."

"Insects fascinate you?" he asked, backing away into the darkness, his features obscured in the night. She could hear his feet crunching the ground below as he walked away.

"Yes, I suppose," was her reply. She sensed that this approach was no more charming than the former.

He appeared once more, close to the fence, now fixing his eyes on her in a mean sort of glance, and said, "I liked you better when you danced," disappearing into the dark again.

"Please don't go," she whispered. "This was all so dull before."

"I won't leave. My name is Lorenzo, I am twenty and live alone, I have no money, and I drink rum and whiskey. Do you still want me to stay?"

"*Sí.*"

"Then tell me your name."

"Josefina Navarro." They spoke low and hurriedly, hiding in the shadows cast by the lanterns.

"Do you know, *mi amor,*" he began, endearing himself to her with the tender mention of love, "I picked you out from that crowd of girls right away. You aren't the prettiest one, you know."

Josefina had not known. Her chest hurt suddenly when he said it.

Lorenzo shifted his weight on the fence. "It's in the eyes, *mi amor.* The others, while they dance, look at their partners' groomed eyebrows, search for wrinkles in their expensive dresses—that sort of thing. But you look around as if the shadows themselves were reaching out to take you. Your eyes are huge, Josefina, like a frog, it seems to me. You are scared of something, I can tell. And just then, when you danced that awful *danzón,* your eyes were bulging out of your face, twitching even, to find something, just like a frog."

Lorenzo's voice had risen in pitch, and his fingers, thin like

bamboo reeds, grasped the iron bars. He sensed Josefina's stillness. Her eyes, quite as large as Lorenzo had noticed, seemed
larger now, and her forehead was the color of cherry red from her
effort to keep from crying.

"Josefina," he continued, "you stared about you, at the shadows
around you, and you found me stuck behind this gate." He smiled
then, barely a smile, so that only one of his front teeth poked out
from between his lips. Josefina stood, not caring who might see
her, and gripped the iron bars. She studied the half smile in-
tensely. The longer she stared, the less human Lorenzo looked. He
appeared to liquefy before her, into one large mass of inky darkness. Perhaps he was one of the shadows he mentioned, poised to
consume her in its fold.

"I won't hurt you. That's what you're afraid of, isn't it?"
Lorenzo said, breaking the silence of her hard stare. Before he left
he thrust a rusted medal into her hand that he had found on the
floor a few days earlier. It was so worn that the saintly relief figure
was unrecognizable. He whispered, "For good luck," and "I'll see
you soon, my beautiful doll," before dissolving into the humid
darkness.

That evening, Josefina crept into Regla's little room downstairs,
her crinoline skirt rustling under the bedcovers as she slipped in
beside the sleeping woman. Josefina shook her, dangling the
medal in front of the maid's leathery nose, and told her the story
of Lorenzo and what he had said.

"He's handsome, Regla, dark and long, like a late afternoon
shadow." Josefina chuckled to herself with the comparison, so
lovely did she think it, but Regla only frowned, remembering the
destiny of this girl before her and thinking that shadows were not
the way to avert a bad fortune.

Regla held the medal to a candle on her nightstand, scratched at
the rust with her fingernail and said, "This, *niña,* is Oshun, the
goddess of marriage," and then, laughing aloud and exclaiming a
series of rapid *"Dios míos,"* Regla grasped Josefina's hands, saying,

"It is a sign of good luck." She kissed Josefina on the forehead and they fell asleep easily that night, with Regla's heavy arms around the girl, one of her fat hands still clutching the medal.

The sergeant did not approve of Lorenzo Concepción, of his white shirts with the frayed hems, of his slick hair, of the manner in which the young man always forgot to remove his straw hat upon entering the house, and the way he leaned on the sergeant's car, tapping his fingers on the hood of the new Ford Coupe, one of the few very modern automobiles in the neighborhood, as he said his afternoon good-byes to Josefina. He did not like the way Lorenzo picked wild flowers for Josefina instead of bringing her roses, as a gentleman would do, and how he often divided the bouquet up and gave half to Regla, who would puff up with pride. As for Lorenzo's means of living, the sergeant was even more disturbed. To the sergeant it appeared that Lorenzo was all things at once. In the summer he claimed to work in carpentry, and a few months later, picking his teeth with a fish bone and putting up his swollen feet on the table in the parlor, he claimed to be a fisherman. And when Lorenzo came to the house one morning with a red carnation sticking up out of his shirt pocket to ask the sergeant for his daughter's hand, exactly one year after the dance where he had enchanted her from behind a fence, Lorenzo held his fist to his heart and swore that he had finally found work binding books in the city.

The proposal had taken the sergeant by surprise, though he could not stay and nurse the blow. He had been invited to a weeklong officers' retreat in the sierras of Pinar del Río province that he could not evade, if he wanted a salary raise for the next year. The hotel where the officers stayed, Hotel Organo, was nestled between two breast-shaped mountains that protruded from flat plains. The policemen who gathered from all of the provinces took many photographs of the formations, pointing to their own copper-buttoned chests, riotous grins on their faces. The valley between the mountains teemed with movement and fretted with the noises of birds in the morning and crickets at dusk, scorning the officers and their crudity.

The night before he left for the sierras, a mountain range he knew as a young boy, when he and his brother first arrived from Spain and were handed rifles, prepared to fight in the war for independence, he stood in the doorway of Josefina's room for a long while. She watched him through sleepy eyes in the bright light of the hallway, his tall figure like a resplendent apparition that pulsed and threatened to disappear. She finally called out to him, "Papá, come in," and he did, sitting on the edge of her bed so that the mattress tipped and Josefina had to shift to maintain her balance.

"Would you like to hear a Tío Francisco story?" the sergeant asked her, his voice timid in the dark. It was the same voice he had used when she was a child, and he told her funny stories of her lost uncle's antics as a boy. The muted way her father spoke of his brother was tender, and Josefina remembered now, in the dark, how well those stories calmed her during tropical thunderstorms that lit up her room like a bursting camera flash, how her stomach hurt from laughter, and how the sergeant never seemed to run out of stories to tell. They were happy, brightly painted stories, but Josefina sensed, even as a child, that there might be more to them, an element of danger, of romance, that her father was leaving out.

"*Sí, Papá,*" Josefina said and put her hand into her father's.

He began, "I've always said your uncle was a Wednesday boy, always in the middle." The sergeant cleared his throat and wiped his mouth with the back of his free hand. "There was this one time when we were about nine years old, back in Spain. There was a hill behind the house with a paved path on it, lined with jonquils that Francisco loved to trample. He had an idea—to ride down the hill on a wheelchair that belonged to our grandmother."

Josefina laughed, because she knew what everyone knew—that riding someone else's wheelchair brought only the worst of luck. She remembered how a schoolmate named Danette, a pretty French girl with unwieldy curls, borrowed her grandmother's wheelchair and rode it to school. The next day, Danette's red-haired cocker spaniel was found crushed to a pulp in the street.

"Because I was smaller," the sergeant continued, "Francisco shoved me into the chair first. He stood behind me, his hands on the handle and his feet dug into my back, as we started down the hill. I remember how the street lamps were a sickening blur as we rolled by. At the bottom of the hill was a road and as we shot toward it, a carriage with a huge, pregnant mare hauling crates of squawking chickens came up the road." The sergeant laughed and so did Josefina. She released his hand to cover her mouth, as she always did when she felt her giggles were becoming loud and gaudy.

"Francisco broke his leg when he landed underneath the fat mare and I tore my elbows open." In the dark, the sergeant lifted his shirtsleeve to show off the scar. Josefina could see nothing in the shadowy room, but she nodded her head.

When the soft, familial laughter died down, the sergeant straightened his back and cleared his throat once more. *"Mi hija,"* he said, "I was never able to change Francisco. He was reckless until the day he died."

"Tell me how he . . ." Josefina interrupted, but the sergeant, his voice no longer timid, would not be interrupted.

"You cannot change a foolish man, even when he is still just a boy. You will not change Lorenzo." The sergeant stood, and the dreamy apparition that Josefina had seen in the doorway was gone in him.

"There is nothing I want to change, Papá," Josefina said and covered herself with a blanket, though the heat was stifling. The sergeant left without another word. He was always that way, in complete control, Josefina thought. She closed her eyes and forced herself to dream of Lorenzo, and the thought of him thrilled her, like an ice cube sliding slowly down her back.

2

The sergeant, at first, did not want to leave his daughter alone in Vedado. He thought of her little room with the balcony that faced east. He thought of her open closet that always spit out dresses and pumps when the doors opened, and of the pianoforte he had given her for her fifteenth birthday, tucked into a specially built niche of the room. He could even hear the tinkling strains of "Clair de Lune" as his daughter played at night. And above all this, he imagined Lorenzo walking in through the front door after sundown and staying with Josefina all night in that very room amid ribbons and porcelain dolls. He believed that Regla would never know, so often did she close herself up in her quarters chanting to her saints. Still, he left the maid with instructions.

Josefina was to stay home from school that week and follow Regla on whatever errand she might have, and more importantly, Lorenzo would not enter the house until the sergeant's return. He had written the instructions in green ink on onionskin paper and copied it several times over—leaving a sheet on Regla's bed, another in the kitchen, another folded neatly on Josefina's dresser, and a final sheet pinned to the clothesline outside, so that Regla would remember her duty as chaperone even while she hung the laundry out to dry.

Thoughts of his daughter had occupied the sergeant's mind thoroughly, so much so, that when one of the security ministers at the officers' retreat patted him on the back, handed him a camera, then stood in front of the mountains posing for a picture, the sergeant was so distracted he was sure that what he had taken was a photograph of the man's large belly, and little else.

He could not even discuss the subject of the urgently called meeting—what was already dubbed the Sergeants' Revolt, led by Sergeant Batista, that had ousted the provisional government. Batista had recruited the police officers, and they gladly joined. The uprising had been brief, and the sergeant was home for his evening meal with Josefina with only a small nick on his forehead as evidence of the coup. The sergeant was typically calm, and his officers tried to upset him often by hiding his coffee cup or putting tacks in his chair, just to see him lose that placidity. But he rarely did. After having prayed for his safety for hours on their knees, Josefina and Regla weren't surprised that he had returned unscathed, his hair still molded into place, his medals shiny, asking for his dinner and about Josefina's school day. So it was that his obsession with Lorenzo surprised even him.

He finally found respite from his thoughts later at the first night's dinner. The sergeant had picked at his pork for some time when Nelson Ruáno, an old friend from the academy, approached him.

"Hello, Spaniard," Nelson called, "what brings you to the backwoods?"

"It has been years," the sergeant said, as he stood to embrace his friend. Nelson tipped his head to one side, turning a large, red ear toward the sergeant.

"What was that you said? Speak into my right." Nelson pulled hard on the earlobe. The dangling flesh shrank back slowly from the tug.

"It has been years," the sergeant shouted loud enough for others around him to stop their chatter. "What happened, *com-padre?*" he asked then, closer now to Nelson's face.

"Let's see. When did we last meet?"

"Ten years. Maybe more."

"Do you remember the uprisings in Oriente? *Los negros,* remember?"

The sergeant nodded, remembering the black rebels who fought in the hills and were blotted out by Cuban officers and American marines.

"One of them threw a stone at my temple, and I lost all hearing then. I never even heard the captain's shouts of retreat." Nelson kneaded his pulpy ear as he spoke.

"1901. We were barely men, eh?"

"Sí," Nelson said, "that same stone would kill me today, I've gotten so old."

When the waitresses, young women who fiddled with their dipping necklines while they spoke or took orders, began serving coffee after dinner, the two men isolated themselves from the massive group of policemen, choosing the smallest wooden table on the outskirts of the tent. They were so far from the general gathering that crickets lit upon their plates every so often. They watched together as the men, drunk and sick from rum and whiskey, took more photographs of the mountains.

"You can't blame them, Antonio," Nelson said, and then, after considering the crowd once more, "but you must question their taste."

The sergeant, consumed once again with thoughts of his daughter and Lorenzo, had not been listening and could only grunt softly whenever Nelson paused in his speech.

"What I mean," Nelson continued, "is that the lady, this lady of the sierras upon whose belly we are sitting, is old, ancient, and dirtied with the hands of Indians and these filthy officers. Give me the breasts of a schoolgirl any day over these elderly hills."

Nelson's joke vividly colored the sergeant's thoughts of Lorenzo's midnight wanderings. "That is not funny," he said, shoving his coffee hard, spilling most of it and sending the cup to the edge of the table. The sergeant watched stiffly as a cricket pounced on the tiny puddle of coffee and rubbed its legs in it.

"So how is your little one? Little Juana, is it?" Nelson asked, fastening his joke and the sergeant's reproach to a child he no longer remembered, who used to peer at him from behind her papá's uniformed legs.

"Josefina. She is engaged."

"And you don't approve. Let me guess to who," Nelson said, clapping his hands and rubbing them together. "A dapper young banker from Madrid. No? A councilman's son? No? *Bueno,* I hope she isn't going to marry a policeman."

The sergeant thought about that final prospect for a moment, and he suddenly came upon a way to delay his daughter's escape and make Lorenzo a man worthy of Josefina.

"Good night, *mi amigo,*" the sergeant shouted into Nelson's good ear. "I'm leaving in the morning. I don't need a raise this year anyway." The sergeant walked toward the green peaks ahead and to his little room nestled in between.

"Send me an invitation to the wedding," Nelson shouted, and laughed when he noted the twitch in the sergeant's shoulders.

3

The newspapers had, for weeks, announced the exhibition of the *Maine* in Havana's harbor, and both Lorenzo and Josefina, after much prodding and nagging on the sergeant's part, agreed to go to the exhibit. That morning, the sergeant wore his dress uniform, his saber hanging against his thigh, matching the pair of tiny brass sabers that decorated his collar. He was a tall man, broad in the shoulders, with a full head of hair. His eyes were small and above them hung thick eyebrows that met in the center. The sergeant shaved closely, twice a day, and had a score of tiny red wounds all over his face as a result. Regla circled him, polishing the buttons and running a comb through the tassels that hung from his shoulders, while Josefina and Lorenzo watched the preparations from their place on the sofa. As Regla sharpened the pleats of the sergeant's pants with her nails, the sergeant began speaking to Lorenzo.

"There will be many police guarding the *Maine* today. It will be quite a thing to see the ship that started the war. Of course, I was done fighting in the Second War of Independence by then. Quite a story."

"Sure," Lorenzo said and breathed deeply. He was bored and hot.

"Ah, what do you know about it?" the sergeant said and waved Lorenzo away. "You didn't go to school or learn our history." The room was then quiet, except for the tinkling of the sergeant's medals as Regla polished them. "If you'd like," the sergeant said at last, "I will introduce you to some of the other officers." The sergeant raised his eyebrows at Lorenzo, waiting for some kind of answer from him.

"If you wish," was Lorenzo's indifferent reply. He had busied himself with twirling Josefina's short curls around his thumb as the sergeant spoke, tickling the curve of her neck with his nail. The eyes that Lorenzo had found so large that night at the dance looked at him, unblinking. They were blue, a color that the sergeant was quite proud of, and gave Lorenzo the impression of a limitless expanse of sky, full of freedom and devotion. Her face was shaded by a large brimmed hat, tilted to the right. Her dropped-waist dress clung to her breasts, which she had wrapped tightly with a scarf to diminish their size, as all the fashion magazines advised, and the bouquet of silk flowers sewn to her collar trembled in the breeze coming through the open window.

The sergeant continued, "You might enjoy police work, and who knows, you might . . ."

"I might not," Lorenzo interrupted, standing and shaking lint and stray hair from his pants. Josefina's cheeks began to redden as she realized her father's intentions, and she, too, stood, announcing, "Let's go. We'll be late."

The harbor was crowded, and as the sergeant predicted, guards lined the cobbled streets, some chatting in groups, others standing straight and alone like lampposts. All saluted the sergeant as he passed, and he would nod his head as if it were on a tight spring.

The remnants of the *Maine* were surrounded by thick chains and more guards to keep the curious out. The ship's twin smokestacks were on display, and its mast, though cracked and splintering in several places, still held lines that dangled almost to the deck. To the left of the smokestacks a portion of the bow stood, the ragged open edges rusted. Around the exhibit were wooden posts that detailed the sinking of the *Maine*. Here were the names of those who died on board. Here was where the battleship was torn in half, and so on. Josefina trailed her fingers on each of the placards, not bothering to read them or even to look at the ship. She was more concerned with the conversation going on between her father and Lorenzo.

"I was a young man when she sank," the sergeant said. Stamping the stone under his shoe and resting his hand on Lorenzo's shoulder, he said, "I was thirteen when I boarded a ship that brought me here. I was almost fifteen when I lied to the officers at the academy about my age." The sergeant held Lorenzo by the scruff of the neck now, and he forced the thin, abrasive face to turn toward a high, yellow wall covered in theater posters. "Over there, Lorenzo, during the second war, was a sign that said, 'Cuba, better Spanish than African.' " The sergeant laughed hoarsely. He swept his free arm across the harbor, as if he were drawing a curtain open to reveal a new play, "Here and in this way," he said to Lorenzo, pointing to the officers like statues of salt around them, "I made my life so rich."

A clatter arose from somewhere near the ruined battleship. Several of the officers abandoned their posts, scattering across the portion of deck that moaned as they ran, as if the boat itself had grown unused to the hard-soled boots of military men. The sergeant stood straighter, anxious to see over the heads of the gathering crowd what was causing the commotion on the boat. Suddenly, he cut through the throng to reach the ship. Lorenzo and Josefina followed him through the milling pack of spectators until they were able to get a good look for themselves.

They saw a woman dressed in rags. Her hands tore at her face and hair. It was because of this, and because of the dented tin cup that hung from her waist, that everyone knew she was likely to be a beggar woman, mad from hunger or want. The officers, nearly fifteen of them, circled her. Every once in a while, one would plunge toward her, like a swallow diving for a worm, only to find that his approach made her all the more wild. A gash across the bridge of her nose, now one on her chin, as her fingernails dripped with her own blood.

The sergeant finally arrived, puffing his chest with a rapidity that made Josefina worry for his heart. The circle of officers turned from the woman to face him. She quieted then, perhaps pleased that their eyes weren't on her anymore, and resumed what she had been doing—unscrewing brass screws from the placards and dropping them into her tin can with a cheery *plink.* The sound of the screws caught the sergeant's attention, and it brought his bullish voice forth.

"Take her already. Use these," he said, pulling his own club, weathered with deep pits in the wood. The circle closed in on the woman, who stood still pulling screws from the brass frames. She scratched at the men when they pushed her to the deck, and she spit when her hands were finally bound. They carried her off, because she would not walk, as one might a prize buck, shot for competition. Two held her head and shoulders, while another held her feet. The rest of the officers took to replacing the brass screws, one by one. The sergeant followed the woman, tapping his club on his shoulder, off the bow of the *Maine,* back toward his daughter. Josefina and Lorenzo got a close look at the beggar woman as she was being drawn away and could hear her spit gurgling in her throat.

The sergeant held fast to Lorenzo's collar once more and resumed his speech, but Lorenzo cleared his throat and eased his way out of the sergeant's grip. The stiff, nodding officers seemed like brutes to him, ready to knock him down, too, and kick him in the face and ribs for walking alongside Josefina and her father. She had asked him to wear his best pants, but he had chosen the ones with the holes in the knees just to prove a point.

"See that fellow over there, Lorenzo?" the sergeant continued. "He was just promoted and his salary will rise to several hundred pesos a year. And that stout one there, he just returned from the academy and look how fresh and happy he is." The sergeant spoke as he walked, pointing to the men in uniform aboard the exhibit. Lorenzo, however, had not spoken for a long time and even refused to hold Josefina's hand when she slipped it into his. Instead, he fixed his eyes on the battleship as they walked. The policemen looked ridiculous to him, bent over, their backsides wide, bovine, as they twisted screws back into fancy moldings. With the officers preoccupied, the tourists and visitors gathered were able to reach the sides of the ship. Some knocked on the wood for luck. Others picked off slivers of it as keepsakes, catching splinters in their thumbs, then turning and cursing at the ship itself.

"Of course, you would have every advantage a new cadet could ask for as my son-in-law, and I will make sure that while you are away at the academy, Josefina is well taken care of, in the manner to which she is accustomed, until your return," the sergeant continued, standing straighter and believing that Lorenzo was persuaded.

"And where is this academy?" Lorenzo asked, stopping suddenly in front of a placard that listed the *Maine's* previous battles.

"It's in El Cotorro. Oh, I know it's far away, but . . ."

"Very far, you say?"

"Near the province border, but it is a beautiful pueblo, and though the people are poor, the academy provides for every . . ."

"You say it's very poor country?"

"*Bueno,* I won't lie to you, son, it is near miserable."

Lorenzo began to chuckle, reaching for Josefina's hand once more and kissing her knuckles loudly. "Why, you've stumbled upon our secret," Lorenzo said, "your daughter and I have already purchased a home in El Cotorro," and then turning to Josefina, "Isn't that right, *mi cariño?*" Josefina, who had never discussed her new home with Lorenzo, could only stand there, stupefied and trembling, mirroring her father's reaction as only a daughter could. "Except, señor," Lorenzo continued, "I won't be entering the academy. I've never found police work appealing."

They went home soon after the discussion, missing the evening fireworks over the mammoth broken thing that was once a battleship. Once arriving at the house, the sergeant took Josefina by the arm and pulled her inside, away from Lorenzo. Before closing the door, he growled, "Wear decent trousers the next time you come to my house." Outside, Lorenzo stood at the closed door for a minute, pulled out a loose nail from the door hinge, and went home, contented, listening to the crack of the fireworks over the harbor.

Inside, the front hall was awash in tints of blue. The setting sun shone through curtains of blue organza, drawn because Regla feared the eyes of peeping strangers when she was alone in the house, and the effect of blue light made the sergeant look more waxen than he already was. He walked to the kitchen and motioned for Josefina to follow. He poured whiskey into two tumblers and placed one in front of his daughter. He took a long sip, accompanied by two loud swallows, and said, "I will ask you once, because you are intelligent, as your mamá was when she lived. Do not marry him."

Josefina said nothing. She knew her papá would make this request. She had made up her mind, long before she had seen Lorenzo's face watching her through the hibiscus at the dance, that governors' sons and the heirs of Spanish landowners were not for her. Still, as long as she had known this, she had never formulated the words that could explain it to her father.

The sergeant noted her silence. "Drink," he said.

"Papá, no quiero."

"Drink." He did not raise his voice, but his mouth shrank into a tiny slit, moist with whiskey. Josefina lifted the tumbler with a shaky hand and brought it to her mouth. The liquor stung her dry lips and burned her throat, tense from holding back tears.

"Now, give me your answer." The sergeant finished off his

whiskey, shaking the glass so that every drop fell into his mouth. Still, Josefina said nothing. She rubbed her thumb up and down the sides of the tumbler so that her skin squeaked against it. She made no other sound.

"So, you have chosen him," the sergeant said, his voice gravelly and harsh, "and you will be hungry and miserable all your life, *hija.*"

In the weeks that followed, the sergeant spoke to Josefina only to bark orders, as if she were one of his cadets. She found him, one morning, sorting through the clothes in her closet. When Josefina asked what he was doing, he said, "You won't need so many expensive things in that slum you are moving to." And he threw some of her prettiest dresses in a bag. Josefina wrote Lorenzo long love letters to pass the time. She refused to eat dinner with her father.

In the evenings, every evening, the sergeant would crack open the door to Josefina's room. The scent of gardenias that filled the air around his daughter always struck him most on those evenings when he was prepared to say something hurtful to her. Every night he readied a few stinging words to share with Josefina. They were usually about Lorenzo, about his frail looks that bespoke an effeminate nature, or of the rumors that were already making rounds in Vedado's society. The night before the wedding, the sergeant whispered his most cruel jab through the crevice between the door and its frame, "*Mi hija,* your mother always wanted a daughter, a foolish and stupid girl that she might one day dress up in frills. I am glad she got her wish."

She had sacrificed all duty to her father—and she *had* been a dutiful daughter, proper when among his colleagues, never letting herself fall into adolescent moodiness, bringing him steaming cups of coffee in the morning—to love Lorenzo. Of course the sergeant didn't understand. He wanted her to marry a boy from a good, wealthy family so that she might live next door, make the sergeant blond grandchildren like the ones in Spain, and populate

Vedado with people like him, people who could readily dismiss the poverty of the island and the corruption of the capital so long as it suited them. All of this so that at the end of their long, prosperous lives they might all fill an angel-decked tomb in the upscale section of the cemetery.

But Josefina found well-bred men hateful. They'd visit her dressed in wool suits (wool suits in Cuba!) and speak with booming voices, addressing most of their talk to the sergeant and not to Josefina. Then they'd want to steal kisses when the sergeant excused himself to go spend ten long minutes in the bathroom. No, Josefina much preferred Lorenzo's way. Lorenzo, whom she called Renzo. Renzo, who climbed up the wooden lattice that led to her bedroom at night, who buried himself under her bedclothes and whispered bawdy poems he had learned. Renzo, whose thin body emanated a heat so intense that Josefina's blood seethed and was soon settled by his embrace.

The wedding was held one morning in a cathedral near the sergeant's Vedado home. Stained glass decorated every archway. Female saints lined the left side of the church, and the male saints marked the right like marble bridesmaids and groomsmen. The church was quite empty, because the sergeant did not want anyone present, an act which angered many of his colleagues in the police department and many of the society mothers from the dances. As Josefina walked down the aisle with her father, the sound of her heels echoed through the church where no solid bodies soaked up the sound. It even traveled into the cloisters, where solitary nuns turned their heads and wondered at the odd, echoed tapping. Regla alone sat in one of the pews, clutching her left hand, which she had burned with an iron the night before while steaming Josefina's veil.

Once at the altar, the sergeant pulled a sheet of paper from his coat pocket and said to Lorenzo, "Sign this."

"What is it?" Lorenzo asked, his mouth forming an impertinent pout.

"A contract," the sergeant said.

Lorenzo took the paper, headed *Contrato de Matrimonio, 1934,* and read it aloud. His tone mocking, he looked every so often at the priest who gave him a knowing smile, so accustomed was the priest to the intrusiveness of fathers. *"Numero uno,"* Lorenzo read, "Lorenzo Concepción will promise to maintain a sizable house for Josefina Navarro in the best area of El Cotorro."

The sergeant bristled in his military jacket as Lorenzo read. Droplets of sweat hung from either side of his mustache.

"Numero dos," he continued, "the aforesaid gentleman will work consistently and during reasonable hours and will keep the seventh day holy for God and his family." He paused, turning on his heels to face the sergeant, then finished reading: *"Y numero tres,* the gentleman will take the aforesaid lady out dancing every other weekend as was her habit when in the custody of her father."

The sergeant already had one hand on his daughter's neck, sure that Lorenzo would tear the contract in two and run from the altar. But it was Josefina who took the letter and folded it. Her eyes were moist and red-rimmed as she pushed the paper into her father's coat pocket. The sergeant looked at her with eyes that burned like a kiln, as if to cook away the emotion he found in her face. She, too, knew that Lorenzo would not sign the contract.

"Papá, por favor, no. No, por Dios." She said this quietly, through the airy tulle of her veil.

The priest, already amused at the severity of the sergeant's face and too drunk from the brandy that had accompanied his lunch to notice the violence that poured and ebbed from the bodies before him, laughed and said, "God's blessing is enough of a contract." Lorenzo grasped Josefina's arm, pulling her away from her father's firm clamp at her nape and turned to look at the priest. The sergeant felt dizzy. The balls of his feet slid around inside his shoes, and he felt as if he would fall forward into the priest's stomach or backward to the freshly polished aisle. He sat at a pew instead, several feet from where Regla knelt crying and closed his eyes to feel the spin of the earth.

After the wedding, Lorenzo and Josefina went to the house in Vedado, with its cool porches garnished with roses and paper lanterns, its old Spanish paintings, and stone tiles. Lorenzo came into Josefina's room and opened her closet where he drew his arms wide and grabbed all her clothes at once, taking them downstairs and letting the delicate cloth drag on the floor. The sergeant yelled at his daughter from the doorway, and Josefina cupped her hands over her ears. She followed Lorenzo out the door, leaving the fresh, open house that the sergeant kept and stepped out into the dusty cobbled streets of the city, her satin slippers tearing with each stumble.

4

The train ride to El Cotorro was quiet. Every so often, Lorenzo would hum a couple of bars from an old ballad, but the sound seemed out of place, and it made the few people in the car shift in their seats with discomfort. Before they had left, Regla had taken the contract the sergeant had written, and she had placed it in Josefina's purse. Josefina now waited until Lorenzo was asleep before she read the contract again.

As she read, Josefina could feel the heat swelling in her throat and into her cheeks. She imagined the sergeant hunched over his desk writing out the arrangement in his careful, pampered cursive. Josefina's fingers curled around the edges of the paper as she remembered the fiasco at the church and how much she had wished, at the moment that her father swooned at the foot of the altar and fell into the pew, that his diseased old heart would have stopped for good.

The truth of that desire, of the horrible wish that her father was dead, washed over her. She crumpled the paper up into a tight ball and threw it under her seat, to be found, unraveled, and chuckled over later the next day, by a group of young men on the way to the university. She tucked her head down onto Lorenzo's lap and closed her eyes. Lorenzo rested his hand on her head as he slept, and she soon developed a headache from the pressure of his palm on her skull.

They arrived in El Cotorro by dawn, and Josefina got her first glimpse of the town. The houses were dipped in pale pinks and blues. Each home had a tiny front patio, and on each patio were pots of different shapes filled with small palms and tall papayas that swayed, top-heavy, in the breeze. Schoolchildren scurried to class in dingy white uniforms. A flock of girls came by with no shoes on their feet, an image that contrasted with the huge, extravagant bows that sat atop their heads, in the fashion of the day, like monstrous butterfly wings ready to carry the wearer into the mountains. They walked through the streets in silence; the same stifling quiet from the train seemed to follow them like a fog. Skinny, battered dogs sniffed their ankles as they walked, then turned on their bony haunches up the street.

At one intersection, Josefina and Lorenzo were taken aback by a crowd that surged around a baker's cart that had overturned. Long, soft bread rolled off the cart and onto the ground as old grandmothers and children pushed each other to get at them. Guava sweets were scooped up into sticky arms, stuffed down housedresses and into purses. Cheese rolls, ham croquettes, and even a large birthday cake with thick pink merengue were harvested from the wreck. All the while, the baker stood atop his crushed cart and shouted obscenities at the crowd. Tears of anger fell onto his cheeks as he took to throwing hard, stale muffins at the crowd to fend them off. Josefina watched, her large eyes still and watery.

Lorenzo released Josefina's hand and ran into the throng. After a few minutes he emerged with an armful of meat pastries. His skin glistened with sugar and syrup, and here and there, small *merengue* puffs stuck to his shirt. He stuffed one of the meat pastries into his mouth before offering another to Josefina.

"Here," he said, and aimed the thing at her lips.

"How can you eat that?" Josefina asked and pointed at the baker who was now sitting on one of the spindly wheels and weeping.

"Don't be so stupid, Josefina," Lorenzo said, and filled his mouth with another pastry. Josefina wished that the sergeant would suddenly appear and arrest them all. But earlier, she remembered, *I had wished him dead.* And with that remembrance and with a resoluteness to equal her father's, she plucked a *merengue* from Lorenzo's shirt. She ate it, though the sugar burned her throat.

"There you go, *mi amor,*" Lorenzo said. "You'll have to be tough to live in a place like this."

Josefina had never seen a place so heartbreaking. The sun that warmed the cold tiles of her father's house was, here, an oven that threatened to mar her complexion. On the street people shouted obscenities at one another and sat on porches playing cards. Flowers were housed in big coffee cans, not terracotta pots. Dust rose from the ground like a cloud. She had read about villages like this in newspapers now and then and had scowled when her French teacher preached about obnoxious privilege in his students. *I'd be happy to share what I have,* Josefina always thought and had said so often to her admiring peers. And when she saw Lorenzo that day, his face dirtied, his clothes torn, she had thought he was the most romantic figure she had ever known. She had imagined herself scouring his clothes with her own hands, of dreamy cottages with cracked plaster that they could call home and where they could live honest lives. That vision had not been accompanied by scores of children coughing in loud, thunderous roars, by dirt paths and shattered glass, by thievery or hunger.

Lorenzo ate his fill as they walked up and down streets lined with tiny cement blockhouses. A FOR RENT sign, written on a white sheet with shoe polish, fluttered on a line in front of one small house. Lorenzo and Josefina entered through a dark parlor then passed through a small kitchen before they found the owner of the house. She was an old woman who sat placidly on her couch, eating bean soup.

"You want to live here?" she asked, without looking up.

"Sí," said Lorenzo.

"Bien," the woman replied through a bean-filled mouth, and she began to show them around. Josefina's nose crinkled as she examined her new home. It smelled like rotting food, and as the old woman opened up the cabinets to show off all of the space in the kitchen, Josefina saw where the stench was coming from. In one of the cabinets the woman had set up an *orisha,* a stone representing a Santería god. It had cowrie shells for eyes and a mouth, and around its base were offerings of stiff steak and eggs, moldy bread, and new packages of chewing gum. Tiny cockroaches walked across the god's face, and the old lady shooed them away with a wave of her crooked fingers.

Josefina had seen these *orishas* before, tucked away in the closet of Regla's bedroom. Except Regla kept her god well fed and she never let any of the food rot or begin to smell. Indeed, she often set mousetraps outside the closet door, to stop any furry intruders from eating her offerings.

"Lorenzo, let's go," Josefina said, "I don't like this place." Lorenzo ignored her and followed the woman into one of the two small bedrooms.

"Señora," he said, "how much?" The woman whispered the sum and kept her eye on Josefina. Lorenzo accepted the offer with a pat on the woman's shoulder and dropped his bag onto the floor.

"But Renzo . . ." Josefina said quietly.

"Enough!" Lorenzo shot back, apologized to their new landlady, and headed out the door to the train depot, to collect the rest of their belongings.

The old woman moved out in two days. She had very little to take with her, since she was going to live with her daughter-in-law and her son. All of the furniture she left behind, which Lorenzo delighted in. She also left behind the *orisha* that Josefina would not go near. The organic little god stayed in Josefina's mind at all times. It haunted her days, seemed to call to her from inside the kitchen cabinets, begging for a morsel. Josefina wrote to Regla about it, and the old woman advised that she keep up the ritual, just in case. So Josefina drew up her courage, cleaned out the god's cabinet so that it no longer stank of rotted food, and left a glass of coconut water for it every morning, making sure to drain the glass and wash it at night. Still, the little god stayed in her thoughts, and Josefina could only banish it from her mind at night, when she and Lorenzo made love so loudly that the neighborhood children threw pebbles at their windows.

As the weeks progressed in El Cotorro, Lorenzo found it hard to work, and he left at least once a month to find employment in neighboring towns. Josefina wrote to Regla every day and received letters just as often, but only from the nursemaid. Her father had said his last to her on the wedding day. She missed Regla as much as any daughter would long for her mother. Regla had known what to do about the abandoned god in her cupboard. She would know, too, what to say when Lorenzo's eyes wandered and he stared too long at the pretty, dark girls on the street. Lorenzo found her crying on the bed one day, her head buried into the pillow, the room hot and dark.

"We'll install a telephone as soon as we can," he said, knowing that she cried for Regla, and Josefina quieted, turned her head, and smiled at her husband. She loved him entirely. As he dried her face with the corner of the bedsheet, Josefina closed her eyes and imagined hearing her nursemaid's voice again, and her father's, too.

It was a week after she had begun dabbing holy water on her pulse points like perfume according to Regla's instructions that Josefina found work in the market. An elderly merchant named Rosa Arias hired her to watch over her shop in the marketplace, selling pet birds—young green parrots that flew freely all over the island. She bred them in her house and hand-fed them scrambled eggs until they sprouted feathers. On those hot, summer market days, Josefina wore an apron and sleeveless dress and sat on a wooden crate. Rosa set the shop up in the mornings and returned in the evenings to collect her birds and her money. Some mornings she would hand Josefina a bird wrapped in a hand towel to break it of its biting habit. At first the young bird would bite and hiss at people. Josefina would swaddle the bird in the towel with only its little round head peeking out until it was moist and exhausted from the effort of trying to reach around the cloth to her skin to nip her. After a few mornings of this mummy treatment, the bird would be broken, like a horse is broken in the country, and would eat out of Josefina's mouth and tickle her ear with its beak.

Rosa had a daughter, a college student named Yesenia, home for vacation, who wore her long hair in braids and read long novels in the shade of a palm while Josefina worked. A college education was a rare thing in the country, and the people regarded Yesenia as one does a politician or someone with an infirm mind. Josefina enjoyed her quiet company and liked to imagine that she had had the chance to go to the university though her father would never have allowed it. In truth, Josefina liked the idea of a place filled with young, brilliant people, but not the books and essays and professors that went with it. The girl read with a pen in her mouth, then scribbled furiously at intervals, muttering, "Hmmph," every so often. Her brown eyes glimmered hopefully whenever Josefina spoke to her. Josefina still possessed that charm she had as a child in Vedado; the charm that had made friends, boys and girls alike, fall in love with her. When Josefina asked Yesenia why she didn't study in the comfort of her home, Yesenia had said she wanted to "be with real people" and then had hugged Josefina to her bewilderment and cooed at one of the parrots.

The young woman, close to Josefina in age, was defiant and confident and brought Josefina novels and poems to read. Josefina thanked her but never read any of them. She had only read one novel in her life, a book with a romantic plot in which the Italian lovers were killed by a jealous husband. Josefina had cried all night after she finished it, cried until Regla made her a special tea and then forbade her to read about sadness anymore. From the deep dent between Yesenia's eyes and the tightness around her lips, Josefina could tell that all the reading caused grief in some way. Josefina felt she was already grieving enough. Eventually, the fall semester began and Yesenia stopped bringing books, stopped coming to read by the shade of the tree, returning again in a few months time, her hair wilder, her ideas more forceful, her novels thicker.

At the market, the parrots squawked all day. Since their wings were clipped, they didn't fly away. They'd hobble about in their little parrot way around Josefina's ankles, inside her pockets. She fed them parsley snippets and bits of banana. Still, the cheerful notes of the parrots were not enough of a distraction for Josefina. She watched the children who didn't go to school and had no place to play but in the muddy puddles of the market. They would steal fruit and even whole fish from stands. Josefina let them pet the birds when Rosa was not around, so they did not bother her or dare take one of the parrots. Most did not wear shoes, and the calluses on their feet and infections in their toenails made Josefina wince. They sucked on sugarcane all day, because it was cheap and the men who made *guarapo* drinks out of the stalks let them have the discards. So their teeth were brown like coffee grinds and rotted. The teeth moldered away as they played and fell out of their mouths, as if the children were old men and women. Josefina watched them and cried all day for the baby she was carrying by then, hoping and praying aloud to the green birds that her child would never be alone and hungry like that.

About this time, too, Josefina started receiving letters from her father. They came in thin monogrammed envelopes. Inside, the stationery was monogrammed, too. She would tell Lorenzo that she threw the letters away. It made him smile and kiss her hard. "I knew you'd come to see we don't need him in our lives." But at night, Josefina would hide the letters inside her shirt, and read them in the bathroom, over and over again. She imagined her father's soft voice telling her all about the new officers at the station, about Regla's sprained wrist. She smelled the paper for traces of his cologne. The tone of the letters was detached, though, as if he were writing to an old Spanish friend, or distant cousin. The only trace of emotion came at the end of each letter when he asked that she write back, and that she leave her husband.

Josefina never wrote to the sergeant. Whenever she tried, the letter would sound too formal, and she didn't know the words to write that would explain to him that she loved Lorenzo, even if he was careless sometimes. When Lorenzo looked at her and smiled, she felt she would do anything for him. Once, in trying to compose a fresh letter to her father, Josefina wrote one line: *Papá—te extraño*. I miss you. But then she remembered the sergeant's final shouts at her as she and Lorenzo left Vedado. He had stood in the doorway of the elegant house and had yelled so that the entire neighborhood might hear. "You took my Ana away from me when you were born! Now you leave like this. *¡Odiosa!*"—Hateful girl!—"Don't you dare come back!"

The memory of that afternoon, of her wedding day, filled her with anger. Josefina sometimes fell asleep with those words trapped in her mind, repeating them like a scratched record. So it was that she always threw away her responses to the sergeant with her dinner's hardened rice.

Josefina's son, Eulalio Miguel, was born in 1935 on a Wednesday. The doctors in the hospital were surprised that he came so quickly. She barely laid down on the bed and Eulalio, called Lalo, pushed his way out of Josefina. His birth was like squeezing an old, soft banana out of its peel. He slithered into the hands of the doctors and whimpered instead of crying.

"So much like you," Josefina had whispered. "My tiny Renzo." But Lorenzo was afraid to hold his son and only looked at him from far off a bit before kissing Josefina's lips and sitting down next to her bed.

Josefina spoke to Regla from the hospital phone. Regla's voice trembled with happiness, and she recommended the name Eulalio, because it had every vowel in it, and those kinds of names were especially lucky. Though this was her first child, Josefina felt only an awkward attachment to him. She was delighted that he looked like his father, pale with a full head of the blackest hair. Even when he had gas, the baby's crooked, gassy smile was like Lorenzo's. But when he was first born, the nurses had laid him on her chest, and Josefina wanted nothing more than for them to take him away so that she didn't have to see him again.

Lalo was a tiny thin boy who cried at the softest sound. For the first year of his life, Josefina thought him more of a bother than anything else. He was colicky, and when letters from the sergeant arrived, Josefina gave them to Lalo to chew, and he would quiet down. The ink would smudge around his mouth, so that later, he would leave blackened kiss marks on his mami's cheeks. The chatter at the market calmed him as well, and he was her daily companion. Rosa Arias loved the arrangement. Ever since the child had begun coming to the market with his mother, sales were up, and Rosa Arias began calling Lalo her "little bird."

As years passed, Lalo grew into a wiry, nervous boy, and Lorenzo had gotten into the habit of leaving Josefina alone in El Cotorro for months at a time. They had stopped paying the rent to the old woman who was their landlady three years earlier. They believed that she must have died, lonely there with her son and daughter-in-law, and so both Josefina and Lorenzo assumed that the house was now rightfully theirs.

Regla made sure to visit at least once a year after Lalo was born, bringing candles, cigars, and statues of saints in a ratty suitcase. Regla was as stout and alive as ever, and every visit was for Josefina like a sigh of relief that lasted a few days. Lorenzo made sure to be home on those days, because he was afraid Regla would cast a spell on him if she caught the scent of another woman on him, and so he sat in the parlor for her entire visit, eyeing her hands for any sudden gestures that might signify a curse.

Even with Regla's blessings, things in El Cotorro seemed to be getting worse for Josefina. Lorenzo had become fatherlike toward Josefina, rarely commenting on her beauty or complimenting the meals she cooked, but at night he was his old self. Josefina pretended that she was back in her bedroom in Vedado and that Lorenzo had climbed the lattice, like Romeo. It filled her with a sense of excitement, of youthful lust, and that carefully crafted mood enticed Lorenzo. At night, they were young still, and their hearts beat faster in each other's arms. In the morning, they would look at each other's sleep-swollen faces and feel the burden of the day ahead, the tiresomeness of being together.

Josefina lost her job at the market after Rosa Arias, the bird woman, died. When the students from the University of Havana protested against President Grau's government, her daughter, Yesenia, was shot and killed by one of the guards. That night, in honor of the girl she barely knew, Josefina tried to read a book by a man named Tolstoy that the girl had given her, but only got through the first page when she realized the book was about funerals. In the market the next day, the vendors told of how they found Rosa Arias and all of her baby birds dead inside her little house with the tin roof, all the windows shut tight and the gas stove turned on. "She could not go on without her daughter," Josefina said to one of the other vendors, and they nodded in agreement.

Josefina mourned Yesenia and Rosa Arias, and those baby birds, frightened then for the baby who would be born to her in a few weeks, a daughter she would name Soledad for the loneliness she felt. There had been many evil signs during the early years in

El Cotorro, and Josefina lamented that she had Regla's interpretations in person only once a year.

Soledad's birth was anything but easy. If her brother had been a soft, pliant banana, Soledad was an anchor lodged on the ocean floor. Lorenzo was in Santa Clara that month, and Josefina walked herself over to the hospital, Lalito seated on her hip because he would not walk when asked. His long legs dangled. Every few yards she would stop, breathe deeply, and go on. No one offered a hand, and Josefina thought the world and its people were cruel, so she wished them all dead.

In the hospital, the nurses locked Lalo out of the room, all by himself. Though he was already five, he was small, and people thought he was much younger. Still, he wailed along with Josefina with each painful push, and she could hear him banging on the door of the room with such ferocity that the cross above the door danced on its nail.

In the torrid heat of a tropical spring, Josefina wrote her first reply to her father's letters, a letter he would never read. It was short, composed quickly at night while Lorenzo was not home. She listed the dates of her children's births (knowing that Regla had already told him everything, she thought it would be a courtesy to announce it all herself), a description of her house, a wish that all was well, a kiss for Regla. The paper was damp with her sweat when she folded it into the envelope. Her next letter, she promised herself, would be longer.

Always in April, when Lenten winds blew the weighty palm fronds off the tops of trunks, the trees outside their house would be alight with avocados, the tiny oblong fruit, like strings of lanterns draped over the branches. By late summer, half the avocados were lost, and Lorenzo believed the fruit fell because someone counted them. They'd lie on the ground, broken and torn, the large white seeds, the size of a fist, sticking up out of the yellow pulp like grave markers. In the summer, Lorenzo would come home again, and he would look through the window that faced the backyard, his eyes scanning the tree outside for fruit, finding only limbs and the luminous green leaves.

"Who counted the avocados?" he'd yell in mock anger and walk through the front door, his slick hair falling into his eyes, his left hand pulling a few thin pesos from his pockets for Lalo, his right lowering a new cane suitcase to the floor. Josefina would follow him as he moved about the parlor, making odd paths around him, straightening his *guayabera* shirt, so stiff with its gray satin embroidery, pressing smooth the handkerchief in his pocket, her hand flat on his thin chest, until he would stop and kiss her hard.

On those days of his return, he would sit with his children on one of the oversized wicker rocking chairs and begin pulling out gifts for them—a rag doll in a blue dress for Soledad, shiny brown shoes for Lalo, sugar candy for both of them. When Josefina would sit on the rocker beside him and begin to ask questions, he would push her aside and sit alone on a stool in the kitchen, waiting for his wife to prepare his first meal at home in months, resigning himself to the idea that he would not have avocado slices to mix with his rice.

On those warm evenings one could hear the people of El Cotorro outside on their rocking chairs, telling dirty jokes, clicking domino tiles on the wooden slats of their porches. It was then that Josefina would come into Soledad's bedroom and push aside the mosquito netting. She'd listen quietly for a second, to make sure that Lalo was sleeping and that his heavy breathing had found its sedated rhythm. Then she would speak.

"Your papá is killing me," she would say, and she would breathe in hard, her chest growing so large in her effort to inhale that Soledad could feel their ribs touching. Josefina would plant her fingers into her daughter's hair, drawing the strands up and away from her neck as she spoke, doing this with so much fervency that by morning, her fingers ached, trapped in a net of curls.

As she wove the hair with her fingers, she would tell Soledad about Lorenzo's lovers and how she could smell the perfume of the women of Havana on his hands and buried in the lines of his face, because those ladies wore violet perfume—deep, purple cologne inside small bottles of yellowed glass. She said she knew he had been to Oriente province, because his tongue was thick with the accent of its women and his back bore the ruby-red scratches of their long fingernails. And she told her of the prostitutes that lounged on the beaches of Varadero and how they had left sweet-smelling grains of sand in his hair. Josefina told her all of these things as if she could read them off Lorenzo's face, or in the secret language of his hands, mannerisms which he carelessly brought home with him from his trips. Soledad believed her then, because she was very young, and because her mother only spoke to her on such occasions as this, when the midnight crickets were quiet, because her papá was outside disturbing their mixed chorus, lifting rotten avocados from the ground.

5

The sergeant, in Vedado, went about his life, pining for his daughter and grandchildren. He had become thin, and his bones showed in his chest, like a cooked snapper. Regla blamed it on Josefina's departure, and the sergeant said nothing to disprove it. Regla returned from visits to El Cotorro with stories about Lalo's foolishness or Soledad's seriousness, about Josefina's *arroz con pollo.* "Just like her mother's," Regla had sighed. Never did Regla mention Lorenzo, and the sergeant was grateful. *Better to pretend that the man was dead than burn with rage,* he thought. The sergeant's mailbox was often empty—a tiny physical void that saddened him. One morning in May, while Doctor Oliveros listened to the sergeant's heart, a messenger arrived with a telegram and a new letter from Josefina.

He had received the doctor early in the morning. Manuel Oliveros dusted his jacket in the doorway with both hands, holding his leather bag between his knees. This had become routine for him, his monthly visits to the sergeant's house. Though he complained that the cab ride was expensive and that he lost profit when he closed his practice in Old Havana for the visit, Doctor Oliveros enjoyed his time with the sergeant.

"*Buenos días,* Antonio," Oliveros said, dangling his satchel in the doorway, like a white flag of surrender.

"Oliveros, come in and poke me." The sergeant held a plate of fried eggs and rice on his lap. The doctor walked into the sergeant's bedroom and frowned at the plate of greasy salted eggs. *Here we begin,* the doctor thought to himself and chortled through his nose.

"Is an officer's bad heart a joke to you, Oliveros?" the sergeant asked from his bed.

The doctor balanced his bag on the bed's thick footboard, cleared his throat, and said, "Sergeant Navarro, please do me the honor of using my title, Doctor Oliveros. Respect, sir, respect." Both men erupted in laughter. The sergeant rose and embraced the doctor.

"Come, sit down and unbutton your shirt," Oliveros said, and pulled a polished stethoscope from his bag. He pressed the cold disk to the sergeant's chest, listening for the missing beat. The arrhythmic heart followed no particular pattern, but its cadence was interrupted by a brief silence every so often.

"Have you heard about the rallies in Matanzas province?" the sergeant asked quietly.

"No speaking, Antonio." The doctor had still not heard the return of the beat. He slid the disk an inch to the right.

"Things are bad, Manuel. I think I'll be leaving soon." The sergeant looked up at his friend's face.

"Nonsense, your heart is strong still. You aren't going anywhere." Oliveros misunderstood. He was aware that he had just lied to his friend, that the missing beat this time lasted too long, and then struck up again weakly before gaining strength.

"I mean I'll be leaving Cuba soon." Again the doctor noted the silence in the sergeant's chest. He put the stethoscope away and brought together the folds of the sergeant's shirt.

"Leaving? Back to Spain, *gallego*?" he asked, using the common epithet for Spaniards that was taken as either an insult or compliment, depending on who used it.

"Perhaps the United States. Things are getting worse, Manuel, and I don't just mean my heart. This country is on the verge of civil war," the sergeant said, and placed his hand over his heart. "Just the other day we arrested thirty-eight demonstrators on the steps of the university, and can you believe? The whole time, Oliveros, one of them cried for his mamá." The doctor shook his head as he tucked the stethoscope back into his bag. "I should never have left my father's home," the sergeant concluded, and dug his buttocks deeper into his bed.

As if to emphasize his point, Regla appeared through the doorway with a telegram newly arrived, and Josefina's letter. The letter he squeezed in the palm of his hand, crumpling the paper a bit, and stuffed it into his pocket to read later. The telegram was already torn open, and from the purple shade suddenly cast upon Regla's cheeks, the sergeant knew the message was not gladdening. He read aloud for the doctor to hear:

1 SEPTIEMBRE 1946

A DEMONSTRATION IN MAR LINDO, THREE MILES FROM THE EL COTORRO POLICE ACADEMY, HAS DEVELOPED INTO A RIOT IN THE PUBLIC SECTORS OF BOTH SMALL TOWNS.

THE STUDENT INSURRECTIONS MUST BE STOPPED. OFFICERS FROM THE PROVINCES BORDERING THE RIOT WILL BE ASSIGNED TO POSTS THERE. SERGEANT ANTONIO NAVARRO WILL REPORT TO EL COTORRO AS SOON AS POSSIBLE.

The sergeant felt his cheek and read the telegram once more, to himself. "Regla," he said, "pack a small bag for me, only the essentials." And then to Oliveros: "You see, my friend, how things are going?"

"Yes, I see," Oliveros said, and helped the sergeant to his feet. "Be careful, *gallego.*"

"*Adiós,*" the sergeant said, and began to dress, pushing his daughter's unread letter into his coat pocket.

He arrived in El Cotorro that night, stepping off the train into the moisture in the air, and felt as if he were swaddled, suddenly, in a wet towel. From the station he could see the outline of the academy and the lights of the fires there, flickering west in the direction of the wind, despite the drizzle that continued to fall. He had little time, though, to take in the sight. Cadets from the academy, their cheeks flushed and beardless still, led the arriving officers in the direction of what once was the ticket area. Now the booths were stocked with rifles, the butts sticking sharply out over the countertops. Old wooden shields, bearing the scuffs and rifts from Cuba's independence, were laid on chairs and benches, so that there was no place for the wounded police to sit. Instead, they leaned against walls, holding bloodied wads of cotton to their wounds, and sat under signs that read, RIDE THE RAILROAD TO HAVANA or TRAVEL THE ISLAND LIKE A KING. The signs belied the island's instability. In just a few short years General Machado had been replaced by Céspedes, then came Grau, then Mendieta Montefur, Barnet, Gomez, Bru, Batista, Grau again. The list of names seemed endless, and the men that alternately took power had been certain that they could make changes. *No matter the name,* the sergeant thought, *blood and loss were always part of the scenery.*

The sergeant stood near the weapons, stroking the cold shotguns. He wondered if he could find the battered rifle he had shared with his brother during the Spanish War. He had carved an *A* onto one side, and an *F,* for his brother Francisco, on the other. The sergeant had never fired his weapon in the war, but he remembered the weight of that rifle on his shoulder, and the way the bayonet would heat like an iron in the sun, scalding his skin. He was sixty-two now, though he didn't look his age, and he still frightened the cadets nearby into standing up straighter.

The sergeant's search for his old rifle was interrupted, and he was led, at last, before a group of twenty cadets. One of them, a boy wearing tiny rimless glasses that reflected the lights of the approaching trains so that his eyes looked like flashbulbs for a moment as the train passed, stepped forward, trembling at the sight of the sergeant's tassels and medals, and handed him a small notice on yellow paper. The sergeant was to lead the group to El Cotorro's Plaza Perla to subdue the mob that had gathered there. He sighed loudly and shoved the paper into his pocket. *"Vámonos,"* he said and began the slow march to the plaza.

The people at the Plaza Perla seemed to quiet when they noted the police walking toward them. Many of the men had begun brawling, slashing at each other with kitchen knives and shards of glass from windows and lanterns. Even they stopped, holding their makeshift weapons toward the sergeant and the young cadets. The crowd was shaking in its anger. It had been the grand hotels that did it. They had seen the postcards—of luxury suites and Olympic swimming pools, of glitter and three-piece suits— and wondered where all the money had gone, while at home, they were telling their children stories of how the cows had stopped making milk.

The sergeant halted the march, placed the shield between his knees and cupped his hands over his mouth. *"¡A sus casas, todos!"* he shouted, his Spaniard's accent incensing the crowd that did not move. An elderly man took a light, cautious step out of the Plaza Perla, his foot leaving the grassy circle and onto the pavement of the road. Several men near him caught him by the shoulders and dragged him back into the ring.

"¡A sus casas!" he yelled again, but still no one turned toward home, nor dropped his weapon. The sergeant could hear the uneven breathing of the cadets behind him and the murmurs of the crowd before him. He looked at the faces, most of them young and dark from being out in the sun. Their hands, he saw, gripped tightly at fragments of glass, yet their tough skin did not split against the biting edges. They hated the state of things, President

Grau, and secretly, the sergeant did not blame them. Though he profited from the fat-faced leader's preference toward the wealthy, though he had fought in the Sergeants' Revolt of 1933, the sergeant knew that Havana had become a corrupt capital. Still, he did what he could to protect the presidency. It was a far cry from his own days as a rebel in the Sierra Maestra, when he and his brother crouched in holes and aimed their rifles at Spaniards to liberate the island. The years had, indeed, changed him.

There was youthful rebellion in the many faces around him, marked by snarling lips and the fantasy each one of them held of drawing blood from a man in uniform. The sergeant thought at once of his son-in-law, who seemed to embody that kind of mutiny. He looked for him in the crowd. Every other face was Lorenzo's, and then the sergeant would blink and he would note how one man had blue eyes, instead of brown, and another was too fat, and yet another had a dimple in his chin that was missing in Lorenzo's taut complexion. He was sure he would find him, and then he could rightfully, and dutifully, knock him to the ground and keep him there. So sure was he in this search and so long did he take to probe the features of each man that when the crowd finally broke before him, slinging dirt and stones, and the cadets turned to run, he did not notice for several seconds.

The error was a grave one. The sergeant found himself alone within the mob. Some of the men did not touch him, but instead pressed their noses to his and yelled, "Down with Grau," or, "Hijo de puta," and then spit on him. He found that his rifle had been wrestled away, and his shield was still braced between his knees. He knew he could not fight his way out from the center of the Plaza Perla where he now found himself, and so he allowed the group to pluck the tiny brass sabers from his collar and the tassels from his shoulders. In fact, as he crouched there, he managed to peek through his fingers at the faces around him, still searching for Lorenzo. He would not be able to bring him down now, but he still looked out.

The crowd milled about him for an hour, tearing his clothes and taking his shoes, then aiming them at his head. Still, no one had really injured him yet. His heart ached, and he thought of death. Why should he die? He had had a life that was rich, full of experience. Other men died. But now, the threat of death was real. Instead of fear, the sergeant thought of his now-lost daughter and felt sad. Sadness above all else. He allowed himself the respite of a kind of half sleep, closing his eyes and breathing through his mouth so as to not smell the rottenness of these men, like milk gone sour. A voice louder than the rest, brought him back from sleep, yelling, "Pull. Harder. *¡Caballeros, duro!*" and he saw a group that was trying to wrench an iron bench from its moorings. The bending iron squealed in the dark, and the sergeant watched through his fingers the funny way in which the skinny men pulled and pulled and grunted, and still the bench would not leave its place. The sergeant was near laughter, in fact, when the bench finally gave way and the men carried it over their heads. The loud-voiced one counted, *"Uno, dos, tres,"* and then the sergeant saw the bench leave their arms and float toward him, there on the ground. It nearly fell apart before striking. Once the bench had landed, and the sergeant found himself sleepy again, all humor gone, he heard the voice say, "Coward," and then nothing.

The four vagabonds who had come upon the sergeant's broken body in the center of the Plaza Perla had rummaged through the fallen man's pockets. They found his wallet, and they found Josefina's letter but did not read it, since they did not know how. Still, the street address was easy to make out, and because of a sense of duty, or perhaps an exchange—the return of the letter for the twenty-five pesos in his wallet—they ran all the way to the little house deep in El Cotorro to deliver the letter.

One of the men, whose left arm seemed to be pulled from its socket in some long-ago fight, so odd did it hang from the shoulder, held the letter. Another, a young man, seemed shaken and asked the one holding the letter, "He was dead, wasn't he, Pedro?" "*Claro, idiota.* He was cold, wasn't he?" Pedro answered. "Was he? I didn't touch him." The young vagrant slowed his step and turned to ask another in the group, "Diego. Diego, listen." "*¿Que?*" Diego answered, gruff and tired, his heels dragged on the ground.

"Did you touch the dead man?"

"I took the money, didn't I? Which reminds me, I get half of the twenty-five pesos."

"Was he cold?" the young one whispered now, clutching his hands together and holding them beneath his chin, like a child begging before a priest for answers.

"*Sí, sí,* cold as ice, Niquito. Now shut up."

The fourth man held the twenty-five pesos. The others trusted him, because he was a religious man, because he crossed himself at dawn and sunset and kissed the feet of statues of the Virgin whenever they passed one as they wandered. The wad of bills pressed warmly against his thigh, and it reminded him to be grateful. He knelt suddenly and crossed himself, then rose and thought of the dead man. He knelt again, as if to speak to the soul of the man in the park, saying, "Be thankful, señor, that you are dead. You're better off, better off."

Once in El Cotorro, they dropped the letter onto the stoop of the proper door and ran, already arguing among themselves of a way to divide the twenty-five pesos they had earned, happy to be rid of the policeman's bloody letter.

Josefina spent the two nights during the riots huddled in her bedroom closet. Soledad slept in her lap, and Lalo sat just outside the bedroom door. Lorenzo had rushed home when he heard about the uprisings and found his wife and children sitting in the dark, surrounded by food brought over from the kitchen, cold things turning warm and going bad. The darkness lasted throughout the day since the shutters were drawn and every crevice that glowed with light was stopped up with towels and rags. It was all Josefina could do before Lorenzo arrived. She could not move, not even about the house. She was trapped by her lack of experience. While neighbors knew they were safe within their homes, that the riots would not come so near their street, Josefina was paralyzed with fear, mainly for herself and her daughter. As for Lalo, he had wanted to go out and join the demonstrators. He had stood before his mother on the dawn of the second day with a machete in one hand and a handmade Cuban flag in the other. His chin was still smeared with that morning's breakfast of eggs and rice.

"¿Adónde vas?" she had asked without looking up. She could see his small shadow at her feet, the outline of his weapon, his pink, soft hands clenched like a man's.

"To the university. To join the fight, Mamá."

"There is no fight. This government will be replaced by another just as terrible. *Mejor sabido que por saber, hijo"*—Better to stay with a known thing than to take a risk on something unknown.

"Me voy, Mamá."

"Children do not fight in men's battles," Josefina said, standing now for the first time in hours, letting Soledad's head hit the ground with a thump as she got up. Her son, she thought, was growing into the type to pick up a cause that had nothing to do with him.

Lalo loosened his grip on the machete and swayed from side to side. His eyes softened.

"Hijito," Josefina said to the reddened ten-year-old, noting the softness and sitting down again, "there is one thing you can do. Pray for your papá to come soon."

Lorenzo did arrive a few hours later to find his son still in the house, still gripping his flag and machete. He had hated to leave the woman in Santa Clara, where he had spent the last month. She had called him her king and had fed him slices of apricots rolled in cinnamon, brushing his eyebrows with her fingertips. This woman knew just how to knead her soft fingers into his angular, delicate shoulders without hurting him. Still, the riots had not reached Santa Clara, and he knew Josefina could not manage alone.

When he came into the house, he had taken Josefina into his arms, sitting with her in the bedroom closet for a while, Soledad crammed between them both. She had let him console her, because she found she did not have the strength to confront him about his lover. He said little, only the words *"Todo bien"* whenever Josefina's cries became audible. He thought he understood well how frightened she must have been, listening to rifles going off at night and the crackle of fires being lit on every road. She cried, though not so much because the night blazed and filled her with dread, but because the sweet smell of apricots and cinnamon wafted from Lorenzo's lips, fresh from the morning.

The night of the second day fell, and the sounds outside seemed to have been quieted. Shouts, belonging to those of officers, punctuated an otherwise silent night. Josefina and Soledad had even begun to move about, and Lalo had dropped his machete and flag on the sofa and slept on top of them. Near dawn, while they all slept, a quick knock sounded on the front door. Lorenzo approached the door slowly, pulling the machete out from under Lalo's hip. He released the lock and pulled open the door to reveal a letter crumpled and stained with blood on the floor. Josefina's letter, pulled from the sergeant's grip by the group of men who found him, stirred in the breeze. The envelope, bearing Josefina's address printed in her own hand, lay nearby. Lorenzo recognized the penmanship, refined and gentle, the hand that must have been trained that way long ago in preparation for the addressing of invitations to benefit balls or long, amiable letters to the wives of mayors and such. Lorenzo picked up the letter, careful not to touch the spots of blood. He pressed the letter into Josefina's hand.

"I wrote this to Papá," she said. "Renzo, what can this mean?"

She had already gone pale about the cheeks and forehead. She had really not meant to ask, and now she wanted to stop her husband from saying it.

"He's been killed, I suppose," Lorenzo said, gathering Soledad in his arms. "Someone has let you know about it. That's a kindness I wouldn't expect in this village."

Josefina stood holding the letter loosely between her fingers. It balanced there for a moment, falling one way and then the other, before slipping to the ground quietly. Lorenzo carried Soledad outside, "to pick at the anthill near the avocado tree," he told her when she protested. Even outside, Josefina's cries could be heard.

"Papá," Soledad asked, "why is she crying? Let me go see her."

"Leave your mother alone for a while. Look at the ants. The big one, see there, do you think it's the queen?"

"But why does she cry?" she'd ask again, standing on her toes and trying desperately to peer through the trees toward the windows. Ants crawled up her legs and bit her thighs.

"Nothing, *niña,* nothing. Your brother spilled milk on her dress, her favorite dress. Let her be sad for now."

When the crying stopped, and the afternoon sun flared overhead, Lorenzo went inside. Lalo, still on the sofa, pretending to sleep and clutching his small flag as he watched his mamá, stood at the sight of his father.

"Go watch your sister. She's outside," he said, noticing the dents the flag's tiny rod had left in his son's hands, so tight was his hold on it. Josefina knelt on the floor.

"*Basta.* You've cried enough," Lorenzo said, gripping his wife's shoulder. He pulled hard, expecting her body to be stiff, but it was not. She flew up with the force of the tug and stumbled, catching herself on a small settee nearby. Lorenzo looked at his wife, her cheek smudged with blood, like a child playing with lipstick. She noticed his stare, and her hand fluttered to her face and began to wipe it. Lorenzo, though not pleased that a man had been killed, was gratified by his wife's reaction. He thought she would be difficult. While he toyed with the ants outside, he imagined that she'd want to do something lunatic, like keep the letter around for days, tucked into her shirt, or read it for advice, or frame the bloody paper. These things had happened before to other women, not unlike Josefina. Still, Lorenzo was thankful that she would not put on that type of display.

Her face looked so composed now, wiped clean of blood and glossy trails from her eyes to her nose, that he told her, "Hurry. Take Soledad and ride the first train to Vedado. Take all you can from the old house before the new sergeant is appointed to live there. Regla will be there, won't she?" Josefina was already rising, and running her fingers through her hair.

"Josefina," he added, "I'll stay and watch Lalo until you get back. The government will require money for the burial, if they find the body. I will send it soon." Josefina watched as her husband found his unpacked suitcase and arranged it by the front door. The scent of apricot and cinnamon was so thick in the air that Josefina thought she could open her mouth and swallow it.

Josefina did as her husband told her. She took her small daughter, dressed her in mourning, and headed out to her old home in Vedado. In her pocket was the bloody letter. Her son she left at home, "to make sure everything is safe." Lalo watched them from the window, his small hand still clenching the dull machete, proud to be doing something of importance at last.

Josefina's hand trembled as she tried to lock the front door of her house. Lorenzo would never remember, and the streets weren't safe. Soledad held onto her mother's skirt.

"Mami," she asked, "why were you crying?" The child was teary-eyed herself, knew how hard it was when her father was not around, and was afraid of losing her mother, too.

"Your *abuelo* went to live with the angels, *mi amor*," Josefina whispered and felt her throat constrict again as she pulled on the door to make sure it was locked.

"Why?"

"It's what *Papa Dios* wanted, Soledad. Your *abuelo* is dead."

"But . . ."

"It was meant to be this way," Josefina said loudly. She swallowed hard and took hold of Soledad's hand a little too firmly. She hadn't meant to, of course, nor had she meant to say that the sergeant's death was meant to be. *It was a colossal error,* Josefina thought. *I've made a colossal error in coming here,* and as she walked with her daughter to the train station, Josefina thought of how nice it would have been to stay in Vedado with her little pianoforte and her big closets full of clothes. With Regla and her father making sure she was happy.

The trains, slowed by the riots, did not leave the station until the next morning, so they slept on the third-class wooden benches. Sometime near dawn, an old woman tapped Josefina on the shoulder to wake her. She heard the tapping before she felt it, and in her dream, the sound was like a hammer being put to her front door, gouging a hole in the wood, deeper and wider with each blow. It was not until a few seconds later that Josefina realized she was being awakened.

"*¿Que? ¿Que?*" she asked, clutching at her purse.

"*Perdón,*" the old woman said meekly, her twisted, shaky fingertip still pressed against Josefina's shoulder. "Might you have a few pesos, for an old poor woman?"

Josefina thought of the crumpled bills in her purse, enough for only two train tickets home. The old woman's eyes, large and mapped with red veins, went from the sleeping figure of Soledad to Josefina's purse, then back again.

"I'm sorry," Josefina said at last. "*No tengo nada.*" The old woman removed her finger from Josefina's shoulder as if she had just burned it on a hot iron.

"Nothing?" she asked, the veins in her eyes began to branch out, giving her the appearance of a red-eyed demon.

"Nothing," Josefina said again. Now frightened, she lifted Soledad to her side and held her about the waist.

The woman did not move for a long time. The muscles around her lips twitched first, then the lips themselves parted to reveal a long, thin slice of tongue and gums. She spat as she spoke: "Miserable, greedy, greed, greed, misery . . ."

Soledad, enveloped in Josefina's fearful embrace, peeked through her mother's fingers and said, "My mamá is not miserable. You are!"

Josefina began to yell for the train attendant when the old woman moved close to Soledad. She pried the child's face out from the crook of her mother's arm. Her gnarled hands cupped Soledad's cheeks, and she hissed, "Don't you see it, child? Every inch of her tells of misery. Misery now, misery to come. Greed, greedy, greed . . ." She continued yelling when the train attendant finally took her away and pushed her out of the train.

Through the rest of the dawn and into the daybreak, Josefina and Soledad heard her yelling outside to all who would listen, about suffering and the trials of a woman inside. "See her for yourself," she'd say, over and over, as if she was a sideshow announcer.

Their journey began near noon. They were relieved when the old woman's voice faded as they moved away and were able to notice the scenery outside the moving train with interest. It changed quickly as they moved out of El Cotorro and into Havana province. Ramshackle shelters with emaciated dogs prostrate at the doorsteps gave way to rolling hills and large farms and men on sturdy horses that ran alongside the train, waving at the passengers. They looked as if there was nothing going on in the island, no guns, no revolutions, no men waving flags and growling at one another. Once the city itself began to come into view, the train slowed, or so it seemed to Josefina, so that the passengers could take in the sight of coral-walled buildings. Even the smokestacks looked pretty, the dark smoke like a painter's careful smudge on the blue sky.

Soledad said little as they walked to the house in Vedado. Her eyes took in every detail—the cracks in the sidewalks and the cigarette butts stuck in between, the sparrows that perched in one long line on every rooftop, peering down at the pedestrians. And she noticed everything that was not there, like the fruit trees and tomato gardens, and she wondered if the sparrows had driven the nightingales away. Soledad carried an empty carpetbag "so we can bring our things home," her mamá said. Soledad marveled that anything of theirs could be so far away in so strange a city.

Once in Vedado the scenery changed again. Open doors revealed great marble staircases and pots filled with fresh flowers. Here the sidewalks weren't cracked and the weepy strains of a child's violin lesson pierced the walls and accompanied the sparrows' chirping. Josefina remembered her childhood in vivid waves that made her cry out. *Here was where I learned to ride my bicycle*, she thought. *And here is where I stood when my Renzo first kissed me, in the shade of a looming hydrangea tree that is gone now.* The stillness of these remarkable gardens and homes—except for the violins, it didn't seem as if anyone were living within the walls—was broken by shouts and crashes at the end of the street, the volume of the sounds growing as they approached.

"Dios mío," Josefina whispered, the very words slowing their steps with their grimness. She stood in the doorway, her daughter's small hand pressed into hers so hard that Soledad felt her knuckles grind together. They looked in to see various people entering and disappearing through the many rooms like light-fearing insects, many of them carrying paintings, satin pillows, and glazed pots. A sheet of newspaper fluttering around Soledad's ankle announced the death of the sergeant and the name of the newly appointed officer. The article's author had written a fanciful account of the sergeant's death—he had been shot once in the chest and his last words, heard by those around him, were, "Down with traitors!" Then, the article continued, the rioters took apart his body, which was evidence of the savagery of the anti-Grau fac-

tions. Still, his allegiance, printed for all to read, did not slow the plunder in the dead man's house.

Josefina took the carpetbag by the handle, dragging Soledad along with it. "Take what you can," she yelled, though now there was little to be had. She had quickly surmised that the thieves would not believe that she was the sergeant's daughter. Her nails were not manicured, her shoes were torn, her hair was not curled and set. Josefina began in the kitchen, pulling a set of porcelain teacups with gilded handles from the back of a cabinet. She retrieved three silver forks from a drawer (all that was left from a set of fifty) and a brocade tablecloth from Spain. All this she threw into the carpetbag. They followed the same pattern in every room of the house, pushing through groups of people who gathered around her pianoforte, touching the keys and laughing at the sound, spitting in the face of one woman who pushed Soledad to the ground to get to a pair of the sergeant's dress shoes. Even Regla's room was ravaged, her saints and plaster good luck roosters beheaded in the search for jewelry or money. Josefina opened the old maid's closet, looking for the bag that held Regla's treasures—thin gold medallions of Santa Bárbara that Regla used to let Josefina bite, making little hammered dents in the polish, and a bag of Josefina's baby teeth that Regla refused to let the sergeant throw away. Her hand groped in the dark, like a blind animal, and touched warm skin. From within, Regla screamed and bit Josefina's hand.

"*Ay,*" Josefina screamed, and then: "Is it you?"

Regla emerged from the dark closet, her hair undone from its rigid bun, her head a blur of gray curls. She clutched her medallions and the bag of teeth in her hands, along with some handkerchiefs and a Bible, all wrapped together with red twine. "My girl, I was so worried," Regla said, and fell into her charge's arms. "They are taking everything, everything your papi worked so hard for."

Then Regla remembered herself. She straightened and stood,

seeing Josefina now for the first time in months. Josefina pulled Soledad in front of her in an attempt to cover her shabby dress. The five-year-old stood just past her mother's waist.

Regla spoke at last, her voice now strong, trumpetlike as it used to be when she was in charge of teaching Josefina manners: "You have not written in months."

People who had been milling around them, stripping chests and dressers clean of their contents, began to give the two women and the girl room, as if they were afraid to enter the space that seemed sacred, and at the moment, overwrought.

Josefina for her part began to cry and gripped Soledad by the shoulders tightly. She hadn't written a single word to Regla in so long. Lorenzo's exploits were the reason. Lorenzo was barely home, and when he was, he slept with his back turned to Josefina. If she reached out to touch him, he'd say he was tired, or too worried about finances to think about making love. "And besides," he said once, "we don't want any more *chiquitos* running around here, do we?" How could Josefina write to Regla and leave all of that hurt out? Better to stop writing altogether. Josefina bent over and touched her nose to the top of Soledad's head. She shook as she held her daughter close.

"*No, no llores,*" Regla said, her voice rising, angry that Josefina had not written in so long, that her girl had, perhaps, forgotten all about her. "And when you see me dead, dead from missing you, cold and stiff in a pine coffin, don't cry then, either." Josefina made a sound as if she had been physically wounded.

Regla yielded. She took Josefina in her arms as she once did and rocked her, humming an old lullaby, crushing Soledad between them. Regla was mother and grandmother, old and still young, able to find a husband yet, but bound to the sergeant's home. How could she leave this place where her little girl, her Josefina, had grown up? Who would stay behind and light candles for her future? Who would make sure no one painted over her childish signature scrawled on Regla's bedroom wall?

"Did you see your father, before he . . ." Regla asked.

"Papá? No," Josefina said. "But someone came and left this at my door." Josefina lifted the bloody letter out of her pocket and gave it to Regla.

The two women sat down on Regla's bed. Josefina held Soledad on her lap, and Regla stroked the fine hair on the girl's legs. With heads brought close together, they cried over the pages dabbed with the sergeant's blood, his life force, dried and brown now on the page.

Soon enough, the house was full of policemen arresting looters. When a young officer began to yell at Josefina and Regla to get out, another policeman who felt the sadness in the room stopped him right away. They were left alone in Regla's little sanctuary.

Once the house was secure, Regla packed a small bag to stay at her sister's house until the new sergeant was appointed to the home. The trio stood outside in the dusky evening and watched as the front door was chained shut.

"I'll tell your father's attorney where you live. You'll get whatever is in his account, but the house goes to the next sergeant." Regla turned and looked at the house in the distance. "Write often," Regla advised, and Josefina nodded. *"Y tú, mi amorcito,"* Regla said, coming down to her knees, her stockings tearing on the asphalt, to reach Soledad's height, "Be good to your mami. She needs you to listen and behave."

The carpetbag became too heavy for Soledad to carry, and some of the contents spilled out over the top. The tinkle of falling ashtrays and candle snuffers sounded behind them as they walked back to the railroad station, but they did not turn to pick them up.

6

The sergeant awoke in the center of the Plaza Perla. He was sure that his nose was broken, possibly in more than one place along the bridge. He tasted that crude mixture of blood and dirt and felt around the jagged insides of his mouth with his tongue, exploring the split tissue on the inside of his cheek and drawing a rush of more blood.

It was morning, and the crowd had disappeared. The bench they had thrown at him still lay across his neck and chest. It had cracked in half over him, never striking with the full force of the group's intention. The sergeant could feel his heart beating too hard. He peered under his shirt and prepared himself to see a purple bruise or welt, the sight so grisly that his heart would finally stop forever. But his skin was unbroken. The bench's armrest, which had fallen on his nose and mouth, lay nearby, but his vulnerable heart was untouched.

The sergeant rose stiffly and made the sign of the cross, in gratitude for his life. The morning was hot. The sergeant removed his coat, which had been stripped of its medals and its left pocket. He checked the coat for his wallet, finding that, too, gone, then tossed the heavy wool thing over the park bench, to soak in the puddles of blood. The sergeant reached deep into his pants pocket and pulled a wad of pesos out. In his shoe were ten more, and sewn into the lining of his underwear were five. His money had been stolen once before, when he was knocked unconscious during the festival of Santa Barbara, trampled on by the partygoers, left penniless for days before someone would acknowledge his badge and pay his ticket home. He did not think it could happen again, but he took precautionary measures anyway.

He wandered about the town and reached Josefina's house midmorning. The sergeant knew he had come close to death. *All these wasted years,* he thought as he walked to his daughter's home. He had a plan, to knock on the door and hold her in his arms again, to bounce grandchildren on his knee, to even forgive Lorenzo and try to embrace him as a son. The sergeant thought he had been given a second chance. And if Josefina wanted, maybe they could all move to the United States together, to escape once and for all this island turmoil, these tropical nights, and try to recapture the civility he had left behind in Europe.

The sergeant looked awful. He knew it without having a mirror nearby. The shop windows as he passed reflected a bloody figure. He wiped the blood from his cheeks with his own spit, and even gathered some water from a puddle to wash his hands. The stores were all closed, and even the fountains in the plazas had been turned off because of the riots.

Josefina's street opened up before the sergeant and he suddenly felt a lurch in his stomach. What would he say? He had never apologized to anyone in his life. And how would he be able to keep from saying, "I told you so"? El Cotorro was poor, frightening, and inadequate—everything the sergeant had predicted. But he told himself he would be good. He would compliment her house and give Lorenzo one of those hugs in which father and son-in-law pat each other's backs loudly.

He saw the house and approached it from the other side of the street. Behind the curtains he could see shapes. The sergeant leaned against a cedar tree across from the house. He felt his hands tremble and his legs go weak.

Suddenly, the curtain at the window parted, and a young boy

peered out. Eulalio! He was strikingly like Lorenzo and his brow was furrowed into tiny lines as he scanned the street. The sergeant ducked behind the cedar. *Ay, he'll make such a policeman that one!* Then the door opened.

Josefina squinted in the light. She had her back to him. She wore a flowered dress and was thinner than she used to be. Her long hair was gathered up, and brown curls sprung out from the clasp. She was shapely and the material of her dress clung to her waist and bottom. When Josefina turned, the sergeant nearly cried out. He felt the tension in his legs, the indecision of his muscles—to run to her or stay here? She was still so beautiful. She wore no lipstick, but her lips were rosy, her cheeks were full, her eyes clear and liquid.

Soledad held on to her mother's skirt. The sergeant began to cry, and hid himself behind the cedar again. *Ay, to hold that little one,* he thought. To remember the days when Josefina was only five and still drank her milk, her *che-che,* from a bottle in the sergeant's lap. How her legs dangled to the floor! How her eyelids drooped, and the sweet breath of her kisses. If he could hold Soledad all of those memories would come alive again.

Just when the sergeant had let go of the cedar, ready to run to her, he heard his daughter's voice, carried on the wind, for the first time since her wedding day.

"Your *abuelo* is dead," and then, angrily, "It was meant to be this way."

The sergeant sank to the floor and watched as his daughter and granddaughter walked away from him, to the train station. Her tone had been so assured, so harsh. "Meant to be," the sergeant repeated. Was it what she wanted, after all? To be free of him?

He sat underneath the shade of the tree and cried. His heart ached, but he didn't care. *Let me die on the spot,* he begged. *Let her find me here, this hateful daughter, and be filled with regret!* He cried until sitting up became difficult and didn't care if he was found, shamed.

It was Lalo who ventured out of the house, machete still in

hand. His father, Lorenzo, had fallen asleep and wouldn't notice his young son unlocking the door. Lalo crossed the street and tapped his foot against the leg of the man he had been watching for over an hour.

"*Oye,*" the boy said. "Get out of here. You are disturbing the peace." Lalo waved his machete in his hand.

The sergeant sat up. "I'm sorry, *mi niño.* I truly am." Then he pulled the boy in a tight embrace, feeling his grandson against him for the first time. Lalo struggled and kicked his skinny legs.

"*¡Sueltame, sueltame!*" Lalo yelled, and the sergeant let go as he was asked. The boy ran across the street and into his house, slamming the door behind him.

Lalo's cries of, "Let go of me, let go of me!" ran through the sergeant's mind as he left Josefina's house behind him. He would let go of his family since it seemed to be what they wanted.

The sergeant was at the docks the next day at noon. He did not want to return to the station and report his catastrophe at the Plaza Perla. It would mean that he would have to explain about Lorenzo, how he had become preoccupied with finding his son-in-law, how he allowed the crowd to overtake him, and how he let the cadets run in horror.

But what he most wanted was to be away from Josefina. The anger he had felt toward her when she married Lorenzo was rekindled. He would go to the United States and live in peace. *Let them suffer this island alone,* he thought, even though he could still feel his little grandson against his chest and the memory of Josefina at her front door made his eyes water. But her words, her cruel "meant to be," pushed him toward the dock and to a new life.

A ferry began loading passengers near where the sergeant sat. Several families, clearly residents of El Cotorro from the way they dressed, smelled, held their bags, began climbing aboard. The ferryman noticed the number of suitcases and called out to one of them, a man whose eyes, too, were rimmed in red, saying, "Where are you going? I would think this is a dangerous time to leave your homes for a vacation. I don't recommend it. Think of your property."

"This is no vacation. We are not coming back here." The red-eyed man helped his wife climb the steep steps, then lifted his young son to his shoulder.

"Where is the ferry going?" the sergeant asked.

"A la Florida," the man said. "We sent for our papers months ago. My wife tires of these fights that keep us indoors. There's a new president every day, it seems, and each one is worse than the one before." The man disappeared into the bowels of the ferry, and another family, similarly clad and composed, followed.

The sergeant watched as the boat filled and its engine began to hum. He ran up the slimy plank that served as a step from the walkway to the boat and found himself inside. It was not long before the ferryman appeared beside him, his long hand extended for the passage fare. The sergeant pulled a few moist pesos from the inside of his shoe and pressed it into the ferryman's palm.

"Do you have a passport, señor?" the ferryman asked.

"Sí," the sergeant lied and pushed another wad of pesos against the man's hand. The sergeant made his way to the bathroom and washed his face in the sink. Tucking his head under the faucet, he rinsed his hair. Using the soap on the sink, he rubbed at the stains on his clothes until they were faint spots and the bar of soap was dimished to a sliver. In the mirror, the sergeant saw a series of cuts on his forehead that stung in the cool air. His nose was stuffy and it was swelling like a boxer's after a fight. But after the washing he no longer looked like a man in trouble. The sergeant left the bathroom and made a space for himself on the floor, where the rumbling of the engine was strongest under his thighs.

The trip was quiet. The passengers slept on each other's shoulders and chests, or looked out of scratched windows at the diminishing coastline, or over the railing where they dropped tears into the sea. As for the sergeant, he did not glance outside, but instead, spoke to the first mate, a young man named Mario, to pass the time.

"Where are you from?" Mario asked. "Is it Madrid?"

The sergeant smiled. *People always say Madrid,* the sergeant thought, *because it is the only Spanish city they know.* "No, no, I am from the Canaries," he answered.

"And El Cotorro? Is that where you've been living?"

"Sí," the sergeant said, thinking that if he mentioned Vedado the young Mario would somehow ask for money, or would begin a series of questions about the nearby capital, the cost of Vedado's houses, or the number of maids he had accumulated.

"Me, too. Did you hear about the man killed in the plaza the night before last?" The sergeant shook his head. "The authorities say he was a colonel or a captain."

"How was he killed?" the sergeant asked, staring at his hands folded before him, his nails still sheathed in a thin crusted layer of blood.

"He was taken apart by the rioters, the papers said. His coat was found at the scene, with the right arm still inside one of the sleeves. They say our president is savage," he said, and then he whispered as if the murderers might be on board, "but his opponents are inhuman."

Mario shook his head and sniffed three times. The sergeant rubbed his arm. It was sore, but still there, firmly attached.

"The rest of him," Mario whispered, "hasn't been found."

The sergeant suddenly began to laugh, whinnying and cackling like a horse at the sight of Mario's wide eyes, the severity in his furrowed brow.

"Maybe the man is alive," the sergeant finally said when he finished laughing, "happy to have lost his arm for the dear *presidente.*"

The ferry arrived in the port of Miami by morning the next day. It was raining, and veins of lightning stretched across the dim sky. In the distance, the sergeant saw the gray beaches and off the docks where the ferry stopped, tiny white-haired men who fished without poles, but with spools of line and buckets of bait. The fifty or so passengers on the ferry cradled their bags in their arms to protect the photographs and small carved saints from the rain. The sergeant carried nothing, but kept his arms folded before him. He felt he was catching a cold, because the chill started deep inside his lungs and made him shiver with every breath.

The line for customs was not too long that morning, so the sergeant placed himself at the end of it. Behind the desk was a tall woman. Her cheeks were smudged with bright shadow as were her eyelids. Her hair was nearly blond, growing silver near the roots, and tied in a loose braid that draped over her shoulder and was caught in her little brass name pin that read, Mona Linde.

When the sergeant's turn came, he looked at Mona and smiled, pulled his hands from his pockets, and slammed his palms onto the desk. "Spain, Cuba, me America," he said, pointing east, then south, and finally to his feet, trying to explain the progression of his life to the stranger.

"Passport, please," Mona said, pulling out blank forms from underneath her desk, her pen readied to begin.

"America. *Sargento* Antonio Navarro."

Mona checked a list of translations taped to her desk. *"Pasaporte,"* she said again, pronouncing the word in one breathy sigh. He did not blink or move at all at her request. He leaned on the counter and nearly looked like he was falling asleep. There were dry gashes on his forehead and his nose was swollen and purpled. Mona felt as if she should bring a bag of ice to that nose.

"Take a seat," she said and motioned to a group of chairs to the side of the room. He did not want to go to jail now, or worse, be sent to a waiting room to await the next trip back. He took out his remaining pesos, damp and wrinkled, and tapped Mona on the shoulder with the money. "Just be seated, sir," she said, and turned to the next person in line.

The sergeant waited for two hours until the end of Mona's shift, all the while replaying the scene outside of Josefina's house. Another woman came to take over for Mona. Mona faced the sergeant. "Come with me," she said, then locked up her papers inside the desk. The sergeant understood and followed her.

The sergeant followed her to an employee restroom. He watched as Mona pulled a handkerchief from her purse and wet it in the cold stream of the faucet. She folded it in multiple squares, pressed the excess water out, and shaped the wet linen over the sergeant's broken nose. He flinched, laid his hand on her shoulder, and then said, *"Gracias,"* so softly, in a voice so much like that of her long-dead husband, that Mona Linde decided to help this man out, as one would a stray dog that is mangy and scabby but still somehow charming.

Mona thought he was dignified. The way he sat so still as he waited for her to be finished with her day seemed like something only a gentleman would do. He was tall, broad-shouldered, had the air of someone of a certain position, a certain class, despite his wounded appearance. Mona had snuck looks at him all afternoon, and with each peek, he reminded her more and more of Jim, her late husband.

On the wall of the restroom was a small, framed photograph of a woman. The young, large-eyed woman in the picture smiled stiffly and wore her hair curled softly on her shoulders. Underneath her countenance were the words "Employee of the Month." The sergeant had noticed it at once, and studied the face as Mona studied his. *Perhaps I have been hit over the head too hard,* the sergeant thought, but the woman in the photograph looked just like his daughter. His nose flared as he looked at the familiar face, and Mona noticed the twitch.

"Pretty, isn't she?" Mona said and balled up the wet handkerchief roughly. "She's dead. Drowned. We keep her picture up."

The sergeant, not understanding a word, looked up at Mona and smiled, then turned again to the picture.

"Dead," Mona said, "dead, um, yes, *muerta.*" She pointed to the pretty face and her finger trembled in the air. He had caught the word and it swept over him in a wave of remorse and what might be. He rubbed his eyes and cradled his head in his hands.

"She reminds you of someone," Mona said, close to his ear. The sergeant stirred and placed his hand on her shoulder again. "You remind me of someone, too," she said, but he did not understand. Mona had been so lonely for so long. She folded, deciding she'd offer this stranger a place to stay the night. One night. She'd turn him in tomorrow.

The warmth of his hand lingered long after she had cleaned his entire face, leaving no traces of blood or plaza dirt, long after she had led him through the basement corridors, past boiler rooms and miles of plumbing, long after they rode the bus together to the riverside town of Miami Springs, where Mona kept house.

As for the sergeant, he had allowed himself to be led in this way, partly because he was fond of this Mona, whose name meant "monkey" in Spanish and sometimes "frivolous" or "adorable," and he liked that, partly because he wasn't thinking of her at all. His thoughts were still of Josefina and Lorenzo, how close he had been to them just yesterday, and how far he suddenly was. He remembered his daughter's letter, still unread, and dug into his pocket in search of it. He wondered if the letter had kind words in it, but he couldn't find it. *It must have gone the way of my wallet,* he thought, thankful he remembered her address so that he could write her later. He thought, too, of his post and imagined vividly the way his officers would laugh at his failure.

Mona's little ranch-style home was decked with hanging bowls of pink azaleas. Tiny lizards darted among the blooms, peeking their elongated heads between the petals as the sergeant followed Mona inside. Her house was heavily decorated. Flea market paintings in ornate frames hung on the walls. Potted ferns covered in brown, scaly spores sat in every corner, growing toward the center of the room, the air vents making the leaves writhe. Little spheres of tangled hair and dust, pushed, too, by the air vents, floated just above the ground, touching the speckled terrazzo every so often. One lighted on the sergeant's toe, and he shook it away in disgust. *This is America?* he asked himself and then watched another dust ball trailing its way between Mona's feet.

Mona Linde resembled her house. She was a little disheveled, her long braid coming apart in blond wisps. Her clothes were wrinkled, but she smelled like lavender, and her nails were neatly painted in pink polish.

Mona stood, the dust ball caught in the arch of her heel. In the kitchen, she began to marinate a pair of pork chops and opened a can of red bean soup, because she once heard that Cubans ate red beans at every meal.

After dinner, he mimed writing with his hands, trying to get Mona to fetch him some paper. He would write Josefina again, he decided, pound away at her from afar. He wasn't the kind of man who could let a young, foolish woman determine his place in the world. Most importantly of all, he would see to it that Soledad and Eulalio were happy, as he had done for Josefina. Mona understood and said, "Check the other room," pointing the way as she began the dishes.

In the living room, which seemed very much alive, like the jungle valleys in Matanzas draped in their creeping lianas, thick and long and always moving somehow, the sergeant began to rummage for paper, and pens, and envelopes. He found a little-used writing kit in Mona's stuffed bookshelf. He blew dust off the paper and had to smack the pen against his thigh several times before the ink began to run again. Once prepared, he sat down to write:

Mi Hija,
    I am sorry I was not able to see you in El Cotorro while I was there. Maybe you want me to be dead. No matter. I've decided you need my help anyway. Though I have lost your letter, I hope that you had only kind words for me. I hope my grandchildren are well. I hope you are well. I hope nothing for the scoundrel you married.
    If you have extra money, send my granddaughter to piano lessons, as you used to do. Cultivate her. Do not let her grow up to be a simple *guajira*. Remember her blood is from the mother country, too.
    I cannot tell you where I am. I fear you would not understand, but I will write very soon.
    Tu Papá

He folded the letter and sealed it within the envelope. He rummaged through the dusty box for stamps, and finding none, proceeded to the kitchen to ask Mona.

"Estampilla," he said, and pointed to the upper right corner of the envelope, outlining an invisible little stamp.

"Is this for your wife?" she asked, a shadow coming across her face. The sergeant didn't understand, couldn't answer. Mona sighed. "One night. One night is all you get," she said, and turned in anger to the linen closet.

She set up a foldaway bed for the sergeant in the living room. The creaky thing screeched as Mona and the sergeant pulled at it from both ends. She laid out white sheets for the sergeant, and brought him old pajamas out of Jim's closet.

In the morning, the sergeant ate while Mona watched. He had already begun to learn a few words. He understood "eat," and "drink," "dead," and "out." English seemed a harsh language to him, resonating with guttural sounds and dull r's. Still, he did not long for Spanish. He wanted to understand the baseness of English, as he had come to know, but not appreciate, the vulgar Spanish spoken in Cuba, and all its veiled meaning.

Mona turned the radio on. She twisted the dial roughly, the cacophony of sound a violent, intrusive interruption to their silence. She stopped the dial on a news station and began to take the plates away from in front of the sergeant. She mumbled, "Oh dear," when the announcer spoke of the war veterans marching on the Capitol for their compensations. "Mercy," she said, when the announcer described the way the soldiers had been turned out, with clubs and gunshots, ordered by President Truman himself.

The sergeant heard the newscast, too, listening for one of the four words he understood. He caught "out" three times, and picked up a new word, "president," so much like *presidente.* Mona turned around then, her hands dripping, the droplets gathered on each of her fingertips like glass spheres hanging on a chandelier.

"Are you listening to the radio? You should be thankful for what I've done for you." She held her hands so still at her sides that the tiny droplets did not fall. "We won the war and still folks can't find work. It's hard times, mister. People are killing one another for money from the government, from their jobs, and I've risked it all to help you." Now Mona trembled, and the droplets shook and fell, making miniature puddles on the ground by her feet.

The sergeant did not dare smile this time. Her face looked all at once like a rotting lemon, the skin yellow and wrinkled. Her chin and her lips quivered, and she swallowed two or three times in succession. He had seen the look once before, on the face of his wife, Ana, in her final moments, when the doctor told the sergeant that the birth of her child was a death sentence for the beautiful, spirited woman. In her death, her mouth, jaw, and throat had sprung into movement in the same way, and her skin, indeed, took on the color of a lemon, except his wife had been young, and so her face was not wrinkled like this Mona's was. Ana had fought death, never seemed to have considered it, had tried to will it away. Mona seemed to be staging a similar battle. The sergeant thought for a moment, *is she telling me that she is dying? Have I come all this way to watch over an aged woman's deathbed?* When color returned to her cheeks all at once, he dismissed the idea.

"I've decided we need one another. I know you have a wife, but she mustn't mean much to you if you're here and she isn't. Judy'll cover for me at work. No one'll ever know you are here." Mona waited for the sergeant to say something. He stared at her.

"I am an independent woman," Mona continued. "No man is going to live off of me for long. Come on," Mona said, and wiped the moisture off her hands with her skirt. The sergeant followed her into her bedroom. She opened the closet and pulled back a white sheet to reveal a row of men's suits and shirts. Beside them was a tiny rack filled with wrinkled cravats and little crushed bow ties. The clothes were not modern but musty and small and, in places, moth-eaten.

"They were Jim's, my husband." The sergeant tightened his mouth in sympathy. The word "husband" he understood, and he knew that the man had died. Death seemed all around this woman, dark and smoky. "Cancer, don't you know. Of the lung. It doesn't give you much time on this earth. Now," she said, pulling out a brown suit, "they'll be put to good use." It had been years since Jim died in their bedroom—his eyes had gone wildly large when he had drawn his last breath—but Mona would not give away his things, even if the cigarette and biscuit smell of them made her cry. She liked remembering Jim in the clothes, each article hung neatly beside her own elaborate prints. She often lifted the white sheet that hid the old suits and pants and looked at the pairings of dresses and suits in rapture. She'd never tell the sergeant how one desperate Christmas morning she laid one of the suits on the bed and slept beside it. In fact, she wouldn't mention Jim again. The gleam in her eyes revealed her emotion at the moment. The sergeant's coming was auspicious. In him, Mona had seen a flicker of what Jim once was—stern, handsome, stubborn.

Mona motioned for the sergeant to put on the suit and walked out, shutting the door behind her. The sergeant inspected the buttons shaped into polished disks, the tips of the collar twisted in opposite directions. He tried on the pants and found he could not button the waist, and then put on the shirt and jacket and found that the sleeves were a bit short. Still, he was grateful not to be wearing the old police undershirt and caramel-colored pants.

Once dressed, the sergeant went to Mona, who frowned at the short sleeves and the moth hole just left of the sergeant's heart. "Good enough for a laborer, I suppose," she said and placed her hand into his.

They walked for a quarter of a mile away from the little ranch house, until the double line of houses on either side of them opened up, suddenly, to reveal a busy circular road. Cars honked as they cut each other off. Black puffs of exhaust dotted the air around the cars, and an advancing truck, with its bumper disconnected, clattered and jangled into the distance. In the center of the circle was a lush green little park, like the peaceful eye of a hurricane. A wooden sign rose up from within a thick rose bush, reading CIRCLE PARK, the letters painted gold. A trail of gold paint had run down the side of the sign and dried there, like a singular gilded vein, feeding the park with loveliness.

Mona and the sergeant crossed the street and entered the park, where the noises seemed to quiet, stifled by the tangled branches of the Florida holly trees and the broad fans of the palms. On his knees, pulling at stubborn weeds in the garden beds, was an old man, nearly twenty years the sergeant's senior.

"Señor Matute," Mona said, as she tapped the old man on the shoulder. He turned, taking a handful of weeds with him as he went.

"Aah, Señorita Linde, how may I help you?" Chelo Matute, Cuban by birthright, American by law, wiped the dirt from his hands before shoving them into his pockets. He often mowed

Mona's lawns or cultivated seedling papayas in her backyard, only to find that in his absence the trees had died of thirst in Mona's care.

"This gentleman is new to our country, Matute," Mona whispered, as if the sergeant could understand and overhear, "and I am afraid he isn't very bright. Might you have some work for him? Be a dear and translate for me." Indeed, Matute found the newcomer strangely mute, but his eyes were not those of a dull man.

"Of course, Señorita Linde. I will take good care of your friend."

Mona nodded her head in thanks. "Tell him he can stay in my home as long as he likes, as long as he's decent." Matute translated and the sergeant forced a half-hearted smile. Mona returned the gesture, then patted the sergeant on the back and turned toward home.

The sergeant knew he was to stay and work. He removed the old jacket and rolled up the sleeves to his elbows. He knelt where the elderly man had been, settling his own knees into the grooves in the dirt set there before, and started to pull weeds. Matute, for his part, began to think that the man truly was deaf and mute and imagined how he would explain next week's pruning with only his hands. As he knelt, too, his arthritic back creaking as he went, the sergeant spoke:

"You are from Santiago, no?" He did not raise his voice above the soft sounds of roots being torn from the earth.

Matute nodded, and said in Spanish, "And you are a Cuban who took a short vacation to Miami and have decided to stay. Am I right?" Matute snorted and coughed.

"You are partially right," the sergeant returned, and said nothing for the rest of the afternoon except to ask whether the white impatiens needed further trimming. By the end of the day, the sergeant was doused in sweat, and in an effort to relieve the heat, he had removed his belt, undershirt, and socks, leaving them in a heap behind a statue of a plump, fat-nosed fairy, meant to look as if it were romping among the vegetation.

"Put away your tools, *hombre,*" Matute said, "and come and get your day's pay." Matute jingled a handful of coins in his hand before tossing them to the sergeant. Then he passed on a few folded dollars.

"Might I have a stamp?" the sergeant asked as the coins flew toward him. Matute disappeared into his tool shed, rummaged there a bit, then returned with a stamp, the bottom corners torn. He gave the stamp to the sergeant and took a nickel from his open hand. The sergeant licked the stamp, found that he had to swirl his dry tongue inside his mouth to retrieve some moisture, then licked it again. The letter for Josefina could now be sent, and for the first time since his arrival, Sergeant Antonio Navarro felt gratified.

As weeks went by, other letters were written, mostly in the early orange evenings of Miami, but the sergeant never sent any of them. They accumulated under a potted plant where he hid them, forcing himself to draw the courage to throw the things in the mail. *She will think I am a coward for running away, for crossing miles and miles of water in fear, as I did as a child,* he would think. And then: *Why should I spend this energy on her? She made her bed long ago.* So, the letters stayed under the pot, paper dampening, ink running.

After a long day of pushing the lawn mower, or spraying the marigold beds of Circle Park, the sergeant would return to Mona Linde's house, sit himself in one of her many wicker rockers, and think of ways to bring Josefina and the children to him. He had considered asking Mona for help. Though his English was improving, she seemed to understand little, and usually quieted his efforts with a kiss. Her lips, thin and papery, did not move once pressed against his. She simply hung the kiss there, like a wind chime on a placid day, and waited for the sergeant to begin. He had tried, in the beginning, to rival her stillness, but she had pinched him hard on the arm and walked off, leaving him without supper that evening. The next morning, she walked with him to Circle Park and said something to Chelo Matute in English. Later that day, Chelo translated:

"I don't know what you've done, *hombre,* but Miss Linde said she would send you back to Cuba if you did not make her happier." Chelo had slapped him on the back and continued setting squirrel traps, chuckling to himself as he went. The sergeant resolved then to kiss her and do what she asked, unbutton her silk shirts, grip her neck, lap at her ear, even though he did not love her, just as long as she kept her promise to harbor him.

On those evenings when the sky was painted in brush strokes of orange watercolor, washing off as the sun set, the sergeant returned the favor to Mona, and when they were done, she would scurry off to the shower, turning the dial so far left toward Hot that steam filled the rooms. In that cloud of vapor, the sergeant would write to his daughter. The letters were short, and he often mentioned the contract that Lorenzo had refused to sign on the wedding day. He would write: "Does he take you dancing, my daughter?" or, "Does he strike you, my daughter? If he does I will send a scourge upon him," or "Does he attend Mass with you and the children? Do not let him doom you."

One morning, after the sergeant had written a letter during his lunch break, Chelo, who prided himself on knowing everything in Miami Springs, read the missive. He was instantly addicted to the drama, the story of the spurned father, and finally felt he understood the sergeant's heartache and liked the sergeant all the more for it. The swarthy gardener decided to help the sergeant, because he worked hard, did not fear plunging an ungloved hand into the heart of a thorny bush to pull out diseased leaves, cut garden snakes in half with a shovel whenever he saw them, and knew exactly the right amount of acid to pour into the ground to make the hydrangeas bloom pink instead of blue.

"*Ven,* Antonio," Chelo called one morning. "I need to speak with you." The sergeant dropped five layers of sod he was carrying to the ground. They broke over his feet. "I know about your daughter. I can help you be rid of that bastard son-in-law."

The sergeant sat down to untie his shoes. He poured the dirt out. "*Habla,*" he said, in such a tone that Chelo suddenly felt sorry for opening the letter.

"You must have been born under a lucky sign. My half brother lives in El Cotorro. His name is Abel Santana and he owns a butcher stand." Chelo paused and searched the sergeant's face for a reaction. Finding none, he said, "I will ask him to find your son-in-law."

The sergeant rose and kicked at his shoes. "I don't want him killed, Matute."

"I never said my brother was a murderer, Antonio. He's a religious man. He kills pigs and chickens for a living. But he can find her and convince her that her husband is an *hijo de puta,* you understand? He can hand-deliver the letters you write. She'll never know where you are. She'll think you are still in Cuba somewhere. You can keep your pride, and protect her from afar. Then he can convince her to come here, to be with you."

"For a price, of course," the sergeant asked, and Chelo nodded.

The sergeant considered finding new work to pay for Abel Santana's "services." But he was an illegal immigrant and didn't speak any English. Theft seemed suddenly appealing. He remembered the teenage boys he arrested in Havana with great frequency. They would steal from merchants in the markets, or prostitute their sisters, or pick the pockets of American tourists. The excuse was ever the same—"I did it for my family," they'd say. The boys were thin, they were uneducated, but the sergeant had always lectured them on "better ways to solve a problem," on dropping out of school, on the need for morality in the poor streets of Havana. Then he'd suck air through his teeth and exclaim, "These things never happened in Spain!"

Now here he was, transformed into one of those boys by a mere ninety-mile voyage. And what was worse—little Lalo and Soledad might also become criminals, or victims. *Better me than them,* the sergeant thought. If there were a way to protect his grandchildren, he would do it.

That evening, while Mona Linde slept, the sergeant searched through her bureau with tears in his eyes. He vowed he'd make it up to this American woman who was so full of kindness. His fingers tingled when he found an old necklace buried behind her nylons, with six dirty rubies hanging from a gold chain. He tucked the chain away into the inside of his work shoes, to give to Chelo in the morning. He removed the moldy letters from underneath the vine-filled plant, and recopied them through the night, each on a separate sheet, then said a prayer over them that they might make it to her safely.

BOOK II

1946-1952

7

For years Lorenzo had thought of Santa Clara, not El Cotorro, as home. There he stayed with Gilda, a short, plump woman who wore jaunty three-cornered hats that were several years out of style. Lorenzo stayed at her house for months at a time, and their nights were long and savory. Gilda spoke to people in a breathless, thrilling whisper. Her voice was unlike Josefina's, who spoke in a penetrating pitch. Gilda wet her lips before kissing Lorenzo, unlike Josefina, whose mouth was dry and chapped. *And Gilda,* thought Lorenzo, *has never known luxury. What I have to give is enough.*

Gilda had been one of those unlucky women of whom it was said, was "never fifteen." For a Cuban girl, fifteen was her most beautiful year. To have never been fifteen was to be plain, unloved, and alone. Gilda had watched as her sisters were married. At twenty-five, she had never even been kissed. When she was young, the boys she knew poked fun at her thick thighs, and they walked with a limp to mock her because Gilda had been born with one leg shorter than the other. As she grew older, the men simply ignored her. But Lorenzo seemed not to notice any of her physical flaws. He found her at the cigar shop where she worked, stuck behind the counter reading a newspaper. He had been thinking of Josefina, missing her touch after a few weeks of a fruitless job search, and he was suddenly attracted to the woman who read and chewed her lip, and balanced on a high stool, her fleshy buttocks spread wide over the narrow seat. Lorenzo asked her to dinner, and Gilda blushed and said, "Of course."

After that, Lorenzo had found that Gilda was not just a temporary replacement for his wife, but an additional companion whom he loved in his own way. Gilda loved him, too.

Lorenzo had been with Gilda almost as long as he had been married to Josefina. When Soledad was born, Gilda bought him a box of cigars, wrapped in pink cellophane. They made love that night in a haze of smoke, in a trance of musky breaths. When the riots occurred in Matanzas province, Gilda had fed Lorenzo bits of apricots rolled in cinnamon, one by one, pinning him to the bed with her heavy legs, keeping him from boarding the train to El Cotorro. She had prayed that night that he would be safe on his trip home, promising to God that she would never cut her hair again so long as Lorenzo would be sound. So it was that a few years later, Gilda's hair already reached the small of her back, and Lorenzo took in the scent of it, spread the fine tresses over his chest when he lay down, and was thankful that she had made the promise.

Gilda often asked Lorenzo to describe his children. It was her favorite conversation. As he spoke about Lalo's childhood lisp, or Soledad's recent fall out of the avocado tree, Gilda sighed and rested her chin in her hand. She had been pregnant three times, though Lorenzo never knew, and each time she had crossed the street to a dark, wooden slat house, paying the old man that lived there twenty pesos for a potion that smoked when opened and stung the inside of her throat. In a matter of hours the baby would be gone, and Gilda would rest for a day or so, counting the days to Lorenzo's return. She didn't tell Lorenzo about the pregnancies. She feared he would walk away. Gilda knew her place, hid resentment from him, and tried to forget that she had never been fifteen.

So it was that she loved the stories of Lalo and Soledad, because she imagined that they were hers. She thought of pudgy baby boys or sweet-smelling girls before falling asleep, to be sure that her dreams would be of mothering children she never knew. The dresses that Lorenzo brought home to his daughter were usually sewn by Gilda, the wood models that he gave to Lalo were also gifts from Gilda. She imagined them both, her son and daughter, loving these things brought from afar and loving her, too.

Lorenzo told the stories of his children because he knew it pleased Gilda, but he never would understand her taste for them. Indeed, whenever they went out onto the streets of Santa Clara, for a quick lunch or dinner, Gilda would point out babies in prams, round, pink cherubs that sometimes cried as she bent down to pat their heads, and Lorenzo would huff, because they were late, he was hungry, and the shrill sound of infant cries hurt his head.

8

Lorenzo did not return from Santa Clara that fall, and winter soon fell upon the family. The money from the sergeant's account had paid for repairs to the plumbing in the house, a new refrigerator, and a telephone in hopes that Lorenzo would call more frequently when he was away. Then it was gone. Josefina took to calling Regla often, and in long, teary conversations, she offered up her loneliness, word by word. When Regla sent her a check—a small, pitiful amount from the maid's salary—Josefina called with less frequency to circumvent the old woman's generosity.

On a chilly Christmas Eve morning, Lalo asked his mother if he could buy the pig for dinner. "Well, you have enough hair on your chest now, *corazón.* You go and take your sister," she said, patting his smooth adolescent cheek with a sticky, sweet palm that had just been lifted out of a ripe mango, her hand wet and nervous like a newborn thing. Upon hearing that she would be going with her brother, Soledad tied a heavy velvet bow into her hair and crushed two rose petals onto her wrists for their scent.

The hair on Soledad's arms was still blond from playing in the sun, and she carried a clutch purse covered in old lace. Inside, crumpled furtively within the silk of the lining, were two pesos. Lalo carried five pesos in his shirt pocket, along with some change that jingled in time with the muffled holiday music coming from behind the fruit stands. The money they carried, money that their mamá took from the inside of a broken cuckoo clock in the front parlor, would be enough for the purchase of a *lechón*. They were surrounded by the sounds of the market at seven in the morning. A man's voice, singing a *bolero* and strumming a guitar, floated from the phonograph behind the butcher's stand, the warm notes blending themselves into the screams of the pigs being slaughtered for a Christmas Eve feast. Lalo and Soledad walked the roads of the market, the brown dirt underneath looking so much like brown sugar that Soledad dipped her thumb into the dirt and licked it. Her brother's bony hip nudged her head with his rhythmic gait, and past every few stands, he would smile and wink at the young girls who shopped with their mothers, and the mothers would jerk their daughters' wrists and make them turn away from the skinny boy from El Cotorro.

They arrived at the butcher stand of Abel Santana. Abel had blood on his apron and hands, and there was so much of it that it was difficult to distinguish the color and severity of his sunburned body from the gore that encircled him. When they approached, Abel had finished handing a heavy pig, tied to a worm-ridden plank, to a customer, and he proceeded to lean against the smooth trunk of a palm and close his eyes.

"*Perdón,*" Lalo asked, interrupting the butcher's dreams, "Which animal can you give me for seven pesos?"

"For seven, *niño,* you can get that spotted one there and slice the throat yourself. I am tired, and you look strong, no? Here." He handed Lalo a machete, the blade dark yet luminous against the wooden handle. Abel kicked lazily at the spotted creature, ushering it behind a towering bamboo screen that waved in the breeze in perfect synchronization with the royal palms that lined the street. The screen hid the act of butchering pigs, but could not stifle the squeals that were trapped between and inside those hollow reeds, or the yelps that filled the market air.

Soledad knew of the horror of an animal's death, because she had already seen Papá twist apart the jaw of a vicious neighborhood dog that attacked Lalo one day and had heard the canine muscles pop in her ears every night for a week. In preserving that memory, she believed herself to be prepared for the death of their Christmas *lechón*. As she watched her brother walk behind the bamboo screen, tapping the blade of the machete against his thigh like a professional butcher, she thought about the dog and how, between the sounds of the dog's dying that punctuated her sleep and the silence that gave her peace, she wished that the dog had taken a chunk of Lalo's rump and run away satisfied, safe from the hands of her papá.

She was not prepared to see her brother running past her from behind the bamboo wall, dropping his machete into the pigs' muddy pen. The spotted pig ran after him, its throat pierced deeply, a dripping ribbon of blood moving like a dancer from its throat, across its spine, and making splashy pirouettes along the tail. The animal did not stop its chase until it collapsed on their front porch.

Abel had watched it all openmouthed, unable to leave his post. He kneeled by Soledad, who had screamed for her brother as he walked past, then had started to cry and lose her breath all at once. A small crowd gathered around her, witnesses to the pig incident.

As the afternoon ripened, the people around Soledad became an assortment of smells without gender or age. The person to her left smelled of turkey basting, the group of people behind her smelled of stale cigars, and the one directly in front smelled of rust or iron or blood. While she did not hear her own wailing, she heard voices around her, speaking to her and about her.

"*Agua, necesita agua.*"

"Someone, talk to her."

"*Niña, escucha,* you need to calm down."

"I was once chased by a crazy goat, little girl. That pig didn't hurt your brother. He stabbed it good."

"Perhaps she's ill."

"Perhaps someone gave her the evil eye at the market today."

"Her mother shouldn't have let her come alone."

And they went on and on, speaking of curses and illnesses and disobedience in the youth of Cuba. Meanwhile, Soledad could not get the image of the half-dead pig running so weakly through the market. It had squealed and opened its mouth in agony, but it ran and ran after Lalo, as if its dying wish was revenge. Soledad thought she might vomit.

It was then that the anonymous voices quieted. Soledad did not see because of the temporary blindness she had inflicted upon herself, but she felt the bristled hand of a man, shoving a cold glass into her own white ghost hands. It was a *frutabomba* milk shake, a sweet papaya concoction, with a long pink straw.

"Oye," Abel Santana said, as he gathered Soledad into his arms. "Your *hermanito* is a brave boy. But you can be a little more courageous, I think. Quiet, quiet. Let me take you home, *linda."* Soledad sipped at the shake and nodded. Then she gave Abel Santana her address.

Abel could not believe his luck. *"Gracias a Dios,"* he whispered, as Soledad led the way home.

Josefina hugged her tall son when he burst through the door. "It's fine, *mi querer,* it's fine. We can still eat him." The pig pressed itself against the door, then collapsed and died at last.

"I don't want to," Lalo cried.

"Where is your sister?" she asked, and Lalo shrugged his shoulders.

Josefina pushed hard against the front door and the pig slid off to the right. She was cursing the butcher who had let Lalo try to do the job himself. *Lo juro,* she swore, *if something happened to Soledad, I'll butcher that man myself!* She was halfway to the market when she saw Soledad perched on the shoulders of a huge man. He had red, red hair, so uncommon on the island, and he wore his blue shirt buttoned all the way to the top. Soledad rode high and slurped at her milkshake. She pointed at her mother.

"He rescued me, Mamá!" she said. "He bought me a *frutabomba* shake!"

"I see," Josefina said. "And you are?" She reached out and took Soledad from his shoulder.

"Abel Santana," he replied. "I'm sorry about the pig. I . . . I thought it would be good for the boy. It's how I learned. I just . . ."

"How could you?" Josefina asked, her hands now firmly on her hips. "My son is just a boy. Just a boy! What a terrible thing to make him do on *Nochebuena.*"

Abel said nothing. He scratched his head and looked down at Josefina. He found her striking. Her eyes were large, and her sculpted eyebrows were raised in anger.

"Mamá, please. Abel is the nicest man. Can he come to dinner?" Soledad asked, and tugged at her mother's hand.

Josefina sighed. What would Lorenzo think? Then the thought came to her—*Lorenzo doesn't even have the decency to be with us on Christmas Eve.* "Señor Santiago . . ."

"It's Santana."

"Santana, yes. Would you join us for *Nochebuena?*"

Abel smiled and winked at Soledad. "Of course. Let me prepare that insurbordinate pig for you. It's the least I can do. Your name?"

"Josefina Navarro de Concepción." Abel's eyes widened. It was the very name his brother, Chelo, had mentioned that morning, along with his Christmas wishes. He knew he had recognized the address as soon as Soledad recited it. The check, Chelo said, would be arriving any day now. Her father wanted Abel to protect her, to keep her husband from harming her or the children. He was to be her guardian angel. This meeting, he thought, was nothing short of miraculous.

Abel gutted and cleaned the young *lechón* and roasted it underground. He covered the hole with palm leaves, and left it there until the ears were crunchy enough to pull off and eat. Some of Josefina's neighbors had been invited, and brought pots of rice, boiled yucca, warm bread, plantains, black beans, and sangria. The spotted pig that had drained its blood along the trail from the market to the house in El Cotorro was delicious. That night, every table in El Cotorro vibrated with Christmas music and laughter, and Josefina's house was no exception. For the first Christmas in ages, the mood was light. The years when Lorenzo had been home were good. He would tell the children stories of *Santi Clo* and his reindeer. He would even help her to cook. But the years when he stayed away during the holidays had been dismal, and the family had often gone to bed early.

That night would have been perfect if not for the teasing schoolboys outside, who dirtied the evening sounds with pig imitations, then quiet, then rounds of laughter that made the windows shimmer.

The neighbors sat down at the table that had been lengthened with wooden boards. They sat on stools, on a rickety piano bench, on lawn chairs they had brought over. It was a loud, festive crowd, except for Lalo. He would be fourteen in January and had his father's pale complexion. He ate his pork with only a fork, tearing at the white, bloodless meat, shredding it and mixing it into his white rice. He was angry and embarrassed, and wished his mother hadn't invited the butcher in.

Josefina noticed his silence and patted his thigh with her hand. She imagined that Lorenzo would have dragged his son back to the market, forcing him to butcher another pig properly. This year, especially, she was glad for his absence. Often, Abel's eyes caught hers, and she felt her cheeks burn.

Abel Santana was the honored guest at the Christmas Eve feast in the Concepción household. Soledad sat next to him and leaned her head on his shoulder. "Sergeant Navarro was your father, no?" he had asked, and Josefina had dropped her fork.

"The sergeant was a great man. I am sorry he is gone. Where is your husband?" Abel asked, and suddenly the meal became cold and quiet. All that was heard was the clinking of cutlery and the clearing of throats as the neighbors tried to be as quiet as possible. Soledad stopped eating and was not reprimanded for it. It was the old man from next door, the one they called Mongo, who broke the tension with a joke about a convent and a male intruder.

Abel Santana stayed at the dinner table long after it was cleared. Josefina made him coffee, the kind that is whipped with a spoon until it develops a creamy froth or until the muscles can no longer take the effort of such rapid stirring. When Soledad washed her face in the porcelain basin in her room, she could hear him talking with her mother. By the time she pulled the night-gown over her head and the velvet bow got caught in the buttons, she had already become accustomed to his way of speaking, rhythmic, like the sound of a drum, then suddenly thunderous, then quiet again. Between his pauses, which were lengthy, Josefina would say, *"Claro, claro,"* in agreement. It was how she had imagined the voice of God in the desert when her teachers read from the Bible. When Soledad awoke the next day, she still heard the butcher's voice, except now it was more distant, because he was outside on the front porch, and he was telling her mamá, *"Adios y gracias."* Soledad wondered how it was that he had spent the entire night talking without losing his voice.

9

Josefina received a pair of letters a few weeks later. One was from Lorenzo, somewhere in Santa Clara. The envelope was thin, and so she knew he had not sent a great deal of money. Josefina felt sad as she weighed it in her hand, not because it lacked the money she needed, but because it spoke of other things—that Lorenzo did not care enough about them to make sure Josefina and the children were well. And she knew, before opening it, that the letter contained no sweet phrases, no *mi sueño, mi muñeca, mi cielito lindo, mi querida, cómo te anhelo.* She longed for the comparisons to dreams, to dolls, to beautiful skies. She wanted to be wanted by him as she was once. Josefina did not dream of Lorenzo at night, though she tried. Awake at night, she pictured him, part by part, as if listing inventory at a store. There were the pale, pale skin, the small dark eyes, the sharp mouth, each like a crack in the porcelain. The slender wrists. His shirt collar that smelled like onions in the morning. Josefina had fallen in love with Lorenzo, with all of him, that day at the dance when she was just a girl. And she still loved him, but she longed for a transformation. Josefina had said to herself, one morning in December, "I don't want to be the same woman I was before, the woman I was for Renzo," and that evening, Abel appeared in her house.

The first few nights with Abel had been exhilarating, like the feeling a child has when it gets lost at the market. First, there was the initial fear. It threatened to take over her chest and come pouring out of her eyes in big, swampy tears. And then, there was that touch of liberty. That moment that was like jumping from a very high place and feeling unspeakable freedom.

In the weeks that followed, Josefina tried to absolve herself of the guilt of the affair. She thought of Lorenzo's other women, imagined them so perfectly that she came to believe she could spot them on the street, and that image filled her with a need for reprisal. Josefina reminded herself that Abel's visits were accompanied by huge sides of pork and sometimes steaks, marinated and sliced already by his large, gentle hands. *If having an affair means my children eat, so be it,* Josefina told herself. Slowly, she thought of Lorenzo less and less, like a dog trained to avoid the pain of its owner's beating. Although Josefina sometimes questioned whether she truly had transformed in that way she had wished, she reveled in the newness of her relationship with Abel, and that feeling was like leaping.

The other letter that came to Josefina that day was not stamped, but her address, written in red ink, was in her father's handwriting. She believed at once that Lorenzo was playing a cruel joke, but the thought soon left her as she read the letter. The spelling was perfect, as was the penmanship, which for Lorenzo was an impossibility. She brought the letter to her nose and believed she could smell her father's hair tonic.

Josefina took the new letter and the old bloodied one, weighing them both in either hand. She had kept, too, the newspapers with her father's obituaries from four separate presses. *El Diario de la Marina* had been the kindest, calling the sergeant "a proud son of Cuba," even though he was born in the south of Spain. And the official telegram sent to Josefina a few weeks later stated:

27 SEPTIEMBRE 1946
WE REGRET THE LOSS OF SERGEANT ANTONIO NAVARRO. YOU AND YOUR FAMILY ARE IN OUR

PRAYERS. THOUGH NO BODY HAS YET BEEN FOUND,
SEVERAL OF THE MEN ARRESTED DURING THE DIS-
TURBANCE WERE WITNESS TO THE SERGEANT'S
DEATH. HIS REMAINS ARE BELIEVED TO BE NEAR
THE PLAZA PERLA. WE HOPE TO FIND THEM AND
BRING YOUR FATHER TO REST.

Each item in the shoebox filled with news and letters detailing her father's death was warped by tears dried on the paper and each carried the musty smell of moisture from being kept closed. But this new letter was unlike the others in every way.

"Maybe you want me to be dead," he had written, and Josefina chastised herself for having wished it so long ago and for forgetting her catechism. Of course, the spirit never really died. Hadn't the presence of her mother in her childhood dreams taught her that?

Josefina had heard of dead people returning in ghostly form. That was the thought that came to her at first, before any other logical conclusion. And she had leaped at the possibility of it, the magic in it, Regla's old magic like a warm blanket. The idea that her father had returned as a spirit hung suspended in the air. She'd heard a young girl in the market just yesterday, speaking of her dead aunt who roamed the avocado orchard in her backyard at night, clutching at her stomach from eating too many avocados. Many a time Josefina herself had been to a funeral and someone had jumped and squealed, "He touched me just now, here, on the shoulder right here," the person would say, pointing to the miraculous spot. Even Regla told countless stories of seances at which the dead would appear above everyone's head, and a special goat sacrifice had to be made or the spirit would haunt the place forever. But Josefina had never heard of a ghost who wrote letters as if he were alive, letters in odd red ink to resemble blood. She never knew of a ghost that told stories about himself, about a past that Josefina never knew existed. She kissed the new letter and put it into a new shoebox, a clean fitting place to begin her correspondence with her departed father.

A ghost letter. It was the only explanation that sat comfortably in Josefina's stomach, the only one that made her feel lighter than she'd been in years.

Abel Santana appeared in her doorway as she put the letter away. *"¿Qué tienes?"* he asked, pointing to the letter.

"You won't believe me." Josefina's fingers trembled over the letter until she decided to lift it out of the new box and give it to Abel.

He read the letter and scratched at his belly. "But you said your father was dead."

"He is," she said, wide-eyed and smiling, "but he is writing me a letter from above."

Abel put the letter into its envelope and dropped it into the new box. He thought about the sergeant awaiting his report in Miami, and the money that had just come in via his brother, Chelo. It was Abel who had quietly dropped the letter off at dawn. The sergeant's money still sat in its own envelope at home. There, in the emptiness of his house, Abel was numb. He imagined saving the money to buy a new car or to expand his shop, but here, in Josefina's presence, he saw himself donating the money to the church or hiding it in Lalo's shoes for the boy to find. She was beautiful, and Abel could not think that her beauty was being exchanged for something dirty—the foulness of money. It was something he had just begun to worry about. With every visit to Josefina's house, he softened. With every kiss, he felt himself grow better. And still, the letter that she held was a lie. He wondered that she couldn't smell the butcher shop on the pages. Abel swallowed thickly and was numb again.

He ran his hand over Josefina's cheek, squeezing the puffiness in it. "Don't be ridiculous. Your father is dead and someone is playing a trick on you. Perhaps they believe you have his wealth," he said, and watched her mouth fall slowly open. "You may live in squalor, but you are the daughter of a prosperous, well-known public servant."

"He knows the names of the children, Abel, and I never told

him that." Josefina smiled and nodded her head slowly, haughty with the weight of the evidence she had just presented, forgetting that she had told him long ago in one of two letters she wrote him, forgetting that Regla had gone back to him after every visit. The magic of it pressed itself upon Josefina and clouded her memory. Abel said nothing and helped her put the two boxes away underneath her bed. He held her hand as she led him out to the kitchen for a snack. *I wonder when a new letter from my papá will come,* Josefina thought to herself as she spread butter over a cracker.

What she hadn't counted on was Abel's coming in the early morning, his silhouette pale against the waking sky, and putting the letter in her mailbox. At first, the fifty American dollars Chelo had sent was enough to convince him that to play postman for this woman would be well worth it. He hadn't counted on her belief in spirits. Abel felt guilty about toying with her faith.

The days that followed were gray ones. There was an unusual chill in the air that made the wooden door of the house condense in size, as if the wood fibers huddled together to escape the cold. Drafts snaked their way in between the door and its moldings, and Josefina stuffed the sides with old socks filled with rice. Still, a column of cold coming from the door divided the house in two and kept the family in the warm kitchen.

The kitchen stove was an electric marvel of iron, painted white. It smelled of burnt milk, sweet yet rancid, from Josefina's morning *café con leche.* When someone rubbed against the sides of the stove, his clothes would catch on the stiff black mosaic of paint and grease that bristled the corners. The countertops were faded and nicked deepest in the place nearest the sink where Josefina used to cut the tip off Lorenzo's cigars in the days when he stayed home. The cabinets, which hung high on the wall, were also scratched, but the fine lines were those of years of scouring and cleaning old grease from the wood. The shelves inside were uneven, and the cabinet's depth seemed infinite. Once, when scavenging for crackers, Soledad's hand came across a collection of glasses filled with water lining the back of the cabinet. The stale water was thick and cloudy inside the glass she lifted. Her fingers examined each glass like a blind mouse in the darkness—one, two, three, two more, five glasses, each filled with water like the first. She was to discover, years later, that Josefina threw the water out at midnight every New Year in an effort to rid the family of that year's suffering collected in the cursed water. She would later fill the glasses again for the next year, expecting those glasses, too, would fill with misery. Aside from the five water glasses, the cabinets were all empty near the end of the month. While they waited for Lorenzo or his money to return, they subsisted on fried eggs and white rice, the yolk always seeping into the rice most disagreeably, making it a wet and salty meal.

During those weeks of rare cold in 1948, they received only one more letter from Lorenzo and fifty pesos. He never telephoned, and Josefina was glad not to hear his voice for fear that she might not be able to stop from crying or pleading for his return. The envelope had no return address, but the onionskin paper inside was watermarked in blue with the city name "Santa Clara" in fancy script. Josefina read the letter in a low voice, holding the thin sheet close to her eyes, the light from outside shining through the paper so that Soledad could see that, indeed, it was her papá's hand, a hand much like hers. Lorenzo and Soledad were both left-handed. When the child learned to write, the teachers tied her left hand to the desk with thread from a spool that they kept in their pockets, thread so thin that it often cut into her wrists. She soon became accustomed to using her right hand, but her penmanship was formless. It tended one way, then the letters became rounded, then arched sharply in the opposite direction. For Lorenzo, it was the same. He once told her that as a child, a teacher had thrust his left hand into a cup of hot coffee when she caught him using it. The result of learning to write: old, thin lines around Soledad's wrist and the polished burn scar between her father's thumb and forefinger. These marks were how Lorenzo showed her that they were the same. As for the letter, it was short, and Josefina read it too fast, so that Soledad always thought that she missed many of the words. It said only that he was busy working in a restaurant, busing tables. There was no mention of "the children" to warm Soledad and Josefina, and they both felt colder after the reading, though they would not say so to one another.

Josefina folded the letter carelessly, the ends of the paper meeting at angles and the creases unsharpened. The scent of almond and cinnamon reached her nose. The smell, so familiar in all his letters now, was actually more of a comfort than it should have been. Whenever she smelled it, in someone's fresh rice pudding or tied in bunches of tulle for good luck at a wedding, she thought of Lorenzo and longed for him to return. She went to Lalo, who had been rummaging through the drawers for the old, rusted scissors he needed to trim his fishing line, and held him by the back of the neck, gently turning him toward the door, and instructing him to "Go and clean the weeds out from under the gardenias." The scissors were dumped into the knife drawer and landed with the blades open, like a foundling bird begging for worms. If she had not been distracted by her son's impudence and the letter in her hand, she might have warned him to close the scissors' blades, because to leave them open, as the old belief went, would be to invite death.

Instead, she watched as Lalo walked out through the door into the wintry air, slamming the door hard enough to drive a puff of air that sent the curtains nearby billowing up like sails. He had become moody overnight, and Josefina blamed Lorenzo for it. *A boy needs a man in the house,* she always thought. Josefina then sat and leaned on the table, spreading the letter out smooth before her. Now Soledad could examine her papá's curlicues, the way his accents flew off the page in heavy strokes, the way his Rs looked like crooked Ns. By now, Josefina's fingers, dancing from nervousness above the page as she read, were blurring Lorenzo's eccentric penmanship. She folded the letter and put it on the counter where it began slowly to absorb a small puddle of dishwater.

Josefina took a seat near the stove. She motioned to the floor and pulled a long comb from her pocket. Soledad cradled her back against her mother's legs as Josefina began to tug at her hair, taking a handful of curls and twisting them into neat ringlets.

"The whiteness of your scalp tells me that you are very smart at arithmetic, and the clockwise swirl at the top of your head tells me that your first child will be a girl." Josefina laughed softly and sighed long. Soledad rested her head between her mother's thighs while Josefina worked on the uneven curls that hung like wrinkled curtains.

"Your grandfather writes to me, you know," Josefina said and clucked her tongue as if even she found it hard to believe. "He writes to me from heaven and tells me what to do. He tells me stories of the past, and he asks about you often."

"I want to see his letters, Mamá," Soledad said, wondering suddenly if her grandfather shared her handwriting, too.

"No, darling. The things he writes about are not for little girl eyes." Josefina twirled another length of hair around the comb and then said, "It would frighten you." She finished the last curl and pushed Soledad off her legs. She pulled the loose hair from between the comb's teeth and from her dress, dropping the strands in midair so that they floated to the floor like shriveled streamers. She closed the scissors that Lalo had tossed and laid them and the comb inside the drawer. *"Ay, mi hijo,"* she said aloud, in a choked voice, thinking about her son. Josefina felt sadness in those days that even her nights with Abel would not remedy. Soledad was her only consolation, and she turned those hours with her daughter over in her mind countless times before going to sleep at night.

She hadn't turned around from the open drawer when she said to Soledad, "Listen to me, *hija:* the day you marry be sure he is a man of skill. This is what your grandfather wants. Marry a banker or a teacher or a carpenter, not someone like your papá. Do you know, Soledad, that when I first met your father, he told me he was a furniture maker, and we would go around town, and he would peek into the windows of houses saying, "See that chair. I made that in the workshop last month," or "Look at the details I put into that cedar chest." Sometimes the house owners would catch us peeking and he'd grip my wrist and we'd run through the streets. When he knew that I loved him, he told me that he had lied, that he was not a furniture maker, but a simple dock worker, and even this I forgave and believed, even though your grandfather told me I'd go hungry."

Soledad had heard this story many times before. First, her papá was a furniture maker, then he claimed to work unloading red snapper off the big fishing boats, and finally, when he came to see that it didn't matter where he earned his money, because, as Josefina put it, "I had already spread my legs for him, and I had been claimed for all time." Then she married him, this unskilled man, this liar, her papá. "Take heed, Soledad," she would say, and Soledad, restless in the chair, wishing she could trade Lalo's chores for hers, could only half listen and count the different shapes of wood grain on the table surface. There were only three—hairline thin, thick like her thumb, and curved, like yellow crescent moons.

As for Lalo, there was a reason why Josefina would send him outside for meaningless work whenever one of Lorenzo's letters arrived. She didn't want to ruin his image of his father. Lalo bragged to his schoolmates and neighbors that his papá was off in New York City playing music in the mambo rooms of the north, or he told them that his papá was sailing around the Spanish Canary Islands to find his pirate ancestors. It wasn't that Lalo was a liar, but the fact was that Lalo never believed what he sometimes overheard Josefina say. Josefina knew this about him. She knew that he shaped his own truth. And so, he and Lorenzo existed in a world apart from her.

Suddenly, they heard Lalo talking outside, every word muffled through the walls. "Get out of here," he said. Then, "You've no right," sounding closer, his voice whistling through the drafts in the front door.

"¡*Niño!*" another voice bellowed, and Josefina recognized its peal throughout the house. "Let me through!"

Mother and daughter ran into the parlor, Josefina's arms crossing instinctively over her chest in the cold. Lalo stood in the open doorway, his arms and feet touching the frame. Abel Santana frowned over him, with one hand on Lalo's shoulder. Josefina stood behind Lalo and placed her own heavy hands on his shoulders—one touching his shirt and neck, the other resting on Abel's hand. Lalo turned to Josefina then, and he saw her mouth the words *"Por favor, Lalito."* Lalo's brow furrowed and changed to red. He pushed his mamá's hand away with such force that her arm was flung backward and her knuckles cracked against the wall.

Mi Hija,

How I miss you. You wrote me once, and now all is for-given. How could I stay angry with you, Josefina, when you look so much like your mother? Your childhood was so dif-ferent from my own. You had dolls imported from Ger-many, dolls you'd carry on your lap all day at school. Regla kept you fat with whipped merengues and rice pudding. I hope that you remember all those things when you think of me with anger in those blue eyes. Think, too, of my own childhood.

My father's household was one of the largest in the Ca-nary Islands. Horses wandered the land around the house, spotted ones that my father bred. On weekends, he'd sad-dle the largest mare, and he'd beat time on the horse's head, measuring the rhythm of the trot. I used to watch from the small, yellowed window, while my mother, a ser-vant of the household, cleaned my father's spare saddle for his Sunday ride. As I'd watch the small figure of horse and man, my father and the mare named Alegria would fade into the morning fog. I'm sorry I never told you about the way I grew up. Do you see why I didn't want you to marry into poverty? Do you see how you suffer needlessly?

You, *mi hijita,* were a lucky child. You had one mother, my beloved Ana, who loved you even though she never saw you, and I think, sometimes, that she gave you her life when she died. But that is another story, Josefina. I was un-lucky. I had a wicked mother and a good one. My father's wife, Olga Maria, used to enter the servant's quarters where I lived with my mother. She'd come with her dirty laundry and release a tangle of smelly stockings from her arms. They'd fall to the floor, all knotted. "Mend these, Dahlia," she'd say to my mother as she walked out, leaving the door open. She never wiped her feet when she came in, and so, the odd tracks of her heels marked our concrete floor. She'd visit every day, leaving her dirt behind. I had to bring out the broom, while my mother lifted the stockings and began letting loose the knots that Olga Maria had purposefully set. I remember once how Olga Maria brought a notebook I had left by accident on the porch. The pages dripped with her morning coffee. Then Olga Maria said, "Antonio, you must be more careful with your things." She must not have liked the face I made, because that same night she came with a bundle of curtains that my mother had spent the day ironing in such a tight ball in her arms that the careful pleats were ruined. Olga Maria said something like, "Dahlia, if only you did things properly the first time . . ."

You would think Olga Maria would have fired my mother. But my father, who loved my mother, never let her. Olga Maria was fierce, but she was no match for my father. I will finish the tale in another letter. I'm sorry I never told you these stories in person.

There is great kindness in the universe, *hija*. I am learning that now. Be good to my grandchildren. Be good to those who deserve it. But I urge you to be strong and independent. I know that Regla and I, with all our pampering, never taught you that. Close your door to Lorenzo when he comes at night. Do not give him any more children so that he can starve them. Listen to me, *hija*, and pray for good things.

Tu Papá

10

The money that Lorenzo sent home to his wife came from Gilda's father, a large man who wore his suits two sizes too small, as if to emphasize to the world his immense size. Gilda's father ran numbers and handled small bets for the tourists who came to Santa Clara to avoid the hustle of Havana's strip. Lorenzo helped the man every once in a while and sent home his earnings in thin envelopes accompanied by plain letters that said nothing.

When the old man died, Gilda cried and clamored for Lorenzo to attend the funeral though he wanted to take the next train home. She threatened to shorten her hair, and so Lorenzo finally agreed. For most of the funeral, Gilda stood next to a candle in a red sconce. The sanguine light sharpened her lips as she spoke and made her dull black dress a luminous thing. Lorenzo held three fingers of her left hand, letting the others dangle in the air, the way lovers do. The other members of Gilda's family, her sisters clutching handkerchiefs, disreputable-looking men with deep furrows in their foreheads, all watched Lorenzo menacingly. Their talk and the talk of the friends and businessmen gathered there were all the same.

"How dare he show himself here?"

"This is a sacrilege."

"We always knew that Gilda was an idiot."

Late in the afternoon, over the gravesite, the sky took on a menacing red glow. Gilda's ancient mother started to cry, "Where is his Santa Bárbara medallion? He cannot be buried without it!"

Lorenzo watched as Gilda left to retrieve the medallion. He followed her away from the cemetery, up the two blocks to the house where Gilda's father had died. Inside, Lorenzo began opening drawers, putting aside numerous bars of soap that kept the old man's underwear smelling clean, a habit Gilda learned, too. Lorenzo dumped a drawer of photographs. There was Gilda, about twenty years old, standing in front of a yard full of blurred chickens. There she was again, carrying a blond baby, perhaps a niece or nephew, dipping the baby's heel into someone's glass of water. Lorenzo liked the way she looked. Her face was alight in a broad smile, tiny creases already developing at the corners of her eyes. He thought he could hear her laughter at the joke she had made. There was a final photograph, one that Lorenzo managed to put into his pocket without Gilda noticing. In it, Gilda was quite young, school-aged, and posed in front of flowery wallpaper. In her hand was a folded fan that she had delicately spread open. It reminded Lorenzo of Josefina, long ago, at the dances when she had twirled a fan like it.

"I've found it," Gilda announced. A silver medallion hung from her fingers, swaying to and fro in the air. She also pulled out two Santa Bárbara statues and held them close to her breast.

Once again at the cemetery, Lorenzo handed the artifacts to the old woman. She put the medallion on the dead man's chest and the statues on either side of him. Lorenzo thought that the old man looked like a child with his stuffed toys nearby. The statues were like fraternal twins, different sizes and shades, but both an image of a striking, long-haired woman in a red robe, a crown atop her head. The priest, upon seeing the idolatry, turned away and waited for the group to quiet down before saying his final prayer and closing the lid.

Then Gilda began distributing roses to her family, so that they could all throw them into the ground. Her motions were polished and fluid, as if she had rehearsed for this role. She would hand a flower over, wipe a tear off her cheek, sniff, then start again. Behind her, her hair swung like a pendulum. Lorenzo thought she was lovely still, freshly coated in a thin layer of sweat from the afternoon sun, but he walked out of the cemetery the moment the priest asked all present to lower their heads in prayer.

The men in the family had not stopped clenching their fists at the sight of him, and Lorenzo felt that the time had come to end the affair.

11

Regla came to El Cotorro in the spring of 1947. Josefina prepared for the visit, making Soledad clean the bathtub with
bleach and sitting Lalo down with a pile of sheets to find the one
without the hole in it for their guest.

"There is no such thing as spring here," Regla said when she ar-
rived, gasping for breath in the hot, stale air. She entered just as
Abel was leaving. When Josefina explained, "He's a plumber,"
Regla sniffed loudly.

"It's been a long time," Regla said, at last, and sat down on a
wooden rocker in a corner of the living room. It creaked musically
as she rocked.

"Has it been five years?" Josefina asked.

"Maybe six, maybe four," Regla said, and hummed a quick, little tune. She was getting comfortable, letting her muscles relax
from the long ride on the train, where she had sat tensely, her
mind full of images of derailed cars and fires.

Josefina brought Regla a lemonade, the glass wrapped in a napkin the way Regla taught her—"So that your guest's hand doesn't
get cold," she had said. Regla's swollen fingers took hold of the
glass tenderly, as if the act of moving them pained her. Josefina
watched her old nanny sip, listened to the tinkle of the ice against
the glass. Josefina felt safe and wished she could sit at Regla's feet
and have the old woman braid her hair again. To feel those fat fin-

gers against her scalp, scratching, pulling, then apologizing for the hurt, was to feel loved. But Josefina couldn't sit cross-legged on the floor again, could she? Her hair was too short now and coarser than it used to be.

"*¿Y los niños?*" Regla asked, interrupting the quiet that had formed around them. She looked around for Josefina's children.

"You haven't seen them in so long. Wait until you see Soledad, and then maybe you can tell me what I can do to make her gain a little weight, eh?" Josefina said. It hadn't occurred to her to call the children as soon as Regla arrived. It was as if, at the moment Regla walked into the house, Soledad and Lalo stopped existing. *If there is to be a child in Regla's presence,* Josefina thought, *it should only be me.* But it was a passing thought, and the urge to display her children overrode her wish to be a girl again. "Lalito! Soly!" Josefina called, and heard her daughter's footsteps coming to the living room.

"Where's your brother?" Josefina asked. "School let out two hours ago."

"Who knows?" Soledad said and leaned against her mother, eyeing the stranger.

"*Aquí la tienes,*" Josefina said and pushed Soledad toward Regla. Soledad had slipped out of her school clothes and was wearing a short dress of green gingham. In her hair was a bow that was six inches wide, from tip to tip. Abel had teased her about the bow the day before, asking if she might take off into flight if the wind came at a certain angle. Soledad became conscious of the bow again when Regla touched it lightly.

"*Hola, preciosa,*" Regla said, then touched the girl's cheek. Soledad recoiled from the touch.

"*Ay,* Soledad," Josefina reprimanded her. "Don't you remember your *tia-abuela?*" Soledad knew that the woman in the rocking chair was neither her aunt nor her grandmother, but she knew, too, that the title, however falsely applied, meant that she had to show respect and love to the old woman. There were other *tia-*

abuelas in Soledad's life—the woman who came once a month to cut her hair and always brought with her a basketful of mangoes, her preschool teacher, Miss Tania, who had kept Soledad indoors from recess on cold days and who made sure she ate all her lunch, and the *Santera* across the street, who blessed the house every time one of them got the flu. But this aunt-grandmother was different, and Soledad noticed it immediately. It was Josefina who gave it away. Her mother, usually stiff and formal when attending to a visitor, leaned back on the sofa, her head tilted to the side. She watched Regla with wide eyes, a broad smile. Every so often, as Regla spoke, Soledad caught tears in her mother's eyes.

"Of course you don't remember me," Regla said. "But you have a *tía-abuela* who loves you very much, little Soledad, and prays for you every night. Now tell me," Regla said and pulled Soledad onto her lap, "how is school?"

Regla was like all the other adults Soledad had known, asking about school, feigning interest in what she was actually saying. Soledad sensed that Regla was sizing her up, looking too deeply into her eyes for something. For a moment, Soledad feared that Regla was secretly some sort of doctor scanning her for sickness. She knew this was her mother's old nurse, had heard the stories, had been told that Regla was as close to a grandmother as she'd ever have, but Soledad felt no tug of affection for the woman. Instead, Soledad was jealous that her mother looked at Regla with so much devotion.

Lalo came into the house just when Soledad had started reciting a poem by Martí, a child's verse about the sincerity of real friendship. Lalo was flushed. As soon as he saw the group in the living room, he tucked something into his pocket.

"What was that?" Josefina asked, and simultaneously Regla exclaimed, "He is the picture of his father!"

"He is," Josefina said, and her face darkened at the mention of Lorenzo.

"*Ven,* let me look at you," Regla said and stood. The motion took her longer than most. The rocking chair creaked as she gripped the arms and pushed herself off. Regla waddled over to Lalo, who had not moved from the doorway. "Just like Lorenzo," she said, then whistled a single note. Regla stood on tiptoe and ruffled his hair. Lalo smiled.

"Like my papi, huh?" he said, and puffed out his chest.

"*Sí, sí,*" Regla said. "You know, *m'ijo,* what they say about boys who look like their fathers?"

"No, what?"

"Their mothers are a little bit in love with them," Regla said. She winked at Josefina.

"No, *tía-abuela,*" Lalo said familiarly, because he remembered the old woman who used to visit him when he was a boy, who always brought with her a bag of chocolates just for him. "Mami wishes I looked like some other man." Then Lalo headed off to his room.

That evening as she lay awake, waiting for her mother's nightly visit and the stories that came with it, Soledad heard the soft squeak of her mother's bed, so unlike the noises that came from that room whenever Abel stayed over. Soledad strained to listen, caught snippets of conversation—"*Ay,* Regla, he cheats on me, you know. Papá was right." Soledad felt she had been replaced.

Regla left in the morning, cutting her trip short when a phone call came from the new sergeant, saying that his wife had invited all the ladies from La Sociedad de Santa Marta on a whim, and they needed Regla back to make dinner and sweep the dining room.

Soledad crouched down in the little hallway that connected the bedrooms to the living room. She listened to her mother crying, heard her say, "Regla, *no me dejes*"—don't leave—"I need you."

"You are strong, Josefina, like your poor father was. You have a boy here, who needs you more than you need me. There's the girl, too. Don't forget about her. I'll come again when I can," Regla said. Soledad heard the door click shut. She was glad the old woman with the piercing eyes was gone.

Josefina watched Regla go from the front window. It had been a long night, and she had told Regla about Lorenzo's absence and Lalo's anger, but not about Abel or the ghost letters. Regarding Abel, Josefina feared Regla's scorn, and as for the letters, she did not want to hear doubt from the one person she trusted most in the world. She could not risk losing the ghost.

Josefina knew very little about what her son did all day. The boy had never really had her sole attention. Before Soledad was born, the crying boy was more a nuisance to Josefina than anything else. She bottle-fed him dutifully, because she hated the feel of his lips on her breast. She had blamed herself later for his thinness, his sickly coloring, and his temper tantrums. As he grew into a young man, she came to see less and less of him, and now, she knew nothing of his fears or desires. It saddened her to think that she had been so loved as a child, but her son was so difficult to love. He reminded her of Lorenzo, but was less passionate. He had his father's short temper, but none of his bravado.

During the week, both of Josefina's children went to school. The schoolyard's gate was made of wrought iron, the pieces twisting and curling and ending in an ugly frozen mass where they were welded together. Wooden benches lined the path to the classrooms, where boys usually sat waving their neckerchiefs at the girls in suggestive hoops around their crotches. Sometimes, they made pig noises when Lalo walked by, the gossip about Lalo in the marketplace having circulated around town, and someone once carved a venemous-looking boar into his desk, its nostrils dark and its tusks pointed upward. The artist had been so careful that on the first day it appeared, Lalo saw immediately that the eyes consisted of two deeply dug holes, with blue marbles resting comfortably in each. He took the marbles and threw them viciously against the blackboard and they bounced and scattered behind bookcases.

Lalo had been befriended by a man known as Duarte on the day that Regla came to El Cotorro. Duarte, tall and fat, wore pressed linen suits and straw hats. The polish of his shoes had glittered in the sunlight and around his neck he wore a gold medal of the Virgin, with a tiny ruby in the center to represent her Sacred Heart. He had fondled it as he watched Lalo. During a game of baseball, Lalo had thrown his glove into the face of three different boys, picking it up and tossing it, then picking it up again. He had run to get away from them and had reached the iron gate, from which Duarte was watching. The teenager was swarthy, fast, and ingenious, and Duarte had liked him best of all the boys on the playing field. Duarte had approached the boy and had shoved a first-class train ticket to Havana into Lalo's hand, saying, "Meet me in front of the Teatro Martí when your train arrives," and then nothing else.

Lalo had read the fine print on the glossy ticket over and over again. He had hidden the ticket from his mother, his sister, and Regla that day when he had returned from school, and by that night, while his mamá had whispered to Regla in her bedroom, Lalo had read the ticket so many times that he could recite the terms of agreement printed on the back. He knew that the man dressed in white linen was not what his mamá would call *buena gente,* but the medal with the ruby had caught Lalo's eye. He had imagined the man asleep in Havana, in a real featherbed that was not stuffed with stiff duck feathers, but true soft down, that was large enough for ten men, his ruby dangling from the bedpost.

"What is that, *mi niño?*" Josefina had asked before going to her room for the night, sitting on the edge of her son's too-small bed and interrupting his reverie.

"Nothing, Mamá," Lalo had responded. He had slipped the ticket under his body. It had been cool against his bare back, a sensation that made him sleepy and content all at once. Josefina's eyelids were heavy, so that she had nodded and had asked nothing else. In reality, she cared little about what her son was hiding. Her mind had been on Regla, who was waiting for her in the bedroom next door. Lalo had taken his mother's indifference as a sign that all would go well in Havana with the rich man.

In the morning, Lalo packed his satchel as if he were going to school. Inside it he hid a sandwich and three extra pesos he took from his mother's purse. As he packed, his sister sat up and watched from her bed. Her knees were drawn up to her mouth, and she rubbed the side of her mouth against her kneecap because one of her molars was loose, and the rubbing loosened it more.

"Where are you going?" she asked, her voice muffled.

"School." Lalo wrapped his tiny bottle of cologne, brought by his father from Marianao, in a thick layer of handkerchiefs for protection, and put that, too, into his bag. It smelled strong, but lasted only a little while, unlike the musk that Abel Santana wore, a stench that clung to the pillows and draperies in his mamá's room. He did not enter her room often, for fear he would retch from the foulness of it.

"No, you aren't," Soledad said. "Where are you going? I won't tell, Lalo." She watched him pack a broken bit of mirror.

"I am going to school, you know-nothing," Lalo said and left the little room without saying another word, hours before his mother or Regla got up.

The station was empty. The attendant frowned at the sight of a first-class ticket in the dirty, chapped hand of this boy. Lalo's shirt was wrinkled, like old paper, and far too big and old-fashioned. His shoes, too, were inherited from his father, and his heels slid out from them with every other step. Still, the morning train to Havana was empty enough so that the single couple in first class would not be too offended by the sight of Lalo slouching in his seat a few rows behind them. The attendant tore the ticket in half, an act that made Lalo wince and then sigh at the loss of the precious souvenir, and showed him to his seat.

Lalo enjoyed the trip in first class. He remembered other trips on the train, sleepy, rumbling rides to the city with his mother to window-shop for things they'd never own. He turned those memories over in his mind until they were polished, idyllic images—of days when Josefina had left Soledad with a neighbor and had draped her heavy arm over him on the train. Of falling asleep there with that wonderful, violet-scented weight pushing him against the seat, in and out of consciousness in time with the bumps on the tracks. How safe Lalo had felt, but always, always they had been far removed from the first-class cars. This ride was different. The chairs were upholstered, not made of wooden planks like the other cars. Long-limbed women brought Lalo piña coladas and coffee cake on plates of white porcelain. When the train stopped, the engineer himself shook hands with all the first-class passengers, even though he wiped his palm on his sleeve after shaking hands with Lalo.

He found his way to the *teatro* easily—it could be seen from the train station. Its walls were embedded with rows of yellow tile. They reflected the sunlight, and the longer Lalo stared at them, the more the world around him seemed to be tinged in gold. The theater doors were covered with old posters, some of a Fred Astaire movie dubbed in Spanish, peeling from the corners to reveal another layer of paper, then another, and another. Before the door stood Duarte, still wearing his ruby medal. He had noticed Lalo stumble off the train but pretended not to see his approach.

"Señor, señor, do you remember me?" Lalo shouted as he crossed the street. Duarte turned slowly and feigned surprise, his mouth forming a deep, dark O. "Ah, yes. I gave you the ticket. Did you enjoy the ride?"

"Very much, *gracias*." Lalo bent over slightly and tried to catch his breath.

"Come," Duarte said. He opened the door behind him. Lalo followed Duarte into a corridor, dark like the mouth of a wolf, as one of his mamá's sayings went. They walked around collapsed wooden crates and fallen support timbers until they came upon the theater proper. The chairs were mostly gone, except for a few left in odd places, and a movie screen glimmered in the dark. On the stage sat two sallow-faced girls, their legs dangling over the edge of what once was an orchestra pit, now furnished with two beds and a small tub filled with cold water, which Lalo could not see. Lalo looked about him in silence. The noises of the theater were loud and hard to ignore. He could hear the skittering of rats in the ceiling, the solitary laughter of a woman, and a bed squeaking somewhere behind a velvet curtain.

"Have you ever been with a woman?" Duarte asked, low, in Lalo's ear.

Lalo took in a deep breath, so deep that it puffed out his chest and made him appear a half inch taller than he actually was. Lalo was almost fifteen. "Of course," he lied.

"Then you understand that a man lives for what a woman can give him. Here, sample one of these two and then we can talk." Duarte raised his arm and pointed at the two girls with his thick thumb.

"Señor, I . . ." Lalo began, but was quieted by Duarte's harsh tug on his arm.

"Never mind then," he said. Duarte did not want to hear a confession from this grubby, nervous boy. He led him to the darkest section of the theater. In the gloom, Lalo could see a pair of chairs covered in cheap tapestry. Duarte pushed him down into the seat and then sat himself.

"There is a great deal of money to be made by a boy like you. The tourists that stroll the Malecón come to taste Cuban women and to play blackjack in the casinos. You will tell them that the prettiest, the cleanest, are at Teatro Martí. They will follow you here. Take these," he said, and handed Lalo a bundle of leaflets, printed with the theater's address.

"You tell them the girls ask for fifty pesos. I will take thirty. The girls take ten, and you, *mi amigito,* take ten for yourself for each customer you bring. But you pay for your own train ticket from now on, eh?"

Lalo felt the bundle of leaflets in his hands, the weight of it bringing him pleasure. He imagined that ten pesos, if rolled the right way, weighted down with a few coins for tips, would weigh much the same as the leaflets. Lalo nodded, and was soon led out into the daylight. The Malecón could be seen in the distance, like the faint brush stroke of an aged painter, crooked and harsh against the horizon. Tourists thronged around the ancient seawall, eager to sit and take in the unearthly blue sky above the ocean, cloudless, broken across only by slashes of seagulls, diving for fish. Duarte pushed Lalo in that direction and shouted, *"Buena suerte, amigito,* bring back lots of rich *americanos."*

Mi Hija,

I've been thinking about my grandchildren more and more. If only I could reach them, I'd hold my granddaughter close to my chest and tell her all about your antics as a girl. Remember, Josefina, when you were a girl and still had nightmares? Those hot nights I'd gather you, so skinny, I remember, in my arms and tell you stories of your Uncle Francisco, *tu tío,* so heroic and funny.

I told one of the Francisco stories to a friend the other day, an angel of a woman, really, who makes delicious pies stuffed with dripping apples, and she laughed and wrote it down with a golden pen. Do the stories still make you laugh, too? Tell them to Soly for me. The stories do not cheer me if there isn't a little child there to fling her arms into the air with surprise or cover her mouth with laughter.

There was much I left out of the stories then. Now I remember how it was that my brother, Francisco, never knew me as more than a friend or a small annoyance. The similarities between us were hard to miss, though. Francisco was tall and skinny. I was shorter, but that was the only real difference. We had the same eyebrows, dark and thick, meeting over our noses. We were born on the same day, so I used to imagine that we were twins, except we had different mothers with different temperaments and different ways of touching their baby's cheek and whispering. I was never allowed to tell him we were brothers, but I almost let it slip once.

We played in the lot that our father owned, an acre set aside for the animals the zoo had no room for. I was the only one of the servant's children allowed to play there, because I was my father's son. Olga Maria knew all along, of course, and hated my mother and me. *Bueno,* in the backyard there were great horn-billed birds that squawked at us when we walked by. The ostriches pushed their small heads through the iron bars of their cage and let me scratch them between the eyes. The turtles crunched away on their lettuce all day, and once, the smallest one bit Francisco's finger and held on tight, so that I had to light a match under its tail to make it let go. We were often injured when we played, and always, Olga Maria would come to the quarters where I lived, which were small, dirty, and built for the servants to share, and slap me if Francisco had been hurt.

One day my brother decided that it would be fun to tease the chimpanzees in their cages. He began to dig up round stones from the earth, wiping the dirt away on his pants. The stones were small, the size of strawberries, and Francisco clicked them together in his hands. We sat a few yards away from the chimpanzees, the stones in a pile between us.

"What's the name of that one?" I remember Francisco asked, pointing at the largest ape, a female with bald patches up and down her arm. And I told him her name was Cuca. Then Francisco lifted a stone and took aim.

I held onto his arms and said, "She's not well. Papi told me so."

"Don't lie to me, Antonio, or I'll tell my mother. You don't know who your father is," and so I had to recover quickly, telling him that I meant that his papi told me. Francisco shrugged his shoulders. "So what's wrong with her?"

"She pulls her hair out, because she is crazy. Her mother left her to die in the cage at the zoo. Leave her alone," I told him.

I remember how Francisco weighed the stone in his hand. "If she's crazy, Antonio, we should put her out of her misery." He laughed, and before I could stop him, he had thrown the small rock in Cuca's direction. The rock struck the ape in her stomach. It had been a weak toss, not meant to harm Cuca, but to infuriate me. Yet, Cuca, who had been busying herself with a patch of hair at her left wrist, picked up the stone and threw it at my brother.

The rock struck him squarely in the forehead and left a small gash there that began to bleed in his eyes, down his cheeks, and onto his white school shirt. He ran all the way to the house and fell into his mother's arms.

So you see that your adventurous hero of an uncle was just a boy, a Wednesday boy, always in the middle of things. Is Lalo a Wednesday boy? Something tells me that he is.

Tu Papá

12

Every Saturday morning, early, near dawn, Lalo purchased a train ticket. He kept the first class ticket stub, from his first trip, tucked into his billfold. The coach stubs he tossed onto the aisle of the train. Once in the city, he would walk directly to the Malecón, approaching single foreign men with his leaflets. In that sleepy city, the shoreline quickly filled with fresh American men and women, who left their cold, northern hamlets and metropolises for the languid sea breeze. And for the taste of forbidden pleasures. The casinos were full to bursting, owned and operated by American mobsters who found it unprofitable to work their magic in the United States any longer and who stuffed their pockets and helped Cuban leaders fill their own. Music poured out of open windows, young couples stood at lampposts and gave one another unhurried kisses. Even the students in their crisp, Catholic uniforms had an air of indolence about them, the girls feline in their movements. The American tourists, tired of news of stocks and wars, of mortgages and restrictions, were caught in a tropical dream. For Lalo, for the tourists, and for the world, it was as if places like El Cotorro didn't exist.

Lalo soon became a fixture on the shoreline and was a point of reference for the regulars from Miami, who loaded onto ferries on the weekends and returned with empty pockets and broad, lazy smiles. Lalo was easy to approach. He was pale like his father, slender, didn't tan easily, and couldn't yet grow a mustache. To the tourists, he could have been a young neighbor or nephew. And so, they came to him and were generous with their tips.

If the weather was sunny, or if the Saturday coincided with an American holiday, Lalo could bring ten or twenty customers back to Duarte. If the day was stormy, the tourists tucked away in their dry hotel rooms, Lalo sat on the seawall and watched the waves, hypnotized by their coming and going. The rushing of the water could not drown the din in his head, of his mamá's whimpering and Abel's grunting on those nights when they both thought that all of El Cotorro was asleep. Abel would come and knock on the door, softly, as though the wood was fragile, and she would pad through the parlor and open the door. Lalo would lie there in puddles of sweat, listening through the walls, to the sound that was carried through the beams that laced the roof. Soledad, a few feet away, would be asleep, lines of sweat running down her face, too. On those hot nights, all the beds were damp with sweat, as if they had all decided, in a moment of inherited resolve, to wash themselves in the sea in the middle of the night.

As for Josefina, she always assumed her son was out in the park, playing baseball or dominoes with his friends. She spent her hours hidden in her room, reading and rereading the stories her father sent her, as if she were a child, craving a bedtime tale at all hours of the day. Lalo would return home after dark, hug his mamá, and go to bed, and Josefina would question nothing. Soledad often wondered why her mamá didn't smell the sea or Duarte's girls on him since she always smelled the perfume of women on her papá. Lalo fell asleep every Saturday night smelling like cigars and rose water and the ocean. Soledad thought it was the smell of something dangerous and unknown. It was sometimes so overpowering that Soledad would take her brother's discarded pants and shirts, and put them outside the room to stink up the hallway instead.

One Saturday in February, Soledad pretended to sleep while her brother dressed. Underneath her covers, she wore her weekend dress that was too large. Around her waist she tied a crocheted sweater, in case her brother went somewhere with chilly drafts. She followed him, hanging several feet back, through the empty, morning roads of El Cotorro. A pair of roosters, separated by a fence, crowed at one another as Lalo walked by, and they crowed again when Soledad passed. She hid for a moment, afraid that the imprudent birds had exposed her, but Lalo continued his quick pace, pausing only once to roll up the cuff of one pant leg.

At the train station, Soledad hid behind a large potted palm, avoiding the red ants that scurried out and over the pot's rim toward her face. She watched her brother purchase a ticket and step up into a rail car at the end of the long line. She ran out from behind her hiding place into Lalo's car. An attendant blocked her path, but she peeked between his legs and called out:

"Lalo, where are you going? Buy me a ticket." Lalo pretended to search his pockets, looked underneath his seat, then out the window, his body stiff in his attempt to ignore his sister.

The attendant lifted Soledad by the shoulders and pushed her off the car. She tumbled to the ground and yelped once. Lalo looked over to where she was and faced the attendant.

"What did you do?" he asked, his face red now, angry with both of them.

The attendant straightened the sleeves of his jacket. "Buy her a ticket," he said, "or take yourselves far from here."

Lalo knew that Duarte was waiting for him. Duarte had said that the Americans were celebrating the day of San Valentín, that many would be on the island over the week, and by Saturday, the men would be frustrated with their wives' chatter, their demand for romance, and would be looking for a Cuban woman who would keep her mouth closed. Lalo had dreamed that night of the Malecón, flooded with rich gentlemen in crisp fedoras, their pockets bulging with dollar bills. In the dream, they lifted Lalo onto their shoulders, chanting, "Take us to the *teatro*." Remembering the dream, he thought to himself Soledad would have to come along, and pulled out the lining of his pocket in search of the money for her ticket. The profit he'd make from this holiday would compensate for the expenditure.

With the ticket in hand, they both boarded the rail car. Lalo pushed Soledad into her seat, with a shove harder than the attendant's. She did not speak during the trip, but only glanced at her brother out of the corner of her eye and saw a tight mouth and his leg bouncing up and down in either anger or agitation. Soledad was not eager to find out which.

When they arrived in Havana, Soledad recognized the train station, the road that had taken her once to her dead grandfather's house, and the dirty, trash-laden sidewalks. She followed her brother, who still had not spoken to her, all the way to a long, lovely seawall. There, ladies carried boxes of cigars, hung around their necks with red ribbons. Little old men sold cotton candy by the handful and cones filled with roasted peanuts, stripped of their papery outer layer and rolled in salt. On top of the seawall, a couple in yellow costumes danced flamenco to no music at all. On the ground was the man's broad bejeweled hat, sprinkled with coins. Their feet flew over the edges of the seawall every so often, and the woman clicked her castanets so quickly that her hands seemed to be sheathed in a blur of shiny black. Her brother, she realized, disappeared to this seaside carnival every Saturday.

She sat on the seawall and let her legs dangle over the side. Every so often, a wave would rush up against the coral wall and spatter water on her bare legs. The day was warm, and the crocheted sweater still hung about her waist. The long sleeves dipped into the ocean, drawing the saltwater up into the fibers and stretching the sleeves with its weight. She watched her brother and the swooping gulls in turn, wondering why the birds circled over different sections of the ocean, as if they were trying to beat a whirlpool into the water with their wings. She observed her brother as he stopped several men who walked along the Malecón and pressed sheets of paper into their hands.

She stood from the seawall, leaving the weighted sweater to drop sluggishly into the water below. She approached her brother just as he spoke to a man with hair that hung a few inches below his collar. It flipped up in the wind, despite the oil he had put on it to keep it down. His front tooth was broken, the edge of the tooth at an angle to the others.

"How much?" the man asked Lalo in English. Soledad was amazed to see that her brother understood.

"Fifty," Lalo said, "beautiful, clean ladies. You say Lalo sent you, okay, mister?" Lalo pushed back against Soledad as he spoke, blocking her view of the man her brother miraculously understood.

"Fifty's too much, boy," the man said, then, peeking behind Lalo, took hold of Soledad's small arm. "Ten pesos for five minutes with this one. ¿Bueno?" the man asked, pulling Soledad closer and slipping his fingers between the collar of her dress and her skin.

"Stop," Lalo began to yell in Spanish. The flamenco couple stopped their dancing, and the woman dropped her castanets. The peanut vendor stood still nearby, and even the gulls seemed to halt their circling.

The man gripped Soledad's arm more tightly. Lalo had taken hold of his sister's other arm, and between them they held her like a wishbone. The man released her and pushed her into her brother's stomach, knocking the air from his gut so that he bent over to catch his breath. The leaflets in his hand fell down and began fluttering along the walkway. Some floated out onto the ocean's surface and were engulfed by a flock of seagulls, fooled into thinking that the papers were food tossed by the tourists. Others rolled out onto the main street where they were run over by the cars that sped by. The man who had held Soledad a moment before, picked up a handful of leaflets, put them in his pockets, then lost himself in the multitude of people.

Lalo stood up finally, after a few long minutes during which Soledad could feel the people's stares, the perimeter of bodies closing in on them there on the walkway.

"Come," Lalo said. She followed him away from the seawall, the music and vendor calls resuming as they disappeared from view.

Soledad assumed they were going back to the train, but instead of purchasing two new tickets, Lalo crossed the street, and entered Duarte's theater. Already inside was the man from the Malecón. "There he is," the man said, and took Lalo by the collar, dragging him to where Duarte stood.

"You don't like to please my customers, *guajiro?* Maybe *guajiros* like you have no mind for the city and its ways." Lalo kept his eyes to the ground, looking at Soledad only once, to make sure she was still where he had left her—behind an empty crate. The man with the broken tooth still held Lalo by the collar, pulling hard at the fabric. Lalo could hear the seams tearing. Duarte pulled Lalo by the ears and swung him, face first, onto the molded arm of one of the upholstered chairs. The skin on his chin ripped against an exposed screw in the wood. Blood soon began to drench his clothes.

"I am not a man who holds rancor in his heart," Duarte said and smiled softly, like a grandfather might, helping Lalo up with one hand, "but do not return here."

Lalo nodded and backed away from Duarte and the man. He bundled up the bottom of his shirt and held it pressed against his chin as he went. On their way through the *teatro*'s dark corridor, they could hear Duarte say, "*Amigo,* if you like them young, Fátima and Rosamaria here are only fifteen. But look at their faces, like the countenance of a baby . . ."

13

Another of the sergeant's letters had arrived, telling a story of the past. At times, Josefina felt as if she remembered the moments her father wrote about, as if she could dig them out from the deepest layer of her memory. She thought she could pick out her uncle and her father from childhood pictures if she had the chance. She thought it funny, wondering how a few words could create such images, when sometimes she couldn't recognize herself in the mirror. Josefina clutched the letter to her breast and looked skyward. Her eyes watered when she read the sergeant's letters. She would often look up after reading, as if the cracked ceiling above, with its splotches of grass-green mold were not there, but instead was the vaulted ceiling of a church. But Abel always sniffed whenever Josefina spoke of her ghostly father.

Josefina tried changing, doing things to please her father, to win heavenly grace. There was the time that she made sandwiches for some farmers who were walking their pigs to the market. They sat in her house and ate and drank, their smiles bread-filled. And when they were gone, so was a pound of sausage from the icebox. Josefina made cotton underwear in her spare time for the children in Soledad's school, because she knew they had none. They really were beautiful things, sometimes embroidered with tulips, or stitched with the child's initials. Had Josefina thought that she could sell the frilly undergarments at the market without shaming

Lorenzo and her family, she would have. Instead, she gave her creations away to the needy children in El Cotorro. And then they'd tease her, call her the "panty lady" when Josefina came with her bundles into the schoolyard, Soledad hiding behind the slide in embarrassment. But Josefina did not allow these setbacks to stop her from doing good to honor her father's soul. Though he had not asked for these "offerings," she thought he would be pleased.

Josefina and Abel were at the dinner table when the children appeared. Abel was eating his meal quietly. The children came into the kitchen. Lalo's chin had been bleeding. The streaks of red were still there, wrapping around his neck and ending somewhere deep within his shirt. As for Soledad, her hair was tangled and her dress disheveled from sleeping on the train.

"What has happened?" Josefina said, cradling Lalo's face into her hands and bending down to look up into the gash on his chin. Abel stood, too, and touched the loose flesh on Lalo's chin. The touch stung, and Lalo pushed Abel's hand away and spit blood at the butcher's feet. His mother released him then, and Lalo stumbled into the street once again, running everywhere at once, like a chicken freed from its cage for the first time.

"The boy needs God," Abel said.

"He was baptized in the church." Josefina spoke with the renewed strength of the offended.

"And the girl?" They looked at Soledad then. Josefina's eyes widened and Abel's narrowed. "No? Then you see why your children carry on so? Come, *mi vida,* there is a Mass tonight. We'll take the girl with us, and the other one"—he looked outside again—"will come if he chooses."

Josefina pushed her daughter through the kitchen and into her bedroom. "Take off the dress," she said, and then: "Be careful not to mess your hair. Where have you been?" she asked and did not notice when Soledad did not answer. She rummaged through the closet, throwing dresses of calico and blue gingham to the floor.

"Aha," she said, "I've found it." She pulled out a dress of ivory sateen, embroidered with rosettes, from the back of the closet. It was the dress that Lorenzo had brought from Santa Clara on the child's sixth birthday. The shoulders had taken the form of the wooden hanger, and the skirt seemed too short. Still, Josefina said, "So here is your church dress," as if church dresses were common things in the house. She said it loud enough for Abel in the parlor to hear as she smoothed out the front with the palm of her hand, then pulled out the stitching of the hem and quickly sewed a longer one. Soledad had only worn the dress once before—when Lorenzo first pulled it out of the box from between the crisp paper and shook out the creases as she stepped into it eagerly, spinning and falling into her father's arms. Afterward, Josefina hid it in the back of the closet, because she said that it reeked of a whore's perfume.

Josefina brought the dress up over Soledad's shoulders, digging her own hands into the long sleeves to catch the arms and pull them through, cautiously, in the way that an infant is dressed. She buttoned the long row of buttons and turned Soledad around to look her over. The skirt was, indeed, still too short, above her knee, and Josefina pulled at the sateen, but it wouldn't stretch. The rosettes on Soledad's chest spread out grossly in an effort to hold the tight material together, and the lace cuffs bit into her wrists like hungry little kittens. Josefina tried seeing another thing altogether—a baptized child or a heroine, blessed with good fortune because of her devotion to God. She kissed her daughter on the forehead, then rearranged the curls, and said, "Offer Abel something to drink. Be a good girl. Remember that we are going to church."

In the parlor, Abel Santana sat on the wicker rocking chair but did not rock. His heels, tucked underneath the feet of the rocker, stopped any motion and scuffed his black shoes at the same time. The wicker squeaked softly as he shifted his body. At that moment, his eyes were scanning the ceiling, resting in the corners where spiderwebs hung lifeless.

"Señor Santana," Soledad asked, *"¿Gustaría café?"*

He circled his stomach with his hands and rumbled a low *"Sí, gracias.*" She felt him follow her into the kitchen, and all her senses were suddenly aware of him. Her ears heard his body shift from the chair, the wicker crackling from the sudden release. She heard the rocker totter on the tile and remembered that her mamá once said that a chair left to sway foretells the death of a child. His shadow moved alongside hers on the wall, threatening to overtake it, and her skin prickled where he stood near to her. Still, she was very careful not to spill the coffee grounds from the brown bag to the pot. She didn't splash any water on herself or the counter, nor did she twist the stove's knob too far left or right. Slowly, she took the porcelain cup and dish from the cabinet, washing them both in case a cockroach had crawled on them at night. Abel Santana would know that she did not harbor the spite that her brother did for him. Lalo would not have washed the cup.

She poured the coffee, folded a napkin into a neat triangle, placed it between the cup and dish, and set it in Abel Santana's red hands. He sniffed at the cup and put it on the counter. "Smells good," he said, then: "Come, let me see," and he reached over and grasped her chin, tilting her head up, and peering closely at her face. In the long months that had passed, Abel had begun to worry about Soledad and Lalo, as a father would. He had worried about where she had been all day, and found himself thinking about the kind of adults the children would become. Abel sometimes lost sleep over them and started arguments with Josefina about their whereabouts. His feelings for Josefina were starting to spread to those that she loved, but the thought concerned Abel. Who was he to love anyone, especially when that devotion was being paid for?

Abel Santana released her chin then, and patted her cheek. "So tell me," he asked, "where were you and your brother today?"

"The playground," Soledad lied. "Lalo got into a fight with Raúl Sotolongo. You don't know him. He's a bully from school." She spoke quickly and stared at her shoes.

Abel let out a noisy breath through his nose. He took his coffee into the parlor, where Josefina waited, her head covered in a veil of black lace, her fingers wound with the beads of a rosary.

The trio stepped outside. Josefina shouted Lalo's name. He appeared slowly from behind a parked car. His hands were thrust deep into his pockets. *"¿Que?"* he mouthed and shrugged his shoulders.

"Come to church," Josefina said, her voice carrying down the street.

"Don't feel like it." Lalo rolled his eyes. Josefina felt Abel tense beside her.

"Ay, just like his father," she said and sighed. Abel fumbled with the keys to the front door.

They walked the mile to the church of San Matéo. Soledad had often passed its porticos and garden statues on her way to school and had seen the little nuns gliding in and out, hiding their faces in the black cloth, but she never had any interest in following them in. She walked with Josefina, holding her gloved hand. The fringes of Josefina's veil fluttered in the wind, and the old lace stung Soledad's cheek. Abel Santana strode behind them.

Josefina had not been to a church in years, and her stomach churned with her nerves. To calm herself as they walked, Josefina gave Soledad a list of rules. "Remember to make the sign of the cross, like so," and she took the child's hand and touched her forehead, chest, and shoulders. "Remember to be very quiet, and remember not to clap your hands even at the end." And then, when they were in sight of the church, she said in a whisper, so that Abel did not hear, "Remember not to cross your legs, *hija,* it brings bad luck."

The church stood on a bit of a hill, its porticos graced with palms and blooming roses. Josefina splashed water on Soledad's forehead from a tiny golden dish. They walked up the aisle, and Josefina and Abel knelt suddenly and crossed themselves. Soledad knelt only halfway down, nearly losing her balance. Then they sat. The women all wore veils like Josefina's, black and old. The woman in front of them kept her veil in place with a long hatpin, stuck into her gray curls and out through one of the lacy scrolls. They were packed into the pew so tightly that the young woman beside Josefina, whose hard, pregnant belly pressed against Josefina's side, broke her rosary. As the Father spoke, his voice circling and landing like crows, the brown beads scattered and clicked noisily throughout the church. What interested Soledad most were the people who sat to the right of the aisle.

There was no written rule as to the seating that divided up the church in this fashion, but it occurred in the same way that families separate during weddings, with the bride's relatives on one side and the groom's on the other, avoiding each other's eyes. The women on the other side did not have veils like Josefina's. Theirs shimmered with lacy iridescence, and she could see that their rosaries were not made of shells or irregular beads, but of perfectly rounded porcelain. Josefina was as enthralled as her daughter. It all reminded her of the days in Vedado, when she was one of those on the right, unaware of those that sat just a few feet away, shuffling and daydreaming about the things they couldn't own, about days that might be easier, softer, kinder. And oh, the little girls on that side were exquisite. Their shoes, in constant motion beneath the pews, shone black and brilliant. They wore white gloves, and caught between all those white fingers were tiny missals, bound in mother-of-pearl, with silver clasps binding the little books together. They looked nothing like her own daughter, Soledad, so dirty and ragged. They were beautiful.

Soledad had noticed the difference, too. One of the girls was, to Soledad, the loveliest. When they stood to sing the psalm, she could see her clearly. Never had she seen a cheek so white and smooth, nor hands that flew so tenderly to scratch at an itchy ear. The lace at her wrist did not cut her, but rested there like an extension of her skin. As Soledad stared at her, the girl turned and met her eyes. They looked at each other for a long time, until the priest rang a bell, snatching her attention away.

With the ringing of the bell, the children on the right of the aisle stood in unison and began forming a quiet line before the priest. Soledad must have gasped aloud because Josefina reached over to her and whispered, "Those are first communicants. You'll do that, too, someday." Soledad watched them all open their mouths, some grotesquely sticking their tongues too far, the meek ones barely opening their jaws at all, so that the priest's hands trembled at having to touch their lips. The exquisite girl presented her open mouth just so and knelt in her pew to pray with bowed head.

After the Father began the recessional, carrying the golden cross high over his head, everyone filed through the rows and out of the church. Again, Josefina and Abel knelt, and again the water was splashed on Soledad's forehead. Outside in the courtyard, Josefina sat on a marble bench, fanning herself with an old painted fan that hung from her wrist. Abel sat beside her, and the fanning stopped. He pulled the corners of the fan in front of him, and together, they looked at the painting. Two horses, their necks strung with flowers and ivy, lunged upward, their back hooves digging into the soft dirt. In the distance, a castle was ringed with fog, and near the base of the fan, almost hidden in the accordion crimp, was a conquistador's helmet, dented but still shiny. Josefina began her litany about the fan's origin.

"This was my mother's fan, and it was her treasure," she said, running her fingers around the horses' manes.

"*Es muy fino,* Josefina," Abel said.

"Yes, very fine and very old. And handpainted . . ."

"Mamá?" Soledad interrupted.

"*¿Qué?*"

"May I go look at the gardens?" She nodded her head and continued looking at the fan and at Abel. Soledad was glad to escape the storytelling. The garden wound itself around the church in neat rows of daisies and colored river stones set like mosaics. Here was a crooked cross, and here someone tried to set an oversized rosary in the dirt, but it looked more like the outline of a noose.

Old anthills poked out of the ground, gray and desiccated, the smell of lye still hanging over the hills like a cloud. Deep in the shade of one of the porticos was a structure like a cave, lit by the flickering of hundreds of candles. Soledad crawled inside, scraping her stockings on the flakes of rock. Inside was a marble Virgin, her eyes closed and her hands stretched across her breast. Her cheeks flickered with blue light, and at her feet were candles enclosed in blue glasses and an iron box with a slot for offerings. Soledad picked one of the slender reeds from the ground, let the tip catch one of the flames, and lit a candle for herself, right near the Lady's marble toe. Just then she felt someone tugging her hair. She turned to see the girl from across the aisle. Her missal was tucked in the sash of her dress, and it, like the Virgin's cheeks, reflected the blue light.

"You need to pay for that," she said, low and kind, as one who helps another to escape reproval.

"For lighting a candle? Why?" Soledad asked.

"Because She won't answer your prayer unless you make an offering." The girl had not yet stepped into the cave except for one polished foot. Soledad did not want to explain to her that she had not prayed at all, nor that she had no money. So, she turned and knelt in the sand, praying for the first time in her life that the girl would be gone when she was done. She stood and crossed herself as her mamá had shown her, but the girl was still there, except now she was within the confines of the cave, leaning on the wall and unbuckling her left shoe. From the inside she produced two centavos, and she put them into the box, the money clinking faintly.

"I hope she answers your prayer," the girl said, and turned to leave.

"What is your name?" Soledad hollered, as the girl stepped over the trim hedges and river stones.

"Camila Flores." She spoke as she walked into the dark night. Soledad was angry at herself, because she had prayed for the girl to leave. She turned and gave the iron money box a timid little kick, so that the tiny flames stretched and broke off from their wicks for an instant before rejoining the fire, and she ran after Camila. The girl was nearly at the church's entrance again when she turned to Soledad and said, "I will see you next Sunday," then mouthed the word *"Adiós."*

While the others were at church, Lalo had spent the rest of the day wading in the cold river, the water numbing his feet, letting the stones rush up to his ankles and scratch at them. It was only that morning that he had lost Duarte, the train, the Malecón forever, all because of Soledad. Lalo waited for his family on the steps to the house. He saw them walking slowly up the street, brown dust floating around them like halos. When they were only a few feet away, Lalo noticed that Abel was carrying a chicken by its neck and a wine jug cradled in his arm. The breeze carried a whiff of incense. Josefina and the butcher stared down at Lalo then, both of them like statues, except that Lalo could see his mamá's arms prickling with the cold, and Abel's breath come out in a fog before him.

"Enjoy your dinner," Abel said, handing the chicken to Josefina and leaving the wine jug near Lalo's thigh. "I won't bother your house tonight." He said all this without turning his eyes from Lalo.

"*Ay,* no bother at all. Why don't you stay?" Josefina pleaded and blushed, pulling the veil from her head and wrapping it around her body, like a shawl. Lalo stood, as if to say, "Enough," ready to pull his mother into the house and spit at the butcher again, but it did not come to this. Abel Santana nodded his head first to Lalo and then to Josefina, and left.

Josefina and Soledad spent the evening cleaning the chicken for dinner. Lalo's stomach growled at the plucking of every feather, at every smack of seasoning on the chicken's breast. He did not want to eat the butcher's meal, but the plate of steaming meat before him was more than he could resist.

14

For Abel, there was no discrepancy between the money he took from the sergeant and his faith in God. There had been a time, yes, when he thought of church as a place where fairy tales were told. His mother, a stout woman with uncommon red hair, giant hands, and wrists like a man's was a staunch atheist. He never knew his father, Ismael Santana, who ran off to New York after Abel was born. Ismael had been a religious man, Abel and his brother, Chelo, were told, and maybe that was why Abel rejected it all. What kind of faith, after all, leads a man away from his sons?

But something changed when Abel came to El Cotorro. There was a languor in the small town that was hard to resist. The people seemed made of air, at times, and swung their arms and hips when they walked to the beat of some silent drum. Even the lizards and cockroaches that scurried here and there seemed to take their time. Abel had come, because he heard business was good, and the people were successful. He opened up his butcher shop immediately. Though times soon turned for the worse, Abel stayed on, making sure his customers were satisfied.

"A female, you say, about a hundred pounds?" a customer might ask.

"I have some of everything," Abel would answer, then dart behind the screen and find the exact pig the customer described. Big and small, fat, young, Abel made sure his stock was always full. And so the lines at his shop were long on Saturday mornings, and particularly so during the holidays. He had money to spare, a small apartment near the beach, and beautiful women who were drawn to a man who could kill without remorse and bring home a thick pork leg to the table besides.

It was one of these women, Carmen León, who demanded long ago that Abel come to church with her. Her husband was a lout, and Abel was keeping her company at nights. It wasn't sinful, Carmen believed, as long as they both went to church on Sundays. Abel acquiesced and saw his first miracle.

It was at the moment when the priest held aloft the goblet of wine, waiting for that instant that it might become blood, the old arms quivering with the wait, the intensity, of the moment. Behind the priest, a golden crucifix hung. Twice the size of any human, the figure of Christ cried out in frozen pain. Abel yawned.

Then came a shout that shattered the silence. From behind the altar, a nun began to scream, and then she ran to the priest who held the cup in midair, shouting, "The wine has been poisoned! Don't drink!"

But it was too late, the wine had been blessed. One didn't simply throw Christ's blood down the drain. To Abel's horror, he watched the priest swallow the drink, turn pale, stumble, tremble . . . then recover. Behind him, the golden crucifix had turned black.

Later, Abel would say it was a trick of lights, and Carmen León would leave him, weeping down the street. But it wasn't the last of the miracles.

Within a week's time, Abel saw the image of the Virgin in the trunk of a tree that was being chopped down, would hear of a man who cured himself of bronchitis by drinking a vial of holy water, and would see for himself the miracle of the sun.

He had been out in the sun, preparing a small pig for a customer. He had removed the heart and liver and wrapped the organs carefully in brown paper. When recalling the day, Abel would remember how he laughed when he noticed the pig's tongue had fallen out of the side of its mouth, cartoonish in its death, at the moment that he saw a strange shadow cast over the animal. Its pink skin seemed blue, all at once, and Abel looked up to see what had caused the change.

There was silence in the market, but for a lone voice singing, *"O Maria, madre mía, o consuelo de mortal . . ."* All eyes were drawn upward. Abel watched as the sun shrank to a pinpoint, then exploded into a thousand orbs of blue light, coalescing again and turning pink, then white, and bouncing in the sky like a ball. Abel watched the ballet of the sun for a long while until it stopped.

He worked on the pig until evening, its skin awash in bits of leftover sun.

Abel saw no other miracles again, as long as he lived, but it was enough for him. When Josefina began to believe that the sergeant's letters were miracles in themselves, Abel, knowing the power of divine wonder, did nothing to dissuade her. He convinced himself that the lie was a miracle in itself, that the illusion of a heavenly father and a guardian angel would keep her bound to him forever.

Sometimes he watched her reading the letters, her eyes wet pools, her lips parted in the wonder of it all. Then he would excuse himself and run home to the privacy of his own bedroom, his heart pounding, his head throbbing from guilt.

Mi Hija,

I will finish the story of Cuca the chimpanzee. Please do not tell this story to Soledad. It will only make her sad. And if you have already begun the tale, finish it in a happy way. You will know how.

It had been a week since my brother threw a stone at the ape and the ape had thrown one back. Olga Maria had not come to punish me in all that time. Then one day she appeared with my father, his leather belt in his hand. My mother, your grandmother, stood at once to defend me, saying, "Francisco threw the stone, not Antonio. Why don't you beat him for once?" She trembled as she spoke. I could see that my father, as strong as he was, trembled, too.

"Ese niño," she said, *"es el responsable."*

And so my father took me into the bathroom. He hit me once across the calves, hard enough to leave a red spot, but no welt. Then he held me, and rocked me, as my mother had always done, and kissed me on the forehead. He let me strike the belt against the sink a few times for the sound to be heard outside before we opened the door.

I made an effort to cry hard, so that my eyes would swell, even though I felt like cartwheeling from my father's embrace. Olga Maria seemed pleased at the sight of my eyes, and she turned with the belt in hand, leaving her awful tracks on the floor.

We learned later that the chimpanzee named Cuca had died. She had picked at the spot where the stone struck her until she tore through the skin, with those nails like steel, and brought out her intestines.

My brother and I cried together at the thought of it.

Tu Papá

15

The sergeant waited by the public telephone in front of Corbett's Pharmacy that Tuesday morning. Abel Santana's phone call was never late in coming, but the sergeant had arrived very early, and as he leaned on the cool phone box, he composed a letter in his head. Soon, he would tell her why he had left Spain, why he had run. Perhaps then she would forgive him for running from El Cotorro that day.

The phone rang, a screeching ring that brought him out of his reverie. The sergeant and Abel discussed the weather first, and then the cost of quality poultry on the island, before getting to the subject of Josefina and her children.

"Sergeant," Abel began, "the children would go hungry if I weren't bringing them food. Soledad's hip bones jut out like pistols."

"¿Y Josefina?" the sergeant asked next.

"Your daughter is lovely, refined," and then the question: "How did you let her marry that animal Concepción?"

"Should I have sent her to a convent in Barcelona instead?" the sergeant said into the telephone, so loudly that Abel heard only static on the other end. And then: "Have you found Lorenzo?"

"His letters place him in Santa Clara. Josefina smells the paper and then starts to cry, as if she could breathe in the life of the women he is with. He never telephones. I don't think he will ever return to her, sergeant. But if he does, I will drive him out and bring her to you." There was silence after this, and Abel listened as the sergeant cleared his throat of the bitter orb suddenly lodged there before he spoke.

"How much do you need this month, Santana?" the sergeant asked, still feeling as though he would weaken and cry.

Abel was quiet for a moment. He had done nothing with the money so far. And when it arrived, he'd hide it away and run to Josefina and bring her a bunch of white carnations, or a side of beef, kissing her ardently, as though apologizing, though she did not know it. "As much as you can send, *hombre*," he said at last. "If you have little, then send little, and I will still do the work. I think of this as a sacred cause, you see."

The sergeant did indeed see and believed that his mission to part Josefina from her husband was somehow holy. Soon enough, Mona Linde's bureau was empty of its contents.

She had noticed the gradual disappearance of her treasures. The sapphire earrings she had inherited from her Canadian grandmother were gone. Her father's gold cuff links were missing as well, and her Christmas bonus, which she had hidden in the fold of a scarf, was gone, too. When she finally decided that she was betrayed, Mona cried in the bathroom during her breaks at work, refused to open the stall door when someone knocked, and even skipped her retirement party, leaving the gifts in the employee lounge. She knew that the sergeant, whom she now called Anthony, was stealing the jewelry and the money, but she could not determine what it was he was buying. He still wore the same ill-fitting clothes from deep inside Mona's closet. She never sensed liquor on his breath, or anything in his eyes or gait that suggested drunkenness. And when she asked what he knew about the horse races in Hialeah, he looked dumbfounded.

He had been kinder to her, though. That very morning, the sergeant had appeared in her bedroom with a plate of toast smeared with orange jelly. "For you," he had said in the accent she so loved and kissed her on the lips. He had begun ironing her clothes, too. He often burned the threads in the seam, but nevertheless, her uniform was crisper than ever. So the missing items were really quite a mystery to her, and as the days went by, Mona Linde became all the more mystified. For the sergeant's part, he had started to love her a little bit, and he was surprised that the feeling didn't come from pity. She was beautiful in her own way, like a moth in its last days, fluttering closer and closer to the ground, missing a beat, trembling on a leaf. Mona Linde told herself that a few pieces of jewelry didn't matter, after all. That she wasn't alone anymore. She had the sergeant's warmth at night, *and besides,* she thought, *sapphires can only offer cold comfort.*

One Saturday, during a hailstorm that sent fist-sized ice raining down on Mona's house to shatter the roof tiles on impact, Mona and the sergeant awaited the bus that would take them to the flea market downtown. The sergeant needed new clothes, since the old ones were bleached from working in the sun and hole-ridden from the pesticides that ate through the fabric, and the flea market sold workmen's clothes cheaply. Mona's large umbrella covered them both as they waited for the bus to arrive, so the hailstones bounced off the nylon easily and landed at their feet. Waiting with them at the bus stop were a black woman and her two children. The children hid underneath their mother's skirt, their ochre-colored legs the only things exposed. When they approached his way, the woman appearing at first sight to be a six-legged monster, the sergeant moved out from under the umbrella and extended his arm for the woman to join Mona. Mona stopped the sergeant and pulled him underneath the parasol again.

Mona Linde shook her head and widened her eyes, and the sergeant seemed to understand, but she noted the sudden hardness in his face, his lips tightly puckered, and his eyebrows coming together to form a little ditch between them.

The little legs under the woman's skirts shifted. A slender little hand swung beneath the skirt's hemline to scratch at an infected ant bite on a knee. The arm dangled there for a moment, then caressed the mother's thick ankle before rising and disappearing again. The gesture was so affectionate that the sergeant was moved once again to give the umbrella to the woman and her children, who were, by now, so soaked underneath their mother's cotton skirt that the material clung to them, and their thin lovely forms could be seen.

"What are you doing, Anthony?" Mona protested, and yanked the handle of the umbrella toward herself again. She had pulled with force and the umbrella fell out of her hands. The sergeant bent to lift it, still determined to hand the thing over to the woman with the children, when one of the stolen cuff links tumbled out of his pocket. He had meant to give them to Chelo that morning, but the hailstorm had begun without warning and the cuff links remained, forgotten, in his pocket. The sergeant picked up the little buttons quickly and dropped them back into his pocket, hoping that Mona Linde did not see.

But she did see, and her thin hand came up to touch the corner of her mouth. The umbrella rolled down the street as she spoke: "Jim's gold cuff links." By now the bus had stopped and the doors were open. The woman had released her children from the shelter of her wet frock, and they stood waiting by the bus, for Mona and the sergeant to enter first and take their seats. As they waited they were pelted by hailstones that the youngest one tried to wave away as if they were mayflies. As for Mona Linde, she made no move to get into the bus.

"Ma'am," the bus driver called, "are you coming aboard?"

"Yes, of course, give me a second," Mona said, still looking at the place where the cuff link had fallen. Though she knew the sergeant had been stealing, had known it all along, Mona had convinced herself that she could forgive him. But suddenly, thoughts of Jim on his last days crowded her mind, of Jim as a young groom, the gold cuff links shining at his wrists.

"Lost something, ma'am?" the bus driver called again.

"Yes. Something very dear," Mona said, and now her eyes shifted to look upon the sergeant.

"Come," the sergeant said, and tried pulling her toward the open door. She looked at him and squinted her eyes, poising herself to say something terrible.

"Come," he said again, and pointed to the family that still waited for Mona to make her decision before they could board.

"They can wait all day, for all I care," Mona said, and the woman, realizing that, in fact, she might have to wait all day, gathered her children under her dress again and began walking north, toward the next bus stop. Mona walked up to the sergeant, who had one foot up on the bus step. She put her hand into his pocket and found the cuff links. She twisted them in the air above her, as if trying to catch whatever sunlight could be found onto their surface. The cuff links were made of hammered gold, and all the little dents managed to shine there in the stormy air. "You may keep them, Anthony," she told the sergeant and put them back into his pocket. She pulled a few loose coins from inside her purse and dropped them into the bus driver's coin box. Then she turned away, walking toward Circle Park and the road to her home.

The sergeant boarded the bus, understanding now that there was no returning to Mona Linde's house. He patted the little gold lump in his pocket and went up the road.

16

Lorenzo left Gilda on the day of her father's funeral to avoid the men in her family, who felt he was the cause of Gilda's disgrace. *She isn't worth the trouble,* he thought and readied himself to go home to the one woman he had fought to keep. Once he was out on the road with his things, he found he could not go home to El Cotorro, to Josefina's constant watching, to the needs of his children. He hadn't seen them grow up and didn't feel any remorse concerning his absence. That Lalo was now fourteen, fidgeting all day, his voice deepening, and that Soledad, at nine years, had forsaken the dolls Lorenzo had bought her as a baby did not cause any pangs of guilt in Lorenzo's heart. He had learned at a young age that life was fleeting, not worth spending on domestic boredom. Lorenzo had lost both parents at a young age to tuberculosis. He barely remembered either one of them. He grew up in the house of an uncle who let him do as he pleased. So Lorenzo played with guns when he was barely out of diapers and decided at age twelve that school was not for him. His uncle thought so, too.

The day he left his uncle's house for Havana was much like the last day he saw Gilda. The sky was gray, as if it might begin to rain but didn't. And the stale puddles on the ground from a few days before seemed black and endless in the mistiness, as if he could fall into them and fall forever. A day like this had led him to Havana when he was a boy, and led him there again as a man.

Lorenzo found himself in the capital in the spring of 1952. He had come by foot, by carriage, by train, stopping at the small towns along the way, always finding the warm bed of a young woman who found his dark eyes hard to resist. He was, as some would say, magnetic. It had taken him nearly three years to make the journey, and in the meantime, he felt like a man liberated. He took odd jobs here and there, sent money to Josefina when he could, drank rum well into the evenings.

Havana hadn't changed since he was last there, hypnotizing Josefina and taunting her father. Lorenzo had avoided the capital since, wanting to stay away from all of the brutal colonels who had been in charge of the island, one after another, as if the city were overtaken by escaped beasts. Lorenzo had lost track of their names. Every year there was a new president, every year new rules to follow. And every year, Lorenzo had less money in his pocket than before.

On the afternoon of his arrival, Lorenzo sensed a buzz in the city. In the distance, a column of smoke rose in the sky. Uncharacteristically curious, he walked toward it, past small painted houses stacked side by side. He secretly hoped that the sergeant's old house was the one ablaze. Suddenly, Lorenzo heard a shot, felt a sharp pain in his arm. More shots followed, and he ran from doorway to doorway, his upper arm bleeding, soaking his shirt. There were shouts of men, orders barked from a megaphone, quiet, then another round of volleys.

Lorenzo pressed himself flat against a doorway, then felt it give way.

"You've walked right into a war," a voice from inside said, then dragged him inside the house by the shoulders. His arm felt like it was being shed of its skin. He closed his eyes to lessen the pain.

"You should wait here," the young woman said. "Wait with me until my papi comes back, please?"

When Lorenzo opened his eyes, he saw a girl, about sixteen,

like Lalo. She was plump and dark. Her eyes were thin slits, and Lorenzo thought she might be part Chinese. She sat before him on the ground, her legs bent at the knee and to the side, the crease at the back of her knee dark and deep. Her nails were polished a golden orange and her wrists were creased, too, like a baby's. The girl wore her long dark hair loose and it made her look wild, like a lost cat.

"Where is your father?" Lorenzo asked.

"Fighting. He's a policeman. It's that horrible Batista who is trying to take over again." She cried without sound and held Lorenzo's hand. Outside, Lorenzo could hear them, the clumsy police shouting orders at the wind and the shots that silenced the voices.

Later, the girl would dress Lorenzo's wound—a surface scratch that hurt like fire—and would cook him a small meal of corn meal and rice. Her name was Dulce, sweet, and Lorenzo thought it appropriate.

He stayed with Dulce for a week, all through the bloody coup, and waited for her father, the policeman, to arrive. With every passing minute, Lorenzo fought the urge to embrace Dulce, to take the soft, firm body and press it to his. But she was much too young, too close to Soledad in age, to Lalo, and Lorenzo restrained himself.

Even when it was clear that Dulce's father was dead, even when Batista came on the radio and said he had abolished the constitution, even when there had been more fighting in the streets, many, many men lined up against walls and shot without the consolation of a final prayer, even then, with Dulce reduced to sighs and trembling, Lorenzo could not offer her even a gentle pat of reassurance, because he feared himself.

He left in the middle of the night, when the streets of the capital were finally safe, and made sure to lock the door behind him.

Mi Hija,

Do not cry when you receive Lorenzo's letters. Do not think of the women he wastes his time with. Instead, look to your mailbox and wait for me. Sometimes I dream that I can fold myself up into squares, flat as a sheet of paper, and stay there, in the envelope, for you.

I have sent an angel to watch over you, *hijita mia.* He will make sure that the children eat, that you don't have to worry about Lorenzo in Santa Clara. But if he wrongs you, dear, I will clip his wings.

Tu Papá

17

That summer, Josefina began to look everywhere for her angel, the one her father wrote her about. When she learned about the coup in the capital, she imagined the angel there by her side, protecting her children with giant feathery wings and a voice like a bell. When the coup was over and Batista was firmly entrenched in the palace, Josefina rejoiced in the wholeness of her family, their safety, and thanked the angel in her prayers. She dreamed that he was tall and golden, casting shadows behind him everywhere he went. Sometimes she imagined that the hazy, wavy mirages that appeared on the concrete in the heat of summer were her angel. Or dust clouds that formed in the church foyer. Or the match that Abel used to light his cigarettes. The sergeant had said the angel was coming, so she looked for him.

Josefina began making crosses from palm fronds, twisting the sturdy, long leaves into shape. She tied them to Soledad's and Lalo's bedposts, and from her own, too. She hung them in the kitchen over the stove, over doorways, the drawers of dressers, buried in the lawn at the base of the avocado trees. She gave them away to strangers in the street, who frowned, then tucked them away into a shirt or a purse, so fearful were they of throwing out a cross of any sort. Neighbors thought she was protesting the new regime, or that she was defending it, mindful of the goings-on in the capital. But all the while Josefina thought that these palm crosses would call down the angel like a lighthouse beacon, and so she didn't concern herself with the trials of politicians and soldiers.

Josefina's constant search made Abel nervous. He'd snap his fingers in front of her nose when she was lost in thought. He'd suddenly say that he wanted to take a walk or mow the lawn or read Soledad a story if the very word "angel" escaped her lips. So it was that Abel took his mission to save Josefina to heart. He realized that he was the angel of the sergeant's letter, and he began to mold himself in that image.

The following Sunday Abel appeared at the house, dressed in white linen, ready for Mass again. To him, Josefina looked like a familiar portrait at the moment, one that is seen in countless brochures, in textbooks, in dreams. She sat in the yellow infant light of the morning. Her white skirt lay in soft folds around her, like a silken cushion. In her hands was a crinkled sheet of paper, striped with disciplined penmanship.

The image was soon interrupted when Josefina saw Abel in the doorway. She quickly hid the letter in her hand, palming it like a magician who is used to hiding cards in his grip. Again, Soledad was pushed into the old "church" dress, and again Josefina wore her veil of black lace, the Spanish fan hanging from her wrist. But the procession to the church of San Matéo was different. As before, Soledad walked with her mother, who whispered rules into her ear to calm her nerves, Abel walked behind, and farther behind still, was Lalo, kicking pebbles off the road and sending them like missiles at Abel's ankles. Once inside the church, the scene repeated itself as before with the exception of the comportment of Camila Flores, who spent a good portion of the Mass waving a gloved hand at Soledad, a misdeed which led to a harsh slap on the thigh from the old woman who sat beside her.

After the Mass, Soledad and Camila met underneath a large tree in the garden, so covered with vines that the trunk was no longer visible. Soledad was in awe of this girl, whose plump arms were so different from her thin ones, whose skin was so light that the bluish veins around her eyes could be seen. Camila poured her rosary from one hand to the other, the crystal beads clicking prettily.

"What do you think of the new president?" she asked. "I heard he is very ugly."

"I don't know," Soledad said, and waved the topic away. She hadn't yet discovered the intricacies of dirty politics, the chatter that was the national pastime.

"Where do you live? Is it far from here?" Camila asked, changing the subject and leaning her elbows on her knees, her chin caught on the tip of one finger.

"Not far," was her answer. Soledad didn't want Camila to come to El Cotorro just yet. She was old enough to understand shame and the lines that were drawn between the likes of Camila and herself.

"Then I'll visit." By now Camila had Soledad's grasped hands, the rosary beads pressing into her palm and marking them.

"I'm not sure you can, I mean, I don't know how you . . ."

"*Por favor,* Soledad. If you let me visit and promise to be my friend, I'll show you my secret." This last was whispered, and Soledad could not stop her eyes from widening and her mouth from watering. She nodded her head and Camila released her hands. Slowly, Camila began to unbutton the back of her dress, first the collar, then the back. She pulled the dress down over her shoulders and pointed at a broad scar high on her chest. The skin folded over itself, like the pleats in a skirt, and in places it formed tiny ruts, like a dry stream, running over her left shoulder.

"When I was a baby I crawled onto a puddle of hot tar while a hole in our roof was being patched. My father waited too long to take me to the doctor, and so now I have this to show for it," she said, and then: "Oh, Soledad, don't cry. I don't remember it at all. Can we be friends now? Now that you know my secret?"

But Soledad could not stop crying or pulling her own skirt up to wipe at her nose. The mournful romance of such a story did not escape Soledad, and she was enamored with the idea that the secret was now hers, too. Her loud sniffling caught the attention of Lalo, who jumped out from behind the tree and stood transfixed, looking at the girl with her dress half off. He thought how different she was from the girls at the theater, and did not see the scar at all but a swatch of ivory skin instead. Camila tried putting her arms into the dress, but could not.

"Lalo, don't look!" Soledad screamed at her brother, but he could not help himself. And he stood there and watched as Camila dressed, kissed Soledad on the cheek, their tears mingling, and ran through the church garden.

Camila Flores lived alone with a woman named Doña Amparo. The affair of the tar was not quite the way that Camila knew it. In fact, it was well known among the adults of El Cotorro and Mar Lindo, because it was a thing they could not forget, that Camila's father had poured the tar over his daughter purposely. Even Josefina had heard the story one day at the doctor's office and now remembered the report and gruesome pictures of the bandaged child in the newspaper so many years ago. There was nowhere Camila could go without whispers in her wake—first of the "accident" and then of her beauty. Soon thereafter, Doña Amparo, who had no relatives to speak of and lived alone in a large home in Mar Lindo, took the scarred infant in. Camila grew up believing that her parents had perished in a fire when she was an infant, and Doña Amparo, who loved the girl as her own, even paid the cemetery to place a pair of false gravestones on a hilly patch of grass with the names of the parents, so that Camila would have a place to bring them flowers and kneel and speak to them. What really happened to Camila's mother was not known, but her father was sent east to Oriente province by a judge in Mar Lindo to live out his life in a sanatorium.

The following weekend, Doña Amparo and her charge appeared at the house in El Cotorro. Camila and Soledad clasped hands and ran to the little bedroom that Soledad shared with her brother. In the parlor, Josefina asked Doña Amparo to sit down while she made coffee. The old woman sat on the worn sofa uncomfortably, shifting her weight back and forth, keeping her tense arms on her lap for fear of having any further contact with the dingy couch. Josefina returned with the coffee in the porcelain cups she had saved from Vedado after the sergeant's death. Though several of the handles had broken off in the rush, three were spared any injury, and, luckily for Josefina, there was only one Doña Amparo.

Neither of the women spoke until Doña Amparo fixed her eyes on a photograph of Soledad and Lalo, the frame's glass cracked down the center in a thin line that was visible in only certain kinds of light.

"Where is your husband?" the Doña asked.

It was an unfair question, Josefina thought. She had not asked, after all, about Camila's own misfortune. Josefina cleared her throat and pulled a thread from her skirt. "He is away. Working, you understand."

"But I saw him at church with you. The man with the red hair."

Josefina felt herself grow very cold, and then, with a smile, said, "He is my brother. The children's uncle."

Amparo seemed satisfied. She pushed herself deeper into the seat. "And how many children do you have, señora?" Doña Amparo asked, refusing to address Josefina with her name. Josefina found that she could not look into the old woman's eyes, so hard was the stare.

"Only the two you see there. Lalo is sixteen now."

"Where is he?"

"In the bedroom with the girls, I suppose." At this, the old woman stood with a speed and agility that did not seem to belong to her. "Señora, what is your son's full name please?"

Josefina was startled and rose also, "Eulalio Miguel Concepción . . . but why are you so angry? What has he done?"

Doña Amparo left the parlor and stood in the entryway of the hall, peering down the darkness and listening for the laughter of the girls. She straightened, formed her hands into a funnel, and placing them around her mouth yelled, "Eulalio Miguel, come immediately."

From his corner in the bedroom, where he had been busy pretending to do his arithmetic while studying Camila's legs, shot out in a V before her, and her shapely white arms as she played jacks, Lalo looked up. He had thought, for days now, of what he had seen of her in the churchyard. The scar, though ugly, did not mar her loveliness for him, and he often found himself wondering if she would lift her dress again, but only for him someday.

Doña Amparo called again. Camila, who not only was unaware of her origin, but furthermore believed that Doña Amparo was her great-aunt on her father's side, said, "That is my *tía* calling. You had better go." Lalo ran down the hall, stopping right before the old woman, one of his feet planted directly onto her right toe. She stepped back, stretching her arm out toward him, as if inviting him into her own parlor, in her own house. Lalo did not have a chance to sit down before Doña Amparo began.

"When my niece"—she, too, had come to believe the lie she had formed—"is in your house, you will be so kind as to not be alone with her."

Josefina, reddening with every syllable the woman uttered, as if the words themselves pricked her, interjected, "But Doña, they are only small girls, children."

Turning on her heel, Doña suddenly faced Josefina. "How old is your daughter?"

"Soledad is only eleven."

"And Camila is thirteen. She is no longer a child, and he knows it." Amparo's starched shirt tightened around her breasts with each heavy intake of breath. Lalo, who had been near the front door, turned the knob and walked out, without saying another word. He decided then that he did not want to see the little house in El Cotorro again.

"Shall I take my niece home?" Doña Amparo asked, but Josefina could only sigh and consider how such a friendship would be beneficial to her daughter.

"No, Doña, it will not happen again," she said.

Finally at ease, the old woman sat on the sofa, interlaced her fingers and cleared her throat.

18

Lalo stood on the edge of El Cotorro's town limits, shaded underneath twin palms that had long ago twirled around each other in a lover's embrace. Few cars went by on the dirt road, and each one sped up as Lalo raised his hand and lifted his thumb. He didn't care where he was taken, as long as it was far away from rules, from decorum, from ancient aunts. If he hesitated for a moment here and there, it was because he thought of Camila, of the girl who didn't laugh, but smiled often, who always looked fresh when the weather was hottest. Though he longed for someone to touch, the desire to get away was stronger. He could not yet find a balance between anger and yearning, between the fury of being only sixteen and the itch of desire.

He had stopped counting cars once the number exceeded fifteen, but soon after, a sputtering black automobile stopped a few yards ahead of Lalo, and a corpulent, woolly arm flashed out of the window and beckoned him over. Lalo approached slowly, watching the driver's reflection in the mirror develop as he approached. First he saw the bristly arm, and then a bright red shirt embroidered with white roses, a patchy beard, and then finally, a face. Lalo stopped again once he could recognize Duarte's face. It had been almost three years since Duarte had sent Lalo sprawling on the floor with one swipe. Lalo's hand went up to his chin instinctively, and he rubbed the tiny scar there.

"Come, Lalo, come," Duarte called. "You have nothing to fear. Times are good for men like us. The casinos are bigger than ever. Millions of dollars, Lalito. They could be yours."

Lalo walked around the car and approached the passenger side. Duarte was the same as he had been three years ago, except now he was heavier and his cheeks burned with a rosiness that had little to do with the sun and more to do with the bottle of rum he consumed every day.

"This is God's will that I've found you, so accidentally, Lalito," Duarte said, and smiled to reveal yet another new-sprung feature on his face—a silver incisor.

"Do you have work for me again?" Lalo asked, his hand already poised on the door handle.

"*Sí, sí.*" Duarte opened the door and dusted the leather seat so that Lalo could sit. "But the business is different. The girls, Fatima, Rosamaria, you know the rest, became sick. Eh, syphillis it was. You understand?" Lalo nodded. "Things have changed. You'll see."

They drove the rest of the day into Havana, and where Lalo thought they would turn onto the road that led to the Teatro Martí, Duarte went in the opposite direction, toward the heart of the capital. He parked the car on the side of the street, between two other automobiles just like his, and walked to an apartment building, sections of it draped in black for fumigation. The effect was that the building looked like an old woman, cloaked in a widow's dress, so disheveled that a thigh here, a breast there, was exposed to the public. The staircase was the only source of color in the black-clothed building. Its steps were made of orange stone, painted with thin feathery lines to resemble marble. It had a tone like rust, and Lalo watched as the color rubbed onto the soles of Duarte's new shoes. He looked for the million-dollar casinos that the new president had sanctioned. Lalo had imagined, on the way there, that he might be a blackjack dealer, or hired as the boy who filled the slots. Maybe he'd be able to smuggle a few coins into his own pockets. But there were no lights, no American tourists. They were clearly in the wrong part of town.

Lalo and Duarte reached an unmarked door. Duarte knocked once and said loudly, *"La mano negra."* The door opened, and Lalo was led inside. The apartment was stifling, since all the windows were shut. The refreshing sea breezes coming from the newly opened door pushed the screen against the glass, and made Lalo's longing for cool air all the harder to bear. On various tables scattered around the room were an odd assortment of items. On one, a pile of fur coats had been thrown, on another, gold and silver watches were arranged by size. Other tables displayed new cane suitcases, emptied, the leather straps polished and softened for exhibition. Every so often, the words *la mano negra* were heard, and a young man would rush in with his arms wrapped around his belly. He would unroll his shirt and two wallets would tumble out, or sometimes a shower of coins and loose bills. He would nod then at Duarte and rush out again. The process was repeated with a dozen or so different boys, and the opening and slamming of the door were the only draft that entered the room to stir and cool the heat.

"This is perfect work for you, son," Duarte said as he opened the wallets that had just been dropped off.

Lalo leaned forward over the table and said, "But I am not a . . ."

"Thief?" Duarte answered. "I know that. Your job is the same as last time. You bring in the customers. You, *mi amigo,* advertise for us." Again a bundle of leaflets was thrown into Lalo's hands, and again, strict directions were given. "You are to tell them to answer, *la mano negra,* whenever asked. No women are allowed here. Ladies have big mouths, you know. Make sure you say that."

Lalo soon found his way back to the Malecón where he was happy to see that little had changed. The flamenco dancers were still there, except now they danced farther north and had a little girl play the accordion for them. The old vendors were all there, too, and the ones who recognized Lalo moved away from him whenever he came near. Lalo could no longer pick out which tourist would make a good customer. In the past, he had been an expert at reading faces. The men who most yearned for a woman had a quickness about the eye. They never looked at any one thing for very long, but let their eyes dart about from one place to the next. Sometimes they fiddled with a seashell found along the way, while others dug their hands into their pockets and rubbed at the material inside. Lalo always found them easy to pick out. But this he found difficult. Which of these men could possibly need a fur coat, he thought, or someone else's suitcase, even if it is very nice and cheap?

It took several hours before Lalo chose someone to speak to. He had tried a few times, finding one man's face "too honest," another's "too angry," and yet a third "too cowardly." One gentleman, dressed in a clean but not altogether expensive suit, had been taking turns speaking to the vendors for some time. Each would nod his head and shrug his shoulders at the stranger's mysterious question. The flamenco dancers stopped their twirling for a moment to speak to the man, and, as Lalo watched, they pointed their slim, elastic fingers at Lalo. The man turned, looked at Lalo, and smiled. He ran to him, and Lalo took several wide steps backward.

"So you deal in women?" the man asked, catching his breath from his short sprint.

Lalo noted the man's fluent Spanish, the island intonations, and guessed this was no tourist. "No, señor, no ladies. But if you are interested in purchasing quality items, follow me."

The man trailed behind Lalo all the way to the apartment building. Whenever Lalo turned to make sure he was there, the man smiled and said, "Go on. I'm right behind you." Once they began climbing the orange steps, Lalo gave the man instructions.

"Say '*la mano negra*' after you knock. Tell them Lalo brought you here," he said, then pointed to the appropriate door. "I must go, señor. Enjoy yourself." Lalo then spun around and proceeded down the stairs.

"Wait, boy," the man whispered, and came very close to Lalo. "I have a secret for you."

Lalo cocked his head to one side so that the man might reveal what he had to say. Instead of whispering, however, the man began to shout into Lalo's ear: "My name is Subinspector Milo. You are under arrest for trafficking stolen goods and the selling of women for sexual . . ." The officer continued to speak, and soon Lalo was facedown on the steps. His cheek rubbed against the stone and drew orange paint from its surface. Lalo said nothing as he was handcuffed and led away, because he found he could not speak. He followed Subinspector Milo down the Malecón, past the flamenco dancers and peanut vendors, with the sides of his face streaked in orange, like the painted-on flush of a silent clown.

Mi Hija,

My brother and I were twelve when we left Spain. Francisco did not decide to come with me until the very last moment, and even then, only because my father had beat him for the first time, over the matter of a house cat that Francisco had tied up like a fresh kill, as if he were some ancient hunter. When my father found that the cat's back was broken and its back legs would not even twitch when touched, he beat Francisco with a belt. Olga Maria cried and cried but could not stop the beating. My own mother had died the year before of a hemorrhage in the brain while she washed the floor of the main house, and so she could not stop Olga Maria from trying to hit me with a hot iron to revenge the beating that Francisco had received. I left the Canaries, away from my stepmother, for Cuba, like Don Quixote on an adventure. I ran away, too, from the final image of my mother. *Ay,* Josefina, her face was so white in the coffin, a pink stain on the side of her mouth where the blood had trickled so mercilessly.

I remember throwing a couple of shirts and underwear into an old carpetbag. From behind me, a pair of Francisco's pants was tossed into the bag. There was your uncle, his arms full of clothes, stuffing his things along with mine. My brother, saying, *"Me voy contigo,"* I'm coming with you. His eyes were red and raw from crying. Your uncle followed me to the port, boarding the boat with me and picking at the welts that the belt had left on his arm.

When we neared Cuba, the first thing we saw from a distance was the yellow and red flag of Spain flapping over every building and on every mast. I remember Francisco saying, *"Ay,* Antonio, the ship has turned around. We are back home,"* with such a quiver of fear in his voice that I thought he might cry.

Once in Cuba, Francisco was frightened at the sight of the thin sailors, cursing at their crates full of flipping, writhing fish and at the dirt and vapors that surrounded the docks. We boarded the ship with the papers I had stolen from my father, embossed with gold stamps, and with the money that Francisco stole from Olga Maria. I would have loved to embrace him then and call him brother, but I did not.

At dockside we were met by a young man, sinewy like Lorenzo, I remember. All the men looked that way, as if they had never tasted the food—fruit, meat, fish—that lay packed in boxes all around them. The impression I had of Cuba then is like the one I have of El Cotorro—of hunger and affliction. The man was a soldier from the Army of Liberation, we later learned. He gave us each a stalk of sugar cane to suck as we walked in that oppressive heat, and we followed him because there was nowhere else for us to go.

My hand aches, *hijita*, from arthritis, I suppose. Expect another letter soon. I will say a prayer for you.

Tu Papá

19

orenzo Concepción slept while he rode a bus back to El Co-torro. Though he did not see it, the forests of palms that rushed by outside were glowing from a fire that had started deep within the mass of trees and vines. The fiery lights coming from the blaze were broken by the trunks of the palms, so that the effect was a flashing that lit the aluminum sides of the bus for an instant, then darkened, only to flare up once more. The passing light revealed a blackened eye and a lip that was gashed nearly in two, causing Lorenzo to sleep with his mouth open, his tongue flicking at the dried blood occasionally, then recoiling at the taste. As a result of his appearance, Lorenzo sat alone in his aisle on the bus, while the other passengers pressed in close to each other. Some even chose to stand rather than share a seat with him. Halfway home, Lorenzo finally pulled his legs onto the seat beside him, and reclined very comfortably.

His injuries had occurred on a small tourist boat that sailed around Cuba's southern tip, on which Lorenzo found work as a steward. On this particular boat, the deck was cleared out and the floor was waxed for dancing. Benches lined the rail for the sight-seers, most of them American ladies who slipped tips into his hand suggestively, rubbing the coin into his palm, and American gentlemen, who huffed and cleared their throats when Lorenzo brought them their drinks, and said, *"Gracias,"* in grating accents, then laughed admiringly at their own nimble management of a new language. It was a gentleman such as this who dealt Lorenzo the worst of the blows.

The day had been soggy with rain, and the passengers herded themselves onto the lower deck. The people swarmed the windows to catch a glance of the view for which their dollars had paid, but were soon disappointed at the haze that developed on all the panes. The more inventive passengers busied themselves with drawing on the windows, their fingers smudging the wetness off the glass. The rest simply sat and pouted, ordering rounds of whiskey and filling the air with such an amount of smoke from their cigars that it became difficult to tell who was who.

As Lorenzo pushed through the lower deck, his hand gripping the pocket in which he kept his tips closed, he felt a woman ring her hands around his neck and lay her head on his shoulder. Her breath smelled like cigarettes, and through the smoke, Lorenzo could see that a sea green tinted the woman's cheeks. "Benjamin, honey," she said in English, the words sounding like the gurgling of rain as it hits a puddle that is already thick with mud and garbage, "please get me to some clear air. This is all too much for me." Lorenzo understood little, but he did sense that the fondness with which this woman cradled his neck and closed her eyes in his arms meant that she was somehow mistaken. And yet, he was aware of a scent other than smoke hanging about this woman. Her breath smelled like rum, her arms like peaches, as did her hair, and he could feel the firm youth of her body against his.

His gesture was a quick one, an almost imperceptible one. As the poor woman hung from his neck, gagging every so often and puffing her cheeks, Lorenzo began to nuzzle his own cheek against the soft hair on her arms and then let three short kisses drop on the sweet-scented limb. The woman revived a little, her hand flying up to touch the mouth that kissed her. In the place of the full clean lip she had loved for over a year, she found a thin mustache, and with this odd discovery, the woman lifted her eyes to see Lorenzo. She pushed him squarely in the throat and began to scream.

It was all over rather quickly. A man about Lorenzo's size, brandishing a brass-knobbed cane high over his head, pinned Lorenzo to the floor and struck him with a closed fist. Several other men circled round, pushing their women out of the circle, and issued random kicks to Lorenzo's legs, back, and chest. Once the beating subsided, the passengers cleared a path for the bartender and the captain, who lifted Lorenzo by the arms and dragged him down into the engine room to nurse his injuries.

There had been little else that changed his mind. Lorenzo decided that it was time to go home, kiss his wife, tousle the hair on his children's heads, and remain there until he was too old to remember life another way. He would, of course, have to make it up to Josefina. And so, before boarding the bus, he bought a watch from a salesman at the station, its face carved from mother-of-pearl, the golden links of the bracelet coming together in a silver clasp.

When he arrived in El Cotorro, he walked straight away to the little house he had rented so long ago, twirling the watch around his finger as one would an odd bit of string tied together in a loop. Inside the house, Lorenzo was disappointed at not finding his children rushing up to greet him, knocking him over with their tumbling embraces. He was aware of the possibility that while he was away, they might have grown too old for such affection. He did, however, hear his wife talking in the kitchen.

"I haven't seen him for two days," he heard her say, sniffling and coughing.

"Two days? *Por Dios,* have you notified the police?" A man's voice suddenly echoed throughout the house.

"No. But I am writing to my papá, Abel. He will find my son."

Abel held Josefina close and whispered in her ear, "And where will you send the letter, *mi querer?* Does this ghost have an address?"

Lorenzo, listening in the parlor, dropped the watch onto the floor, which stopped the hands from ever moving again, and went into the kitchen. There he found his wife, leaning over a sink filled with milk-soaked glasses, wiping at her tears with milky fingers so that the limpid drops that fell from her eyes were soon cloudy like the dishwater. The man was large and shirtless. His belly, covered in red, wiry hair, protruded over his belt. Lorenzo saw him in profile only, because the man now had his hand on Josefina's shoulder. His nose was fat and bulbous, though not particularly crimson in the way of a drunkard, and his hair hung about his eyes and reached almost below his neck where Lorenzo thought a collar should have been.

"*¿Qué es esto?*" Lorenzo asked, appearing on Josefina's left side and staring across her face and at the strange man.

Josefina straightened, and at that moment, her tears seemed to multiply, and her little nose flared. "Nothing, Renzo, nothing. He is the . . ."

"A carpenter. I came to replace the timber on the front porch. It's termite-ridden." Abel Santana lifted his hands, his palms facing the ceiling, the eyebrows arched in innocence, his shoulders lifted in the same upward motion of the rest of his features.

"And were you going to ask the police to rid the house of termites?" Lorenzo asked in the caustic way he had used all his life.

"Renzo," Josefina interrupted, "Lalo has not been home for days. He's lost. I've lost our son." With this, Josefina flattened herself against her husband, wiping her wet little nose on his shoulder. Lorenzo did not circle his arms around her. In fact, he raised one in the air and pointed it to the door saying, *"Sal de aquí,"* to Abel. Josefina adjusted her face on her husband's shoulder to watch her lover walk out of the kitchen, lift his shirt from where it lay in a heap near the door, and exit the house, stomping his feet on the porch so that the wood creaked as if it did, indeed, have termites. Lorenzo released his wife and looked at her, turned her face, and examined her cheeks and neck.

"This time I'm staying," he told her and went outside, calling Soledad's name. Lorenzo found his daughter in the shade of a mango tree that was still too young to bear fruit. She was playing with a doll given to her recently by Camila. The doll wore a tiny dress of wine-colored satin, with cuffs that turned up at the wrists in a different color and pearl buttons that cut across the bodice, their placement marking off the pleats in the skirt. The doll's dress was prettier than anything she'd ever worn.

"Mi niña," Lorenzo said, and Soledad looked up, dropping the doll into a small dirt mound that Soledad had decorated with shells and marbles.

"Papá!" she cried and threw herself into his arms. He kissed her neck and cheek, and she sniffed at his collar for the perfumes that, according to her mamá, always lingered. It had been three years since she had seen him in life, but in her dreams, Lorenzo was always there, and so when her father came outside, out into the bright light of day, she knew him at once. Her memory did not fail her.

"Did Mamá tell you about Lalo?" Soledad asked after being put down and patted on the head.

"Sí."

"Then how will we find him?"

"We simply will."

Soon thereafter, Lorenzo began knocking on the neighbors' doors, with Soledad behind him and Josefina at home, sobbing over the bland meal she was cooking. Many of the women around the pueblo would not open the door to Lorenzo. Instead, they would stare at his bruised visage through heavily curtained windows and ask, *"¿Qué quieres?"* Once his story unfolded, the women either apologized for not being able to help, or sent their husbands out to form a search party. Despite what they knew about him, that he had abandoned the family, that the boy was troubled, that the woman was sleeping with the butcher from the market, they could not deny his request for help. If he were to ask for help years later, when the revolution had turned neighbors into spies, brothers into enemies, the response would have been a different, colder one.

By late afternoon, a parade of men followed Lorenzo throughout El Cotorro, sticking their heads into abandoned houses, breaking open the locks to the school with hammers and calling out, "Lalo, where are you?" in their deep voices that bounced off the houses and resonated in the quietude of the night. Soledad thought the assembly a delicious array, and enjoyed the men who patted her small shoulders, saying, "We'll find your brother." She had tried to keep the image of her brother foremost in her mind, fully aware that the very reason for the search party was to find him, but it was a difficult task. There was far too much to keep her mind occupied, like counting the number of bald men as opposed to the hairy ones, noting how the young men lagged behind and did not do much searching, but talked politics instead. She reveled in her father's nervous demeanor, which caused him to reach his arm out and grab Soledad, holding her close as if he feared he might lose sight of her next.

The dawn came slowly, but still it came, coloring the roads in its red brilliance. The men, sleepy and saddened, walked home feebly, giving Lorenzo a few words of encouragement, each of them sure that Lalo would "appear soon enough." Lorenzo took his daughter in his arms, and her little head hung down and bobbed with every lumbering step that her father took. At home, he put her to bed, not bothering with the delicacies of undressing and covering her with a blanket. He, too, went to bed that morning, passing his wife who still sat in the kitchen over a now cold stove, whimpering.

As Josefina cried, her mind would not focus on either Abel or Lorenzo. One moment she sobbed for the man she had lost, aching already for his large hands that trolled her body for warmth. The next, her tears were a relief that Lorenzo was finally, solidly home. She had missed his chaotic affection, even his bursts of anger, and she wondered whether she was one of those masochistic women, who love only men who swagger and brawl like apes. Josefina hunched over the sink a long time until her back began to throb. Sluggish, she unpacked Lorenzo's bag and began to mend the holes in his underwear, in his socks, picking out loose buttons from his pockets. This, she found, made the torrent of tears, the yearning for two men at once, stop for a while. Dully, she realized she had no tears for her lost son.

At noon the next day, both Lorenzo and Soledad were still asleep. Abel Santana, who had spent the morning searching the pueblo and the neighboring town of Mar Lindo for Lalo, appeared at the kitchen window. He tapped on it lightly to get Josefina's attention, and when she saw his face, she held her hands to her mouth and ran outside and embraced him. The bout of crying had left her with a nose that was chafed from so much wiping, the skin peeling off in dried flakes.

"So now I've lost you, too," she said, and began crying again in such a violent flow of tears that Abel was taken aback.

"Do you mean that he is staying?" he asked.

"He says he won't leave me again."

The two embraced. Josefina wanted to remember the feel of his chest against her face but found she could not keep hold of the moment. She mumbled something to him, something about never finding another, something that she thought was incredibly stupid, and then a sound coming from inside the house made them separate with a jolt. Abel pushed her toward the front door and she stumbled, pausing to catch her breath because the sobs were coming again. Abel, however, was not yet ready to leave the Concepción domicile. Crouching down, he crept to the back of the house, and looked into the window of the room where he knew that Soledad slept. Again he tapped on the window, and the child woke. Through blurred eyes, she saw that it was the butcher and she slid open the window. Abel reached his hand into the house and passed his thumb over her lip, prohibiting her speech.

"You will see me again, child. For now, *adiós*."

"But where are you go . . ." Again he pressed his thumb on her mouth to quiet her.

"Adiós, niña." And Abel Santana dissolved into the trees outside.

Soledad sat on her bed and gathered her bedsheets around her neck. She suddenly felt cold and afraid, partly because the window was still left open, and also because the hurried whispers that hauled her from sleep were like trespassers in her home. And as she sat there, frozen with what Abel had said to her, her mamá appeared in the doorway. She entered quickly, turning to close the door and shoving the back end of her shoe into the crevice under the door like a wedge. Josefina clambered over her daughter's rigid body and shut the window. It was then that the light shone on her face, and Soledad could see that her mother had been crying, except it was not like the calm, almost theatrical, crying she had seen before. This was frantic and genuine.

"Know, *mi hija,* that I love your father. But you must not tell your papá about us, about Abel, do you hear me?" Josefina had her daughter's arms clasped by the wrist, like fleshy shackles. "Never say his name again, to anyone," and now she covered her daughter's mouth, as if to seal in the name forever. "Or I will write to your grandfather and tell him to take you away, do you understand?" Soledad stared as her mother stood and began straightening her daughter's bedclothes, going to each corner and tucking the sheets in tightly, all the while saying, "You must be quiet, quiet like a tiny rabbit, eh?" Her limbs shook as she moved out of the room, lifting a shaking finger to her lips as one final reminder to her daughter. When she left the room and closed the door, Soledad felt that the walls themselves were shaking, too.

That afternoon a telegram sent to El Cotorro was delivered into Lorenzo's hands. They hadn't called, Lorenzo knew, because they assumed that *guajiro* families from El Cotorro did not own telephones. The telegram detailed the arrest of twelve Havana thieves and required two hundred and fifty pesos for the release of an Eulalio Miguel Concepción. Lorenzo reached the subinspector's office by that evening. Inside, a phonograph played a jazz tune, and the aluminum shelves vibrated and accompanied the tinny sound of the record. When he pushed open the door, a surge of cigar smoke met him, and through the haze, he could see the silhouette of his son, cut across by the vertical bars of a jail cell.

"*¿Lalito, qué has hecho?*" he asked, blinking through the smoke and stepping into the office. He could see Lalo better as he moved closer, and noticed his son wrapping his arms around his head when he heard his father's voice. Subinspector Milo stepped out from a tiny room filled with books and loose newspapers, in the back of the office.

"What he has done, señor, is sell off silly girls in the street and corrupt our country and our president Batista's good name with thievery," Subinspector Milo answered. "He allowed himself to be used by a criminal. Your son is very stupid."

Lorenzo, after his ordeal on the boat and his search for his son, looked like a crumpled newspaper, faded and illegible. The lip and the faded clothing strengthened the subinspector's ideas about people from the pueblos, and led him to say, "Since you do not have the fine, we will have to transport your son to the Rural Guard and let them decide what to do with him. Then, you will have to . . ."

Once the subinspector was done talking, he looked up from his papers and saw that the boy and his father were gone. All that was left of them were two hundred and fifty pesos fluttering, landing near the subinspector's feet, and the echoes of their footsteps, the father leading his son out into the rainy evening.

They arrived home the next morning, after a long bus trip that cost Lorenzo twenty-five more pesos for two tickets. The house was dark, except for a tiny glass lamp that burned in the corner of the parlor, lighting up the wall and casting odd shadows against it, so that the inside of the house looked, all at once, as if occupied by still, smoky spirits. Lalo could hear the rustling of his sister in the bedroom, readying herself for school, and the vigorous snoring of his mother.

Lorenzo had not spoken to his son since they left the office in Havana. Neither had Lalo spoken. He had thought of Duarte the entire night and still could not rid himself of Duarte's image. It was Soledad who interrupted his meditation, rushing past him in the morning darkness, unaware of her brother's huddled figure in the corner. She tugged at her stockings as she ran and yelled to her sleeping mother, "I am going to Camila's house after school, Mamá. Don't forget." Josefina mumbled, and Soledad ran out the door.

His sister's words jarred Lalo from his stupor. The image of the hairy Duarte, imprisoned somewhere in Havana, was replaced by that of Camila. He imagined that one day she might fall in love with him, and then there would be no need to rush off to the city and sell whores and rob tourists. She could buy him whatever it was he wanted with her generous allowances. He would have money to spare and a beautiful girl besides. With that thought, Lalo finally found slumber.

20

The sergeant did not return to Mona Linde or to his work at the park. He had sold the gold cuff links for twenty-five dollars and rode the city buses all day, asking passengers who understood his broken English whether they had any work for him. He avoided the park where he had worked in case Mona Linde would come looking for him. To pass the time, he wrote letters to Josefina, sitting on park benches or in the shade of a billboard featuring a plump woman in a blue bathing suit with a smear of thick tanning lotion on her thigh. On the third day of his wandering, on a bus bound for South Miami, seated by a window that jostled in its aluminum frame, the sergeant saw a familiar face reflected in the glass. Chelo clapped his hands onto the sergeant's shoulders. "Come, my friend," he said, and slid across the vinyl seat and made room.

The sergeant sighed. "She's been looking for you," Chelo said, "in and out of Circle Park all week. When she asks me where you've been, I tell her I don't know." The sergeant listened and nodded, not surprised at Mona's change of heart, and then, as if to echo the sergeant's own thoughts, Chelo said, "She needs you, my friend."

"But I do not love her," the sergeant lied. "I loved my wife, and I love my daughter, but not that *americana.*"

"Liar," Chelo said, and the sergeant did not respond.

The next stop was on Le Jeune Avenue, and Chelo stood and stretched, the smell of dirt on him, moist and rich. Without speaking, the sergeant followed Chelo off the bus.

They walked two blocks to Chelo's apartment. It was a two-story building painted green, connected to other green buildings by covered walkways. Each building had a large creature made of mosaic tiles on the side of the wall. "I live in Dragonfly," Chelo said, pointing at an orange and yellow dragonfly of glass and stone. One of its wings was half gone, the stump jagged where the mosaic had come off. Inside the apartment, the smell of tomato sauce was strong, and whenever the air-conditioning started up, the smell became stronger.

Chelo washed his hands in the kitchen sink and put a pot of water on to boil. He threw a box of linguini on the counter, because it was the easiest thing to make, because Cuba was so far away with its rice and beans and salty stews. Chelo picked up the phone, dialed a number, and whispered into the receiver. The sergeant watched and picked at his sparse beard, growing coarse and white now on his chin. He remembered how he had been embarrassed in the police force as a twenty-two-year-old whose cheeks were still smooth and unblemished by even a single hair. The other officers patted his face, and the more daring ones called him Antonia and kissed his cheek. Even now, after three days, he had but a little stubble on his chin.

Chelo sat down on the sofa next to the sergeant. The sergeant looked at his friend, at the fleshy jowls and the puckered lips. He wondered whether Abel looked anything like this half brother. He thought of Josefina then and the infrequency with which Abel had been calling. He drew up his courage and asked, "Chelo, has your brother betrayed me?"

Chelo stood and lifted his eyebrows in surprise. He knew that his brother, Abel, had made a career off women like the sergeant's daughter. He looked after them and fended off violent husbands and, in return, he found a home, a bed, and a woman indebted enough to keep him company at night. Abel was a good man, an honest man, but the sergeant, who sat there, his eyes rimmed in red and the fine wispy tips of his hair trembling atop his head, would not understand. Nor would Chelo tell him of what Abel had said in a letter a month before—that Lorenzo had returned and kicked him out of the house.

"My brother, Abel, has kept your bastard son-in-law away, hasn't he?" The sergeant shrugged his shoulders. He did not know if any of it was true. For all he knew, his letters to Josefina never reached her.

"He has," Chelo said, angry now. "What a selfless person, *mi hermano,* Abel. He is selfless like Miss Linde, who you steal from and who you left alone in that house," Chelo said, eager to take the focus off his brother.

The sergeant shifted and rose from his seat. The two looked like old roosters poised to fight, the kind that are so old that the owners throw them into the pit simply for the blood sport, to make enough money to buy a new animal. It was then that the doorbell rang. Before Chelo could turn toward it, the wooden door creaked open. Mona Linde appeared, framed in the afternoon sun. She wore a purple hat on her head, with a delicate lavender veil and a peacock feather. Her suit was new, the sergeant noticed, and a small tag from the department store still hung from the hem. It flipped and swung in the breeze. When Chelo called earlier, she took off her nightgown, tearing a button that had been hanging by a thread, and put on the new suit and hat.

The sergeant stepped back, looked at Chelo and sighed again. "Call your brother," he whispered. "Tell him that I'll send the next payment soon." Taking Mona by the hand, he pulled her outside of Chelo's apartment and toward the bus stop.

On the bus ride home, Mona released the peacock feather hat from her head, the long hat pins resting on her lap. She laid her head against the sergeant's shoulder and whispered to him, "No more stealing, my love. What I have is yours. Take what you want, and I will not ask why." The sergeant took in the scent of her hair, lavender soap, and tea, and thought how much he missed the rose perfume he used to buy for Josefina. She used to splash it onto the carpets in her room, and even onto Regla when she was not looking, so that the old woman smelled like a garden. But lavender turned the sergeant's stomach, and he breathed through his mouth the rest of the way home.

The sergeant explained at last, as best he could, about his daughter, leaving out Chelo and Abel, saying that the money he got from Mona's jewelry was sent to feed his grandchildren. Mona had cried at the telling of it, and it was as if she cried for herself, for the time after Jim died and she had been so alone, with no one from afar worrying about her. At church on Sundays, she prayed for Lalo and Soledad and Josefina, the names mangled in English, but the prayer was earnest. She was nearing seventy, like the sergeant, and her heart accepted the names of the children as if they were her own grandchildren. She longed to send them Christmas cards and back-to-school outfits, but the sergeant forbade it.

During the months that followed, the sergeant stepped up the pace of his letter writing. Nearly every day he sent a letter to Abel to be delivered to Josefina. He never wrote about Miami, about the United States or Mona. How would he explain his failure at her doorstep? That he had longed to hold her again, but that her words had pounded him like a wave? He had been good at keeping the secrets of his childhood from her. He had a knack for the art of imprecision. He imagined Lorenzo laughing when he learned how the sergeant had run away, like a wet-nosed boy. *No,* he thought, *it is better that my place remains a secret for now.* The first letter he wrote after returning to Mona's house read:

> *Mi Hija,*
>
> I know that the children are going hungry. If I could send you ten hams and a thousand pounds of rice, I would. But from here, there is little I can do but give you wisdom and direction. If I believed in old Regla's witchery, I would have asked her to dissolve Lorenzo from your life with bloodless goats and honey baths. But I do not believe, or else I would have become a shepherd and a beekeeper.
>
> I will write again tomorrow, *mi niña.*
>
> *Tu Papá*

Another letter was written that same afternoon, after the sergeant had found another stamp. He suppressed a laugh when he found the tiny thing, brittle from its long place in the drawer, and ran to the kitchen table and composed another tiny missive, the memories of the riot in El Cotorro still crowding his mind:

> *Mi Hija,*
>
> Have I told you about the Plaza Perla? When the bench struck my head, I imagined Lorenzo was there before me, laughing and pointing his thin, knotty finger at my broken skull. I thought he was my undoing that long ago day when he married you in that desolate church and took you from my house down the crude streets of la Habana. But he was my undoing then, too, at the plaza where every face was his hideous face and I lost all concentration, all that years of training had done for me. My every breath utters a curse for him.
>
> I feel I have not convinced you of him. I know I have not.

What would I give for my grandchildren not to bear the name Concepción. But fear nothing, there is someone near who will lift the misfortune that eats away at you.

Tu Papá

He sent the pair of letters to Chelo's address, and hoped they would find their way to Josefina.

BOOK III

1953-1958

21

Many months passed, and Lorenzo kept his promise. He stayed and played the part of father and husband. He painted the houses of El Cotorro and Mar Lindo for income, but he never ventured farther than that. He thought of Gilda often, and though she sent word with merchants who came through El Cotorro, Lorenzo did not respond. The last letter from Gilda came tucked inside a large package. The letter was cradled in a heavy lock of dark hair, tied with two golden ribbons. Lorenzo gasped when he saw the shorn mane and kept it inside an old shoe in his closet. He did not return to Santa Clara, though he often craved apricots when they were in season.

With his first real paycheck, Lorenzo installed telephones in the kitchen and the bedroom so that he could check on Josefina during the day and so that she could not rely on the excuse, "I ran to get it, but wasn't fast enough. I'm not a young girl anymore."

"You'll have a telephone at your fingertips, no matter where you are," Lorenzo said, smiling, as he crouched on the ground with a tangle of wires in his hands. The black boxes rang constantly, and the ringing was so loud it would set the roosters next door to crowing. It drove Josefina wild with anxiety, but Lorenzo thought only of the man he had seen in his kitchen, Josefina in his clasp. She gained value in his eyes after that, like silver that shines more with use and age. Gilda's luster, for Lorenzo, was long gone, lost in heavy folds of skin and masses of long hair.

Still, he soon became known around the housewives in the towns as a seducer of sorts, asking them coyly for a drink of water after painting their houses and then slipping into the kitchens behind the women and leaning on the door frames, his hip cocked to one side and his lips pursed and shiny. Though no one ever told Josefina about his goings-on, she knew that besides his presence in the house every day, little else about her husband had changed.

The one real difference was in his nighttime ritual. Every evening, before he bathed, he would check the beds in the house. He would run his hands over the cloth, over the pillowcases, over the mosquito netting. He was checking for short hair that was lighter than his own. If there was the slightest stain on the bed, he would drag Josefina over by the arm and point to the discoloration and yell, *"¿Qué es esto?"*—Who was here? Then it was that Josefina would have to explain, *"Mi amor,* it is the orange juice Soledad spilled this morning. It is your own sweat from last night. They are the tears I cry from misery." And she would be telling the truth, because she hadn't seen Abel at all. Lorenzo would slow his breathing then and touch the stain with his fingers. "You are right," he would say, then kiss her cheek and go to his bath, which waited for him, warm and soapy, every day.

Regla had advised her never to ask about the long dyed-blond hairs tangled around his belt buckle. Or the button that was sewed with a stitch different from her own. And because Josefina prized her old nursemaid's letters and infrequent phone calls filled with advice nearly as much as her father's missives, she remained silent during Lorenzo's tirades. Whenever she found these things—the button, the blond wiry hairs, the napkin from a restaurant in his pocket—she took them and put them in the box with her father's letters. She envisioned the women who lost these items being visited by a strange and beautiful ghost at night, of strong fingers wrapped around their delicate necks, the smell of her father's cigars choking them, filling their lungs with smoke. This she prayed for, quietly, smiling, while her husband tore off the bedsheets in search of evidence of Josefina's adultery.

After one evening, when Lorenzo took all the sheets, including Soledad's and Lalo's, outside, holding them up to the light in search of a testimony that would seal Josefina's fate, Josefina decided to take action. She telephoned Regla, still a devoted servant to the household of the new sergeant in Vedado, and requested that a *trabajito* be done for her. Josefina remembered the chanting and spells cast in the darkness of Regla's room in Vedado. She could picture the plateful of coconuts hidden behind Regla's dresser and the slices of cake that Regla would leave there as a gift to Oshun. She knew, too, of the bad things, the things Regla always said she could do to those who hurt her or the ones she loved. Like leaving rotten eggs on the person's front porch to bring diseases. Or dropping pennies in their houses to leave your bad luck with them. Regla would release Lorenzo from those women who kept drawing him away from home, wanting to find proof that Josefina had been unfaithful, proof enough so that he could leave his wife with reason and be with them. Josefina and Regla talked at least once a month on the telephone, but Regla had not been to visit in a few years, and Josefina longed to be held by her old nurse again.

Regla arrived during the day a few weeks later, while Lorenzo worked. She carried a suitcase that bulged and seemed to grow as she walked. She had not been to El Cotorro in a long while. The new sergeant was more demanding, his duties more secretive, and Regla was seldom allowed days off. They ate a small lunch of bean soup, and Josefina told her all about Lorenzo and about her new life on the back porch, underneath the tinkling of a wind chime made of spoons and forks. Regla was still wearing her maid's uniform, so quickly had she left Vedado and the new sergeant's house. The only sign of a life outside of servitude was wrapped around her thick-lined neck—a row of tiny yellow beads, the color of her patron saint.

Josefina did not worry about Lorenzo's happening upon them there, since she saw how he had selected his very best socks and doused himself with cologne before leaving the house—precursors of a full night out. So the women talked for hours, well into the early evening. Their talk was like the chattering of birds, punctuated by moments of deafening quiet, then building up again into breathy sighs. The cycle of noise went on and on through talk of the sergeant's death, Lalo's recklessness, Soledad's thinness, Lorenzo's women, the price of ground beef, the opposition to Batista that was stirring in the mountains.

Finally, when the sun had begun to set and the air had taken on the scent of warming dinners, Regla took her old charge by the hands and sat her on the ground outside. She took a cigar from inside her uniform and tore off the tip with her teeth. She spit the tobacco flakes of leaf onto the ground and wiped her mouth. Regla lit the cigar, and as she puffed hard trying to get it smoking, she tore palm fronds from the trees that grew in Josefina's backyard. Then the circling began.

As she walked around and around Regla puffed smoke into Josefina's face and shook the palm fronds above her head. Two wasps were released from the palm as Regla shook. One of them alighted on her neck and stung her there, but Regla did nothing to note the pain or the swelling that began immediately, her flesh pressing against the row of beads.

She chanted, too, muffled words spoken through lips that clenched the cigar. Josefina closed her eyes and felt the warmth of the smoke in her face. She thought of her father, imagined him there, with pen in hand, writing another celestial letter for her to keep. *Sí, this will work,* she thought, and lay down on the grass, oblivious to the itch and the heat. Regla stopped and crushed the cigar underneath her foot. The palm fronds she nestled back into the small tree, as if they could reattach themselves and grow again.

She put her hand to her neck and went inside, leaving Josefina asleep in the sunlight.

When Josefina awoke, she found Regla inside her house, clutching a bag of ice to her neck. The beads had grown so tight around the swelling that she could not open the clasp, and so she snapped them off. The tiny beads swirled on the floor, pushed around by drafts and inclinations of the ground. In the kitchen, Soledad was making coffee, and telling Regla about her new religion teacher, who used to be a nun. When Regla saw Josefina come into the kitchen, she said, "Keep the *cafécito* warm for me, Soly," and pushed Josefina into her bedroom.

"*Ahora,* Josefina, we must light this candle." Josefina watched as Regla took out the candle with Lorenzo's name carved into the wax five times. They placed it in the parlor, behind the record player where Lorenzo would not find it. "Now we will dress the candle in five different oils," Regla said, and produced several glass vials from her purse. They smelled like incense burning and, appropriately enough, when Regla spoke, the words sounded hollow, as they would inside a church. "The first oil is called, 'I Can and You Can't,' the other, 'Follow Me . . . ,' " and so on and so forth, Regla went on naming the colorful oils. Josefina peered over Regla's shoulder, sniffing the scent. It made her dizzy, but she did not care.

Once all the oils were applied to the candle, Regla lifted a fishhook, and swiftly, before Josefina could protest, she pierced Josefina's finger with the hook, drawing blood.

"This," she said, "is so that Oshun can catch your husband like a fish and keep him drawn to your blood." Josefina sucked her finger.

That night, Regla, Soledad, and Josefina sat in the living room and traded jokes and songs. Regla read Soledad's fingernails and predicted a happy marriage and a baby girl, and said she saw miles of ocean between Soledad and Josefina. The girl had outgrown her shyness and felt comfortable around Regla, at last. When Lalo came home, late in the evening, he kissed Regla on the cheek and said, "I'm tired, *tia-abuela*. Good to see you again," then went off to sleep. Later, Josefina watched Regla pack her things. In the morning she would be gone again, to the busy, glistening streets of Vedado. She would give her charge a long kiss on the cheek, and then amble out the door and onto the street. But not yet. One day, one night, was all Josefina had with Regla, but she would make the most of it. There was one more thing to show her.

When Lalo and Soledad were asleep, after Regla had read the prayer of San Luis Beltrán over their sweaty, drowsing bodies for health, Josefina brought out the ghost letters. She had not told Regla about them before, because she did not want to be told that it was a trick. But now Josefina felt cleansed, rejuvenated, sure that Lorenzo would never stray again, that the cloud cast over her home had been blown away in a warm wind, and so the ghost letters were more convincing than ever.

"*Mira,*" Josefina whispered as she put the box of letters in Regla's ample lap. "They are from my papá." The letters shifted and the rustling of paper against paper was like a sigh.

Regla said nothing, but her hands shook as she touched the letters, a sign that filled Josefina with hope. Regla opened them each and read slowly, pointing at words she didn't understand, because she had never been schooled and had been taught to read by the sergeant himself. That the hand was the sergeant's, Regla was sure. She had seen psychics prove their worth in the darkened homes of *Santeros,* had watched the sun leap miraculously in the sky, as Abel had, by an intervention of the Virgin herself, known a person's bad luck to change overnight after the sacrifice of a rooster, but she had never heard of ghostly letters.

"Yes, they are your father's words," Regla said at last, and Josefina's chest ached with joy. "Water, please," Regla said. Josefina dashed to the kitchen. The old woman ran her hands over her face. She could not imagine that the sergeant lived. She had seen the headlines, had read Josefina's description of the bloody letter thrown at her doorstep, and been to the memorial mass given by the government in his honor. Candles had been lit and prayers had been said. *Está muerto,* she decided, though her heart wasn't in it.

Josefina returned with the glass of water. Dawn was breaking outside, and the golden light was framing her in a halo. It was a ridiculous image, Regla thought, and lightened her mood. "They must be ghost letters," Regla said, "or else your father lives and is watching you. There are no other explanations."

Josefina's mood fell a little. If her father lived, then this was just a trick, and the resentment she once carried for him in the days of her adolescence flared up again. Regla saw it, felt the flash of emotion, and scolded the woman.

"To think that you are happier believing that your father is dead rather than living!" Regla's voice boomed through the house and shook the glasses in the kitchen.

"No, Regla, no. Don't believe it for a second," Josefina pleaded. "I only wanted his guidance, like an angel, you understand?"

"Sí, mi niña," Regla said quietly. And then: "I am sure that he is an angel."

Josefina's lips parted and she cried softly, lowering herself into Regla's open arms. The old maid began to pray again, again to San Luís Beltrán to "Watch over this woman who is all faith, all believing."

When the sun was high overhead, Regla took her leave. The children slept on, as if drugged by her presence in the house. Regla had come and gone with little notice, taking with her the candles and oils. A new ghost letter awaited Josefina on the doorstep as she saw Regla out. Regla ran her fingers over the envelope and thought she could still feel the warmth of someone's touch. There was the faintest smell of blood about the letter, too, but Regla did not mention it. She kissed Josefina lightly on the cheek and drew a small cross on her forehead before descending the porch steps.

"Write soon," Josefina called out as Regla walked away.

22

"Why did I choose to come to this town?" Abel Santana asked himself grimly in the days after Lorenzo caught him with Josefina. It would have frightened Josefina to see how quiet he had become in those days. He forgot to go to the marketplace and three of his best pigs were stolen from him. The lazy days he had so relished became a chore. The sultry airs put on by the women in the market, an irritant.

He went to church daily and could not clear his mind of Josefina. He saw her in the shapely statue of Santa Bárbara that was nailed to the wall. In mirrors, he thought he caught her reflection in place of his. And, like the sergeant, he wanted nothing more than for Lorenzo to drop stiffly to the floor one morning, a corpse.

Every day, the sergeant's letters arrived at his home. Then, according to the instructions he'd been given long ago, Abel would remove the letter from the stamped envelope, refolding it carefully. Sometimes, the sergeant tucked a new envelope in with the letter, addressed to Josefina in his hand, in his red ink. Always, the letters smelled like hair tonic.

The sergeant was getting old. Abel had guessed he was in his seventies, and he wasn't far off. The handwriting had taken on the characteristics of the elderly—the fluid cursive of youth lost, the letters now sharp, the pen pushed hard into the paper, so that at times the paper was punctured. Still, the argument was as healthy

as ever. Abel could see why Josefina believed in the ghost so readily. Never did the sergeant mention the turmoil in Havana, the ex-
ecutions and the gambling palaces that were making world
headlines, nor the life he led in the United States. It was as if the
world was of no concern, as if all that mattered was that Lorenzo
be gone from it.

For a while, Abel saved the letters he had received since he last
saw Josefina, but he eventually surrendered and brought them to
her house. He had feared approaching it. It wasn't that he feared
Lorenzo, but what he might do to her. Every night he fell asleep
imagining Josefina. In the mornings he awoke with her name on his
lips. To rouse himself from that stupor, he would spend the day in
the church, helping to polish the pews, trying hard not to look at the
womanly figure of Santa Bárbara. One afternoon he watched as a
man in the market barked orders at his wife, throwing bags of veg-
etables to her, who, loaded with a multitude of bundles, only sighed.

This will be Josefina someday, Abel thought wildly. That night he
gathered the sergeant's letters, and with a sense of duty, and of love,
he waited outside the house of El Cotorro. He waited until he could
see the lights turn off, one by one, until he heard Lorenzo's snoring,
until the only sound coming from the house was the drip-drip of
the faucet in the kitchen. Then, Abel climbed atop an old milk
crate set underneath Josefina's window to peer in and make sure
she was all right. He watched her sleep, hypnotized by the up and
down of her breast as she breathed. He scanned her limbs for any
marks, any bruises, and never found any. But her eyes were swollen
and her nose red, from crying, and it made Abel tremble in anger.

Before dawn, he made sure to leave the letters in a place where
Josefina, and not Lorenzo, would find them. So, he tucked them
safely into the canvas bag that hung on the clothesline, the one
filled with wooden pins for hanging laundry.

It would be four years before he spoke to Josefina again. He
called only once, and hung up when he heard her voice, a voice
that made his heart cry out and his hands tremble. He fought the

temptation to speak to her every night as he continued the ritual of his visits. Though the neighbors noticed him crawling about in the moony darkness, they never said a word to the Concepción family. "That family is very strange," they'd say to one another, deciding the nightly adventure was better left unspoken.

Mi Hija,

The rural districts have changed little since the time I first arrived in Cuba. The people have always been poor and ignorant and superstitious. The women bear children in the fields, then sling them onto their backs and continue to harvest sugar. In the rural districts of Cuba, it feels hotter and stickier than anywhere else on this Earth. I hate to think that you live this way.

When your uncle and I first arrived, we followed a man who called himself Toledo. I still do not know if that was his real name, but the men in the Army of Liberation called me Navarro and never Antonio. Francisco did not like my using our father's name, and he told me so, though with a weakness in his voice that was unlike him. The tropical heat had made him weaker, less the bully and more the persecuted. He no longer invented complex roles of adventure for us to play. I often thought, and think still, that the change did not come from the heat at all. It was Olga Maria who had given my brother strength. Without her, he was so small . . .

It never bothered me that these men and young boys were out to kill my countrymen, to obliterate my beautiful Spain from their tropical paradise. I accepted the offer to impersonate a Cuban and join the rebels, to kill Spaniards, because I saw the wretched Olga Maria in those Spanish faces. The soldiers taught us to speak without a Spaniard's lisp, which could get us killed in the rural country. I learned quickly, happy to be more like these muscular young men with their foul mouths and moist, ever present dangling cigars. Francisco only lisped harder. That was his one act of rebellion while in the Army. The men we were with hated Spaniards, despised that country so far across the sea, wanted nothing more than a free Cuba, a Cuba without a king.

We did very little, militarily speaking. Every day we marched through the village roads, stopping at random houses for meager lunches, or baths, or head shavings by kind women to keep the lice away. Always, always, Toledo cut stalks of sugarcane for us, and Francisco, who took up cigar smoking, too, had lost three teeth by the time we were fourteen.

I might have stayed with the Army of Liberation right into the Second War of Independence. I probably would have been shot right off of my pony. But Francisco's lisping, his quiet, baffling mutiny would clear another road for me.

Keep your windows closed, Josefina. When the wind changes from night to dawn it brings with it bad luck, straight off the ocean. Regla always said so. I will write soon.

Tu Papá

23

Lalo had begun going to Sunday Mass with Soledad, "to watch over her," as he told his parents. They, in turn, were happy that he had stopped taking long walks and crying out in his sleep. Soledad's interest in church was solely in meeting with Camila afterward, and it was also a place for her eyes to take in vast amounts of wealth and beauty—enough to last her through the week until the next Sunday. Lalo's purpose, too, was anything but churchly. His thoughts during the week percolated with images of Camila. It was on Sundays, when Soledad and Camila spent time under the shady trees of the garden, that Lalo would perch on one of the limbs and watch Camila and listen to the girls talk, while Doña Amparo, who did not like Lalo any more than she had the day of their first meeting, sat on a stone bench opposite him. On one particular Sunday, Lalo overheard something that pleased him very much.

He had woken very late that morning, so Soledad was allowed to walk to church alone. When Lalo did finally wake, he dressed and rushed to the church, because his weekly turns of being near Camila were now quite a habit for him. Lalo sometimes sat with them at Mass, and sometimes sat on the pew behind her, to watch the gold in her hair catch the candlelight. This day, Lalo found them in their usual place in the garden. He slid quietly into the heavy parted limbs of the tree and listened to their chatter. Doña

Amparo, too, noticing the absence of Lalo that day, had gone home early, kissing Camila on the cheek and reminding her to come straight home. Lalo was overjoyed in knowing that, for today, Doña Amparo was gone and that he was invisible to the girls, and thus, their speech was freer.

Camila, who was now fourteen, spoke animatedly, her legs draped delicately to the side, her hands loosely grasping the toes of her leather boots. She had, as of late, lost the roughness of girlhood, a fact that enticed Lalo all the more. He listened to them almost dumbly, stiffly, so as not to rustle the leaves.

"Come on, Camila, you promised you'd let me know today," Soledad said.

"I'll tell you this much," she said, "he is not very tall, and his eyebrows arch, like this," she pointed at her own brows, "and when I see him, he watches me in the oddest way."

Soledad could not suppress her joy at the thought that her friend had a secret admirer, because Soledad, too, was growing up, and boys had begun to draw her attention. Lalo stared at the girls like a feral cat that is suddenly approached by a person intent on catching it. *Could it be,* he thought to himself as he heard the conversation below, *she will be so easily led away?* He tried to imagine this other fellow with the shapely eyebrows and wondered at his age, his background, his true intentions for this girl. The existence of another wasn't a possibility that he had dismissed altogether. He didn't even want Camila, he told himself, but this information, the giggling that went on below him, was painful to hear. And the pain was quite real, beginning deep in his chest and rumbling there, then moving up to his throat in a surge of sour bile. He wanted to open his mouth and relieve himself of the pain and the hot liquid in his throat, but to do so would reveal him, so there was little else to do but swallow hard and listen.

"And where does he live?" Soledad asked.

"Not far. He goes to school here in El Cotorro." Camila's blush had now managed to cover every inch of her face, including her eyelids. Lalo, who had noticed the progression of the blushing, also heard the fact of this boy's location. He could only be a student at Lalo's school, and he vowed to find him out.

"Please tell me his name, oh please, please." By now Soledad was itching with anticipation.

"I can't," was Camila's timid reply.

"His initials then."

"Well, very well. They are E and M and C," she whispered and looked at her friend with very wide eyes, waiting for the moment when Soledad knew who he was. Meanwhile, Soledad, who prided herself on knowing the names of the boys who went to school with Lalo, could not find any matches to that particular combination of letters. As for Lalo, the whispered letters were spoken too softly to be made out from the heights where he sat, and so he fumed in frustration, willing his sister to make a guess of it so that the culprit might be revealed.

"That does not help, Camila, and besides, it's not very fair." Soledad's irritation nearly equaled that of her brother.

"Come, you know who it is," Camila said, "you know him very well."

And the way she said this last, tugging at her friend's wrists, Soledad suddenly knew that Camila spoke of Lalo.

"My brother?" she asked, not really wanting to believe that it was true. And when Camila said yes, Soledad felt her face change into a sullen mask, stiff and pale. She had come to know her brother in the past months better than she did before. She didn't know whether her perceptions had matured or whether his behavior was odder than it had been in the years past, but she did understand that he was not for Camila.

Up in the tree, Lalo had a different reaction to the news. The pain in his chest was overtaken by a nervous itch, the effect of which was still the same. He tasted the bile in his throat that swelled upward at such a pace that Lalo found himself jumping out of the tree and running out of the garden, vomiting the last of his breakfast onto the exposed roots of an aging palm.

The sudden noise frightened the girls. Though they did not get a good look at the figure that ran out of the garden, they were both keen enough to know who it was and why he had run off so quickly. This knowledge turned Camila's rosy face into a pale mask, much like Soledad's, and so they parted with kisses, and both went their separate ways.

Camila stopped running when she reached the Avenida Madero, a broad road filled with the youth of Mar Lindo, buying ice creams for each other and making plans for the next holiday. She wiped at the black scuffs on her shoes and tucked loose curls behind her ears. Despite her run, she still looked as if she had just come from her home after hours of primping before a mirror. The thought of how Lalo had found her out crumpled the easy spirit that made her good looks all the more pleasing to the eye. She walked at a brisk rate down the avenue until she arrived upon the quiet park that marked the center of Mar Lindo. Within its confines, one could stroll past rows of imported maples, their growth stunted by the heat, or watch the children, each one dressed in a sailor's outfit more expensive than the next, being pushed on swings or down magnificently polished slides by their nannies. It was the latter pastime that Camila chose—to sit and watch and catch her breath.

Lalo, who had followed her at a distance, felt that the nannies were far too much like Doña Amparo. They were gruff and over-weight, and each looked after her own charge sternly, careful that no other child went too near. These women made Lalo feel as if he was being watched, even here. He stood between the malformed maples for a few moments in which everything around him seemed to slow, as if he was drunk and his eyes were playing tricks on him. He took one more long look at Camila's back before the trembling overtook him again, and he ran away.

Camila, who had been watching Lalo's reflection on the polished metal slides, turned to see him disappear out of the park and toward El Cotorro. She was sure now that Lalo had an interest in her. Satisfied, with the blush returning to her cheeks, Camila walked to her own home, assuring herself that she would have to spend more time visiting Soledad from now on.

When Lalo finally arrived home, he found Soledad waiting for him in their stifling little bedroom. Rivulets of sweat ran down her cheeks, and Lalo could tell that she had run home in order to get there before him. In her anger, she forgot to open the windows to let in some fresh air. The way in which Soledad stood there mutely, her hair in little girl ribbons, made the pain return to Lalo's stomach. *This child, this baby, is Camila's dearest friend, a fact which makes her a child, too,* Lalo thought. He swallowed thickly and pushed passed his sister.

Soledad, who had a similar pain in her own stomach, spoke before Lalo could throw himself on the bed. "Do you love her? I mean, the way she says you do?" she asked, and the question was more a plea than a demand.

"Be quiet, Soledad," Lalo said as he finally did drop down on the bed, rolling over on the hot sheets.

On this rare occasion, Soledad was not to be quieted. "If you do love her, I will tell her to run far away!" She screamed the last into Lalo's uncovered ear, which rang and buzzed as if to confirm that the threat was a real one. At this, Lalo sat up and watched his sister, who quavered in spite of her own will not to. "And I will tell her that if she doesn't run, then you will sell her away like a whore, like you did before to the other girls."

At this, Lalo wanted nothing more than to cover his sister's mouth, to stop her from speaking to him or to Camila. She always knew it all, as if someone had come in the night and told her, keeping her up late with scandals and chatter. There was no way that Lalo could think of to alter what Soledad already knew. Realizing that she was still a child who could be tricked, Lalo found that his only resort was to lie.

"I do not love her," he said, trying very hard not to grimace. "She's a terrible liar. Now be quiet and open the window, will you?" Lalo lay on the bed once more, curling his spine into a U to ease the pain in his stomach and to calm the retching in his throat the lie had caused.

But Lalo did not fall asleep. Instead, he lay there until late in the afternoon, listening to the movement of the family outside the room. He heard when Lorenzo arrived from work, shouting at his mother because the meat she had packed for his lunch had been raw. He heard when Josefina dropped a kettle and noted the extent of the splash, and so he imagined that the soup, or broth, or whatever it was, had doused the parlor. All of this he listened to, each new sound interrupting a different version of his morning in Mar Lindo's park with Camila. He might have walked up to her, saying that he understood her affection for him, but, she'd understand, it could never be. Or he might have run to her instead and lifted her from the place where she sat to hold and kiss her and link arms with her. And it was this vision that lingered the longest in his mind, only to be suspended by another sound from the noisy house.

The front door had been thrown open, the knob thudding against the wall loudly, and a series of voices mumbled and rose in pitch until the talks were now shouts instead. Of all the voices, the clearest was that of Doña Amparo. It was her grating voice to which Lalo was most attentive. He lay still and held his breath to hear all that the old woman was saying.

"You will be so kind as to tell me, señora, what your son intends for my niece," she said, and Lalo could barely make out the blundering retaliation of his mamá before Doña Amparo continued.

"My niece arrives home and her skin is flushed and I ask her, '*Mi niña,* what is wrong?' and she tells me that all is well. And at dinner she does not eat her food, and I ask again, 'What is wrong?' and again she tells nothing, but you see, I know well that a lost appetite is a signal of lust, and so I say to her, 'It is the Concepción boy, isn't it?' and her cheeks burn red again, and I know that it is so. Look at her," she says, and Lalo understands that Camila has been brought to the house, too.

"She still burns to think of him. And now she has told me everything." Lalo could hear the murmuring of his mamá, surely apologizing out of respect for the wealth and good standing of the woman. Her murmurs went on for a long time before Doña Amparo cracked the quiet with her own rumbling voice.

"My niece will not go about public parks with small demons such as your children," and then, as if to mark the sudden sadness of the prohibition, Camila moaned the tiniest of moans, a sound that Lalo felt pierced his breast. Upon hearing the sound that came from her niece, Doña Amparo, too, must have felt a stitch of pain, because in a lower voice she said, "If he is to be around my niece, he must learn the respect that he was never taught here, and he will visit like a gentleman on Friday afternoons between the hour of five and six in my parlor and in my presence. Come, Camila." And the pair made their way out of the house, Josefina giving an audible sigh of relief. Lalo sighed along with her, overjoyed that his courtship of Camila could begin.

Mi Hija,

My brother, Francisco, was a Wednesday boy. He was stuck in the middle, always. The streak of rebellion he had lost when we first arrived slowly made its way back into his voice, his smile, and his very walk. He moved deliberately slowly, far behind the marching men, like a serpent in the way he swung his hips and took in the sights of the rural districts. I walked with the soldiers, and I could hear them grumble about Francisco, calling him a "dirty Spaniard," or a "lazy woman." And the angrier they became, the more Francisco lisped in an exaggerated Spanish way.

"What are you doing?" I asked him finally, after I watched one of the soldiers cock his fingers into an imaginary gun and fire three invisible bullets at my brother.

"I want to go home, Antonio," my brother said, and I remember how he blinked wetly. I wanted nothing more than to stay and fight at last—to fight in the mountains that the Spanish did not understand, to swing from the vines and drop on the Spaniards like quiet rain. The soldiers would not let Francisco go freely, because he might give away our plans to the Spanish. They feared that he would turn traitor and that all could be lost on account of one small boy.

The men could taste independence. When the Americans arrived with their armies, they could see it plainly. They talked about their girlfriends, their wives, and the children they did not yet have, born in a free Cuba, a Cuba without Spaniards like my brother and me. So I begged Francisco to stay and be quiet. I pointed at the rifles slung on the backs of the ponies. My brother nodded and draped his arm around my shoulder.

The next morning the men awoke to see a small Spanish flag set around the head of one of the ponies, like an old woman's kerchief. The animal munched slowly on the grass beneath it while the sun glared overhead, setting the red and yellow bars of the flag aglow. Francisco, wrapped in a blanket beside me, began laughing a low moan of a laugh. His mirth became louder and louder as we watched the soldiers tear the flag off the head of the pony and stomp it into the ground. Toledo himself drove a knife through the heart of the flag, then a soldier named Concepción spit on it until the flag was little more than a wet rag.

It was this same man who shot Francisco in the stomach that afternoon as we ate, when my brother wondered aloud what the King of Spain was having for lunch.

Do not imagine, Josefina, that I am angry that you share the name of a murderer. Lorenzo's people are innocent of that butchery. There are thousands of Concepcións in the world.

Tu Papá

24

On the day Soledad turned fifteen, Josefina decided that she was somehow trapped. Little had changed in her life, except that now she looked aged, her hands were covered with so many brown spots that they did not seem to belong to her body anymore. As for her husband, he suffered from headaches that were bad enough to keep him in a dark room all day. She'd retrieve the ghost letters from the bag on the clothesline. She had been surprised when she'd found them there the first time, but the new location was just further proof that her father was watching, that his wisdom beyond the grave told her to hide the letters from Lorenzo. She and Lorenzo argued, and still she went to Soledad at night, lying down next to her and crying into her hair about Lorenzo's infidelity. And she finally read her the old ghost letters.

Josefina went to her daughter one night when Lorenzo was gone. Soledad's bare legs were entangled in cotton sheets, and her left arm hung off to the side. Josefina stood in Soledad's doorway, noting the woman her daughter had become, thinking to herself, *My God, she's fifteen already*. The years had passed so quickly, in a way that Josefina could never have imagined. The passage of time felt unreal. She sometimes felt unreal.

Fifteen was a magical year, a girl's prettiest, it was said. It was a time when the wealthier families threw lavish parties, introducing their daughter to society. Josefina herself had been one of those beautiful debutantes. In her pink, ruffled gown with matching cape, she had danced a waltz with her father across a slick marble floor, with all her classmates watching, giddy from the night's festivities. The sergeant had given her the best *quince* Vedado had ever seen. *Now, what do I have to give my own daughter?* Josefina thought as she stood there in the dark.

Josefina explained to Soledad that night, after an hour's worth of combing her daughter's hair, that Regla's *trabajito* had not worked fully. Though Lorenzo no longer searched the beds of his house for remnants of lovemaking, he still prowled the neighborhood. He still reeked of rotten fruit on Fridays, when Josefina knew that he visited Gloria Ramos in the market. His belly would still be full and tight when he came home Sunday nights after visiting Sara Barrera, who everybody knew cooked the best *yuca* and steak in El Cotorro. "Oshun," Josefina said, "must be angry at your grandfather's interference."

Josefina pulled the box out from the inside of her closet and brought it to Soledad.

"This little one arrived last week," Josefina said. "Some of the others are much longer," and then she began to read:

Mi Hija,

What anguish at the thought that you might still be miserable. Regla used to say, long ago, that you were destined for it. I did not believe her then, and still, I do not. I grow tired of this place, and wish I were home.

Tu Papá

Josefina held the paper to her lips and kissed it, then lifted the sheet to Soledad's lips for her to do the same. Soledad brushed it away.

"Tell me the truth," Soledad said, softening her tone. "Who

wrote this?" she asked, and thrust her hand into the box, so full with letters that the lid would not close and was held tight by a rubber band.

"Your grandfather. He writes to us from heaven." Josefina kissed the paper once again. "I told you once, when you were young," Josefina said. She watched her mother and was reminded of the paintings she had seen in books of saints in ecstasy, because they had seen God, in a flash of light, in the moment before death, in a burning candle, in a dark cell. It was a look she had seen once before on the face of Camila when she caught her and Lalo behind the house one rainy afternoon, naked together. It was that look now that cautioned her to say nothing.

"They are wonderful, Mamá," she managed to say, and left the room. Later that night she took the box out of the closet and read the letters. Though the handwriting was not her mother's rigid script, it was similar enough, and Soledad came to believe that her mother, in an inspired craze, had written them, so obsessed were they with her father's faults.

The family had fallen into routine. Lalo was twenty, had finished school, and loved wearing suits that he could not afford. He had grown handsome, and he made Camila's eyes water with emotion whenever he was near. He had been happy the past few years with Camila as a companion. Her devotion was complete. As for Soledad, though she was fifteen, she had no lovers of her own, and so she spent her days chaperoning her brother and her friend, in their walks to the shipyards and cemeteries, and any other abandoned place they could think of. They would walk ahead, their arms linked, and Soledad would dawdle far behind, far enough so that she did not have to hear the sopping sound of their kisses.

She did not particularly like this chore forced upon her by Doña Amparo. The old woman had taken her by the shoulders, saying, "They met because of you, so now you must watch them," and she had hobbled away. The matter was settled. Lalo and Camila did nothing without Soledad somewhere behind them. And it had been this way for nearly four years now, so that no one remembered it any differently. For Soledad, it was a kind of bitter revenge, too. She knew that there was little they could do when she was around, and it sometimes made her happy to think it.

And so, on her fifteenth birthday, while she looked at those around her holding out presents wrapped in colorful paper and tied with silk ribbon to mark this year that was said to be a woman's most beautiful, she, like her mother, began to feel that she was trapped and that things would always be the same.

But things were changing. All around the island it was coming, and the people felt it as if they were swimmers in a deep sea, the chrome-colored fins of a shark circling in wide gyres. And there was a tremor of hope, too, that the change would finally be good.

For Soledad it came in the winter of 1956. She was nearly finished with school, and was tired of the political gangs that had formed among the young men, baiting the girls and the weaker boys about which side they were on—the rebels in the mountains or Batista in his palace. They had taken to growing beards, long and scraggly. Those who were unfortunate enough to have smooth cheeks tried all kinds of tonics, green mixtures of avocado, lime, and kerosene, to force the follicles into action. There was even a rumor that little Rubén Pozo had glued pubic hair to his chin to avoid criticism. Political alliances were tied closely to hair—the bearded had their hearts in the sierras, the clean-shaven in Havana.

Secretly, Soledad loved the coarse faces. She imagined kissing one of them, as long as he wasn't talking about injustices, liberation, or corruption. One of the novice rebels, in particular, made Soledad feel as if she had swallowed a lead weight whenever he came near. Julio Cuadras was tall. His forearms were detailed in thick veins that disappeared into the crook of his arm. Green eyes and a brown beard completed the portrait. Most importantly for Soledad, there was the laugh that started off low, grumbling, and then broke out into fits of joy that made her want to cry out with desire. Julio Cuadras was the first person she had ever desired, and she did so with a cupidity that made her lose her appetite.

Josefina teased her at the kitchen table. "Not hungry, eh? Must be a lover." At which Lorenzo would scowl or tell Josefina to shut up. Soledad's mother had asked her incessantly about her crushes, where her heart was stowed, since she was eight years old. It was Josefina's favorite topic. But Soledad kept Julio Cuadras to herself.

In truth, Soledad had little contact with the boy. He flirted with her mercilessly. He'd said to her once, "If you weren't so thin, I'd pull you into the bushes with me. But I'm afraid I'll break you." And later, from inside a crowd of other boys, "Soledad, if I get you, I'll wet you," but he ignored her most of the time. It was said, too, that he had gotten his girlfriend, Simoneta Perez, pregnant, and that they were to be married after graduation. Still, Soledad pined for the handsome boy and began to believe in him, in his causes, in the handsome baseball player whose picture she saw in the newspapers, the one named Fidel, who was leading the insurrections.

Those wars in the misty hills seemed like bedtime stories. What were they compared to the reality of having too little to eat, a mother who corresponded with ghosts, legs that were thin like a chicken's?

In December, as the nuns at her school forced the students into recreating the nativity scene, singing "Pastores á Belén," over and over until it sounded like a monk's chant instead of a Christmas carol, Julio Cuadras, who had been absent for a week, much to Soledad's dismay, and other young boys attacked an army barracks and didn't come back.

That night, after she'd heard the news and the president's triumphant speech, about how he'd killed so many boys in one afternoon, Soledad shut herself in the bathroom, and cried big, splashy tears onto the tiled floor.

Mi Hija,

When you asked me, all your life, how your uncle died, I did not want to tell you because I always thought that life for you, Josefina, should have been easy, like an afternoon picnic or a swim when the waves have died. Why should you have to know about the hours I spent burying your uncle, his blood drenching the earth and the birds that perched on his chest as I dug? Or the months that I spent alone in the sierras, begging from house to house? Or the blisters on my feet, like large onions? Every man I met was like the one who killed your uncle.

After months of loneliness and walking down the mountains and through the vine-trapped valleys, I ran into a fence surrounding a yard, and in that yard were hundreds of boys in green uniforms that were ironed almost as well as the clothes my mother had pressed. They were like a legion of aphids, covering the grounds together, training to be police for the nearly independent state of Cuba. You see, we had not yet won, not until years later, but Spain had been beaten back for a while. It was not until I came to that fence that I learned that independence had not really been gained. Part of me had prayed that we would not win, that the man who killed Francisco might be trampled by a horse, or worse yet, shamed into wearing the colors of Spain. But it was the grief that had taken over. The truth was, I had come to love the idea of independence, of freedom. It was why I left my stepmother's rule behind, it was why I first held a rifle in my arms like a baby. But it was why my brother was killed. So you see the confusion I was feeling.

One of the cadets stuffed buttered bread through the fence for me when he saw me standing there, and I was won over. It was that easy, the choice between hunger and discipline. I'm sure you've learned by now, *mi hija*, that resignation is a loyal friend. I told them I was eighteen, and I vowed my allegiance to the island. Some days, I longed for my mother and the propriety in Spain, the glitter of her capital, the bullfights and the jonquils that lined paved roads in the north. But most of the time I was happy to be part of this resurrected island.

Life in the academy was good. I am surprised still that your husband did not join the force when I asked him. We awoke at dawn to exercise and practice shooting. We ate large meals cooked by volunteer grandmothers, eager to help the country reestablish itself. And on the weekends the unmarried cadets were invited to the dances held by the Santa Marta School for Girls. There is where I met your mother, Ana.

I remember it well. The breeze was cool underneath the tent, and some of the girls wore dresses that were too exposed, and so their skin prickled with goose bumps. Ana wore a new shawl wrapped around her slim shoulders. It was covered in golden beads that clicked musically in the night air. Ceramic bracelets circled her wrists and her cheeks had a newly pinched look, like tiny wild strawberries. I watched as she and several other girls disappeared behind a curtain, and I waited for the folds of the velvet drapes to move again, announcing her return.

Aware of any slight movement in the curtain, the tiny drafts that sent the ends of the fabric swinging gave me shivers. At last, the sisters chaperoning the dance clapped their hands to begin the show. A group of girls strode toward the front of the room and lined up according to height. They wore frilly tutus in different pastel shades, their hands clasped behind their slim backs. Ana stood in her costume, looking like a chick in its new, yellow down, in the center of the line. The cadets around me sighed at the sight of the Santa Marta Ballet Club, and I sighed with them. My anxious comrades, I'm sure, thought of bedding all of these girls later that evening in their youthful, arrogant dreams, but I saw only Ana. And when the strains of the piano began, your mother danced, *mi hija,* as if she were moving through water, in a slow, mesmerizing way. At the end, the girls all fell to the ground, but your mother draped herself over a nearby chair, left there by accident, I'm sure, and the very tips of her fingers touched the floor and lay there, still. I wanted nothing more than to put those fingers in my mouth.

She disappeared again and put on her shawl and her bracelets. And then, after all my waiting, she danced all night with a cadet named Ivan! He was a boy with a large, immovable body. I knew that it was immovable, because during the last dance I tried to cut in several times, and Ivan, a cadet not known for his patience, swung his tree trunk of an arm, and my forehead caught his wrist. And though I thought that Ana would find me weak and defenseless, she pushed the doltish Ivan with her small hands and knelt beside me.

Then, Josefina, the breeze caught her hair in its invisible fingers and lifted the scent of gardenias, up and out of those curls. I'd like to believe it was that scent and not the bump on my forehead that made me swoon, mute and giddy, in your mother's slight arms.

I watched all of her recitals and clipped the news articles that featured her in a classic ballerina's pose as the best dancer in the region. I burned those articles the day she died, but I wish I hadn't, for you, for myself. How could I tell you about all this when I saw her eyes in yours, your thin face an echo of hers? How could I say it without crying? *Los hombres no lloran.* It's true that a man can't allow himself to cry in front of his daughter, in front of anyone.

We married a year after we first met in the mess hall of

the academy with the nuns of her school and my commanding officers in attendance. I asked her to carry a bouquet of gardenias, and I remembered how she complained, "No Antonio, gardenias are fragile and they wither as soon as you cut them off the branch." I insisted, and in her hands she carried a bunch of gardenias, brown and dry. But the smell, *ay mi hija,* how it lingered.

It was the same smell that was like a cloud over her grave whenever I visited. And there were times that I caught the aroma of white gardenias in full bloom on your breath when you'd say, "Good night, Papá."

Tu Papá

25

As a child, Josefina would go into her mother's wardrobe. The trapped air inside was hot and sultry, and Josefina inhaled the scents and stroked the dresses against her cheek. The sergeant would hear her knocking about inside the wardrobe and yell, "Leave your mother's things alone!" On better days, the sergeant would sneak up on Josefina, touching the fabric and say, "She liked this one best," or, "That one suited her legs." Josefina had always felt that the information, like quick melting candies, was all she needed to know about her mother. With the ghost letters from her father, she began to hunger for more than something so fleeting.

Josefina had not known her mother was a dancer. She looked at herself naked in the mirror for an hour after she read the letter. *Why have I not inherited a dancer's body,* she asked herself. Her legs, she noted, were a little bowed, and her thighs pressed together now more than ever. She joined her heels and pointed out her toes. First position. She had learned that in school, but could never keep her balance. The years had not perfected her equilibrium, and she teetered toward the mirror and caught herself before she fell. Josefina tried again, and again could not keep herself still. Her legs quivered with the effort. After a fourth try in which she banged her nose on the glass, she gave up. *If my mother had lived,* she said aloud, *she could have given me lessons.* Massaging the beginnings of a cramp in her left calf, Josefina hobbled to the kitchen to prepare dinner.

The vision of her mother in a tutu, flitting about a stage like a dragonfly over water, would not leave Josefina. She heard the old music she used to play on her little pianoforte in Vedado in her head now as she shopped for fruit in the market, or as she fingered every single bolt of tulle in the fabric stores. At night, she began to wonder whether her mother, Ana, even cared for the ballet. Perhaps she did it to stay trim, to meet boys, to please her own mother. But in the daylight, the anchor of reason and reality let Josefina loose, and she imagined ways to make a tribute to her mother, the woman her father in heaven adored so much. She owed her at least that, Josefina thought, after so many years of pretending she had never existed, after so many years of forgetting to light candles or visit her mother's grave.

It did not take any more long looks in the mirror for Josefina to know she would never dance. Not even a short cha-cha-cha with her husband was suitable for her anymore. And as she sat, drumming her fingers to music no one else heard, watching her daughter float in and out of the kitchen, Josefina suddenly thought of a way to make her tribute.

That morning Josefina resumed her old sewing, making underwear and slips for the women of El Cotorro to wear underneath their rags. She completed them in a day and sold them the next. The women believed Josefina when she told them these hidden clothes would make them beautiful and attractive to their husbands. After all, the wife of Lorenzo Concepción should know, and they bought the flimsy things by the armload. With the money, Josefina purchased three tickets to the ballet.

The following evening, Soledad accompanied Lalo and Camila to the Mar Lindo teatro. Soledad, who was economical and bashful in big crowds, had protested, of course, but Josefina argued that the tickets were a gift for her fifteenth birthday, and the girl could not refuse. Josefina smiled as she helped her daughter get ready, and she envisioned the spirit of her mother, Ana, taking possession of Soledad, inspiring her to be more graceful, encasing her in a maternal love.

Soledad had grown quickly, so her clothes did not fit her well. They never had, really, because they were donated things, but now that her mother could make her modern pencil skirts and tight-fitting, buttoned shirts with Peter Pan collars, Josefina found that her daughter's figure was not easy to dress. She was too thin and never stood straight during fittings. Though some of the boys of El Cotorro thought her beautiful, Josefina never looked at her daughter's face without feeling a pang of guilt, as if she was at fault for Soledad's pinched look—lips pursed tightly, eyes close together, a muscular but thin neck. There was a delicacy about her that Josefina did not seem to notice—the way her slender fingers toyed softly with whatever she held, her rounded, high cheeks, her small breasts.

The young couple dressed in their finest clothes—Camila in a long satin skirt in deep purple, with a heavy satin belt in a lighter shade and Lalo in a suit he had bought that very morning, the lapels crisp, the buttons still tightly sewed on. Soledad wore a simple dress of brown taffeta. She might have looked as if she were attending Mass instead of the ballet, if Josefina had not pinned a white moonflower from the vine outside the door into her hair.

Josefina waved them good-bye as they walked into the dark. She hummed a few bars of "Clair de Lune," a piano piece she had once learned to play for her father as a girl, then sat to read her letters again.

At the theater, Soledad found herself lingering far behind her brother. Lalo, who held Camila tightly about the waist, walked about the lobby as if he were at home, and all of the furniture and fabrics and brass trimmings were nothing new. Soledad could not help walking slowly on the broadloom rug, trying to feel the plush newness of it through the hard soles of her shoes. When she touched the brass railings that led into the theater and up the steps, she wiped her fingerprint off with her skirt. And when a petal fell from the moonflower in her hair, she bent down to pick it up, because she thought that a place such as this would be sullied by even a flower's petal. The program that a young usher in green handed to her seemed perfect—the paper heavy and porous, the raised script with the ballet's name *Giselle* on it, glossy and smooth to the touch.

Inside, the theater was lined with rows of chairs covered in golden velvet. Above them the high ceiling was decorated with painted angels, each one malformed in some way, as if there had not been enough money in Mar Lindo to engage any artists of real talent. The cherubs that floated directly above Soledad, Camila, and Lalo were long and thin, more like wraiths than plump babies, and Soledad was glad when the lights finally dimmed, and she could no longer look at them in the dark.

A peal of cymbals rang through the darkness, and music that Soledad thought was sinister enough to accompany the dancing of the strange angels above began. But this soon softened, and the lights above the stage illuminated a rough set of cottage houses and the peeking eyes of the dancers glowing behind paper trees and wooden boulders. Soon the dancers began to appear, clad in scanty peasant clothes that exhibited their calves and ankles and plump arms. The plumpness, paired with the darkness of their hair and the soft brown color of their skin, quickly revealed that the dancers had not come to Mar Lindo from some faraway Parisian company, or even Havana for that matter, but they were girls from nearby towns and provinces, once again making it clear to Soledad and to the two or three men in the left wing, who hooted and whistled when the buxom dancers appeared that the money in Mar Lindo, though good enough for velvet theater chairs and brass railings, was perhaps not enough to fund any performance of reputation.

When Giselle finally appeared from behind one of the cottage doors, she, too, was thick and fleshy, but she seemed to drift inches above the stage, and it was easy to see that she was the lead dancer. In the same way, Soledad thought, that a person who is striking, not because of beauty, but because of something quiet and hidden, is easily spotted in a market crowd.

Soledad felt Camila clutch her hand with emotion at the moment when Giselle finally began to dance with Albrecht, her lover. At the strange touch, a touch that Soledad had become unaccustomed to since Camila and Lalo had found each other, Soledad looked toward her brother, who sat dumbly, his chin resting on his palm in a way that made his mouth open and exposed his red, inflamed gums. His left eye was already closed in sleep. Soledad did not pull away from her friend as she thought she would, but instead relished the closeness with a kind of bitter happiness. She imagined, too, that for a moment she was Giselle herself, and Albrecht had become the dead Julio Cuadras, the rebel she had loved from afar.

Since the time that Lalo and Camila began their love affair, Soledad had found herself quite alone in the world, with only her mamá to come and speak with her, and this was nothing like a kindred friendship, because Josefina had not changed. Her nighttime visits to Soledad's room were more frequent now, and she told of women at the market and at the bank whispering among themselves whenever she happened upon them, and every so often, she'd hear the name Lorenzo spoken among them, and a hushed chorus of breath pulled in too quickly in anticipation of some great rumor. And then, when dawn neared, Josefina would begin to fall asleep, her lips slack, and she would garble, "But I loved once. I loved once, and he sent him away," and then she would finally sleep, and Soledad would wrap the sheets around her mother's clammy body and prepare breakfast.

Here, at the ballet, Camila's touch was nothing like Josefina's. It didn't demand tears, or secrets. But the touch did not last long. As Giselle was driven to madness by her lover's betrayal, and the dancer staggered through the cottages, dragging a sword by the blade, the handle clinking along the wooden slats of the stage, Camila released Soledad, and in tears at the thought she might have to mourn Lalo someday, like Giselle, she leaned over to Lalo, and with a nudge to wake him, she embraced his arm and cried onto the sleeve of his new suit.

Camila's shift toward Lalo was little noticed by Soledad. What intrigued her most were Giselle's death throes—leaping wildly toward the mother who warned her not to dance so, spinning up near the rafters, it seemed, and then their fingers almost touching before she collapsed, only a few feet away from the possibility of a final embrace. By this time, Camila was crying as if she were Giselle herself, her delicate sniffs and the choking sound coming from her throat causing those around her to pity a young woman so sensitive, and some of them could not resist patting her pretty shoulders and petting her hair. But Soledad sat there with her jaw clenched tightly at the injustice of the story, and only Lalo, who happened to glance at her over the hands that reached out to Camila, noted the severity of his sister's face. He pinched her cheek playfully, a pinch that was hard enough to leave the mark of a little red half-moon on Soledad's flushed skin.

The slow walk back to El Cotorro seemed, to Soledad, to go on for an eternity. The night was humid and sticky, and there was little breeze to cool them off. Despite the thickness of the air, Camila clung to Lalo and lamented the death of Giselle. Her tears were now replaced by a talkative mood, and her voice echoed through the streets.

"Can you imagine, Lalo? To die from a broken heart."

"She must have had a weak heart, I suppose," said Lalo in a distant sort of way as he examined the tips of his brown shoes as he walked. There was a tiny rip on the right shoe, and he was thinking of taking it in to work the next day and repairing it when no one was looking. He had wandered into the factory one stormy afternoon to dry off. The foreman handed him a bundle of wrapped leather, pointed him in the direction of the cutters, and left. Lalo officially began in the Capote Shoe Factory that day. Still, whenever Doña Amparo frowned at the rancid smell of untreated leather that lingered like a dust cloud around Lalo, he told her that he would one day do what his papá had done and find meaningful work in a city with more opportunities to offer. Amparo usually sniffed and waved him away, but Lalo had learned not to mention his plan around his mother, who would begin to weep whenever she heard it.

Camila held both of Lalo's hands in hers and said, "To think, that even after death she loved him so. *Ay, mi amor,* that is how I would be. If I were turned into a ghost, I would still love you," and at that, Lalo laughed and held her close, distracted for the moment from his shoes.

With every tittering compliment that the couple paid one another, Soledad slowed her step until they were both small specks in the distance. She had been whistling the melody of the overture to the ballet, repeating the same notes over and over because she could not recall the rest. Her thoughts had been straying for quite some time now, from her mamá to her brother and back to the ballet.

Soledad carried the three tickets in her hand, each one torn in half. She had meant to keep them, to put them away as souvenirs. Halfway home, she found that the ink from the paper was smudging blue-and-yellow stains onto her palm. They didn't fit into her tiny purse, a purse made of mother-of-pearl shaped like a clam that Josefina had found at a flea market. Soledad was afraid of the tickets getting crumpled, and so she held onto them tightly, her heart skipping when the wind made the tickets tremble in her hand. She paused then, watching her brother and Camila walk farther away in the dark, and decided that they could fend for themselves for a moment, while she washed her hand.

Nearby, she knew, was a small fountain that decorated the entrance to the bank of El Cotorro. She found it quickly and plunged the stained hand into the cool water, careful to hold the tickets in her other hand, far from the fountain. Soledad rubbed her palm against the tiled sides vigorously. When she was done and the stains were gone, she stood there, her hand and sleeve dripping, with nowhere to dry herself. With her arm outstretched she began to walk, squinting to catch a glimpse of Lalo and Camila. They were too far ahead, so she quickened her pace.

When the neighborhood lights began to glow in the distance, Soledad finally slowed, and wiped at the sweat on her upper lip with a hand that was still damp and cold. It was then that a tall man approached her, offering a handkerchief, saying, *"Para la señorita."* Soledad, who was by now tired and agitated, took the handkerchief roughly, and, placing the tickets in her mouth, began to dry her hand. She was still drying with the crumpled cloth when she began walking again.

"Espera," he said, and grabbed her roughly by the shoulder. Soledad stiffened, and her eyes searched for her brother in the darkness. She felt the heavy hand that stopped her lift, her skin feeling suddenly cold where the touch had been.

"Do you remember me?" he asked, and with that, Soledad turned around and began to examine the face above hers. It was a thin face, with lines around the mouth that revealed at once that the face had been fat years before. His eyes were topped by eyebrows that came together in a way that suggested unkindness. This trait was offset by the way the man stood, with both hands tucked into pockets now and the legs oddly apart, like a boy being chastised. She could not decide right away whether to run to her brother or stay and talk with this man. She also could not decide upon an answer to his question. He was somehow familiar to her, as if she had known him long ago or had seen him in passing somewhere. Soledad wished for light. Here in the darkness, it was hard to tell who it was.

"You don't remember, *niña?*" he asked again, standing straighter and almost growling. Now Soledad could not help backing away, away from this madman of changing moods. It was too dark, there were too many shadows. The face was familiar, the voice echoed memorably. Soledad was afraid, and she moved toward the lights of the nearby lampposts, watching him watch her in the murky night. He followed her, and once they were in the hazy light, she recognized Abel at last. He had been to her house earlier, delivering a letter.

"Can I have my handkerchief, please?" he asked, holding out an immense hand.

"Of . . . of course," Soledad said, and released the crumpled thing she had been holding so tightly. She looked at it and frowned at its condition before dropping it between the large, curled fingers.

"What happened to your cheek? Roughhousing with Lalo again, eh?" Abel asked.

She touched her face where Lalo had pinched her. They had stopped in the middle of El Cotorro's only pretty road, each lamppost garnished with baskets of pink and white impatiens. Soledad felt as if the velvet curtains she had seen at the theater were now parting somewhere in her own memory, revealing Abel before her.

She had linked the memory of him with the days when her papá did not come home, and now she remembered that he was kind to them and that for some reason Lalo was not kind to him. Though only four years had gone by since Abel was thrown out of the house by Lorenzo, they had been long years for Soledad, had taken her from childhood to womanhood, and had erased the image of Abel from her mind, leaving only a shadow.

Soledad had no way of knowing that Abel had seen her often. At least once a week, he delivered letters to the house in El Cotorro, and he peeked into the windows to watch over the family he had come to love, and the woman who meant the most to him in the world. The next day, he'd make his dutiful call to the sergeant and report that all was well. Abel had grown attached to the voice on the other side of the line, a voice that had grown more ragged with each passing year. He would do what he could to protect the sergeant from grief, even if it meant lying. So this was Abel's routine—skulking to the house in the dark of night, a phone call in the morning. If he had been caught by a roving policeman, he would have been taken for a peeping tom, a pervert of some sort. But Abel looked on Soledad as a father would his sleeping child. The last four years had been difficult, like walking slowly in a nightmare from his apartment to the little house and back. Seeing Soledad now, awake and grown, was like seeing the morning for the first time in years.

"Good evening, Señor Santana," she said.

"No, *por favor,* call me Abel, just Abel. You have grown so," he said, admiring her frame and height, and Soledad, obviously pleased, drew closer to him and took the crushed handkerchief from his hand, folded it carefully, and returned it to him once more.

"May I walk you home?" Abel asked, and Soledad, searching the horizon for her brother, and concluding that he was long gone, nodded.

Their street was quite dark at night. It lacked the faint light of the lampposts that made the rest of the town seem to glow. Soledad stumbled on lifted cobblestones, or the exposed roots of trees, and with each blunder, Abel grasped her arm. When they reached the house with its little concrete porch and the windows clouded over with scratches and fingerprints, Soledad invited Abel in.

"Oh, Mamá would be so happy to see an old friend. I'm sure she is still awake."

"No, Soledad, old friends are easily forgotten," he said, and seemed to lose himself for a moment. When he finally drew himself out of his reverie, he asked, "Would you meet me tomorrow at the market, around noon?"

Soledad, sensing a way to escape her duties as chaperone at least for one afternoon, readily agreed. With a small peck on the cheek from Abel, she hopped up the porch steps and went into the house.

She found her brother and Camila kissing in the front room. When she appeared, the couple separated, and did not ask her where she had been, but instead smiled at her. At once, Soledad noticed that Camila was no longer wearing any lipstick in that berry color that suited her so well, but rather, the pink stain had left its oily remains on her chin and on Lalo's white collar. Soledad excused herself and went to bed. After a while, she could hear Lalo and Camila leaving the house, on their way back to Mar Lindo to drop Camila off. Kissing in Doña Amparo's parlor would just not do, and so they often stopped in El Cotorro for some time alone in the dark.

Later, Soledad would hear Lalo snoring in the little room he had built for himself. He had thought it too awkward sleeping in the same place as his sister, and so he spent one summer raising the walls of a little shack behind the house. He built the frame for his bed, too. It took him two weeks at the shoe factory to earn enough for a mattress. His snoring, heard through the open windows at night, and that of his father's across the hall, combined to form a horrible melody—one high note, one low note—repeated throughout the night.

Inside her dark room, Soledad had the immediate sensation that she was not alone, and as her eyes adjusted themselves to the dark, she began to make out a slumbering heap on her bed, stirring just a bit.

"Mamá, what's wrong?" asked Soledad.

"*Nada, nada,* how was the ballet?" Josefina rubbed her eyes like a child and sat up, spreading the sheets smooth next to her, readying the space for Soledad.

"Beautiful," Soledad said, and began undressing in the dark, letting the dress fall to the floor. She stepped on the brown taffeta as she pulled on her nightgown, the starchy material crunching under her feet.

"Be careful, that dress cost so much. Hang it up, hang it up."
Josefina was lying down again, impatience marking her voice. She
wanted to begin talking to her daughter, and Soledad, who noted
the impatience, was taking too long. Soledad took a wooden
hanger and slowly draped the dress over it, and then sighing,
preparing for a sleepless night, she sat next to her mamá, who
pushed her down onto the bed and held her about the neck and
shoulders.

"Tell me, what did you think of the ballet?"

"I said it was beautiful, Mamá."

"But did it move you? Do you feel like dancing now?" Josefina
leaned into her daughter's face, her own eyes wide and teary.

"What is wrong, Mamá?" Soledad asked again.

"I have a new letter from your grandfather today. Every day I
expect his letters," Josefina said, and held her hands open, the letter crumpled in her hands. "There is so much you don't know, so
much I wish you never to know," she said. "A dress like that was
nothing to me when I was a girl. I could wear it once and throw it
out, just like that. And now I am lucky if I even have a dress for
each of the seasons." Josefina slipped in deeper beneath the heavy
blanket. "Your grandfather gave me all those things. All I have
now are these letters." She paused, and drew in a long, whistling
breath. "Those others that your papá is with, those are like dolls,
I tell you. They are probably beautiful and thin. They probably
don't have *masitas* like this," she said, and grabbed at a layer of fat
on her stomach. "And they laugh at me in their tight dresses and
don't care about my feelings." Again she stopped, she laughed a
bit, then said, "But they are unfortunate, you know. They don't
have someone in heaven guarding them as I do."

By now, the tears had begun, and Soledad could feel them on
her neck, making their slow progression down between her
breasts and onto her stomach before finally trickling down onto
the bed. She felt her muscles tighten with each word from Josefina. She wanted to be alone, to think of the ballet, of the lovely

theater, and of the old friend who had taken such an interest in her. And she wondered whether telling her mamá about the encounter would make her quiet for a while.

"Mamá, I met someone tonight, he's . . ."

". . . and your papá, he tells me, 'Be quiet, woman, you are a crazy woman, I'll have you sent away.' "

"He's very nice, Mamá, and he knows us all from a few years ago. His name . . ."

"And I say, 'Yes, you were happy when the sergeant died, and you were happy when you sent *him* away. You took them both from me,' I say, 'I should be the one with that power, to send all those fancy women away from you.' "

". . . is Abel Santana, and Mamá, oh, don't you remember him, because I do."

At the mention of his name Josefina became very quiet and very still. The wriggling hand had stopped moving through Soledad's hair. The stillness was unsettling. It was odd, like death in a way, because nights like these were usually filled with movement to the point of exhaustion. Josefina sat up a little, and the sudden gesture startled Soledad. The stillness continued for a long while before Josefina spoke again.

"You were much younger, you remember? But that was love, what we had then."

"You and Papá?" Soledad asked, pleased that the talks had turned to memories more cheerful.

"No, *mi querer,* Abel and I. And on certain nights, when I long for him most, I believe that I smell him all around. I smell him now, in your hair and on your arms." And Soledad grew very still herself. To hear her mamá talk of ghost letters and Papá's lovers was one thing, because Soledad didn't really believe any of it anymore. The ghost letters were clearly forged, and Papá seemed so frail now with headaches that ravaged him night and day, but to hear of Mamá and Abel was another thing altogether. Here it was, infidelity confessed to. And to see her there in the dark, smiling with remembrance . . .

"But I told you, long ago, never to mention his name," Josefina said, with a bizarre kind of calm about her. She cleared her throat and sniffed. "Did you say you saw him somewhere?" she asked, and the agitation of her hands and the quivering in her limbs began again.

"No, Mamá, no. I simply said that I suddenly remembered him, like a long ago dream. I'm sure he's far away. I'm tired, can we sleep now, please?" Josefina nodded and kissed her daughter, breathing in the scent of her, and him, deeply.

"Buenas noches," she said, and fell asleep quickly, caught between then and now.

26

Soledad did not sleep well with her mother's head lying on her breast. There was little Soledad could do to make herself comfortable enough for sleep, *and besides,* she thought, *I can think of nothing but Abel right now.* The scent of him, which her mamá had noticed, indeed lingered, and Soledad caught herself lifting her forearm to her nose and sniffing where he had gripped her, finding the scent of him still there. But she had already dismissed the idea of meeting him at the market the next day. She would not be able to enjoy herself or his company, because she was sure that Josefina's voice would hover over every conversation between them, her eyes would be reflected in every shop window they might pass, and he would touch her only because she looked like a younger version of her mother. These were the thoughts that crowded Soledad's mind that night. Toward dawn, when the neighbor's three-year-old rooster began to crow its discordant song, her thoughts began to change. Surely here was a way for her to finally keep a secret of her own. And when her mamá would come at night, Soledad would have something to hide from her, or perhaps, something to tell.

As agreed, Soledad arrived at the market at noon. The sun was high, and she burst into a heavy sweat quickly. She tried standing underneath a fruit vendor's tent for shade while she waited for Abel, but the vendor pushed her away with both hands flat on her waist, saying that others could not see his produce because she was in the way. She stood underneath the fish vendor's tent then, but after a few minutes, she decided that the stink of shrimp and the fat groupers that lay side by side with their tails cut off and shoved into their gills to enable buyers to examine the meat would adhere to her clothes, so she walked back out into the sun and leaned on the iron flag post in the center of the market, which burned her back and left a red mark that she would not notice that day.

After a few minutes, some of which were punctuated by moments of relief from the sun, when rain clouds floated overhead and cast passing shadows over the market, Abel appeared. He wore pants of white linen. They were tinged brown around the cuffs from the dust that he kicked up with each step. When he saw Soledad standing by the flagpole, he opened his arms wide, then brought them together in a loud clap, as if he had just discovered something astonishing about her. Soledad found the gesture alluring. No one ever showed such enthusiasm upon seeing her, unless it was followed by a request of some sort. When he reached her he opened his arms again, clasping Soledad's hands, then twirling her around so that her hair spun into his face and he tasted the saltiness of her sweat mixed with the bitterness of the perfume she had sprinkled into her hair.

"*¡Que linda!*" he said and spun her around once more.

"*Muchas gracias,*" Soledad said and curtsied in a way she had once seen Camila do when Lalo complimented her. Abel curled his arm and placed Soledad's hand through the crook of it. They spoke quietly as they walked through the market and out of it, and Soledad wondered why they had met there at all if not to stay a while.

"Does your mamá bring you to Mass?" asked Abel, suddenly releasing her arm and looking her over much as he used to, his eyes peering down his nose at her, his hands folded behind him.

"No. She says she doesn't believe in the church anymore. She says that her father, my grandfather, is her only god." Soledad held her hand over her eyes to shield them from the sun. "She writes letters and says they are from him, as if his ghost were only occupied with correspondence." Soledad lowered her head and spoke in a hushed voice: "Sometimes I wish his ghost would appear and throw things in the house, a potted plant all over the kitchen floor, or shatter a coffee table in half. Then perhaps Mamá would change her mind about spirits. Was she this way when you knew her?" Soledad asked, and lowered her hand when a cloud floated overhead.

"She has always been the same," Abel said, and then, indifferent to Soledad's sigh, asked, "And your baptism? Have you been baptized?"

"No."

"I suppose I should finish what I started, hmm? Come." He smiled, cocked an eyebrow up, took her hand. They walked the mile and a half to the church. It had changed much since the first time Soledad was brought to it, but she did not notice the changes, in the same way that she did not notice the changes in her face and figure when she looked in the mirror. In the years to come, the nuns would be sent into hiding, the church would be closed for good, and the state would become the new deity. But this was far on the horizon, and now all that Soledad could see was that she was with Abel and that he had chosen her for this sacred moment. She quivered with excitement.

The stone cave where she first met Camila was boarded up with fresh planks, because the stones had begun to fall, crushing the plaster Virgin inside. The gardens themselves were now covered in gravel. As more and more automobiles had come onto the island, more and more people began driving to church, and the garden served as a suitable parking lot. Inside, the people of El Cotorro now sat to the right *and* left, and there were no longer any pearl-handled fans, or lace dresses, or big donations for that matter, since the town of Mar Lindo had opened its new cathedral.

What had stayed the same through the years were the cloisters, where the nuns continued their daily shuffle to and from the church. The stone wells that marked each corner of the cloisters were intact, and the tiled murals on the walls of San Matéo penning the New Testament, of Cuba itself, cradled in the arms of the Virgin were polished every afternoon. Abel walked Soledad through these halls and past the nuns who polished, dipping their rags in soapy water every so often. He stopped at the smallest well and plunged his hand inside.

"This will do. Come," he gestured, and Soledad came up to the well and looked into the darkness of it. It was not as deep as she thought it would be. Instead of a gaping hole into the earth, the well was nothing more than a carved-out sink that held a small amount of water. She let her own hand fall into the water and swirled it about. It was cool, and the walls of the well were somewhat slimy, as if the nuns who spent so much of their time polishing the mosaics found no time at all to clean out the wells. Suddenly, she felt Abel's hand embrace her neck, his thumb brushing against her cheek. When she looked up at him, he brought another hand to her forehead, and he made a small cross there with his finger, dripping and cold. He stepped back to look at his work and watched as a thick drop made its way down her brow and onto the bridge of her nose. This final drop he wiped away with a handkerchief.

"I baptize you, *en el nombre del Padre, del Hijo, y del Espíritu Santo. Amen.*" But this solemn blessing he said with a smile.

"You can't baptize me. You don't have that power," Soledad said, wiping at her wet face with the back of her hand. She had thought that he was going to take her to a priest and that her baptism would be a sacred moment, filled with all those beautiful little rituals and chants that made things sacred. And here was this man, dousing her face with filthy water as if he could change anything.

Abel still smiled at her and proceeded to explain: "Look here, here is the holy water in this well. And that nun there, no, the other one, with the nose like a fish hook, yes, her, she is your god-mother. And I," he said, patting his chest, "am your godfather. I am to make sure that your education in this world is complete."

She was about to ask, "And what am I to learn first?" when she bit her lip to stop herself. It sounded too saucy, too much like something her mamá might say in response to him. Instead, she rolled her eyes daintily and walked down the corridor, listening to his steps as he followed her out. Once outside, the oddness of the day struck her again, and she began to think of Josefina, and what he still thought of her.

"Abel," she began, "you really should see Mamá. She hasn't aged at all," she lied, "and I'm sure she'd be overjoyed to see you again, such a dear, old friend." Soledad watched him, her eye-brows unwittingly arched in anticipation of his response. In truth, she wanted him to meet her mother again and to be shocked, horrified, by the old woman she had become. It was a cruel thought Soledad allowed herself to enjoy before brushing it away guiltily. Soledad had, in the course of an afternoon, fallen in love with Abel.

"So you know. And she told you, I am sure." Her eyebrows fell and her eyes widened as he approached. "Aah, but I see that she doesn't know you found me again. You are too confident, too bold." He laughed then. "What I did was for you and your brother. You should have seen yourselves. There was no food, your hip bones stuck out and showed through your dresses, your clothes were tattered, you didn't know what the inside of a church looked like . . ." Abel had not noticed Soledad watching him with eyes large and wet. She seemed to him still the vulnerable girl he once knew. His thoughts were consumed with Josefina, at all hours, and if there was any delight in being with Soledad, it was because she sometimes resembled her mother when she smiled.

"What you did was not for us," she said, angry now that he was defending himself. She wanted him to be sorry, to say that his thoughts were only of her now.

"If you despise me, Soledad, then please leave." He stared down at her and watched as her fingers twitched and her face tensed at his demand. She could not force herself to move, to leave, to walk away, and to go tell her mamá.

"Very well. I'll walk you home," he said, curling his arm, and Soledad took it once again, and they walked in silence the rest of the way.

2 7

Lorenzo had been yelling for twenty-four hours about his headache. The light bothered him, the smell of chicken cooking was excruciating, and Josefina's questions, "Are you better? Let me call the doctor," made him want to wring her neck.

"Let me die in peace," he shouted at the ceiling at last, and it had driven Josefina out onto the porch for some peace of her own. So it was that she saw them, Abel turning the corner, her frail, dark daughter arm in arm with him.

"*Dios mío,*" she whispered, and her chest tightened. She thought for a moment that this was a vision, that either they or she were dead, and this was the final moment, the final recognition of an earthly life before sinking into the dark forever. The strong winds of the evening sent a palm frond from the yard across the street crashing down, rattling its hollow bones with a crunch. *No, no, this is real,* she thought. She could see Abel clearly even from a distance, thought she saw the veins in his arms, the wet patches of sweat growing into larger circles on his chest.

It did not take long for Soledad to notice her mother, a wavering figure in the distance.

"Stop here," she said to Abel. "I can walk alone the rest of the way." But it was too late. Josefina had left the shade of the porch and was now running, barefoot, toward them. She dashed through a puddle and mud splashed onto the bottom of her house dress, all the way up to her knees.

Abel let go of Soledad's arm, as tenderly as a father giving up the bride at the altar, and met Josefina halfway. They stopped and faced each other, then silently embraced. Her muscles went watery, relaxed as if they wanted nothing more than to be still forever. Curtains in the windows around them parted, the game of stickball going on behind them ended, and Soledad walked the rest of the way home, kicking stones with her feet, cursing the one secret that had been only hers for a while, as it slipped away.

A light sprinkling of rain fell in El Cotorro and washed the dust off the streets. Josefina came in from the rain, flushed and nervous. Her large eyes, eyes that Lorenzo had once called froglike, were bigger than ever. Upon seeing her mother inside again, Soledad pushed past her, shoving Josefina out of the doorway with her slim hips. Josefina followed her daughter outside, the humidity clinging to their lungs at once.

"You shouldn't be with him," Soledad said, her voice dripping venom.

"You are being stubborn," Josefina said. She turned her daughter around.

"Mamá, you have lost your head! You can't have an affair right under my father's nose!" Soledad yelled and her voice was carried up by the wind and caught in the laundry hung to dry on the balconies above. As she yelled, Soledad knew this wasn't about her father. He had become a breathing corpse, took up space, never offered to help around the house, never showed her mother affection. It wasn't for him that she was angry. Soledad had never had a thing of her own, never had a thing she hadn't shared with her mother or with Lalo. Abel could have been that thing, and her heart ached for him as it did for Julio Cuadras.

"Come, *mi vida,*" Josefina said, trembling, "why shouldn't I have some love in my life, too? Your father has had every woman in El Cotorro, and then he comes to me at night and touches me and wants me to be his wife. I haven't let him come near in four years. Four years! I love Abel in the way your father should love me."

There was silence for a while. Regla had once said, during one of her visits, that Soledad was the strongest person in the world. That her heart was immobile as a mountain's. At this moment, Soledad felt her heart pounding, could swear it had burst inside her chest, wanted to scream, "I love him, too! Can't I have a little happiness?" She remained silent. Inside, Soledad measured her words. She weighed her thoughts. Mountainlike, she stood straighter.

"Papá says he sometimes thinks you are crazy, and I could have confirmed that for him. I could have told him about Abel, and Regla's *trabajito,* but I didn't." Soledad had both hands on her hips now, and the scene unfolding before the opened windows was getting louder. "And now you want me to accept your affair? You're ridiculous."

Josefina was straightening her dress all the while that Soledad shouted. She tucked a few stray curls into the clip in her hair at last, cleared her throat, and said, "Your grandfather has sent Abel to me, to us. He is our guardian angel made into flesh."

"And Papá sleeps with a thousand women a night, doesn't he? And those letters in the shoebox are from heaven." Soledad cupped her mother's cheeks in her hands, both of them sweating from heat and rage and sadness. "Not everything, Mamá, is destiny and witchcraft."

Soledad expected her mother to cry, to apologize, to see apparitions, but Josefina simply kissed the hand that clutched her face. She entered the house once again, sitting on a hard, cane-backed chair, fanning herself with a magazine she lifted from the seat next to her. She was thinking that she should never have shared the ghost letters with Soledad long ago. Her daughter, she thought, was a bit ungrateful, as ungrateful as she was as a child when she forgot she had once had a mother. *Young people,* Josefina decided, *cannot understand holy things.*

Outside, Soledad turned away from the scene. She was hot and tense, anticipating the touch of her mother again. She thought about Abel, about the dreams she had had of him the night before, how she had moaned in her sleep and woken herself up. And she thought about the ghost letters. The sergeant. How she wished she had known him in all his uniformed toughness. At times, she was more like her mother than she liked to admit, and there, under the just breaking rain clouds, she thought she could feel the sergeant looking down on her where she sat, and the tropical heat felt more like rays from heaven, warming her skin. She closed her eyes and prayed the Our Father, the way Abel had taught her when she was a little girl. "*Anda,* come inside," she imagined the sergeant saying to her. "Make your sad mamá happy."

Josefina nearly cried out when Soledad came and sat by her, but she held her hand to her mouth to keep from waking her husband.

28

Lalo's friends had urged him to propose. Camila's friends looked for a ring on her finger, and Doña Amparo expected the request any moment. But it didn't come. They had been together for more than five years. Though most of Lalo's friends were either engaged or enlisted, Lalo and Camila lived like teenagers, despite the fact that they were in their twenties, romping about in the backs of cars, taking advantage of their homes when they were empty. Lalo did not want the pressure of having to maintain a house, having to use his salary from the shoe factory on bills. Camila wasn't quite ready to give up the life she lived in Mar Lindo, a life of comfort for the poverty that would come with being Lalo's wife. But change came upon them, suddenly.

Doña Amparo died of a fever in the summer of 1958. She had been ill for days, and Camila spent the sunlit hours placing wet towels on her *tía*'s forehead, feeding her chicken soup and bean broth. On Friday, when her aunt finally fell asleep, trusting that the old woman was well enough to spend the evening alone, Camila took the opportunity to go out with Lalo, unchaperoned. She returned from a night of dancing at Mar Lindo's society hall to find her great aunt in bed, her eyes open, staring up at the ceiling, her hands clutching the wet towels so tightly that the water had been wrung out of them, forming puddles on the floor.

The doctor who examined the body later that evening shook

his head when he asked Camila where she had been all night. He looked at Doña Amparo's stiff remains and said, "Aah, she must have died from worry." From that moment on, Camila, who had been crying endlessly since she found her aunt's body, was like a woman turned into a slab of marble. Her eyes no longer widened with surprise or fear. Instead she kept them narrowed, so that a deep crease formed over her nose. Her cheeks, usually raised high on her face, now sank below the gray half-moons under her eyes. Her posture was affected, too, and she no longer stood with her little hands folded delicately before her, but, instead, dug them into the sleeves of her clothes and scratched at her arms. The change, as the Concepción family soon learned to call it, was immediate, and the cheerful, frivolous Camila they once knew was gone.

The entire Concepción family stayed with her in Mar Lindo that night. At home in El Cotorro, the announcement had prompted an excursion, with Josefina ironing the family's best clothes and Lorenzo climbing the narrow attic to pull out suitcases and an old carpetbag that hadn't been used in years.

Once in Mar Lindo, Josefina brewed cup after cup of tea for Camila, bringing it up the stairs on a silver tray with real linen napkins tucked underneath. In her youth, Josefina had had a home such as this, and teacups and a staircase with iron railings—all things that she felt she should never have lost. Like Abel, these beautiful things would return to her someday, she was sure.

Camila stayed in the bedroom with her aunt all evening. Lalo sat on an ottoman near her, not wanting to touch her yet or to speak a word. The light from the lamppost outside shone a thin thread of light over Doña Amparo's forehead and across one eye, having a ghastly effect of making it appear that the pupil underneath the lid was twitching, as it might in sleep. Twice that evening Lalo tried to adjust the curtain so that the light would not shine through, but it was no use. The wrought-iron lampposts and their light, which were the hallmark of Mar Lindo and its wealth, were now a curse to Camila, because she believed that this image of her dead aunt, with the single moving eye, would haunt her always.

In the morning, Josefina and Soledad undressed Doña Amparo and bathed her. Her nightgown had begun to take on the smell of a cadaver, even before her body did. With their large sponges and buckets of cold soapy water, the pair washed and lathered the old, wrinkled woman, soaking the mattress. Then they dried her and dressed her in an ugly black dress with a calico print. Soledad could not bear to send a pretty dress into the grave. Josefina combed and lifted the woman's hair into the chignon she had so often worn, while Soledad smudged the withered lips with lipstick. They did all this with a cold sort of efficiency. All the while, Josefina thought about how she was glad she had not had the chance to do this for the sergeant, her papá, and how hard that would have been. Soledad imagined the awful day she would have to do this for her mamá. And so they worked in silence, each one lost in her own morbid vision.

At noon the men arrived with the coffin. It was black and lacquered, and Soledad could not help touching the silver handles as the box went by. Upstairs, the men, skinny gravediggers who left clumps of dirt from their shoes all over the house, lifted Doña Amparo with surprising ease and arranged her in the coffin. One man placed her hands over her breast while the other straightened the knees, which had hardened overnight, so that when he pulled, the bones clicked loudly. By now, they had all pulled their funeral clothes out from their stale suitcases and put them on. Only Camila needed Josefina's help. She would not dress herself, and Josefina found that dressing the niece was harder than dressing the aunt.

Outside, the converted limousine arrived. The men who had come with the coffin were the same men who placed it inside the car and drove it to the church, and later, the cemetery. Seeing that the family had no transportation to the gravesite, they allowed them all to sit alongside the coffin, on black leather seats that were so close to the casket that they all had to bring their knees up to their chests and hold them in place. No one wanted to touch the box with Doña Amparo inside, and no one spoke, except for Lorenzo, who said at least twice before arriving at the graveyard, "Feel this leather, will you? What do you think they put on it to keep it so soft?" he asked no one in particular, rubbing his hand over the upholstery.

Once at the cemetery, the family worked themselves out of the car and walked to the open grave, where the entire town of Mar Lindo, or so it seemed to the Concepcións, had gathered for the burial. The whispers among the townsfolk became hurried when they saw the band of miserable-looking people emerge from the car. One of the women, who had gripped her husband's arm at the sight of them, rushed forward and embraced Camila, pulling her away from the group and toward the mouth of the grave, where a seat had been provided for her, the bereaved, Doña Amparo's only relative. The men and women from Mar Lindo crowded around that chair, holding golden rosaries and bunches of roses, and each took a turn, one after another, placing their white hands on Camila's shoulder and squeezing for a moment.

The Concepcións had been relegated to the back of the crowd, where the turf had grown muddy, and Soledad and Josefina felt their best heels sinking into the wet earth. Lalo strained to see the priest who stood mumbling as the coffin was lowered into the ground, and Lorenzo counted the number of funeral-goers and priced their suits and dresses in his head.

The burial was soon finished, and the car that brought them all over was long gone. Camila was taken by the arm, by the same woman as before, and escorted into a blue sedan. The people from Mar Lindo dispersed then, in their own automobiles, and left the Concepción family standing, yards away from the open grave to contemplate how they would get home.

It took them more than an hour to walk back to their home in El Cotorro. By the time they reached the small house, each one of them looked bedraggled in his or her way. Lorenzo's tie had been flung to the ground somewhere near the market. Lalo developed a significant limp from the blisters forming on his feet; his shoes were new for the occasion and not broken in yet. Soledad and Josefina had hiked up their long skirts and waved them about to cool off their legs. They walked in silence, none of them wishing to discuss what had occurred at the funeral, how they had been unseated as Camila's caretakers, how they had been made to walk home after all they had done for her. And all of this while they wore their best clothes and had spent their morning shining themselves up.

Lalo felt this rejection most keenly and refused to go and find Camila that evening, even after his mamá urged him to. In fact, none of them saw Camila for two weeks after the funeral. Their only sight of her was in the Mar Lindo newspaper, where, in a small, faraway picture, the funeral was shown, and Camila, installed in her chair and surrounded by the wealthy of Mar Lindo, sat meekly.

The days went by slowly, curiously empty without the cheerful, delicate girl coming by for visits. Soledad had just graduated and was working at a local beauty shop, sweeping up hair from the floor, to earn enough money to attend the university. Lorenzo nursed his migraines, Josefina met Abel in his apartment for lunch every day, and Lalo sulked at work and at home over his girlfriend. That had become the routine of their lives until Camila came back to them.

It was on the Sunday of the second week that Camila opened the creaky door of the house in El Cotorro without knocking and sat herself on one of the rockers, folding and unfolding a document in her hands. She might have sat there all morning had Josefina not come into the parlor to search for her purse.

"*Mi niña,* what are you doing here?" Josefina asked.

"I . . . I've been alone these last days and didn't know what to do when this arrived."

Indeed, Camila's appearance revealed that there was no one looking after her as she was accustomed to. Her hair was loose about her shoulders and uncombed, the strands lying dead on a white collar that was dirty and wrinkled, over a neck that was dark with sweat and dirt. Her once chubby face was now marked by a pointed chin and hollowed-out eyes, and her pale bottom lip was nervously tucked under a row of teeth.

"Let me see," Josefina said, taking the letter from Camila. She read it, and it took her a long time to read, so long, that before she was finished, Lorenzo and Lalo appeared in the parlor. Lalo looked at Camila, who would not meet his eyes, and felt his stomach turn.

"What is that?" asked Lorenzo, his hand placed on his forehead, a permanent fixture now to relieve the pressure.

"Amparo's will, and a letter from *la Doña, que Dios la tenga en la gloria,*" she said, glancing up at the cracked ceiling and crossing herself.

Lorenzo read as slowly as Josefina had. For Josefina, there was little she could do to stop herself from smiling, and the corners of her mouth twitched uncontrollably. Lorenzo tapped his foot on the ground as he read, a quick knocking rhythm that would not ease. And as for Lalo, the old tightening of his stomach returned, and he bent forward a little as he read, to lessen the pain. It read:

Mi Querida Camila,

If you have received this letter from the lawyer, my beautiful niece, it is because I have died. You must be strong. The house is yours. Everything is yours. There are approximately two hundred thousand pesos in your name at the bank.

Do what you must to be happy. Marry Lalo if you wish. There is no shame in marrying poor. To be quite truthful, your parents were even poorer still. But they were kind, above it all, remember that they were kind and loved you despite what they did. I often wondered why you were so drawn to the Concepción boy and thought perhaps that it was in your blood.

Remember me and above all, be happy, *corazón*.
Tu Tía Amparo, if not through blood, then through devotion.

Lorenzo and Josefina thrilled at the mention of Lalo as part of
this inheritance. In light of this, they were both willing to dismiss
the old woman's comments about the poor, for Lorenzo never
considered himself poor, though Josefina, who once knew what it
was to live in wealth, did. Lalo's thoughts, too, lingered on this bit
of information, but Camila had come to them, not for a marriage
proposal but for an explanation about her ancestral poverty, her
parents, who she had always thought were as rich as Amparo.

Josefina walked Camila home that night after having fed and
bathed her. It was like caring for an infant, or so Josefina thought,
because the girl's arms were either limp or stiff and unyielding.
When feeding her, Josefina found that she had to issue commands
for the eating: "Open. Chew. Swallow. Swallow, Camila. There.
Now open," she'd say, holding her jaw with one hand, lifting the
spoon filled with cornmeal in the other.

Camila had not said a word after the family read the letter.
Though she wanted to speak to Soledad, to ask her questions that
she could answer, Soledad was out, strolling about, they had said,
and they did not expect her soon. So, the questions lingered in
Camila's mind, about her *tía,* her parents, herself, her money. As
she walked, she slipped her arms into her sleeves, touched the scar
on her chest with her hands, like prostitutes who know how to
tuck their hands into their blouses and unhook bras and underwear from the inside out. By the time they were half a mile from
Doña Amparo's house—*now Camila's house, someday Lalo's
house,* Josefina thought—the girl's movement was making her nervous. She pulled Camila's arms from inside her dress and smacked
the tops of her hands lightly. Camila stopped then, and looked at
her escort in horror.

"No one has told me anything," Camila began all at once, "and this, this, is the key." She opened her dress with one vicious rip, the rose-shaped buttons snapping and scattering to the sidewalk. The scar was now red, as if it, too, was infuriated with the deception imposed on its origin. "Tell me. Tell me," Camila yelled, grabbing Josefina by the shoulders, the girl's torn dress now puddling around her ankles.

It was a story so infamous that the whole island had heard of it, even if they weren't able to connect the sweet girl from Mar Lindo to it. It was one of those stories that people repeated, turned into gruesome legend. Perhaps it was because of her past that Josefina had come to love her like a daughter. Josefina, who was so expert at telling Soledad every awful truth, could not bring herself to tell this delicate, lovely girl that all she had was illegitimate, that she was really no better than they were. And so, Josefina clucked into Camila's ear, wrapping her arms around her and pulling her dress on. In this way they continued walking, the lights of the houses dimming behind them.

The next day, after making breakfast, Josefina excused herself with a "trip to the beauty parlor." Lorenzo grumbled about the cost of a woman's haircut and nodded off to sleep, his head wrapped in cold cloths. Josefina spent the day with Abel again. All the while, as Abel whispered in her ear, she thought of Lorenzo, singing to her in their youth in his beautiful voice. And as she thought of Lorenzo, she felt guilty, an ache in her chest that wouldn't weaken. After all, he had come first, long ago when she was just a girl and her father still loved her in life.

She and Abel boarded a bus to the coast and wandered through the fish markets and near the docks. They watched as the boats pulled in loads of snapper, the large red fish openmouthed and jumping wildly for air. The tails were cut off while the fish still wriggled, and then they'd go stiff, ready for the grill. Josefina and Abel sat down for a meal of shrimp and rice, fried for them by a woman who cooked there every day and sold meals to the fishermen for a few centavos. She would twist the heads off the shrimp and throw them into the air behind her, where giddy seagulls would swoop down and catch the heads before they touched the water.

After lunch, Abel took Josefina by the hand and into a small, oceanside hotel and restaurant with terrazzo floors in pink-and-black fish designs. He nodded to the clerk, a young man with tufts of blond hair coming out from under his cap, and the young man raised an eyebrow at the couple in return.

They sat at a small round table in the lobby for drinks. In the center of the table was a crystal vase and a single lily. He ordered a *cerveza* for himself and one for her. Abel's talk that day was as frothy as his beer, while Josefina's grew quiet and pale, the foam settling away.

"Why are you so quiet?" he asked.

"I'm not so quiet," she said, but knew she had lied.

"It seems an impossibility, doesn't it?" Abel said.

"Us?" Josefina asked and Abel nodded. He sipped his beer and thought how even on this hot, sticky day, Josefina had a certain early morning quality, a fresh beauty, about her.

"You are beautiful," he said, then, "You haven't changed."

Josefina responded with a terse "hmm" and pushed her beer into the center of the table, bumping her glass with the lily vase, as if it were some sort of toast. She thought she could sense her father shaking his head in dismay, was sure that Lorenzo would know the flush in her cheeks at once, know that it wasn't caused by his caress. Their meal, when it came, settled uncomfortably in her stomach.

When they finally returned to El Cotorro, Abel kissed Josefina's hand and felt it tense and cold as her fingers snatched themselves away from his. Inside, Josefina would compose a letter of apology to her father that he would never read.

As for Abel, he walked away slowly, deliberately slow, and he, too, began to wonder at the situation in which he found himself. Why had he returned to this house? He owed the sergeant nothing. Theirs was a business transaction. But there was more, of course. Abel felt a duty to the family, a need to care for them, but there was little he could do. He had no money, and neither had Josefina. He would be taking her from poverty to more poverty and shame. He thought all of this as he walked. When he had arrived at his small apartment, he still had not found a solution.

In the little parlor at home, Josefina was surprised to find her husband, sitting in the dark, laughing with Lalo and flipping Amparo's wrinkled letter between them. Josefina noticed the emptied glasses that circled their feet, and the still upright bottle of rum, its bottom covered in a light film of the dark brown liquor.

"Mira," Lalo said, "Papá let me have it." He balanced a small ring on his thumb, and as Josefina looked closer, she saw that it was her wedding ring, dulled over the years, but still dainty. She had once been told that gold went brown when not used, when not stroked by human hands, anointed with human oils, and indeed, her gold ring seemed bronze, not golden at all, from disuse.

"What do you think, eh?" asked Lorenzo. "You won't mind." His eyes were glassy and his lips formed a sneer. Josefina felt cold. *Lorenzo knows,* she thought. *He has seen me with Abel and this is his way of letting me loose, of saying good-bye forever.* A knot in her throat, fat as a lemon, pulsed.

"She doesn't quite care about the old thing like she once did," Lorenzo said then to Lalo, and the two men laughed gustily, like windstorms blowing suddenly through the house. The moment passed. Lorenzo was happy still, unaware, believing that when Lalo came into Amparo's money, he would be able to buy diamonds as big as their house.

"Where is Camila? Soledad?" Josefina asked, breathing heavily with relief. Lalo was now trying to balance the ring on his nose.

"In *la Doña's* house," said Lorenzo, yawning and scratching his throat. Josefina left the house then, decided upon seeing Camila, and in the distance, she could hear the men in her life laughing again. On the way, she thought about Abel, about all she had come close to losing if Lorenzo had discovered her secret, and all there still was to lose.

The house in Mar Lindo was dark when she arrived, but the iron door, usually bolted for fear of robbers in the night, was open, a slit like a mouth exposed to the outside. Josefina came into the house and locked it behind her. She found her daughter in Camila's room. Camila was asleep on the large bed, the mosquito netting with the pretty lace trim pulled tightly around the mattress, and Camila herself, dressed only in a short camisole and nothing else, slept restlessly, her chest heaving and her brow furrowed. Soledad had fallen asleep on a chair next to the bed, and her head hung to the side. To Josefina, in her state of mind, her daughter looked as if her neck had been twisted.

"Hija, hija, despierta," Josefina said, shaking her daughter's knee. Soledad moaned and lifted her head, wiping at the saliva from her mouth with the back of her hand.

Josefina tried to smile, though Soledad could not see it in the dark. "Has Camila confided in you? Will she accept Lalito's proposal?" Soledad nodded and closed her eyes again.

Will we be lucky at last? Josefina thought to herself. *Such a house with so many rooms . . .* "And we can go, hand in hand," Josefina said aloud now, though Soledad was sleeping again, "you and I, *m'ija,* into the new cathedral in town, and we'll say we are Camila's long-lost cousins, and then you can go to society dances like I used to . . ." Her voice had risen in pitch, hammering away at the confusion regarding Abel, at the guilt she felt when she gave Lorenzo his aspirins at night, and with each marked change, Camila grunted in her sleep.

Soledad stirred, "What are you saying, Mamá? You don't mean to say . . ."

"*Sí.* I'm sure that Camila will want us here. I've been so good to her, you know." Soledad winced. "Your grandfather in heaven has taken good care of us." Josefina opened the netting and passed a smooth hand over Camila's forehead. "The girl is feverish. Go fetch some wet towels," she said. Then she lay down next to Camila.

Mi Hija,

I will write to you today of your mother, Ana, and the events that surrounded your birth. When she was pregnant a terrible thing happened. One day, while I was at work, your mother came home from a visit to a friend. Inside, she found couches overturned, clothes torn in two, and all of her jewelry gone. Stabbed into the polished wood of our china cabinet was a large knife that wasn't our own. Your mother, *que Dios la cuide,* ran out of the house and circled the neighborhood for hours, tiring herself out, so afraid that the robbers would return.

When I arrived home, I saw Ana waiting for me in the doorway, her belly bulging too low, it always seemed, drenched in rainwater from the afternoon downpour. She shook for days, because she was cold and afraid, and she could barely feed herself, her hands trembled so much.

The doctors had warned that she might not survive the delivery. Her body was weak. I told her they were wrong. And I remember that she nodded, accepted my advice, kissed me sweetly. But she was changed after that. Ana became defiant. She began to buy only baby clothes that were suitable for girls. There were pink bonnets, crocheted dresses, small blankets with polka-dotted giraffes embroidered on the corners. One day I argued, "What if the child is a boy?" She jutted her chin and ground her teeth, and through that grating noise she said, "Then I will dress him like a beautiful girl, foolish and pink."

Then, Josefina, in one of those horribly dramatic moments that was her one flaw, she pulled her curly hair with two tight fists.

You were born only a few hours later. Your mother was still in the fog of ether, mumbling about bonnets and tiny petticoats that could be bought in the capitol, when she was suddenly, coldly still.

I think that had you been a boy, had you been Antonio the third, of a long line of men nicknamed Tonito or Ñico, of men with eyes that are often mean and passionless, I would have dressed you in bonnets, so long as Ana would have stirred at that moment.

Tu Papá

29

L alo arrived at the Mar Lindo house in the morning. The door
clicked open when he knocked, and so he walked in unan-
nounced. He found his mamá in Camila's room, lying down
alongside her, her fingers tangled in Camila's hair. The girl wore
only a small shirt, and Lalo could see the tips of the scar that
trailed off near her navel. He fumbled with the ring in his pocket
as he stood there and watched, and he would have stood there all
day had not Soledad come in.

"*Indecente*," she had said to Lalo, as she covered Camila with a
blanket. His sister's presence awoke him to his purpose. At once,
Soledad saw the ring being lifted out of his pocket and balanced
on his fingertip. He approached the bed and knelt beside it. He
touched Camila's forehead, then her lips, and finally her eyebrows
before she stirred. There was a slight tremble to his touch,
matched only by the softness of it. He had thought of her all
morning long. He knew he loved her, of this he was sure, and the
union between them would benefit the others, so there really was
no conscious decision to marry. It was simply a fate that was
handed down to him—by his mamá and papá, by his own shabby
room, by the moth-eaten curtains in his mother's parlor, and by
the growling in his belly at night.

Camila was startled at the sight of Lalo so close to her bed when
she could feel herself naked underneath the covers and Josefina

nearby. Her left hand grabbed at Josefina beside her and she stirred now, too.

"I have something to tell you," Lalo said at her waking. "I think we should get married, you and I." He noted her silence, her lip curled just so in the way it always did before she cried. "We have nothing else," he added hastily, when the quiet became unbearable.

"Yes, I have nothing else," Camila said, still feverish. She turned her face from him, to avoid his nervous stare, and found another pair of staring eyes beside her.

Josefina smiled at the look and patted the girl's thigh beneath the blanket, whispering, "We'll be good to you, like a daughter, you'll see," into her ear, "and for your wedding day we will order the finest dress for you . . ." Camila felt Lalo slipping the ring onto her finger and then kissing her forehead.

"Sleep, *mi amor*," Lalo said. "We'll talk in the morning."

Soledad, who had watched the proposal from the doorway, backed away now, letting the threesome alone in silence—Lalo stroking Camila's cheek while she slept, and Josefina bustling around the room, twirling old cobwebs around her hands and picking up little dead moths in the corners with her fingertips, tidying up what she had already planned as her new bedroom.

The wedding was held a few months later, when the last heat of summer was upon them. Josefina had taken the role of mother of the bride, using Amparo's bank account to send engraved invitations to the wealthier families of Mar Lindo. She had Camila's gown sent in from a French boutique in Havana and ordered the cathedral to be filled with lilies, which were out of season on the island and had to be imported from the States. The wedding was going to be as lavish as any Mar Lindo had ever seen, and Josefina spent her days going to and from the bank, crossing herself and blowing a kiss into the sky for Doña Amparo, who had made it all possible. Though Josefina did not know it, the celebration she was planning would be like a closing chapter in the island's history, an end to the days when big "society affairs" would be tolerated.

As for Camila, she had little of a bride's blush to her cheeks, rather, they were drawn and gray, and mention of the wedding brought only a sigh from her. She often wandered to the town cemetery, standing long over the graves of her parents. Their gravestones were massive things—high stone crosses with deep, curled designs chipped into them. They were the largest pieces in the cemetery, casting long, straight shadows over the other graves, so long, in fact, that even Doña Amparo's marble cherub, recently placed a few yards away, was overtaken by the specter of the crosses. The names at the base of the crosses were often covered over with grass, so that Camila found herself pulling spiky weeds away so that Julia and Benito Flores could be read.

Camila had no memory of either of them, or at least, no memory that she could believe. She thought she remembered her father and the buckets of tar, and his face grimacing at her as she lay writhing on the roof of a large house, but she knew the recollection of it was faulty. It was something she had pieced together, long ago, from stories she was told.

And she had often wondered how they had died. Was it the smoke that killed them or did they burn? If she unearthed the coffins would they have scars to match hers? Was Amparo her mother's sister or her father's? Was she ever told? And now that her aunt had died there really was nothing else, as Lalo had said. In this state of mind, Camila left the cemetery in the afternoons, not really minding the sun that burned her arms and made sweat trickle between her legs.

The morning of the wedding, Josefina awoke quite early and went into Camila's room. She had already taken up residence in Mar Lindo, because she felt that Camila could not be left alone. She walked daily to El Cotorro to pick up her mail, one of her father's letters coming in every other day or so. The others still slept

in El Cotorro, amidst boxes full of their things, ready to be trans-
ported a few miles across town after the wedding.

She laid Lalo's suit on his bed, pressed and scented with the bay
leaves Josefina had folded in the pockets. Once Soledad's dress
was hung up to air out and Lorenzo's pants were let out a few sizes
in the waist, Josefina turned to her own ablutions. She shaved her
legs in the shower, cautiously running Lorenzo's old straight edge
over the ridges of veins behind her knee. She washed her hair with
soap, then lathered it in egg white for shine and rinsed it away.
And then, looking like the morning, she left the house in the hours
before the wedding to meet with Abel in his apartment, sidestep-
ping the puddles left over from the market day of slimy blood and
shards of bone.

She imagined that this was her own wedding day, that the time
spent in Abel's bed was her honeymoon.

"You look like the bride herself," he had said as he helped her
dress again.

Josefina clothed Camila and cooed over her, painting the girl's lips
and fingernails and kissing her cheek whenever they crossed
paths. The day was a delight to Josefina, who thought more than
once that it did not matter now if Soledad ever married, because
she was living this role well. She thought of her own mother, too,
who died at her birth. *How she would have hated my own wedding, so shabby and solemn,* Josefina thought.

The two women arrived at the church at the appointed time,
one giddy, the other sullen, to find that the cathedral was empty.
The invitations had gone out, the word had been spread, and still,
no one came. Inside the vast structure, only a few figures dotted
the pews, and these were the familiar faces of Josefina's family.
Even the priest had not arrived yet. Though they would never
know it, the social gatherings of Mar Lindo in the past months
whirred with gossip about Amparo's "niece" and the miscreant

she was marrying from El Cotorro, and how Amparo's money would soon run out and the girl would soon know the truth, although no one volunteered to tell her. The invitations which had cost so much and had been sent with such care (Josefina even paid an extra charge to have the words *"En recuerdo de Doña Amparo"* printed on the envelopes), were promptly thrown away or kept on someone's foyer table for the purpose of ridicule.

Josefina released Camila's arm, and walked up the aisle, past her husband whose face was reddened in anger, past her son who sat on a pew and bowed his head, past her daughter, who went to Camila to console her. Josefina opened a door behind the altar with such fury that the knob struck the wall behind it and cracked the plaster. Inside, she found a tiny room, scattered with papers and clouded over with cigarette smoke, and huddled in one corner, asleep on the crook of his arm, a lit cigarette dangling from his lips, was the priest. She paused at the sight of him, as her conscience pricked her with the memory of Abel.

"Padre, despierta," Josefina said, taking the cigarette and putting it out on the desk. The wood sizzled for an instant then stopped. The priest yawned.

"¿Qué? ¿Qué es?"

"My son," she said, "is getting married today. Now, at this hour."

The priest looked at his watch. Confused, he wondered at the silence outside and looked over Josefina's shoulder. "Where are the people?" he asked, thinking that perhaps this was some kind of trick, for surely, this woman, though dressed finely, was not from Mar Lindo.

"They did not come. But check your roster, *Padre,*" she said, lifting a sheet from underneath the priest's elbow. Then, pointing at the names scheduled for eleven, she said, "there they are, Eulalio and Camila. Now, get up." Josefina turned and closed the door, allowing the priest time to get ready.

By now, Camila was sitting in the pew next to Lalo. They held hands limply, her veil in his lap and his collar on the floor. There they remained, even when the priest appeared between two thick candles, and his hands, like two points of light from where they sat, pulled them to their feet. Josefina rushed to place the veil back on Camila's head and pinched her son so that he would return his collar to its place. The priest hurried through the ceremony, mumbled his words often, and yawned in between long phrases of speech. He blessed them both with sprinkles of water, and then, without music, since the organist, too, had failed to come, bid them farewell.

At home, the caterers had come and gone, and the family found themselves surrounded by dishes filled with roasted pork and rice, sprigs of mint around the edges of the plates, and bottles and bottles of red and white wine. They ate in silence and then each went to sleep, on velvet couches, on featherbeds, and leather divans— there was no lack of furnishings in the large house—surrounded by food and drink and open windows, so that the smell of the food wafted outside and filled the air, attracting flies and small lizards into the house.

30

The sergeant and Mona had aged together in the little Miami Springs home. He was now seventy-four, but still robust. He dyed his hair often and left dark smoky stains on his pillowcase. Mona now wandered about the house, stiffly, with both hands on a cane, and the sergeant often had to reach the high shelves for her. She would call, "Anthony, Anthony, dearest," and the sergeant would rise from his lounger in the living room and amble toward the kitchen to bring down a box of oatmeal or a new canister of salt. At night, he helped her change into her nightgown, careful not to tug too hard at the delicate arms and the pale, spotted skin that bruised so easily now. The air-conditioning rattled through the night, and several times a week the sergeant would hear the squeal of a rat outside, caught within the unit's blades. He would rise early in the morning, to hose down the bits of fur and gore that splattered on the wall, so that Mona, while tending to her violets outside, would not see the carnage.

As for his work in Circle Park, Chelo Matute had died earlier that year. The sergeant had worked with him until the end and was the one to tell Abel in Cuba the sad news. Abel had sobbed hoarsely into the telephone, because he had no one else to cry to, because Josefina could not know about the phone call lest he reveal the sergeant's secret. Chelo had been chopping at the trunk of a gnarled, old lemon tree that bore more thorns than fruit when a car came by the edge of the park too quickly, and struck him, throwing him against the lemon tree with such force that the trunk finally splintered and gave way. Afterward, the city began to bring prisoners, tied to one another with massive iron chains, to weed and trim the park. The sergeant had not returned again, because the sound of the prisoner's chains saddened him and because the warden, who accompanied the men, never carried stamps in his pocket for him.

As for his letters, he had not stopped sending them. Abel had vowed to deliver the letters, even without the small checks he had received over the years. Now, after more than ten years of life in Miami, the sergeant let Mona watch as he wrote. Sometimes she cried as his hand trembled with arthritis, and then she would retreat to her room and count her earrings and pendants, checking each stone to make sure it was secure in its prongs.

Around this time, the sergeant had come to believe that he would die in Miami, be buried in the tiny, weed-covered cemetery on the south side of Miami Springs, and have no one to mourn him, for surely, when he died, Mona would follow. He began to collect brochures from travel agencies nearby. Though he rarely spoke to the agents, they let him collect as many pamphlets from the wall as he wanted, since he reminded them of their own grandfathers at home. His favorite pictures he pinned to the wall next to his bed. One was of the shoreline of the Canary Islands. He had stared at that photograph the longest, desperately trying to remember the foamy cusp of the waves from his childhood. The other photo was of the cemetery in Havana, the coffins encased in stone aboveground, up and away from the sea and its putrid moisture. The great families, the Bacardís, the Martís, housed entire generations there, in lovely angel-clad crypts, and Josefina's mother rested there, too, her name engraved on a slab of coral and inlaid in bronze. The sergeant had his own empty tomb, waiting for him there. Sometimes he dreamed of that cold empty space, and lost his breath.

One morning, the sergeant awoke from a dream in which Josefina was still a child, and he, a young man, and they walked hand in hand across the old plazas in Vedado. The ground beneath them was sprinkled with sawdust, as if they were walking inside the rings of a circus, and the swish and crunch of their shoes on the tiny grains made Josefina laugh and pull at her father's hands. The squeal of another dead rat woke him, and his eyes opened to the picture of the cemetery. If he squinted, it looked as though he was actually there, standing at a distance, and his hand, tucked underneath his body, felt the warmth of a child's grip still. Laced with portent, the dream lingered even as he brushed his teeth. He took the brochure from the wall and dangled it before Mona's nose as she sat, dipping her spoon into an overripe grapefruit.

"More pictures, Anthony?" she said, and waved the pamphlet away with her spoon.

"We will go to Cuba," the sergeant said, demanding something from Mona for the first time. The tone he used had been the one he was once accustomed to in Cuba. He had used it with the officers beneath him, with his servants, even with Josefina when she misbehaved. "I no want to die here, Mona," he said and sat down beside her.

"And I will not die in a country where tourists can dance the mambo on my grave." They had seen a clip on their new television set, in which men and women dressed in frilly ruffles shook across Havana dance floors, swinging their full backsides to and fro. Mona had sniffed and waved her hand at the set, and had asked, "Whatever happened to the fox-trot? The 'Chattanooga Choo Choo'?" The sergeant had said nothing, but sat before the small black-and-white television and touched the screen every so often as if he could pass through it into that familiar scene.

His face held the same rapt anticipation as he gripped the brochure. Mona attempted a dramatic rise from her chair and grimaced when her legs would not lift her. "Anyway, I am too old. You are too old," she said. "And it's dangerous, Anthony."

"Dangerous?" the sergeant repeated. He sniffed loudly.

"Aren't you watching the five o'clock news? There's all kind of trouble there. Fighting and whatnot. We're staying here."

"Dangerous?" the sergeant asked again. "Danger in Cuba means nothing. *Presidentes* come and then they go. So what if they fight in the mountains? We're no going to the mountains. I keep you safe and soun'." The sergeant had learned English fairly well and had even adopted a few sayings into his everyday speech, phrases like "safe and sound," and "dead as a doornail."

"Be quiet, Anthony. You're making me dizzy with all this Cuba talk."

The sergeant pushed the little kitchen table away from him, driving the edge of it into Mona's breasts. The sergeant's anger did not soften. He pressed the table close to her body and said, "Say what you want. But hear to me," he said and pounded his chest as if he were reviving himself from a heart attack. "I going to Cuba, with you or no with you."

Mona pushed her chair away from the table and wiped tears from her cheeks and upper lip. The brochure fell then from the sergeant's hand, and Mona bent to pick it up. The glossy paper, once stiff, was now soft from his touch, and in places, the paper was greasy from his hair tonic. She crumpled the brochure in her hand and threw it at the sergeant. The ball went up weakly and missed hitting him just short of his nose. With one quick swipe Mona dug her spoon into the grapefruit and lifted a massive chunk of pulp. This she stuffed into her mouth and chewed for a long time. For the next few weeks, Mona ate nothing more.

The sergeant did not notice her hunger strike for several days. He rose early, and his breakfast of coffee and crackers spread with butter was always ready for him. As Mona watched him eat, he would remind her, between mouthfuls, that "I going soon." Mona would nod and smile, and the sergeant thought, for once, that he had won her over. At lunch and dinner the routine was the same, and it went this way for several days before he noticed that she was not joining him at meals. When the notion that she was not eating finally struck him, he sat her down on her bed and forced a glassful of milk into her mouth. The milk poured out from between the crack of her lips and was sopped up by her nightgown. As he tilted the glass toward her she waved the crinkled brochure over his head. "Don't eat, then," he had yelled at her more than once whenever the brochure went flying like a flag, not of surrender but of war. It was her old body, growing thinner by the day that kept him in the house in Miami Springs.

While she slept and her mouth hung open, the sergeant would spread a spoonful of peanut butter onto her teeth for protein. She would awaken, try hard not to lick at it, and fail, swallowing minuscule bits. Other times, he poured some beef broth down her throat when she slept, and she would wake up, coughing and gagging, but this, too, she would swallow. He harassed her so much as she slept that Mona stopped dozing altogether, and simply sat up, her eyes red-rimmed and lifeless as the sergeant waited, poised in the kitchen to deliver another surprise spoonful of food to Mona Linde.

Worried, the sergeant decided to weigh Mona Linde one afternoon. Outside, he hung a pulley and strung a rope through it. On one end he strapped a strip of leather to work as a seat, as if he were building a swing for a child, and the other he tied to a pair of concrete blocks, which easily weighed one hundred pounds together. He believed she could no longer weigh more than seventy pounds. He hefted her body onto his arms easily, and Mona, weak and quiet now, did not protest. Outside, the mayflies blackened the air, and they flew into the sergeant's nostrils as he walked, making him sneeze. Slowly, he sat Mona onto the leather sling, wrapped her fingers around the rope to steady her, and then let her go. The concrete blocks rose in the air about an inch, hung there for a moment, then settled onto the dirt once again. Mona did not weigh enough to lift even the concrete blocks. Seeing that, the sergeant felt the same old pulse in his chest that had never gone away, and thought for a moment that he would die out there in the backyard. Mona, feeble as she was, would not be able to bring herself down from the makeshift scale.

The throbbing in his chest died down, and the sergeant was able to lower Mona without getting too winded. He walked with her in his arms through the house, picked up a crocheted blanket on the way to cover Mona, and left through the front door. He waved a taxi that took them to the hospital, which was, mercifully, the sergeant thought, just three blocks away. The sun was setting, and the sidewalks were dusky paths from which they could see the red lights of cars ahead and the hospital signs glowing blue.

By the time they reached the hospital, the pain in his chest had begun anew. Inside, the cold blast of air-conditioning gave Mona goose pimples, and her skin took on a blue cast. A pair of nurses gasped behind their desks at the sight of Mona's skeletal frame, and a doctor rushed out and took her from the sergeant's arms, through the double doors of the hospital. The sergeant sat then and waited between a boy with incessant nosebleeds and a woman whose daughter was being attended within, her clavicle broken in two places. The grayness outside gave way to a night so black, so complete, that the glowing hospital signs did not seem to be able to break through the obscurity. The sergeant slept in short fits and was often awakened by the opening doors of the hospital, the sucking of air like a vacuum that blew by him whenever a new patient entered.

As dawn approached, crows bobbed over the hospital's lawn outside, pecking at the bloated worms that had not yet crawled into their earthy dens. The sergeant watched this, his eyelids heavy, his arms crossed before him. One of the nurses tapped him on the shoulder, and he found that he could not turn away from the sight of the crows. She touched him again.

"You may go in to see your wife now," she said and helped him rise with her steady, young hand. Inside, the sergeant saw rows upon rows of beds, and on the farthest one, lay Mona, an empty tray at her side, the plates cleaned of their food.

"So you have not left yet," she said, her voice hoarse from days of disuse. She coughed, and a spray of saliva came out in a fine mist before her. "Well, you should go. I won't be here long." The sergeant kept one hand on her thigh, the femur like a gnawed bedpost under his touch, and the other on the bed rail. "I am tired of this life," she whispered, as if the revelation was a secret between them, so that the doctors would not come bearing more needles and more food to keep her alive. She fell asleep then, so deeply, that she did not awaken when she was moved to a room upstairs. The nurses brought a heavy iron cot for the sergeant to sleep on. The cot creaked and whined as it was opened, and twice it toppled over, the crashing sound resonating through the hall and waking more than one patient. Still, Mona did not awake.

When dinner was brought around to the rooms, the nurse did not stir Mona. "Let her eat when she wakes up," the nurse said to the sergeant and rested her hand on his shoulder for a second. Through the night, as the sergeant slept on the hard hospital cot, no one came to disturb Mona, and she lay there hushed and serene. By morning a new nurse appeared, removed the untouched dinner plate and replaced it with a little bowl filled with oatmeal.

"You must eat, Mrs. Linde," the new nurse said as she shook Mona's shoulder. Her papery nightgown slipped down her arm and revealed a breadth of her collarbone and chest, where a blue tinge had suddenly been cast. "Mrs. Linde?" the young nurse asked again and, getting no response, ran out of the room and down the hall. The sergeant himself did not awaken until a group of doctors brushed past him, knocking his pillow out from under his head. He awoke, groggy and breathless, to the sight of human backs shifting about over Mona's body. They yelled at one another for a moment, their white-sheathed arms flying up like flashes of light, and then, abruptly, they became very quiet. Slowly, one by one they turned to look at the sergeant with downcast eyes. As each left the room, their forms uncovered, first, Mona's bare bedpost legs, then her arms like vine shoots above the blanket, and finally the shape of her face, hidden beneath a flimsy cotton sheet.

The bowl of oatmeal, knocked down in the ruckus, lay over Mona's feet. The grayish porridge dripped around her ankle and between her toes, onto the mattress and along the bedframe. A nurse picked up the bowl as the sergeant bent and cleaned the mess with a handkerchief. He ran the sticky linen square under the running faucet in the bathroom and left it there, draped over the fixture. His hands moist now, he touched Mona's arms, felt the short hairs there, and then covered her limbs with the sheet. Her feet he wiped with the comforter, and then covered them. For a moment, the sergeant thought how he might transport her corpse to Cuba. He did not wish her body to lie alone and forlorn in a neglected grave. At least in Havana she would rest next to Josefina's mother, and by him, too, when his time came. The more he thought of carrying her body to Cuba, the more jumbled his thoughts became. *How will the authorities allow it? Perhaps the cemetery in Havana is full now. Then what will I do with Mona Linde?* He spent the next few hours in this meditation beside Mona's body. When two boys, orderlies dressed in blue, took Mona's body from the bed and plopped it onto a stretcher for the mortuary, the sergeant finally arose and shook his head. The brochure that now held permanent residence in his pocket slid against his thigh. The sergeant, taking the paper's caress as a sign, left the hospital and rode a bus to Mona Linde's house, ready to start preparations for his trip home.

The sergeant gathered Mona Linde's belongings—from jewelry to kitchen appliances—and sold them and the modest house. The money paid for a humble funeral, a tiny plot under the slim shade of a cypress tree, and a ferry ticket to Cuba. The ferries would soon be gone, the ninety-mile stretch of water desolate for the next fifty years. The sergeant, lacking Regla's clairvoyance, did not sense the largeness of the moment, the immensity of what he was reading in the Miami newspapers, and he did not give the Florida shoreline a second glance. While others like the sergeant, old friends from the academy even, were fleeing the island like packs of dogs, noses in the air, sniffing the danger that was coming, the sergeant was coming to it.

He saw her, his long-lost pearl, in the distance like a mirage. The dark sliver of land grew and grew until it swallowed him whole. And when he stepped onto the dock, it was like that time long ago, when he had his brother by his side, and they were coming to something, but they didn't know what it was. It was like that now, and the sergeant wept at the memory.

Mi Hija,

How is it if I told you that I am making plans to see you soon? Would you wrap your arms around me and love me once again, or do you still hold rancor in your heart? I will see you again in life. There are pictures of you and of Cuba that I hold dear. There you are, in my mind, posing on your fifteenth birthday, wearing your mother's white dress, a hibiscus in your hair.

Was I right, *mi hija*? Does he love you still, Josefina? Does he take you dancing?

Tu Papá

BOOK IV

1958-1969

31

Soledad felt she had to leave Mar Lindo for a while. There had been a storm of change in the months following Lalo and Camila's wedding. The family had withdrawn, and Soledad was tired of the silence in the echo-filled house. The quiet was unnatural, awkward, an affront to the character of the island itself. Lorenzo sold the little house in El Cotorro. Some of the money he gave to Josefina for her keeping. The rest he hid in vases around the Mar Lindo house, because he did not trust the banks. He had shown Soledad where all the money was, had drawn her a map to the various bundles, then asked her to keep it secret from Josefina. Soledad, the keeper of secrets, agreed. When not worried about his money—it was a small fortune, the profits from the house and Camila's inheritance, and he could not think of a way to use it—Lorenzo locked himself away in the afternoons to sit in the dark and eat the apricots that were in season.

Lalo and Camila rarely laughed, as if their marriage had ended their ardor, extinguished their fretful touching. They seemed to practice a cold kind of celibacy now, a mood that was both dark and quiet.

Josefina, meanwhile, seemed to grow lovelier, though older. The change of scenery was good for her. She seemed to belong in Mar Lindo. Though the society wives did not accept her, she transformed quickly into one of them—manicures once a week, dinner every night on fine china—all at Doña Amparo's posthumous expense. She'd had a moment of crisis after another of the sergeant's letters appeared. He had said he would see her soon, and Josefina, for a week, believed with all her heart that she was dying. She recovered quickly, and Soledad was sure that visits with Abel had been the cure.

Even Cuba itself had begun to wear on Soledad, peeling away her layers one by one. It was in the little things, like the paint that flaked off the buildings of El Cotorro in big chunks, falling to the ground like dead butterflies while the homes of Mar Lindo were dressed up with wrought-iron fences, and their owners spent weekends in Havana's pleasure palaces. Like the Elvis hits hour that wouldn't come through clearly on their old radio. Like the fact that they had not eaten any meat but stringy chicken while they had lived in El Cotorro, and now stuffed themselves with pork chops and applesauce—a recipe that Josefina had seen on Amparo's black-and-white television set on the American channel that came in fuzzily.

She was tired, too, of the ocean in all directions, of feeling trapped, drowned but alive.

Soledad wandered into her old neighborhood, winding her way to the school where she scanned the old playground for a leftover image of herself, perhaps there, in the bodily composition of the child on the swing set, or in the heavy teenager leaning against the palm, reading a novel. But the girls were foreign beings, really, no longer her peers. School had ended, and there was nowhere to go. Soledad had begged her father to let her attend the university in Florida, because she felt that if she did not cross the ocean she might drown in it. He had said, "Only whores leave their fathers before marriage."

Soledad had responded, in a voice not quite her own, "Only insane people stay on this island," and had looked at her mother, pointedly, when she said it.

Though Lorenzo had never lifted a hand against her, he balled his fists and held them like a boxer, urging Soledad to take a swing. Soledad thought it a sad thing. Suddenly, her father looked old, but not wise, senile, rather than affectionate, so she dropped the subject.

It wasn't because of the coming revolution that she wanted to leave. Those who could afford it seemed to be going in droves, as if they had just heard of a shiny, new neighborhood with good schools for their children. No, the triumph of the shabby, little revolution in the mountains was a day she looked forward to, though it did seem a hopeless endeavor. She had dreamed one night of Batista, tied with rope and stood up against a wall. In the dream Soledad's long-ago rebel, Julio Cuadras, had pulled the trigger of a shotgun and aimed it squarely at the president's throat. Despite the promises of revolution, of Fidel and Che, Soledad longed for visions of skyscrapers and new cars, for rock 'n' roll and hamburgers.

Soledad still thought of her boyhood love, Julio Cuadras, on occasion, and it was because of him that she had begun making large pots of rice and beans for the rebels who would sometimes come out of the mountains and ask for sustenance. Josefina and Lorenzo did not mind, since they had a vague notion that a Cuba without Batista would be a better one. However, they didn't watch television beyond the variety shows, and they didn't read newspapers, so the pair was in a fog when it came to the forces that drove politics in their country.

Julio's boyish face often crossed her mind, and Soledad had given up on Abel. She considered him a passionate, sudden, misplaced crush, and she received his fatherly affection with carefully constructed grace.

One day Soledad's wandering brought her back to her old house in El Cotorro. An old man, whom Soledad took to be a beggar because of his dirty and haphazard clothes, was standing on the porch, peering into the windows of the empty house.

"Can I help you?" Soledad asked. They looked each other over.

The elderly man was foreign—his clothes were too new, his gaze uncertain, unlike the Cuban men who smirked condescendingly at women her age, his cologne not quite strong enough.

"Señorita," he asked, "have you lived in El Cotorro all your life?"

"*Sí,*" she responded and instinctively clutched her purse. Her legs tensed, prepared to run from the odd old man.

"And do you know a woman named Josefina Navarro?"

Soledad froze. "*Concepción,*" she said. The sergeant blanched at the correction and made a queer sort of face, angry and confused all at once. Then, he lurched forward to grab Soledad's shoulders and examine her face more clearly. Soledad turned on her heels, running down the street.

"Soledad," he shouted after her, pronouncing every letter slowly, declaring with his utterance not only his granddaughter's name, but the culmination of his loneliness brought to the brink.

The sergeant felt his heart quivering inside his chest. More color had drained from his face, and he seemed, at the moment, to be an apparition. He took Soledad's fear to be a sign that Josefina was dead, cold somewhere like Mona, the way all of Cuba believed he, too, was.

The sergeant followed her for a few feet, then felt an acid pain in his chest and stopped running for fear he would collapse. He caught his breath and leaned against a tree. So much had changed. The animated people he had once embraced as his own seemed deflated now. The billboards along the road were faded where once they were vibrant. The lawns that had once been lush were now yellow and unkempt. Even the sun seemed more punishing. El Cotorro had always been poor, but now it was pitiable. The sergeant's narrow eyes looked toward the bright green hills in the distance. *I hope the men hiding there can find some success,* he thought. *I hope they can restore this place to life.* He remembered when he was one of them, fighting a different war, and filled with hope and youthful negligence. He found a sturdy-looking crate, empty of its load of fruit, and sat on it. The sergeant leaned his head against the trunk of the tree and fell asleep.

He slept for two hours. He dreamt of Mona, those last moments he had spent with her, dressing her scrawny little body. And he dreamt of Lorenzo as he was in his youth, the sly eyebrow that would lift at the sight of the sergeant, the lean lips that had kissed Josefina when no one watched. The sergeant thought of Lorenzo's grip on Josefina's arm the day of the wedding, the way her smooth, pink flesh purpled underneath his fingertips. The warm breezes, brewing off the northern coast of Cuba, chilled a little, bringing a frigid draft to wake the sergeant. He sat up, rubbed his temples, and straightened his clothes.

The sergeant, Josefina's address in hand, knocked on the door of Josefina's old neighbor. From the window he could see an elderly woman, peeking out and frowning. Moments later, a young, plump woman, opened the door. She stood before him, the door clamped tightly in both her hands, and asked, "What do you want?" The cries of many children could be heard inside, and the dark circles around the woman's eyes spoke of diaper washing, fevers, and the vomit of unfamiliar children, all cared for for very little pay.

"Señora, excuse me," the sergeant bowed his head, "I have been away a long time and have forgotten. I am trying to find the Concepción family."

The woman looked at the sergeant for a long time. A toddler wandered through the front door and lodged himself between her knees. "They don't live here anymore, but I know them. The husband once installed a sink for me. Badly, too. The thing leaked and rotted out the wood in the floor. No, mister, they are gone," she said at last, "to Mar Lindo." She smiled when she saw the sergeant's face turn from concern to deep worry. "May the Virgin spare me for talking about this, but their new money is not the husband's. He is a lout. It's well known." She drew her hand to her throat and whispered, so that the sergeant had to lean into her. "It belongs," she continued, "to an innocent girl they've swindled." The woman shut the door, unwittingly leaving the toddler outside, who wrapped his arms around the sergeant's leg and bit his knees. He drew the child away from him and left him there on the steps to dig his little hands into a mud puddle at his feet. The sergeant watched the child for a moment, before turning toward Mar Lindo.

32

Josefina often invited Abel to come to Mar Lindo on days that Lorenzo was out working, to spend the afternoon in the thickly padded rooms with their upholstered sofas and lush carpets. Lorenzo had taken on fewer jobs, since bills weren't as worrisome as they once were, and so visits with Abel were harder to come by. Josefina had become careless, sometimes wishing that she might be caught and that Lorenzo would then end this thing he should never have started.

Abel disliked the house in Mar Lindo and wished the family had stayed in the country. He had wandered into the old house in El Cotorro before it was sold one day out of curiosity, to see the place empty, the spots where the furniture once stood bright and new on the otherwise dingy floor. He had roamed through the rooms, in the bedroom where he had embraced Josefina, in the parlor where he had first observed the light swing in Soledad's young hips. He rambled about this way in the dark, humming softly.

He recalled how the emptiness brought him relief. If only Josefina would disappear into Mar Lindo society forever, he sometimes thought. He would not have to explain to her then all that he had been thinking. That he could not give her marriage. That he had conspired with her father. That she would one day find another to replace him and that everything would be well. Despite weekly confessions, Abel could not shake off the guilt.

It was not as if he had not done it all before. In the days when he was younger, Abel would often find women, young and old, most of them poor wraiths, staring at the huge sides of meat with water in their eyes. He would take them by the arm and into his life for a while—to feed them, to clothe them, to love them a bit. And Sergeant Navarro was not the first person to come to him and beg him for help. There had been a grand dame of the old days, who was willing to pay him a ship's passage to New York if he could help her daughter escape from a drunken husband who hit her so hard that she often fell unconscious and woke days later. And though the girl's mother asked for nothing more than protection against the brute, the broken girl found a tender, loving touch and a companion through the lonely nights. Others had followed once the drunkard finally ran away. Abel Santana built a reputation among the women in his town—a secret well kept from the men, and so he never boarded the ship to the States. Though his services had gone unsolicited once he set up his butcher shop in El Cotorro, his brother, Chelo, had rejuvenated his cause with the case of Josefina and her lazy husband. Some men rescued children from collapsing caves. Some men built real homes for the *guajiros* in the countryside with church money and town donations. Abel Santana loved the women who needed it most. So it was that when Lorenzo Concepción finally glared at him over Josefina's hunched shoulders, after having been gone for so long, Abel felt he had broken some rule that was not stated. There were no bruises on Josefina's body, no explosive violence in Lorenzo's disposition. Perhaps Josefina did not need him in that way, after all.

In her old bedroom, he had opened her closet. Cockroaches scurried from within, up and over his shoes and out the door. A single dress had been forgotten, and it hung limply, like a rain-wilted feather. Though beaded, the dress did not glitter when Abel held it up to the window, and he could see now why the sad, old thing had been left behind. He replaced the dress, stamped on a few roaches nearby.

The Mar Lindo home was cavernous in comparison. As Abel approached, feeling warm and lethargic as he thought about Josefina in his arms, he noted the fine curtains with tiny, embossed *fleur-de-lis* appearing every so often. The French theme was echoed in an oil painting of a Parisian street in the dining room. The house had been carefully decorated according to Amparo's good taste, and the colors, ruby red and emerald in one room, pale salmon and lavender in another, were the colors of the wealthy.

As he walked toward the front door, Abel heard a stirring in the kitchen. Inside he found her, sitting on a kitchen chair, her legs drawn up and her head resting on the still slim kneecaps, girlishly. Her hem hung low, revealing a patch of darkness between her legs.

"Josefina," he said, his hand flying up to his throat where a knot had begun to form suddenly. He could not stop himself from thinking of that priest long ago, who had taken the poison and created a miracle. Josefina was like that poison, or like a strong bottle of rum. "Where is everyone?" he asked.

She did not answer but drew his arms around her neck. The smell of her—of Russian violet perfume—lingered. All thoughts of leaving her, of disappearing into the interior vanished in the folds of scent, in her curls, into the soft press of her curves against him.

"*Ay,* Abel," she said, and they fell to the floor of the kitchen, Josefina's hair dusting the tiles. Her voice, he thought, was the most musical sound in the world, and her movement beneath him was both violent and peaceful like a passionate fugue. They made long brushstrokes clear of dust on the kitchen floor.

This was how Lorenzo found them. He had been sent home from the hospital job because he was caught with stethoscopes from the supply closet in his pockets. He was bringing them home for Soledad, as if she were still a girl who liked odd playthings. His mind had been slipping in that way, forgetting that his daughter was almost eighteen now, asking Camila about the health of her Aunt Amparo. But his mind was sharp when he witnessed the scene on the kitchen floor.

They lay partly clothed, Josefina's skirt hiked up around her waist, her shirt undone. Her legs, legs that might have been a dancer's in another life, were draped over Abel's waist. They had fallen asleep there, on the kitchen floor, as if they were voracious teenagers or newlyweds. The light from the kitchen window cast shadows on their limbs and speckled their faces with sunspots.

Lorenzo sprang without bending his knees, his hands twisted into claws. A throaty gurgle escaped his lips and his sleeve tore at the seam. All this happened so quickly that Josefina barely had time to awaken, to shield Abel, to yell, "No," before it was all over. It was in midair, fury heating his body like an oven, that Lorenzo felt the sudden twitch in his face, the tightness in his jaw. He fell to the floor, unconscious.

Soledad slowed when she saw that the old man who knew her name was nowhere near. Her legs tingled as she brought them to an unhurried pace, as if they wanted to keep running of their own accord. The sky was dark now and Soledad could see the moon reflected on all the windowpanes. It looked to her that the miniature moons were cut out of paper, hung from the window moldings inside. The images even fluttered, as if drafts were straying into the house and rustling the paper moons, the wind striking the loose panes and making them shift and bang through the night. The sound of the glass followed her all the way to Mar Lindo, and flimsy moons were reflected in all the windows she looked into, including the little stained-glass alcove window at Doña Amparo's house, where the moons floated in puddles of blue and red and yellow.

She did not think again of the old man until her hand touched the cold knob of her new house in Mar Lindo—cold, cold like the man's grip on her wrist—and only then for a moment, because the shouting inside cut short the thought.

"Renzo, Renzo darling," Josefina had said, but her voice rose until she was screaming at him, "¡Lorenzo, *despierta!*"

"He's not waking up, Mamá. He's not waking up. Camila, stop making such a fuss."

"*Mira,* his mouth is moving. ¡*Despierta!*"

"Camila stop crying. Go to bed."

"Maybe it's an epilepsy, Josefina."

"Who's there? Lalo, go see who walked in. *Despierta,* Renzo! Please, wake up. I'm so sorry. So sorry, so sorry," Josefina held Lorenzo's hands and cried into them.

"It's me, Mamá," Soledad said. She went over to her father. She did not notice Abel, half-clothed, standing in the corner of the room. Lorenzo was facedown on the seat of an armchair, his legs spread underneath him on the floor. His eyes were open now and looking at Josefina, focusing on her nose and then moving side to side, examining the tiny moles on her face. She kissed him then, murmuring into his cheeks, his forehead, his chin, and when she pulled away, he was studying her nose again.

"What's wrong, *mi amor?*" she asked, and still, his eyes did not waver. His mouth looked as if the jaw had come unhinged, and his tongue lolled about on his lips.

"He's awake now," Lalo said.

"You call this awake? Help me lift him. Help me." And Josefina and her son lifted Lorenzo by the waist and shoulder, his legs dragging and bumping into the furniture, and they put him in bed.

Soledad went over to Camila, who was sitting on the floor and sobbing at what she had seen. "What happened to my father?" Soledad asked, now sobbing herself, louder than Camila. No one would answer.

Soledad could see that her father wasn't dead, but frozen in a terrible moment, like a wax figure in a haunted house. It was Soledad who had the presence of mind to call a doctor, to answer question upon question before the hospital receptionist said that a doctor was on his way. She hung up the phone and dug her fingers into the palms of her hand until her fingers cramped and went numb.

When Soledad rose from the quiet of the corner where she sat and went to the room where Lorenzo lay, she saw Abel and thought that he had brought this misery on. She dared not say a word, but she felt a tingling hatred for her mother, just then, for having betrayed her father, for herself for having kept the secret. Soledad was the first to sit on the bed with Lorenzo. She stroked his face and listened to his heartbeat.

The house was quiet as they waited for the doorbell to ring, bringing with it the doctor who would make things right, prescribe medicine, administer a shot, something, anything to bring him back. The quiet was impenetrable as they strained for the sound of bells that would mean hope.

In the meantime, Abel had found his pants and shirt and was leaning against the wall, trying very hard to disappear. He was finding it difficult to breathe, to think, and his mind raced to those moments when he had witnessed glory in the skies, at an altar. The thoughts brought no relief from the shame he was feeling.

It was Lalo who broke the silence at last, taking long strides to the kitchen, his polished, wing-tipped shoes striking the wood floor loudly. A jangling of steel was heard from within, and he emerged with a steak knife in hand, pointing the thing at Abel.

Abel, his face burning, laughed bitterly. "I've seen you handle a knife before," he said, remembering that long ago day when Lalo had tried to kill a pig.

"I will kill you," Lalo said, his voice already breaking as his hand trembled. Stillness embraced the room. Only Lorenzo's hoarse breathing filled the space, and filled it completely. "I'll kill you," Lalo said again, and then, more silence.

"No. It's her fault," Soledad said, not looking at her mother.

"*Sí*, it's true. I've become the thing I hated most." Josefina crumpled against Abel and looked up at the ceiling, "*Ay*, Papá, help me, come for me." Josefina was choking now, wishing for death, and her tears were soaking her shirt, running down her nose and commingling with her spit. She squeezed Abel's hand. "Leave now," she said to him, and Josefina ran out of the room. Abel buttoned his shirt and said a prayer for Lorenzo. The family watched him go. Down the road he walked, stopping every so often to spit.

Late that night, when the doctor, who had examined Doña Amparo, finally arrived, he twisted his mustache in the same grim way he had before and said, "Stroke," so soft that no one heard it. He had to say it again. The second time, the word resonated through the house, making itself known. Other words followed—"nothing," "helpless," "infant," and "death," but those words did not fly through the house and impose themselves on every bit of expensive fabric and fine china, silver tray and thick blanket in the way that "stroke" did. The doctor left promptly after saying it and did not utter another word until he was outside on the front lawn. He had turned around and called out to Josefina, "Try to feed him something. Bean purée or mashed avocados. So long as he doesn't have to chew," he had said, then went down the road. The doctor would have recommended a stay at the hospital had he not known that Lorenzo Concepción was the man who had slept with his wife a few months ago. *That El Cotorro bastard's lucky,* he thought to himself, satisfied, *that I came at all.*

They spent the afternoon taking turns at trying to feed Lorenzo. At first he would not open his mouth to accept the spoonful of mashed plantains. Josefina pried the lips apart with her thumb and forefinger, and he would draw them together and bite on her fingernails. Soledad noted her mamá's frustration when the woman began cursing in a low breath—at the lips that wouldn't open, at the tiny, blue bruises underneath her own nails, and the eyes that would look at nothing but her nose. And soon she took the spoon from her mother's hand and tried feeding her papá.

She, too, tired of the effort. Her papá began opening his mouth now but would not swallow. The food lay between his cheek and molars until his mouth was full and then would dribble out of his mouth and onto Soledad's lap. All the while he stared at her face with a dull sort of grin about his lips. Soledad soon waved the spoon at her brother, who sat on the sofa near her, signaling his turn at nursing their father, but instead, Lalo stood in the hallway and yelled for Camila. When she did not come, he went in after her.

Camila appeared a few minutes later with Lalo behind her and his hands gripping the back of her neck, directing her way to Lorenzo. She trembled like a leaf rocked from its mooring, dangling from a final thin fiber. She felt the space around her was like the vast open vineyards in Matanzas province she had heard about but never visited, where in the old days, when they were just deep valleys, Taíno Indians, unseen behind palm fronds and thick, ribbed trunks, would surround lost Spanish soldiers. The parlor where she found them all was just so silent and ominous. Lorenzo and Soledad sat in the far corner of the room, hidden behind a tall, fringed lamp. Josefina sat in the other, her head swaddled in her arms, bent low to her waist. And Lalo had disappeared down the hall, so that it felt as if everyone was trying to get far from her. Soledad finally did stand, and crossed the gap that was like a valley between them, placing the sticky spoon into Camila's hand.

She sat down in front of Lorenzo then, with the spoon waving in her shaky hand. She dipped it into the mash, just the tip and presented it to the limp mouth, and as she did so, she hovered in close to his ear and whispered. At the soft murmur, Lorenzo opened his mouth and swallowed, mechanically at first, and then with relish, sucking the goopy plantains from between his back teeth. Though he still gazed at her nose and little else, Camila's whispering stirred him.

It would soon become a daily and sacred bond between them—the dormant old man and the frightened girl, she whispering to him between mouthfuls of beans, boiled so long that they broke up in the bowl, and he swallowing and smiling at her nose. No one knew what it was she said to him, and in fact no one asked.

33

The boys who lived on Abel's block were still in the midst of a ferocious baseball game when he got home from Mar Lindo. Abel sat on the porch of his apartment and watched these boys who knew nothing of love affairs yet. They were grim players, their teeth set as they waited for the pitch, flexible like little lizards, and fast, too. They had dreams of playing for the States' big leagues. And they were good enough to do it. Abel watched them enviously, wishing that he could be young again, could begin anew.

The sun set quickly on the ballplayers, and soon all he could see of them were their shadowy shapes running in the night, and all he heard was the soft padding of the ball against gloves. Though he couldn't see the children, in the darkness he could see Josefina clearly. She was disheveled, her lips still smeared in lipstick, her forehead shiny. She was standing in front of her husband, and she was telling Abel to go.

It was what he had wanted, wasn't it? He had wished for some release, for a chance to start over, and here it was. But now that it had come . . .

Abel sat on the porch through the night, let the salamanders come and crawl on his feet without shaking them away. He imagined Josefina's every move—putting on her thin pink nightgown, first the left arm, then the right, putting lotion on her hands, caressing them the way a lover might, slipping into the sheets and thrusting her fists underneath the pillow, her body jackknifed, occupying most of the space on the bed. But Lorenzo would be there, too. Perhaps he had regained some function in the evening and could get into bed himself. Or maybe Lalo and Josefina had had to carry him to it.

Again, he imagined her, alone, beautiful, and again Lorenzo imposed himself on the vision. This went on all night. When the morning broke, luminous, like a miracle, Abel had come to a decision about Josefina. He had been wrong to help the sergeant carry out his deception, and he had been wrong to love a married woman. And so Abel would make amends.

In the morning, he went to the market as usual. He sold his pigs—every last one of them—for half price. His stall he sold to the fish vendor on his right. He telephoned the *finca* where he usually went to pick up livestock and told the farmer he was out of business. In the afternoon, he cleared his apartment and sold the furniture on the front lawn. To the ballplayers who congregated in the street every day, Abel gave old decks of cards, bottles of cologne, frying pans, novels. They grinned and shouted, setting their bats and gloves down for just a moment.

Finally, Abel removed the money the sergeant had sent over the years from the wooden box in which it was kept. Now he knew what to do with it. He would make things right with the Concepción family, if only in a small way, if only for one of them. Then he would leave for the monastery in Baracoa and begin to see miracles again.

But there was one last thing to do. Abel sat down on the floor of his empty apartment, with a pen and sheet of paper. *Dearest Josefina,* he began, *I loved you desperately. Please know, I am not a ghost. . . .*

34

It took the sergeant another week to find Doña Amparo's house. The people of Mar Lindo did not seem to know the family and could not tell him where to go. There were three Concepción families in the phone book. He had called them all without finding the right people. The sergeant had tried the Navarros listed, too, in the hopes that his daughter had reverted to her maiden name. Finally, he had resorted to ringing random doorbells the first few days, and was nearly arrested by the neighborhood police. He slept on park benches, laughing at times when he thought of the plaza and the one bench that had nearly ended his life.

Eventually, a watermelon vendor the sergeant asked had pointed the way with such a look of disgust when the name Lorenzo Concepción was uttered that the sergeant's face, too, changed, inadvertently mimicking the scowl. Once at the door of the house, ivy and rosebuds intricately cut into the wood, the sergeant paused. The door was open, just a bit, and he peeked in, holding his breath. His old eyes caught nothing of the indoor parlor. He loitered there for many long minutes, thinking, at last, *I must make a noise. Any noise will do.* He coughed first, thumping his chest as he barked out a throaty sound. Then he sighed a long, diminuendo of a sigh, holding the last note for a moment. When no one appeared to push the door open, the sergeant leaned on a potted fern by the door, purposely, so that it tumbled down the steps.

A few moments after the sound of the ceramic pot's shattering faded, Josefina appeared in the doorway, bringing along with her the harsh stench of disinfectants that grazed the sergeant's nostrils. He held his hand to his nose and met her eyes. She was thicker than she used to be. Her neck was no longer the slender porcelain thing it once was. But there was something youthful still about her. Her brown curls had only just begun to show signs of graying. They touched the sides of her face lightly. Her hands were raw and red from too many washings. The thinnest of lines formed a *V* above her nose as she frowned.

They held each other in a silent gaze for some time before Josefina's eyelids began to flutter and her eyes crossed and uncrossed, like a day-old infant learning to focus. She stumbled then, and the sergeant caught her by the forearm.

"Papá, how is it that a spirit can hold me?" she said, staring at the hand clasped around her arm.

The sergeant looked at his daughter, at her large eyes, her smile. He had expected to be turned away, to hear those words again concerning his death, "It was meant to be." But this welcome was odd.

"A spirit? What do you mean? I'm as real as you are."

Josefina's smile faded. *The letters,* she thought. *Where did they come from?* "You are a ghost. Yes, a ghost. And you sent a guardian angel."

"I am not a ghost, *mi hijita.* Is that what you thought all these years?" Josefina's knees weakened, but the sergeant caught her by the shoulders. "I've been away," the sergeant said, "in America. Miami. I . . . I've missed this. You." He tried to put the words in order, to pull her toward him, to quench the need to hold his little girl, but Josefina was stiff.

"How could you?" Josefina asked, her voice small.

"Ay, mi hijita, mi hijita," the sergeant said, over and over. Josefina would not come near. She eyed him as if he was a malevolent spirit and her body shook.

"You bastard," she screamed at last, and the sound startled him. She pushed the sergeant with both hands. "All those years, all those years. I was such a fool crying over your letters. How I suffered without you. All I wanted was to say, 'Papá, I am sorry I left you alone in that house.' I had nothing. I needed you . . ."

"I didn't know. I . . ."

"No, Papá. I trusted you. My children don't even know you. And all along you've been playing with me. Like a child."

"My child," the sergeant said and grabbed hold of Josefina. He could see it, how the moment had hung years on her face. *"Mi niña,"* he said—my little girl.

The sergeant pulled her again, and this time she yielded. Josefina crushed herself against her father. She could feel the bones of his ribcage. The burly man he used to be was gone. His familiar hands, grown more stiff and calloused, ran through her hair. His crying began to match her own, until they were both sobbing together.

"Perdóname," the sergeant said at last, and Josefina nodded against his chest.

"Papá, how I've longed for you," she whispered, and the sergeant hugged her close.

She could still feel his touch, so human, so warm, even after he let her go. "Even if you are alive," she said and laughed uneasily, "I knew you would come and save him. *Gracias a Dios.*" She led the sergeant by the hand through the house. She indulged in the warmth of his mortal hands, and he gaped at all the things inside. The photographs were not the ones he remembered leaving in Vedado. They were of strange people, wealthy, yes, but not Navarros, nor could he imagine that these were Lorenzo's people. The pictures were framed in gold and matted in red and green silks. The glass that covered the photographs was dusty and dull from long months of grime collecting there, layer upon layer. He saw delicate ballerina figurines, their tiny lace cuffs trimmed in silver paint, scattered about the parlor—on a mantle there, a tea table here.

Josefina drew her father by the hand toward the screened-in porch at the back of the house. She pushed aside a curtain made of cheap gingham to reveal Lorenzo with a wet rag on his forehead. His mouth lolled open and his eyes wandered to the left. In only a week his left hand had begun to bend at the wrist toward his body, like a claw, hardening so that no effort on Josefina's part could straighten it.

Josefina had expected the ghost to chant, to snap his fingers and bring Lorenzo back. Instead, he laughed. "I see that life is just," the sergeant said, and he slapped his thighs and roared. "So the old devil has gotten his reward, eh?" and he turned and kissed his daughter, then squeezed Lorenzo's nose with his fingers. "*Cabrón,*" the sergeant said at last.

This really is no ghostly being, thought Josefina, trying to think above her father's laughter. She looked up at her father, no longer the spectral figure she imagined, but real and old and imperious as before. Here was the flesh. The fantasy of the past decades had been a lie, had been a kind of madness.

"I thought you had come to help us!" she shouted, feeling the familiar rebellion she once knew. Suddenly, Lorenzo was once again the bright young man who would show her a new life, away from society dances and prim, white gloves, and piano lessons. Her Renzo. She defended him as she had done so long ago. "Why have you come back, Papá?" she asked and knelt beside her husband, his mouth open and pressed against his wife's neck as she cradled his head.

The sergeant tried to take hold of Josefina and pulled her away from Lorenzo, saying, "*Ven, mi hijita,* his misfortune is catching." Lorenzo held his hands in tight fists, as he had done in his youth, and his open eyes stared out at the sergeant in aged defiance.

"Let go of me, *demonio,* let go, let go," Josefina began to yell, and she pulled her arms out from the sergeant's grip and pushed him against the wall. The frustration had returned to her father's face, and she stood before Lorenzo, still fearing the power of a spiteful ghost. Lorenzo gurgled behind her, and the sergeant twitched at the sound. "Can you help us?" Josefina asked, her hands open, palms facing the ceiling.

"I've come to help you, *hijita mía*," he said. Josefina dropped to her knees and crossed herself, muttering a prayer underneath her breath. "Your husband," he began, "has received a just punishment." Josefina's muttering stopped. "If you stay you will end like him, drooling and stirring in your own waste." Josefina huddled on the ground, her forehead touching the carpet, her fingers woven and clasped over her head. He had come back for this? All of those years of missing him, of wanting nothing more than to return to the days in Vedado, the days when her father held her tightly and told her he loved her, and here they were again. It was as if she were a child still, with the sergeant flinging desperate insults at the boy she had first loved.

Lorenzo himself, as if he understood the insults thrown upon him, was roused from his stupor and began to cry. The yellowed eyes watered thick like syrup, though they were focused on the lamp across the room. His chin quivered and, wearily, wearily, a soft moan escaped his lips. Lorenzo reminded the sergeant at that moment of his Mona. At this, the sergeant felt a pang in his chest. "*Dios mío*, there is no mercy in this. None at all," he said and looked at his daughter's face, so dark and tired. *Yes,* he thought, *she has changed so much. She had a lover's rouge about the cheeks when I saw her last. I have hurt her more than he has,* and his gaze fell upon Lorenzo, still crying at the lamp and moaning every so often. Now, the sergeant, too, was crying, syrup tears like his son-in-law's.

The sergeant went back through the house and opened the front door. The moment felt familiar. *Here I am again,* he thought to himself. He stood on the porch and thought about going, could feel the anger in his throat, the bile coming up. *How could she?* he asked himself. He thought about the payments he'd sent to Abel, the stealing, bringing himself down so low for Josefina. *For what? For more rejection? She still chooses that man over me,* he thought.

"Papá," the sergeant heard spoken behind him. Josefina stood in the doorway, wiping her face with her sleeve. "You can stay. You have to stay. But Renzo is my husband still. And even after everything he's done, I love him. No, Papá, don't shake your head. I don't understand it, either." Josefina looked down at her slippers and twisted her foot to reveal the worn sole.

"Come in, Papá, and tell me where you've been all my life."

By morning the sergeant was already a fixture in the house. Though his grandchildren would not come near him, they accepted that this was the historic grandfather of stories they were told, that this was the ghost who had written his daughter for so many years, and that kind of loyalty they respected.

For the first few days he sat on a sofa, in a suit Josefina bought for him. He would stand to use the restroom, to eat, then back onto the sofa he went. Soledad and Lalo thought he was crazy. Now they had two invalids to deal with in the house. But the sergeant was watching, investigating. He didn't like what he saw. Soledad's shirts were too tight. Her bosom stretched the fabric and the buttons strained against their holes. And Lalo was not the gentleman the sergeant had hoped. He didn't pull out the chair for his wife, ignored her most of the time, then at turns would chase her around the house, pin her against a wall and kiss her. *Like his father,* the sergeant thought.

Sometimes he'd yell at them from where he sat. "*Oye, niña,* where are you going?"

"Out," Soledad would yell, grabbing her purse by the door.

"Without a chaperone?" the sergeant would bellow. But the door would slam before he received an answer.

Once, he asked Lalo to sit with him, and he lectured his grandson on the attributes of real men, suggested the police academy as an alternative to factory work. Lalo responded with an "Okay, *abuelo*," and went about his business. Though Camila thanked the sergeant for talking to her husband with a kiss on the cheek, she didn't really see a change in Lalo.

When the sergeant was young, he once imagined a slew of grandchildren living in Vedado. The girls would attend society dances, like their mother, the boys would go into public service. There would be chaperones to worry about and courtships to plan. He had seen the young people in America dancing on television, rotating their hips to rock and roll, had seen young women smoking cigarettes and tanning on top of cars. But he had thought that Cuba had not changed. The sergeant imagined his island trapped in a glass bowl, a museum piece, a relic of better days. But the second half of the century had come across the water and found willing participants along the valleys, among the palms.

He found respite in the moments he had alone with his daughter. After attending to Lorenzo, Josefina would come with some coffee for her father, or a small sandwich. They would sit together and the sergeant would tell her about the States.

"*Ay,* everyone is so busy. No family time at all. Can you imagine, these people are so cold they don't kiss or hug one another when they come to your home. And everything is big—big markets, big clothing stores . . ."

Josefina listened, her round eyes wet. He was the same old sergeant, but she knew now that she had missed him despite his severity. She knew now that there was another side to her father, one revealed in ink.

35

Josefina circled her husband those days like a gull around old bait, eyeing the rotting flesh from afar and swooping in occasionally for tiny pecks at a time. She did not interrupt Camila during Lorenzo's lunch and dinner and would touch him only to walk him to the toilet six times a day. Though he no longer spoke, he paced the house as long as someone held him by the elbow. If he were released, he would fix himself at the spot, remote and quiet, and would slowly, slowly, fall asleep standing. During these moments in the cramped bathroom—where Lalo nailed broad planks to the wall for his papá to hold on to—Josefina found that she could finally, truthfully, talk to her husband.

"You see how things go, *mi amor?*" she would say, undoing his pants with one hand and lowering him onto the seat. "Where are they now, *mi amor?*" And then, feeling guilty about bringing up those women, about Abel and how she had cheated, too, she would say, "If I were to meet you again at the dance in Vedado, I would follow you once more."

There was something wild about him she had loved from the beginning, so unlike the constraints of the upper class. She missed his vulgarity, how he could never keep still. *There was a passion in that,* she thought, *that not even Abel had.* Josefina wished that she might have said all of that earlier, when Lorenzo still stalked the house like a prize cockfighter, and perhaps he might have set aside his pride and returned the compliment.

There had been a letter from Abel that had made her feel as if she'd been punched in the chest. In it, he revealed the sergeant's ruse, his own role in it, and vowed to love her until death. There was also a promise to "make amends" when the time was right. Josefina had grown weary of letters. Her life had been one long correspondence—with her father, full of stories and protection, with Lorenzo and his meager checks and lies about his whereabouts. And now Abel? More promises, more declarations of affection. Josefina tore the letter to shreds and sent the pieces down the drain of the kitchen sink.

She could no longer rely on the power of her dead father, who was very much alive, to make things better. He now spent his days writing more letters to dead companions, hoping that one would find its way to someone who was alive, someone with the power to find him a job, make him a resurrected hero. The sergeant understood at last when Soledad explained that the Cuba of the present was no longer interested in heroes, but in the murmurs of revolution and new beginnings. The sergeant sighed and said, "I know of revolutions," and threw his pencil into the trash.

In desperation, Josefina spent hundreds of Doña Amparo's pesos and the money Lorenzo had hid on doctors from the University of Havana. They would arrive in taxis, paid for by Josefina, and would smile broadly when the large house came into view. Though they often spent days in the house, prodding Lorenzo with needles, stretching and massaging his limbs, peering into his eyes, snapping their fingers behind his ears, they all left saddened, not so much by the man's condition, but because they could no longer think of any new tests to bill Josefina for. She wanted to shake them, to have them spend a day in her shoes as Lorenzo's nurse, sponging the limp form that she once loved and hated all at once.

Her final resort had been to send a telegram to the Vedado district in Havana once again, as she had a few years ago, to the home of Regla's newest employer, a certain Judge Don Emilio Cruz, to request a leave of absence for his ancient maidservant, Regla. Don Emilio's reply was curt, demanding that Josefina pay him the maid's monthly salary, so that he might find temporary help while she was away. He made no mention of paying the costs of Regla's train ride. The sum total all but closed Doña Amparo's bank account forever, but Regla was soon on her way. In the dim moonlight in which Josefina sat, holding the judge's telegram, watching her husband watching her nose, Josefina began to cultivate a bit of hope.

Regla arrived at the train depot in Mar Lindo during lunchtime one Sunday. It had been a few years since she had made a visit. The judge she now worked for was dictatorial, his wife shrewish, and Regla could not get away for any length of time. And she had gotten old, and train rides were tiresome events. Josefina waited for her in the shade of a towering hibiscus bush, swatting away wasps that circled her face. When the old woman appeared, Josefina rose to touch the leathery face, the nose that dipped down to the little divot over her top lip, the eyebrows that were barely there now, and white as tufts of stray fleece from a ratty sweater. Regla had arrived to touch her, too. Except she bent low, uninterested in Josefina's face that sagged about the eyes and cheeks now, and instead, went to take the hands she knew so well. Regla's own hands trembled with age, and as they lifted Josefina's fingertips into view, an inch from her eyes, Regla began to cry. The white flecks that had inflicted a bad fortune on Josefina as a child were gone now. But the old maid felt as if the daisy and honey baths, the *trabajito* a few years back, had not worked.

"Now, now you've come," Josefina said, wiping at the wetness in her nose, and like a child pleading, said, "You can make it better."

"Por Dios," Regla said and cried again.

They rode to Mar Lindo in a taxi, the ride itself being so expensive that Josefina refused the driver a tip, and the man, incensed that a woman wealthy enough to live in Mar Lindo was so miserly, drove off, with most of Regla's clothes still in the trunk of the car. When Lalo had gotten engaged, Josefina had called Regla, had hoped that she could make it for the wedding, but the judge demanded her service on that day, to polish the silver for a banquet in his home in honor of President Batista. On the ride, Josefina explained the reappearance of her father, since she feared that the sight of the sergeant would send Regla into a stroke of her own. Regla nodded and said nothing when she heard he was alive and doubted whether it was true at all. Once inside, Josefina took her old nursemaid to Lorenzo's room, where Camila sat with him, whispering in his ear and touching the corners of his mouth as she spoke. Soledad was there, too, closing windows and drapes at the sight of Regla, so that those outside, walking their dogs in the afternoon, pushing children in prams, would not see anything they weren't supposed to.

"Reglita," the sergeant said, appearing in the doorway.

Regla turned and embraced the sergeant, and they stood there, in each other's arms for a long time, each one feeling the delicate bones of the other. Regla cried onto the sergeant's shirt and left a dark stain there that spread then dried over his shoulder. When they released each other, Regla straightened his clothes, and buttoned a button that he had missed. It was as if time had never passed at all.

"I don't believe it," was all she said and then Regla went over to Lorenzo and kissed the speckled forehead.

"How you've changed," she said, remembering the youth who had been so imprudent with the sergeant and his wealth, wishing Josefina to know his poverty as he had always known it, bringing wildflowers, picked from the sergeant's own gardens, for Regla because he felt a kinship with the maid who, day to day, earned as little as he did.

"What can you do for him?" Josefina asked, peering from the maid's face to her husband's. "Who has put this spell on him? Was it a woman? Can you tell?" Josefina's eyes glinted with anticipation. She would not tell the old nurse what Lorenzo had witnessed on the dusty kitchen floor. Josefina, in fact, tried to convince herself that it was not her infidelity that brought on the stroke. Rather, she had been thinking, for weeks now, that one of Lorenzo's women had done this to him, prayed that he would fall ill. Perhaps he had left her, or perhaps he had drunk too much of her good liquor, but whoever she was, she was powerful.

"No, *mi hijita,* this is a disease of the body. No one created this, no one could have stopped it. But if you wish it, I will pray for him now." And the old woman rose and pulled a vial of water from in between her breasts, sprinkling droplets about the room and chanting in a rhythm that was at once beautiful and unsettling. For Soledad, who stayed by the window, lifting the corners of the drapes occasionally to look for passersby, the chanting made her stomach quiver. This, she thought, was nothing like the hymns during Mass, nor was it anything like the verses children jumped rope to. This was something alien, imported, the words sounding as if they were all pronounced in the old woman's throat instead of inside her mouth, as if her tongue was suddenly paralyzed. And she shook herself about her papá, waving her arms around his head so that he flinched in time with her dancing.

Lalo walked into the room and stopped to watch. He did not like the chanting, which he did not understand, and which, somewhere deep inside him, was frightening. "This will not help my father," Lalo said, and then: "We don't need two lunatics in the house, *Mamá.* Please, be reasonable."

"This is not lunacy," she whispered, and gripped his arm. "The saints have taken care of us. Don't you live in a fine house? Don't you have a beautiful wife? You are an ingrate, Eulalio Miguel." Her cheeks kindled red.

"They have not spared us this," Lalo shouted, and pointed to Lorenzo who sat there, staring dumbly out.

"Misery!" Josefina pushed her son. "We have been spared our share of misery!" It was as if Lalo had not picked up a newspaper in ages, as if he hadn't seen the beggars who were entering the confines of Mar Lindo's walls. Josefina knew that life could be much, much worse. She flew to where Regla was, hoping that she had not heard her son's impudence.

But Regla had not heard, and her dance continued for quite a while. Long enough for Josefina to find a seat and for Soledad to begin leaning on the windowpane. Though her song seemed as if it was far from over, her voice having just reached a high pitched crescendo, Regla suddenly stopped in the middle of the room. She turned on her heels slowly, and floated her arms to her side, like a music-box ballerina winding down, until her eyes met Camila's. Camila, who had been sitting with Lorenzo, praying silently that the woman would do him no harm with her devil's chanting, began to tremble.

Regla sprang from her spot, her old hands, like dried branches, clinging to Camila's shirt. "*Niña,* what did your father do to you?" she asked, as the branches took the form of nimble fingers and tore open Camila's shirt, exposing the long scar.

"Nothing," Camila said, crying, "nothing. An accident, an . . ."

"Accident?" Regla asked, her eyebrows raised in disbelief, and as her mouth pursed on the threshold of revealing the vision she had seen, Regla quieted and sat down. She had been praying for Lorenzo, but not wholeheartedly, of this she knew. She understood what Josefina could not—that Lorenzo was ill of no one's doing, and no prayer could change what the saints had planned. While she prayed, she thought of other things: of the stains on Josefina's nails, of Don Emilio Cruz and his wife who demanded that Regla curl her hair with an iron every morning, of Josefina's daughter, Soledad, and her twitchy, restless body. And all at once, a new thought emerged, of a girl-child being pinned to the ground of a dirt lawn, and a man, red-faced and confused, tilting a basin of tar over the child's chest. She had seen Camila's face change when she mentioned the "accident," and decided that it was best to comfort her.

"Your father, *niña,* I have seen him in a vision and know that he thinks of you, though he is far away."

"*Sí.* He thinks of me in heaven," Camila said, her breath returning to her. She had pinched Lorenzo's arm when the woman began looking at her, and she felt now, without looking, that she had left a mark on his skin.

"No, precious girl, not that far. He is somewhere east, I think. Santiago de Cuba would be more precise."

"He is dead, in a fire, they both were killed, my mami and papi, and I was saved," Camila argued, pinching Lorenzo's arm again and raising beads of blood on his skin. Regla stood and walked cautiously up to Camila. The others had receded into the wallpaper, dispersed into crystal candy dishes, melted into the plush of the Oriental rugs, all to avoid Camila's gaze. Only Regla and Lorenzo were close enough to hear the girl's raspy breathing, and the whistling in her throat accompanying it.

The nursemaid, now shaking herself, came to believe her powers as a prophetess for the first time. The evidence of it was now not only in the nail bed of her old charge, but in the spittle puddling on Lorenzo's chest, Soledad's eyes shut tight, and on the bosom of this other girl.

Regla placed her palm over Camila's breast and throat and whispered, "What have they done to you?" The hand, so tenderly placed, willed into a healing thing, was pulled suddenly as Camila stood and ran, and Regla was knocked to the ground.

On the floor, Regla cried. It had been too much, she thought. Daisy petals and honey could never have worked.

Soledad listened to Camila's footsteps down the hall and out the front door. She heard her brother's footfall, too, and then the shouts of "Where are you off to? Come back, crazy woman, now," and then Camila's howl at him. It was a sickening cry, but it made Soledad stand and open her eyes. She saw the old black woman, crying on the ground herself, and her mamá huddling over her, so that the two looked like one impressive mass of cloth and salt-pickled flesh. She followed the echoes of the howl out the front door and caught a glimpse of Camila, rushing across dark streets and tripping over exposed roots of trees.

Soledad ran from the house and followed her through the park, past the grove of withered maples and the empty playground, and into the cemetery. Dusk had fallen quickly around them and Camila's form blended into the shadows. Soledad found her once again, catching glimpses of white skin here and there, at the foot of her parents' grave. It was then that Camila noticed Soledad's presence. She gestured for Soledad to come closer.

Camila poised her mouth above Soledad's ear, the tiny gold hoops tickling her lip, and said, "My father tried to murder me and yours, yours has slept with women from all six provinces, you know. And isn't it funny? Your mother turned out to be the biggest whore in Mar Lindo. Aren't we lucky daughters?" Soledad stood frozen. She had not followed her for this. She had come to stroke her hair, dry her wet cheeks, and bring her home for some warm milk. She watched as Camila gripped her skirt, hitched it above her knees, and began jumping from one grave to the next, thumping the ground with her foot then crouching to the dirt and laying her ear on the graves.

"See, Soly, no echo. There's a body down there." And then, jumping to the next grave, the headstone carved with a cross and a porcelain doll laid next to the marker, she thumped the ground and listened again, saying, "Poor creature, so young, so young . . ." And this she repeated for a few long minutes, patting the headstones as she went by them, crossing herself every so often, until she reached her parents' graves once more. Here she knelt, crunching twigs and dried leaves beneath her, and she patted the ground, then listened. And patted again to listen, and when she was done, and her ears and cheeks were blackened with the earth, Camila began to dig.

"Stop it, Camila, *por favor,* stop," Soledad yelled, pulling at Camila's shoulders, but it was as if the dirt itself held her in place, and her hands were like roots clinging to the earth.

"They aren't here. There's nothing down there. Nothing," she said. She tore at the ground with one hand, and touched her chest with the other. "And this," she said, still touching the old scar, "this was no accident." Finally, Soledad was able to pull Camila free, and both, exhausted, tumbled on their backs onto the grave, looking as if the bodies of Camila's parents were unearthed and laid side by side on the mounds.

Regla left for Vedado in the morning. She had prayed over Lorenzo through the night. When she was spent and ready to go, she kissed her girl, Josefina, on the cheeks and touched the heads of Soledad and Camila who lay on couches asleep and muddy.

The sergeant kissed her on the forehead as she stood at the door, and Regla, in turn, held his hands and said a prayer for his well being. During the prayer, Camila stirred and watched Regla lumber toward the taxi that waited for her.

Camila noted the straightening of the sergeant's back, his hands coming down to hang, defeated, at his sides. Camila stood then and said, "You were supposed to have died, long ago?"

"I am alive, *niña,*" he said, and pressed his hand to her cheek. "Alive, as you can see."

"No one stays dead anymore," Camila said and she walked over to where Lorenzo was and took her seat by his side once again.

36

A single check had arrived in the mail that winter from Abel. It was made out to Soledad with the express purpose of helping her begin her education, at least partially. Without Lorenzo to impose old-fashioned ideas about a girl's studies, Soledad was free to go to the university, and she set her sights on the States.

There was very little familial chatter in the house, save the light voice of Soledad talking to anyone in sight about her enrollment in the university. She hummed Elvis tunes and learned English out of a book, saying, "Thank ju berry much," to the postman, and, "Es-sweet dream, modder," to Josefina at night.

The sergeant, too, who in days past filled every empty space with the thunderous bass of his voice, was now quiet. He disapproved of Soledad's plan. He took her aside and asked, "Why is it you want to go?"

"Because there is nothing for me here, *abuelo*." The sergeant was not offended. He recognized the need for flight now as a family curse, a recurring illness that the generations could not wipe out.

"Bueno," he said, patting her shoulder, "be careful. Remember that your mother and I love you." Soledad had hugged him then, said, "I love you too, *abuelo*," and even doubted, for a moment, whether she should leave all this behind.

He now took an interest in his son-in-law's health, and shaved Lorenzo's face slowly with a straight edge. At first, the sight of her father with the blade so near her husband's throat made Josefina hold her breath and cringe. But soon she saw the tenderness in the sergeant's face as he worked, as if he were trying to remedy a wrong from long ago. It was at these times that Josefina would bring up the ghost letters to her father, expecting him to laugh at her mistake. But he would not acknowledge the letters.

"Papá," she would say, "your letters were so beautiful."

"*Ay hija,* you know I can barely write," the sergeant would reply, running the straight edge over Lorenzo's slack cheek.

"But Tío Francisco and my mother . . . why didn't you tell me before?"

The sergeant would stiffen and dunk the blade into a bowl of water. "Put those musty letters away, Josefina," he would say, then, "I don't know where they came from."

It seemed to Josefina, at times, that she was a girl again. Her father was gruff and believed he was in charge. Then it would pass. Still, his past was, once again, a nonpast, not existing in the thickness of his memory. He had been himself, truly Antonio Navarro, only twice in his life—while he wandered through the mountains with his brother and in his exile in Miami as he wrote long, story-filled letters to his daughter.

For the first time, Josefina was not cold in the shadow of a man. Her father had grown so quiet, nursing pains in his chest every day now. And Lorenzo sat noiseless in his chair, his limp hand placed into Josefina's in the afternoons, on the porch. She cried there with him countless times, and she wished she could conjure the smell of apricots and cinnamon so that he would seem alive again. She found him easy to forgive in his stillness.

And she dreamed of Abel at night and felt that he would return again, like a phoenix. It was his way, she told herself, and she did not lament his absence, even in her heart, because she felt it was temporary.

Josefina's sewing quickened her blood and kept the family fed. Some of the still wealthy of Mar Lindo, those who still had huge *quinceañera* parties for their daughters, enlisted Josefina as their seamstress. She would make the girls large, petticoated pink gowns with garlands of beads at their back and pink organza capes to tie at their necks. Now that Lorenzo could no longer complain or make accusations, Josefina had turned the entire downstairs into her workroom. The ottomans were draped with chiffon and taffeta in blues and mint greens. The east corner of the house was dedicated to wedding dresses and *quince* gowns, the tall lamps acting as shapely mannequins with the right amount of cotton stuffing here and there. She had bought a used Brother sewing machine and a zigzag machine for the heavy fabrics that required double stitches. These two "monsters" as she called them, sat quietly in the corner of the kitchen until Josefina's hands brought them to life. Little tin spools wrapped in colored thread rolled all over the house, and the whir of the machines filled every dormant corner. As she put together costumes, wedding dresses, baptismal gowns, and mourning wardrobes, Josefina recited portions of her father's letters to herself, keeping her mind free of distractions. She could not think of Lorenzo's new feeding schedule or the workings of the politicos in Havana while putting together the delicate feathered cap of Mar Lindo's prima ballerina.

Of course, they could have used more money to pay for Lorenzo's new wheelchair and the sergeant's heart medication. They were lucky to have Camila, who looked after both men as if they were her fathers, at a time when nurses were considered luxuries. She put lotion on Lorenzo's bedsores and watched the sergeant's diet. The sergeant had suggested that they sell the furniture in the parlor—fine wooden chairs from Spain, with gilded arms and mother-of-pearl designs encased in the wood. Camila, in a voice permanently meek since Regla's visit, blushed crimson at the thought that her old aunt's things, all that was left of her, would be taken away. She managed to raise her voice just enough to say, "You may sell them to pay for my casket if you wish. But not before." It was as if Doña Amparo had returned for a moment in the body of her niece to protect her inheritance. But the moment was fleeting, and Camila was soon yielding and vulnerable again. They had no way of knowing that the house and everything precious inside would be gone in a year, the house divided into thirteen apartments for the sake of the revolution, the furniture distributed among the poor in El Cotorro.

37

The sergeant and Josefina rode a bus to the beautiful streets of Vedado. Every minute she was with the sergeant, Josefina wanted to ask him about Miami, or the riot so many years ago. She wanted to know more about her mother's death, the pall of her skin, her last words. Sometimes, Josefina wanted to shake her father, or knock him down for lying all that time. And then, she wished he were still writing letters, so that she might cull the truth from them. She had felt the same way as a girl, but then, she'd only imagined that her father had other stories to tell, that the world outside Vedado was more exciting. Now that she knew what some of the sergeant's stories were, now that he had carved out a little window through which she could view his life, she wanted more. Every detail.

Once in Vedado the sergeant walked slowly. Josefina had bought him a cane, with the flag carved into the side. The sergeant leaned on it heavily, and it creaked. Still, he looked as if he belonged on that street, walked with a slow ease that was missing from his step in Mar Lindo. This, more than any other place, was his home.

He had missed the balconies most. The way apartments faced each other in a courtyard, the clear view of a neighbor's kitchen, the sounds of men on the balconies, talking to friends on the ground. He hadn't seen them since he left Cuba years ago, and now as he walked through old Vedado with Josefina, the sergeant stared up at the various windows, saw the scrolling wrought iron, noted the cracks in the mortar, and breathed deep.

But there were changes, too. Now tall hotels scraped the sky. Hundreds of cars crowded the streets. Tour buses played loud music and stopped traffic as the guides pointed at the old buildings sandwiched between the new, announcing, "You see folks, just like New Orleans," and then the sound of tourists clapping.

"Want me to buy you a *cafecito?*" Josefina asked, curling her arm around the sergeant's elbow. He shook his head. "*Bueno,* how about an ice cream? A *guarapo?*" She pointed at the various vendors as they walked, and the sergeant said no, again and again.

They had been walking for an hour when the sergeant stopped. "Sit," he said, and pointed his cane at a bench in the center of a small courtyard. It was painted white, and was set on a circle of tiny white stones. The pebbles crunched under their feet and the bench sank into the ground a bit and settled when they sat. The two of them were quiet for a long while.

"Papá, please. Why have we come here?" Josefina asked. It had been his idea. Josefina had awoken just after dawn, as was her normal routine. If she was early enough, she could feed and change Lorenzo, sweep the floors and bathe, all before breakfast. Usually, she crept about the house, padding in her slippers, setting down spoons softly so that the others could continue sleeping. But this morning had been different. Josefina was still rubbing sleep from her eyes when she saw the silhouette of her father in the living room, a box on his lap.

The sergeant had found his old letters in the bottom drawer of the china cabinet where Josefina had hidden them. He had been sitting in the dark, ruffling through the box when Josefina found him.

"Papá, can we talk?" Josefina had whispered.

"No," the sergeant had said and smashed the lid on the box. Then he shuffled back to his room. But a few hours later, after Lorenzo's feeding, and after Josefina emerged from the bathroom smelling like rose soap, the sergeant was dressed and standing at the door, tapping his cane.

"Vámonos," he had said.

"Where? What do you mean?"

"A Vedado." The sergeant had turned around then, and stepped out into the sunlight. Josefina grabbed her purse, yelled at Lalo to "Wake up and watch your father," and went out the door.

But he hadn't said why he wanted to go, or what place he had in mind. Now here they were, sitting on a bench in silence. The wooden slats of the bench were beginning to cut into Josefina's thighs and she felt the tension knotting up the muscles in her body.

"I don't understand why we . . ."

"Josefina," the sergeant interrupted, "what do you think of this place?"

"Here? The city?" The sergeant nodded. "It's good. Crowded, but good."

"Don't you miss it?"

"Sometimes." Josefina listened to the clink of silverware from an apartment above, and to the honking of car horns. She watched a man and woman kissing against a tree in the park across the street, counted the cars that zoomed past. "I miss it very much," she said after a while. "You?"

The sergeant drummed his fingers on the top of the cane. "Every moment I was away, I thought of these streets, and of you. We are both fools for running from here."

"Papá, let's not start this," Josefina said.

"Mi hijita, I am old. Am not going to be around for much longer."

"Shh, Papá."

The sergeant looked off into the distance. The sun was beginning to set and his face was awash in a yellow glow. He would not look at Josefina, but groped about for her hand, then held it. The sergeant spoke in a slow, deliberate way. "It's the truth. Truth, *mi hijita,* is such a difficult thing to manage. The truth is I am sorry. I should have given you a beautiful wedding filled with guests, and I should have helped you buy a bigger house in El Cotorro, should have been there with cigars and flowers for the birth of my grandchildren. *Ay,* so many 'should haves,' I could fill a book. And what do you have? A box of letters from a ridiculous man."

"It's all done with, Papá," Josefina said, wanting him to stop. This was not easy, listening to his voice crack, watching him furrow his brows in the effort to maintain composure.

"*Ay,* there's no way to pay it all back. I missed the very best years. Every Christmas, every summer, and every moment I spent like a fool without you, without my people, my country. *Ay, mi hijita,* I can't make it up to you." He was talking so fast now, no longer mindful of the people walking by and listening.

Josefina held her father's hand in both of hers. It was a beautiful day, the late afternoon sky clear of clouds. She could see the dome of the firmament, from right to left, without a tall building or mountain to block the view. It was limitless.

"*Ven,*" he said, and stood slowly. Josefina followed her father as he turned onto a familiar street. Away from the noise of the hotels and the new construction, the road narrowed and was flanked by massive homes painted in pink and yellow tones. The ironwork was painted white on most of them, though aluminum fences marred the landscape. Josefina felt herself breathing with ease, felt her shoulders relax, drop away from her ears where she'd held them. *One more block,* she told herself, *and we'll be home.*

The home had been newly built when Josefina moved in with her father. She was a little girl, but remembered the boxes, the new furniture, the beautiful echo whenever she called out for the sergeant. Vedado was a trendy neighborhood, a burgeoning city unto itself. The name Vedado means "forbidden," and it kept out those who could not afford the soaring rents. But for Josefina, standing before the pastel yellow mansion was humbling, like returning to her mother after so many years.

The sergeant tugged at his shirt and tapped the door. A child opened it. Josefina was surprised not to see Regla, though she knew the old nursemaid no longer worked in the home.

The little girl who opened had dark, dark eyes. She was no more than six, hadn't learned yet about strangers, or evil, and so she offered her cheek to the sergeant for a kiss hello as she had been taught to do with all the relatives who came for a visit. The sergeant stooped and kissed the smooth cheek.

"*¿Cómo tú te llamas?*" she asked. A small dog rushed up to her ankles and growled at the sergeant.

"Antonio," he said. "Can I come in? I want to show my little girl something."

"She's not so little," the girl said, eyeing Josefina. But she stepped aside, and the sergeant walked past the child and into the kitchen. Josefina stood in the doorway.

"Hurry up," he yelled behind him, and it was as if Josefina was the six-year-old, as if she was late again for lunch, or had forgotten to wash her dish. Josefina laughed and found she could not rush. She walked slowly, noticing the changes her childhood home had undergone, and also what was untouched. There was still a shadow on the terrazzo floor where her father's massive china cabinet once stood, the one that held trophies and medals instead of fine dishware. The high ceiling was still painted in the lightest blue. In the kitchen, the family had taken down the sunflower wallpaper. A scrap of it remained near the ceiling and Josefina wanted to reach up and take it with her. But the sight of her father atop a chair, perched on tiptoe, his cane raking the top of a cabinet, distracted her. "I know I left it here," he mumbled, stepped off the chair and moved it to another spot, then climbed again.

"What are you looking for?" Josefina asked as she held onto the trembling chair.

"*Fotos.* Of your uncle. And your mother."

There was a loud intake of air from Josefina. She felt her hands grow cold. There had been no pictures of her mother in the house, save for the one her father kept in his closet, the one she sometimes snuck in there to see. In it, Ana was so young. Her lips were painted a deep, dark color. In her hair was a dark flower, and she was wearing a black dress with full sleeves. It was her engagment portrait, but the sergeant had kept it in the dark. The portrait had been lost when the house was ransacked after the sergeant was presumed dead. Josefina had never seen a picture of her uncle.

She shook with anticipation as her father searched. In the background, she could hear the little girl who had opened the door singing. *What luck,* Josefina thought, *she hasn't bothered to tell anyone we are here.* Josefina began to imagine everything she would learn from the photographs. She felt certain they would find them. After all, the owners had not even bothered to remove all of the wallpaper. They weren't as careful as they should have been in cleaning their home.

Josefina found her mouth watering. She bit her lower lip. Who did Soledad resemble? Did Ana have a full figure? She imagined the picture frames she would buy in Mar Lindo and the wall she would use to showcase them all, her family, her heritage, intact again.

"Coño," the sergeant cursed, "they aren't here anymore." He came down off the chair after the long search. He kicked it, and then pulled it close again to sit. Just as quickly, he started to cry. *"Coño, los hombres no lloran,"* he said to himself—men don't cry—and he swiped at his nose with the back of his hand. Josefina wanted to cry, too, for those pictures she had envisioned for a moment, so real already in her mind. She wrapped her arms around her father's neck.

"If only we had found the pictures . . . I could tell you so much," the sergeant whispered.

They were quiet for a long while. The little girl outside the kitchen was still singing. It was an old Christmas carol, and she repeated the line *"El Niño tiene sueño, bendito sea, bendito sea"*—the baby is sleepy, bless him, over and over. Josefina imagined her rocking a doll in her arms. Such bliss. Josefina remembered the times she played in the front room, lining up her porcelain dolls and the cloth ones Regla made, and singing songs to them, her still, sweet audience. She recalled the torrent of gifts on the sixth of January, left for her by those three generous kings. She remembered the sergeant scooping her up and kissing her neck, asking her, "Who loves you? Who takes care of you?" and her response, *"Tú, Papá, siempre tú."* The pictures seemed like a silly thing to want, all of the sudden. "Papá," she said and lifted her face to look at her father. "Tell me a story."

The sergeant composed himself, took his daughter's hands to his lips, and kissed them. He leaned back against the chair and rested the cane across his lap. "My father had a large farm, this of course you know. He had two dogs. One named Bowtie for the patch of white fur at his neck, and another named Listen Here. One time, your Tío Francisco . . ."

Epilogue

I t was New Year's Day, 1959, when the radio announced that the
rebels in the sierras had finally overtaken the regime and that
Batista had fled with his family to the Dominican Republic. Josefina
was sitting amidst a mound of old lace, fluffed up around her like
a cloud, prickling her skin with its finely cut edges when she heard
it. The announcement was like a trumpet call, and soon streets all
over Cuba were filled with people cheering and clapping, and crying on their doorsteps. Those with nothing cheered the loudest,
expecting, finally, fairness and good times. Mar Lindo was quiet.
Those with the most to lose began packing their things, afraid of
the redistribution of wealth that they heard was coming. Batista
had been good for them. They were troubled by the youngsters
who had been shouting, "Fidel! Fidel! Fidel!" and "Che! Che!"
Long-haired, rebellious, atheist, ambitious—they represented
everything they had tried to suppress in their own children. Despite the silence in their neighborhood, Josefina pushed Lorenzo
in his wheelchair outside, and she linked arms with her daughter
and danced in the road. The sergeant stayed inside, watching the
dancing from the window.

In El Cotorro, people shot Spanish war-era pistols, and poor,
barefoot children ran into Mar Lindo, taunting the owners of the
imposing homes with shouts and lighting sparklers, writing their
names and Fidel's in the air. In Havana, people wrapped their bod-

ies in flags, honked the horns of their cars, and watched, rapt, as rioters took apart Batista's casinos, slot machine by slot machine.

In a year's time, the revolution would drive Soledad and Lalo to America. Camila, it was decided, would be "sent for" later, when the others had earned enough to pay for her visa and when Soledad had finished her studies. The night before her flight, Josefina sat up with her daughter in silence, both of them lying in the bed together. Josefina did not know if she'd ever see her children again. How could she leave the island with a sick father and husband in her care? She could never learn English, she thought, or get used to new ways, new street signs, a place with snow and ice. All night, Josefina swallowed thickly to keep from vomiting. The thought of losing Soledad forever was terrible. Soledad slept fitfully, for her part, youthful and sure that they would visit again and again. "Only ninety miles," she'd say, as if the airways and ocean would be open to them forever.

At the airport, Josefina fixed a frown on her face to keep herself from crying. Colorful threads were stuck here and there in her curls, a permanent fixture of her appearance now, as if she were not going gray, but rainbow. Josefina had filled Soledad's pockets with letters, one for each day to fill a month. And she had told her to "sit by the window and look for me." Soledad never found her mother in the squirming crowd below, but she wrote in her first letter that she had and that the island had shone in the sun and could be seen from Miami.

When the sergeant died years later, Josefina cried for weeks, stopping here and there to eat, crying right through her baths and as she waited in line for food rations. There were no priests anymore to attend the wake. So Josefina said the rosary aloud by herself and gave him the best last rites she could, imagining what the ritual was like since she had never seen it herself. It had been the same when she had heard of Regla's death in Vedado. She was orphaned for good this time, and Josefina could not undo the feeling of stark loneliness that came with that fact. The house in Mar Lindo had been converted into apartments as part of the new government reforms. Josefina sold what little she could in the black market before the place was overtaken, letting Camila howl inside as she watched her aunt's things being bartered and sold. Josefina, too, allowed herself the luxury of tears, now that Lorenzo could not yell at her sentimentality. She was able to mourn her father in earnest, this time, and a part of her thoroughly enjoyed it.

On the day he died, the sergeant told her one last story of an eccentric uncle who played pranks, and he told her about America in the dark, safe from the neighbors who might barge in and hear and then squeal to the neighborhood police about the *gusano* traitor living in apartment 4B. She held his hand, thanked him for coming back to her, and kissed his neck. "Who loves you? Who takes care of you?" he asked, and she answered, *"Tú Papá, siempre tú."*

The day after the sergeant's funeral, Josefina waited by the mail, expecting a posthumous letter from her father. When it didn't arrive, she felt as if the sergeant had died all over again. The feeling was worse than finding that bloody letter at her doorstep years ago. It was worse than losing Lorenzo to a stroke, or saying goodbye to Soledad, waving at the dot in the sky that was her plane until her arm gave out.

That afternoon, Josefina finished a set of airy silk wings for her granddaughter in Miami. Soledad had married a Cuban-American banker, a slender man who stuttered when he spoke Spanish, and their daughter, a beautiful girl with a name Josefina could not pronounce well—Ashley, which Josefina pronounced "Ach-lee"—took ballet classes in Coral Gables. Though she was only four, the girl was able to do a split, her little plump toes pointing north and south. The child signed her letters, "I love you, grandma," even though Josefina wished she could hear the word *"abuela"* from those small foreign lips.

Josefina also wrote a four-page letter to her daughter, her words overwrought, thinking about the day those letters, too, might stop coming. She packed the wings and the letter well in a box and sent them via airmail to the States. Inside she had tucked a few guava-filled candy bars for the hungry soldiers who would inevitably open up the package and search the contents. She had imagined their disappointment at finding only fabric and nothing to steal.

And as she predicted, Abel returned to her one Christmas night, when the kitchens all around were buzzing with preparations, despite the rationing, despite the ban on the holiday. His longing for a miracle and his brief stint with the fathers at the monastery ended with the revolution. God was a forbidden thing, talk of miracles cause for imprisonment. He had escaped the storming of the monastery by hiding up in the rafters. Abel's tears fell from the ceiling onto the soldiers as they beheaded statues and pissed into chalices, forcing a young novitiate to drink, pulling the veil off her head. He came back to Mar Lindo, his clothes in shreds, his eyes sunken, his stomach tingling at the thought of falling into Josefina's arms again. Abel knocked on the door and they did not say a word to each other. She had let him in and washed him with a sponge as Lorenzo sat in a corner, sleeping. Abel prayed in his sleep, alternately crying out, and then falling into the rhythmic tones of the Credo again. The noise comforted Josefina as she slept.

Josefina's sewing, too, was prohibited as long as she was making a profit. She began to work by hand, needle and thread the way Regla had taught her, so that there would be no noise from a machine. At least two of the neighbors worked for the local party, and Josefina had caught them spying into her kitchen window on occasion. Josefina's home was silent except for Lorenzo's snoring and Camila's shuffling between the bathroom and bedroom.

Together, they prayed for Lorenzo, each one hoping that he would awaken one day, cleansing them of guilt. Josefina was glad Abel was back, had forgiven him for lying about the ghost letters, and loved him so much that it ached. And she stayed up at night imagining life without him again, how awful it would be without his bone-crushing hugs. Then, spurred on by the thoughts, she'd turn to him and kiss his fingertips.

She still loved Lorenzo, too. Would whisper, "My Renzo," into his ear when she bathed him and fed him. She couldn't explain it, even to herself, how she could love two men so much. Yet she did, and had stopped questioning the feeling long ago.

Abel and Josefina talked of leaving the island—by boat, by air, by raft—and often lost themselves in that reverie. To start anew, to leave the old lives behind, to forget about curses and ghosts, to never wait in line for milk, to open up a butchery, to have enough soap, to celebrate birthdays with granddaughters and real, toy-filled piñatas, to read newspaper editorials, to make love in English. But then, Lorenzo would cough, hacking and snorting in his bedroom, and they knew they could never leave him to an institution. They were bound to him through love, through sin. And then there was Camila.

Camila, a faithful, quiet mouse, seemed to float in and out of rooms. There had not been enough money to bring her to the States, back to her husband. Whenever Lalo called, or wrote, it was to say, "Never enough money to bring you. But soon, soon," and Camila would shut herself in her room and cry. He wrote to her of breaking his fingers at the tire factory, of taxes, and of the rising costs of his apartment, but she did not believe him. She could not comprehend the rushing around that he described or the pace of life in the States. It was as foreign to her as poverty, and Camila could not adjust to either.

Despite Abel's return, Abel, who kept her up every night, Josefina thought of her father's letters. No matter how many pages she received from her daughter, cheerful letters full of vivid descriptions of Miami's oceans, its buildings, the funny, odd ways of America, Soledad's course work, no matter the number of fresh, perfume-scented, youthful, hurried notes that arrived once a week, it was the ghost letters that were ever present in Josefina's mind.

On one damp, moonlit night, after Josefina put a finishing row of sequins on a corseted bodice, she burned the ghost letters outside, like leftover fronds on Palm Sunday, because it would be a sacrilege just to throw them away. It was Abel who suggested it, hoping that the act might relieve the burden. Her hands quickly blackened with ash, and neighbors propped their heads on the fences to see where the smoke was coming from. From the open window above, Josefina could hear Camila's muted singing to Lorenzo and the murmur of the radio she had left on, tuned to yet another long address by Fidel. Their street had not been outfitted with speakers to blast the multiple-hour speeches into the air as it did in other places.

Josefina left the fire and the letters burning. She wished for a blaze to lick the walls of the converted mansion. She craved the light show that would occur when the porch collapsed, sending lit splinters toward the neighbors who would watch from the lawn.

But it was a passing wish. Abel waited upstairs, and Josefina would inhale full drawn breaths of him that evening and forget about time and place. Humming notes from "Clair de Lune," Josefina's voice went up in the air like morning birdsong, pinging its way into the open windows above. As she wiped her hands on her apron and then the sweat from her face, Josefina climbed the steps to her apartment, her thoughts already turned to composing another letter to her daughter.

Acknowledgments

The Spanish word for exile is *destierro*. Un-land, or no-land, is a closer translation. And yet, as a child of exiled parents, of *destierro*, I remember how I used to strain my eyes looking out at the horizon, sure I would be able to see Cuba from my place on the beach if the day was clear enough. Though I had never been there, I was attached to that slender chunk of land out in the ocean. Sometimes I swore I saw her. Impossible, of course, but I was fed on stories of a dream island where all things, nightmarish and beautiful, were possible. The stories filled me with a longing for a breeze I've never felt, a street I've never walked, distant relatives I've yet to meet.

This book would not exist without those stories. I owe that yearning, the insistent desire to retell and invent, to my family, to every moment that loving group of people came together to recount the past, to revisit that island that for them is trapped in time. I thank them with all my heart.

In particular, I want to acknowledge *mi abuela,* María Asela García. *Tita, tus cuentos y memorias son mi inspiración.* I'm thankful, too, to my parents, who teach me daily what it means to love. *Gracias.*

I want to extend my gratitude to Judith Weber, my agent, for her guidance and wisdom. For treating this story with so much care, and for finding a place in the world for it, thank you. Thank you, too, to Nat Sobel, for sending a letter to Pittsburgh that serendipitously found its way to Connecticut. To Catherine, Kat, and everyone at Sobel Weber, many blessings.

Thank you to Diane Reverend, my wonderful editor, whose skill and instinct made this a much better book. Thank you for believing in it. To Gina Scarpa and all of the talented people at St. Martin's Press, *muchísimas gracias*.

I am indebted to Lester Goran, my mentor and friend. Henry James wrote about the madness of art. Thank you for keeping me sane. Your friendship means the world to me. Thanks, as well, to the University of Miami for the gift of time and learning.

¡Colorín-Colora'o, este cuento se ha acaba'o! Except for one last thing . . .

This book is dedicated to my husband, Orlando. I love you. Thank you for everything.